Anna Bowman Dodd

In and out of Three Normandy Inns

Vol. 2

Anna Bowman Dodd

In and out of Three Normandy Inns
Vol. 2

ISBN/EAN: 9783337327767

Printed in Europe, USA, Canada, Australia, Japan

Cover: Foto ©Andreas Hilbeck / pixelio.de

More available books at **www.hansebooks.com**

IN AND OUT

OF

THREE NORMANDY INNS

BY

ANNA BOWMAN DODD

AUTHOR OF

"CATHEDRAL DAYS," "GLORINDA," "THE REPUBLIC OF THE FUTURE,"
ETC.

Illustrated by C. S. REINHART and others

NEW YORK

LOVELL, CORYELL & COMPANY

43, 45 AND 47 EAST TENTH STREET

TO EDMUND CLARENCE STEDMAN.

My Dear Mr. Stedman :

To this little company of Norman men and women, you will, I know, extend a kindly greeting, if only because of their nationality. To your courtesy, possibly, you will add the leaven of interest, when you perceive—as you must—that their qualities are all their own, their defects being due solely to my own imperfect presentment.

With sincere esteem,

ANNA BOWMAN DODD.

CONTENTS.

LIST OF ILLUSTRATIONS.

VILLERVILLE.

AN INN BY THE SEA.

THREE NORMANDY INNS.

CHAPTER I.

A LANDING ON THE COAST OF FRANCE.

NARROW streets with sinuous curves; dwarfed houses with minute shops protruding on inch-wide sidewalks; a tiny casino perched like a bird-cage on a tiny scaffolding; bath-houses dumped on the beach; fishing-smacks drawn up along the shore like so many Greek galleys; and, fringing the cliffs—the encroachment of the nineteenth century—a row of fantastic sea-side villas.

This was Villerville.

Over an arch of roses; across a broad line of olives, hawthorns, laburnums, and syringas, straight out to sea—

This was the view from our windows.

Our inn was bounded by the sea on one side, and on the other by a narrow village street. The distance between good and evil has been known to be quite as short as that which lay between these two thoroughfares. It was only a matter of a strip of land, an edge of cliff, and a shed of a house bearing the proud title of Hôtel-sur-Mer.

Two nights before, our arrival had made quite a stir in the village streets. The inn had given us a characteristic French welcome; its eye had measured us before it had extended its hand. Before reaching the inn and the village, however, we had already tasted of the flavor of a genuine Norman welcome. Our experience in adventure had begun on the Havre quays.

Our expedition could hardly be looked upon as perilous; yet it was one that, from the first, evidently appealed to the French imagination; half Havre was hanging over the stone wharves to see us start.

"*Dame*, only English women are up to that!"
—for all the world is English, in French eyes, when an adventurous folly is to be committed."

This was one view of our temerity; it was the comment of age and experience of the world, of the cap with the short pipe in her mouth, over which curved, downward, a bulbous, fiery-hued nose that met the pipe.

"*C'est beau-tout de même*, when one is young—and rich." This was a generous partisan, a girl with a miniature copy of her own round face—a copy that was tied up in a shawl, very snug; it was a

bundle that could not possibly be in any one's
way, even on a somewhat prolonged tour of observation of Havre's shipping interests.

" And the blonde one—what do you think of her,
hein ? "

This was the blouse's query. The tassel of the
cotton night-cap nodded, interrogatively, toward
the object on which the twinkling ex-mariner's
eye had fixed itself—on Charm's slender figure,
and on the yellow half-moon of hair framing her
face. There was but one verdict concerning the
blonde beauty; she was a creature made to be
stared at. The staring was suspended only when
the bargaining went on; for Havre, clearly, was
a sailor and merchant first; its knowledge of a
woman's good points was rated merely as its sec-
ond-best talent.

Meanwhile, our bargaining for the sailboat was
being conducted on the principles peculiar to
French traffic; it had all at once assumed the aspect of dramatic complication. It had only been
necessary for us to stop on our lounging stroll
along the stone wharves, diverting our gaze for a
moment from the grotesque assortment of old
houses that, before now, had looked down on so
many naval engagements, and innocently to ask a
brief question of a nautical gentleman, picturesquely attired in a blue shirt and a scarlet béret,
for the quays immediately to swarm with jerseys
and red caps. Each béret was the owner of a
boat; and each jersey had a voice louder than his
brother's. Presently the battle of tongues was
drowning all other sounds.

In point of fact, there were no other sounds to drown. All other business along the quays was being temporarily suspended; the most thrilling event of the day was centring in us and our treaty. Until this bargain was closed, other matters could wait. For a Frenchman has the true instinct of the dramatist; business he rightly considers as only an *entr'acte* in life; the serious thing is the *scène de théâtre*, wherever it takes place. Therefore it was that the black, shaky-looking houses, leaning over the quays, were now populous with frowsy heads and cotton nightcaps. The captains from the adjacent sloops and tug-boats formed an outer circle about the closer ring made by the competitors for our favors, while the loungers along the parapets, and the owners of top seats on the shining quay steps may be said to have been in possession of orchestra stalls from the first rising of the curtain.

A baker's boy and two fish-wives trundling their carts stopped to witness the last act of the play. Even the dogs beneath the carts, as they sank, panting, to the ground, followed, with red-rimmed eyes, the closing scenes of the little drama.

"*Allons*, let us end this," cried a piratical-looking captain, in a loud, masterful voice. And he named a price lower than the others had bid. He would take us across—yes, us and our luggage, and land us—yes, at Villerville, for that.

The baker's boy gave a long, slow whistle, with relish.

"*Dame !*" he ejaculated, between his teeth, as he turned away.

The rival captains at first had drawn back; they had looked at their comrade darkly, beneath their bérets, as they might at a deserter with whom they meant to deal with later on. But at his last words they smiled a smile of grim humor. Beneath the beards a whisper grew; whatever its import, it had the power to move all the hard mouths to laughter. As they also turned away, their shrugging shoulders and the scorn in their light laughter seemed to hand us over to our fate.

In the teeth of this smile, our captain had swung his boat round and we were stepping into her.

"*Au revoir—au revoir et à bientôt !*"

The group that was left to hang over the parapets and to wave us its farewell, was a thin one. Only the professional loungers took part in this last act of courtesy. There was a cluster of caps, dazzlingly white against the blue of the sky; a collection of highly decorated noses and of old hands ribboned with wrinkles, to nod and bob and wave down the cracked-voiced "*bonjours.*" But the audience that had gathered to witness the closing of the bargain had melted away with the moment of its conclusion. Long ere this moment of our embarkation the wide stone street facing the water had become suddenly deserted. The curious-eyed heads and the cotton nightcaps had been swallowed up in the hollows of the dark, little windows. The baker's boy had long since mounted his broad basket, as if it were an ornamental head-dress, and whistling, had turned a sharp corner, swallowed up, he also, by the sudden gloom that lay between

the narrow streets. The sloop-owners had linked
arms with the defeated captains, and were walking
off toward their respective boats, whistling a gay
little air.

> " *Colinette au bois s'en alla*
> *En sautillant par-ci, par-là ;*
> *Trala deridera, trala, derid-er-a-a.*"

One jersey-clad figure was singing lustily as he
dropped with a spring into his boat. He began to
coil the loose ropes at once, as if the disappointments in life were only a necessary interruption,
to be accepted philosophically, to this, the serious
business of his days.

We were soon afloat, far out from the land of
either shores. Between the two, sea and river meet;
is the river really trying to lose itself in the sea,
or is it hopelessly attempting to swallow the sea?
The green line that divides them will never give
you the answer: it changes hour by hour, day by
day; now it is like a knife-cut, deep and straight;
and now like a ribbon that wavers and flutters, tying together the blue of the great ocean and the silver of the Seine. Close to the lips of the mighty
mouth lie the two shores. In that fresh May sunshine Havre glittered and bristled, was aglow with
a thousand tints and tones; but we sailed and
sailed away from her, and behold, already she had
melted into her cliffs. Opposite, nearing with
every dip of the dun-colored sail into the blue
seas, was the Calvados coast; in its turn it glistened, and in its young spring verdure it had the
lustre of a rough-hewn emerald.

"*Que voulez-vous, mesdames?* Who could have told that the wind would play us such a trick?"

The voice was the voice of our captain. With much affluence of gesture he was explaining—his treachery! Our nearness to the coast had made the confession necessary. To the blandness of his smile, as he proceeded in his unabashed recital, succeeded a pained expression. We were not accepting the situation with the true phlegm of philosophers; he felt that he had just cause for protest. What possible difference could it make to us whether we were landed at Trouville or at Villerville? But to him—to be accused of betraying two ladies—to allow the whole of the Havre quays to behold in him a man disgraced, dishonored!

His was a tragic figure as he stood up, erect on the poop, to clap hands to a blue-clad breast, and to toss a black mane of hair in the golden air.

"*Dame! Toujours été galant homme, moi!* I am known on both shores as the most gallant of men. But the most gallant of men cannot control the caprice of the wind!" To which was added much abuse of the muddy bottoms, the strength of the undertow, and other marine disadvantages peculiar to Villerville.

It was a tragic figure, with gestures and voice to match. But it was evident that the Captain had taken his own measure mistakenly. In him the French stage had lost a comedian of the first magnitude. Much, therefore, we felt, was to be condoned in one who doubtless felt so great a talent itching for expression. When next he smiled, we had revived to a keener appreciation of baffled

genius ever on the scent for the capture of that
fickle goddess, opportunity.

The captain's smile was oiling a further word of
explanation. " See, mesdames, they come! they
will soon land you on the beach ! "

He was pointing to a boat smaller than our own,
that now ran alongside. There had been frequent
signallings between the two boats, a running up
and down of a small yellow flag which we had
thought amazingly becoming to the marine landscape, until we learned the true relation of the flag
to the treachery aboard our own craft.

" You see, mesdames," smoothly continued our
talented traitor, " you see how the waves run up on
the beach. We could never, with this great sail,
run in there. We should capsize. But behold,
these are bathers, accustomed to the water—they
will carry you—but as if you were feathers ! " And
he pointed to the four outstretched, firmly-muscled
arms, as if to warrant their powers of endurance.
The two men had left their boat; it was dancing
on the water, at anchor. They were standing immovable as pillars of stone, close to the gunwales
of our craft. They were holding out their arms
to us.

Charm suddenly stood upright. She held out
her hands like a child, to the least impressionable
boatman. In an instant she was clasping his
bronze throat.

" All my life I've prayed for adventure. And at
last it has come! " This she cried, as she was
carried high above the waves.

" That's right, have no fear," answered her car-

rier as he plunged onward, ploughing his way
through the waters to the beach.

Beneath my own feet there was a sudden swish
and a swirl of restless, tumbling waters. The
motion, as my carrier buried his bared legs in the
waves, was such as accompanies impossible flights
described in dreams, through some unknown
medium. The surging waters seemed struggling
to submerge us both; the two thin, tanned legs of
the fisherman about whose neck I was clinging,
appeared ridiculously inadequate to cleave a successful path through a sea of such strength as was
running shoreward.

"Madame does not appear to be used to this
kind of travelling," puffed out my carrier, his conversational instinct, apparently, not in the least
dampened by his strenuous plunging through the
spirited sea. "It happens every day—all the aris-
tocrats land this way, when they come over by the
little boats. It distracts and amuses them, they
say. It helps to kill the ennui."

"I should think it might, my feet are soaking;
sometimes wet feet——"

"Ah, that's a pity, you must get a better hold,"
sympathetically interrupted my fisherman, as he
proceeded to hoist me higher up on his shoulder.
I, or a sack of corn, or a basket of fish, they were
all one to this strong back and to these toughened
sinews. When he had adjusted his present load
at a secure height, above the dashing of the spray,
he went on talking. "Yes, when the rich suffer a
little it is not such a bad thing, it makes a pleasant change—*cela leur distrait.* For instance, there

is the Princess de L——, there's her villa, close
by, with green blinds. She makes little excuses
to go over to Havre, just for this—to be carried in
the arms like an infant. You should hear her, she
shouts and claps her hands! All the beach as-
sembles to see her land. When she is wet she
cries for joy. It is so difficult to amuse one's self,
it appears, in the great world."

"But, *tiens,* here we are, I feel the dry sands." I
was dropped as lightly on them as if it had been
indeed a bunch of feathers my fisherman had been
carrying.

And meanwhile, out yonder, across the billows,
with airy gesture dramatically executed, our treacherous captain was waving us a theatrical salute.
The infant mate was grinning like a gargoyle.
They were both delightfully unconscious, apparently, of any event having transpired, during the
afternoon's pleasuring, which could possibly tinge
the moment of parting with the hues of regret.

"*Pour les bagages, mesdames——*"

Two dripping, outstretched hands, two bérets
doffed, two picturesque giants bowing low, with a
Frenchman's grace—this, on the Trouville sands,
was the last act of this little comedy of our landing on the coast of France.

CHAPTER II.

A SPRING DRIVE.

 THE Trouville beach was as empty as a desert. No other footfall, save our own, echoed along the broad board walks; this Boulevard des Italiens of the Normandy coast, under the sun of May was a shining pavement that boasted only a company of jelly-fishes as loungers.

Down below was a village, a white cluster of little wooden houses; this was the village of the bath-houses. The hotels might have been monasteries deserted and abandoned, in obedience to a nod from Rome or from the home government. Not even a fisherman's net was spread a-drying, to stay the appetite with a sense of past favors done by the sea to mortals more fortunate than we. The whole face of nature was as indifferent as a rich relation grown callous to the voice of entreaty. There was no more hope of man apparently, than of nature, being moved by our necessity; for man, to be moved, must primarily exist, and he was as conspicuously absent on

this occasion as Genesis proves him to have been
on the fourth day of creation.

Meanwhile we sat still, and took counsel together. The chief of the council suddenly presented himself. It was a man in miniature. The
masculine shape, as it loomed up in the distance,
gradually separating itself from the background of
villa roofs and casino terraces, resolved itself into
a figure stolid and sturdy, very brown of leg, and
insolent of demeanor—swaggering along as if conscious of there being a full-grown man buttoned
up within a boy's ragged coat. The swagger was
accompanied by a whistle, whose neat crispness
announced habits of leisure and a sense of the refined pleasures of life ; for an artistic rendering of
an aria from " La Fille de Madame Angot " was
cutting the air with clear, high notes.

The whistle and the brown legs suddenly came
to a dead stop. The round blue eyes had caught
sight of us:

" *Ouid-a-a !* " was this young Norman's saluta-
tion. There was very little trouser left, and what
there was of it was all pocket, apparently. Into
the pockets the boy's hands were stuffed, along
with his amazement ; for his face, round and full
though it was, could not hold the full measure of
his surprise.

" We came over by boat—from Havre," we murmured meekly ; then, " Is there a cake-shop near ? "
irrelevantly concluded Charm with an unmistakable ring of distress in her tone. There was no
need of any further explanation. These two hearty
young appetites understood each other ; for hunger

is a universal language, and cake a countersign
common among the youth of all nations.

"Until you came, you see, we couldn't leave the
luggage," she went on.

The blue eyes swept the line of our boxes as if
the lad had taken his afternoon stroll with no other
purpose than to guard them. "There are eight,
and two umbrellas. *Soyez tranquille, je vous atten-
drai.*"

It was the voice and accent of a man of the
world, four feet high—a pocket edition, so to speak,
in shabby binding. The brown legs hung, the
next instant, over the tallest of the trunks. The
skilful whistling was resumed at once; our appearance and the boy's present occupation were mere
interludes, we were made to understand; his real
business, that afternoon, was to do justice to
the Lecoq's entire opera, and to keep his eye on
the sea.

Only once did he break down; he left a high *C*
hanging perilously in mid-air, to shout out "I like
madeleines, I do!" We assured him he should
have a dozen.

"*Bien!*" and we saw him settling himself to
await our return in patience.

Up in the town the streets, as we entered them,
were as empty as was the beach. Trouville might
have been a buried city of antiquity. Yet, in spite
of the desolation, it was French and foreign; it
welcomed us with an unmistakably friendly, companionable air. Why is it that one is made to feel
the companionable element, by instantaneous process, as it were, in a Frenchman and in his towns?

And by what magic also does a French village or
city, even at its least animated period, convey to
one the fact of its nationality? We made but ten
steps progress through these silent streets, fronting the beach, and yet, such was the subtle enigma
of charm with which these dumb villas and mute
shops were invested, that we walked along as if
under the spell of fascination. Perhaps the charm
is a matter of sex, after all: towns are feminine, in
the wise French idiom, that idiom so delicate in
discerning qualities of sex in inanimate objects, as
the Greeks before them were clever in discovering
sex distinctions in the moral qualities. Trouville
was so true a woman, that the coquette in her was
alive and breathing even in this her moment of
suspended animation. The closed blinds and iron
shutters appeared to be winking at us, slyly, as if
warning us not to believe in this nightmare of
desolation; she was only sleeping, she wished us
to understand; the touch of the first Parisian
would wake her into life. The features of her
fashionable face, meanwhile, were arranged with
perfect composure; even in slumber she had preserved her woman's instinct of orderly grace; not
a sign was awry, not a window-blind gave hint of
rheumatic hinges, or of shattered vertebræ; all
the machinery was in order; the faintest pressure
on the electrical button, the button that connects
this lady of the sea with the Paris Bourse and the
Boulevards, and how gayly, how agilely would this
Trouville of the villas and the beaches spring into
life!

The listless glances of the few tailors and cob-

blers who, with suspended thread, now looked
after us, seemed dazed—as if they could not believe in the reality of two early tourists. A woman's head, here and there, leaned over to us from
a high window; even these feminine eyes, however, appeared to be glued with the long winter's
lethargy of dull sleep; they betrayed no edge of
surprise or curiosity. The sun alone, shining with
spendthrift glory, flooding the narrow streets and
low houses with a late afternoon stream of color,
was the sole inhabitant who did not blink at us,
bovinely, with dulled vision.

Half an hour later we were speeding along the
roadway. Half an hour—and Trouville might have
been a thousand miles away. Inland, the eye
plunged over nests of clover, across the tops of the
apple and peach trees, frosted now with blossoms, to some farm interiors. The familiar Normandy features could be quickly spelled out, one
by one.

It was the milking-hour.

The fields were crowded with cattle and women;
some of the cows were standing immovable and
still others were slowly defiling, in processional
dignity, toward their homes. Broad-hipped, lean-
busted figures, in coarse gowns and worsted kerchiefs, toiled through the fields, carrying full milk-
jugs; brass *amphorœ* these latter might have been,
from their classical elegance of shape. Ploughmen appeared and disappeared, they and their
teams rising and sinking with the varying heights
and depressions of the more distant undulations.
In the nearer cottages the voices of children would

occasionally fill the air with a loud clamor of speech; then our steed's bell-collar would jingle, and for the children's cries, a bird-throat, high above, from the heights of a tall pine would pour forth, as if in incontrollable ecstasy, its rapture into the stillness of this radiant Normandy garden. The song appeared to be heard by other ears than ours. We were certain the dull-brained sheep were greatly affected by the strains of that generous-organed songster—they were so very still under the pink apple boughs. The cows are always good listeners; and now, relieved of their milk, they lifted eyes swimming with appreciative content above the grasses of their pasture. Two old peasants heard the very last of the crisp trills, before the concert ended; they were leaning forth from the narrow window-ledges of a straw-roofed cottage; the music gave to their blinking old eyes the same dreamy look we had read in the ruminating cattle orbs. For an aeronaut on his way to bed, I should have felt, had I been in that blackbird's plumed corselet, that I had had a gratifyingly full house.

Meanwhile, toward the west, a vast marine picture, like a panorama on wheels, was accompanying us all the way. Sometimes at our feet, beneath the seamy fissures of a hillside, or far removed by sweep of meadow, lay the fluctuant mass we call the sea. It was all a glassy yellow surface now; into the liquid mirror the polychrome sails sent down long lines of color. The sun had sunk beyond the Havre hills, but the flame of his mantle still swept the sky. And into this twilight

A VILLAGE STREET—VILLERVILLE.

there crept up from the earth a subtle, delicious
scent and smell—the smell and perfume of spring—
of the ardent, vigorous, unspent Normandy spring.

Suddenly a belfry grew out of the grain-fields.

"*Nous voici*—here's Villerville!" cried lustily
into the twilight our coachman's thick peasant
voice. With the butt-end of his whip he pointed
toward the hill that the belfry crowned. Below
the little hamlet church lay the village. A high,
steep street plunged recklessly downward toward
the cliff; we as recklessly were following it. The
snapping of our driver's whip had brought every
inhabitant of the street upon the narrow sidewalks. A few old women and babies hung forth
from the windows, but the houses were so low,
that even this portion of the population, ham-
pered somewhat by distance and comparative isolation, had been enabled to join in the chorus of
voices that filled the street. Our progress down
the steep, crowded street was marked by a pomp
and circumstance which commonly attend only a
royal entrance into a town; all of the inhabitants,
to the last man and infant, apparently, were assembled to assist at the ceremonial of our entry.

A chorus of comments arose from the shadowy,
groups filling the low doorways and the window
casements.

" *Tiens*—it begins to arrive—the season ! "

"Two ladies—alone—like that ! "

"*Dame ! Anglaises, Américaines*—they go round
the world thus, *à deux !* "

" And why not, if they are young and can
pay ? "

"Bah! old or poor, it's all one—they're never still, those English!" A chorus of croaking laughter rattled down the street along with the rolling of our carriage-wheels.

Above, the great arch of sky had shrunk, all at once, into a narrow scollop; with the fields and meadows the glow of twilight had been left behind. We seemed to be pressing our way against a great curtain, the curtain made by the rich dusk that filled the narrow thoroughfare. Through the darkness the sinuous street and rickety houses wavered in outline as the bent shapes of the aged totter across dimly-lit interiors. A fisherman's bare legs, lit by some dimly illumined interior; a line of nets in the little yards; here and there a white kerchief or cotton cap, dazzling in whiteness, thrown out against the black façades, were spots of light here and there. There was a glimpse of the village at its supper—in low-raftered interiors a group of blouses and women in fishermen's rig were gathered about narrow tables, the coarse-featured faces and the seamed foreheads lit up by the feeble flame of candles that ended in long, thin lines of smoke.

" *Ohè—Mère Mouchard !—des voyageurs !* " cried forth our coachman into the darkness. He had drawn up before a low, brightly-lit interior. In response to the call a figure appeared on the threshold of the open door. The figure stood there for a long instant, rubbing its hands, as it peered out into the dusk of the night to take a good look at us. The brown head was cocked on one side thoughtfully; it was an attitude that ex-

pressed, with astonishingly clear emphasis, an
unmistakable professional conception of hospitality. It was the air and manner, in a word, of one
who had long since trimmed the measurement of
its graciousness to the price paid for the article.

"*Ces dames* wished rooms, they desired lodgings
and board—*ces dames* were alone?" The voice
finally asked, with reticent dignity.

"From Havre—from Trouville, *par p'tit bateau !*"
called out lustily our driver, as if to furnish us,
gratis, with a passport to the landlady's not too
effusive cordiality.

What secret spell of magic may have lain hidden in our friendly coachman's announcement we
never knew. But the "p'tit bateau" worked mag-
ically. The figure of Mère Mouchard materialized
at once into such zeal, such effusion, such a zest
of welcome, that we, our bags, and our coachman
were on the instant toiling up a pair of spiral
wooden stairs. There was quite a little crowd to fill
the all-too-narrow landing at the top of the steep
steps, a crowd that ended in a long line of waiters
and serving-maids, each grasping a remnant of
luggage. Our hostess, meanwhile, was fumbling
at a door-lock—an obstinate door that refused to
be wrenched open.

"Augustine—run—I've taken the wrong key.
Cours, mon enfant, it is no farther away than the
kitchen."

The long line pressed itself against the low
walls. Augustine, a black-haired, neatly-gar-
mented shape, sped down the rickety stairs with
the step of youth and a dancer; for only the nimble

ankles of one accomplished in waltzing could have
tripped as dexterously downward as did Augustine.

"How she lags! what an idiot of a child!"
fumed Mère Mouchard as she peered down into
the round blackness about which the curving
staircase closed like an embrace. " One must have
patience, it appears, with people made like that.
Ah, tiens, here she comes. How could you keep
ces dames waiting like this? It is shameful,
shameful!" cried the woman, as she half shook the
panting girl, in anger. "If *ces dames* will enter,"
—her voice changing at once to a caressing fal-
setto, as the door flew open, opened by Augustine's
trembling fingers—"they will find their rooms in
readiness."

The rooms were as bare as a soldier's barrack,
but they were spotlessly clean. There was the
pale flicker of a sickly candle to illumine the
shadowy recesses of the curtained beds and the
dark little dressing-rooms.

A few moments later we wound our way downward, spirally, to find ourselves seated at a round
table in a cosy, compact dining-room. Directly
opposite, across the corridor, was the kitchen,
from which issued a delightful combination of
vinous, aromatic odors. The light of a strong,
bright lamp made it as brilliant as a ball-room ; it
was a ball-room which for decoration had rows of
shining brass and copper kettles, each as burnished as a jewel, a mass of sunny porcelain, and for
carpet the satin of a wooden floor. There was
much bustling to and fro. Shapes were constantly

passing and repassing across the lighted interior.
The Mère's broad-hipped figure was an omniscient
presence: it hovered at one instant over a steam-
ing saucepan, and the next was lifting a full milk-
jug or opening a wine-bottle. Above the clatter
of the dishes and the stirring of spoons arose the
thick Normandy voices, deep alto tones, speaking
in strange jargon of speech—a world of *patois* removed from our duller comprehension. It was
made somewhat too plain in this country, we reflected, that a man's stomach is of far more importance than the rest of his body. The kitchen
yonder was by far the most comfortable, the warm-
est, and altogether the prettiest room in the whole
house.

Augustine crossed the narrow entry just then
with a smoking pot of soup. She was followed,
later, by Mère Mouchard, who bore a *sole au vin
blanc*, a bottle of white Burgundy, and a super-
naturally ethereal soufflé. And an hour after, even
the curtainless, carpetless bed-chambers above
were powerless to affect the luxurious character of
our dreams.

CHAPTER III.

 ONE travels a long distance, sometimes, to make the astonishing discovery that pleasure comes with the doing of very simple things. We had come from over the seas to find the act of leaning on a window casement as exciting as it was satisfying. It is true that from our two inn windows there was a delightful variety of nature and of human nature to look out upon.

From the windows overlooking the garden there was only the horizon to bound infinity. The Atlantic, beginning with the beach at our feet, stopped at nothing till it met the sky. The sea, literally, was at our door; it and the Seine were next-door neighbors. Each hour of the day these neighbors presented a different face, were arrayed in totally different raiment, were grave or gay, glowing with color or shrouded in mists, according to the mood and temper of the sun, the winds, and the tides. The width of the sky overhanging this space was immense; not a scrap, apparently, was left over to cover, decently, the rest of the earth's surface—

ON THE BEACH—VILLERVILLE.

of that one was quite certain in looking at this vast
inverted cup overflowing with ether. What there
was of land was a very sketchy performance. Opposite ran the red line of the Havre headlands.
Following the river, inland, there was a pretence
of shore, just sufficiently outlined, like a youth's
beard, to give substance to one's belief in its future
growth and development. Beneath these windows
the water, hemmed in by this edge of shore, panted, like a child at play; its sighs, liquid, lisping,
were irresistible; one found oneself listening for
the sound of them as if they had issued from a
human throat. The humming of the bees in the
garden, the cry of a fisherman calling across the
water, the shout of the children below on the
beach, or, at twilight, the chorussing bi....s, carol-
ling at full concert pitch; this, at most, was all the
sound and fury the sea-beach yielded.

The windows opening on the village street let
in a noise as tumultuous as the sea was silent.
The hubbub of a perpetual babble, all the louder
for being compressed within narrow space, was
always to be heard; it ceased only when the village slept. There was an incessant clicking accompaniment to this noisy street life; a music
played from early dawn to dusk over the pavement's rough cobbles—the click clack, click clack
of the countless wooden sabots.

Part of this clamor in the streets was due to the
fact that the village, as a village, appeared to be
doing a tremendous business with the sea.

Men and women were perpetually going to and
coming from the beach. Fishermen, sailors,

women bearing nets, oars, masts, and sails;
children bending beneath the weight of baskets
filled with kicking fish; wheelbarrows stocked
high with sea-food and warm clothing; all this
commerce with the sea made the life in these
streets a more animated performance than is commonly seen in French villages.

In time, the provincial mania began to work in
our veins.

To watch our neighbors, to keep an eye on
this life—this became, after a few days, the chief
occupation of our waking hours.

The windows of our rooms fronting on the
street were peculiarly well adapted for this un-
mannerly occupation. By merely opening the
blinds, we could keep an eye on the entire village.
Not a cat could cross the street without undergoing inspection. Augustine, for example, who,
once having turned her back on the inn windows,
believing herself entirely cut off from observation,
was perilously exposed to our mercy. We knew
all the secrets of her thieving habits; we could
count, to a second, the time she stole from the
Mère, her employer, to squander in smiles and
dimples at the corner creamery. There a tall
Norman rained admiration upon her through wide
blue eyes, as he patted, caressingly, the pots of
blond butter, just the color of her hair, before
laying them later tenderly in her open palm.
Soon, as our acquaintance with our neighbors
deepened into something like intimacy, we came
to know their habits of mind as we did their facial
peculiarities; certain of their actions made an

event in our day. It became a serious matter of
conjecture as to whether Madame de Tours, the
social swell of the town, would or would not offer
up her prayer to Deity, accompanied by Friponne,
her black poodle. If Friponne issued forth from
the narrow door, in company with her austere mistress, the shining black silk gown, we knew, would
not decorate the angular figure of this aristocratic
provincial; a sober beige was best fitted to resist
the dashes made by Friponne's sharply-trimmed
nails. It was for this, to don a silk gown in full
sight of her neighbors; to set up as companion a
dog of the highest fashion, the very purest of
caniches, that twenty years of patient nursing a
paralytic husband—who died all too slowly—had
been counted as nothing!

Once we were summoned to our outlook by the
vigorous beating of a drum. Madame Mouchard
and Augustine were already at their own post of
observation—the open inn door. The rest of the
village was in full attendance, for it was not every
day in the week that the "tambour," the town-
crier, had business enough to render his appearance, in his official capacity, necessary; as a mere
townsman he was to be seen any hour of the day,
as drunk as a lord, at the sign of "L'Ami Fidèle."
His voice, as it rolled out the words of his cry,
was as *staccato* in pitch as any organ can be whose
practice is largely confined to unceasing calls for
potations. To the listening crowd, the thick voice
was shouting:

"*Madame Tricot—à la messe—dimanche—a—
perdu une broche—or et perles—avec cheveux—Ma-*

dame Merle a perdu—sur la plage—un panier avec —un chat noir——"

We ourselves, to our astonishment, were drummed the very next morning. Augustine had made the discovery of a missing shoulder-cape; she had taken it upon herself to call in the drummer. So great was the attendance of villagers, even the abstractors of the lost garment must, we were certain, be among the crowd assembled to hear our names shouted out on the still air. We were greatly affected by the publicity of the occasion; but the village heard the announcement, both of our names and of our loss, with the phlegm of indifference. "*Vingt francs pour avoir tambouriné mademoiselle!*" This was an item which a week later, in madame's little bill, was not confronted with indifference.

"It gives one the feeling of having had relations with a wandering circus," remarked the young philosopher at my side.

"But it is really a great convenience, that system," she continued; "I'm always mislaying things—and through the drummer there's a whole village as aid to find a lost article. I shall, doubtless, always have that, now, in my bills!" And Charm, with an air of serene confidence in the village, adjusted her restored shoulder-cape.

Down below, in our neighbor's garden—the one adjoining our own and facing the sea—a new and old world of fashion in capes and other garments were a-flutter in the breeze, morning after morning. Who and what was this neighbor, that he should have so curious and eccentric a taste in

clothes? No woman was to be seen in the garden-
paths; a man, in a butler's apron and a silk skull-
cap, came and went, his arms piled high with
gowns and scarves, and all manner of strange odds
and ends. Each morning some new assortment of
garments met our wondering eyes. Sometimes it
was a collection of Empire embroidered costumes
that were hung out on the line; faded fleur-de-lis,
sprigs of dainty lilies and roses, gold-embossed
Empire coats, strewn thick with seed-pearls on
satins softened by time into melting shades. When
next we looked the court of Napoleon had vanished, and the Bourbon period was, literally, in full
swing. A *frou-frou* of laces, coats with deep skirts,
and beribboned trousers would be fluttering airily
in the soft May air. Once, in fine contrast to
these courtly splendors, was a wondrous assortment of flannel petticoats. They were of every
hue—red, yellow, brown, pink, patched, darned,
wide-skirted, plaited, ruffled—they appeared to
represent the taste and requirement of every cli-
mate and country, if one could judge by the
thickness of some and the gossamer tissues of
others; but even the smartest were obviously, unmistakably, effrontedly, flannel petticoats.

It was a mystery that greatly intrigued us. One
morning the mystery was solved. A whiff of to-
bacco from an upper window came along with a
puff of wind. It was a heated whiff, in spite of
the cooling breeze. It was from a pipe, a short,
black pipe, owned by some one in the Mansard
window next door. There was the round disk of a
dark-blue béret drooping over the pipe. "Good—"

I said to myself—"I shall see now—at last—this maniac with a taste for darned petticoats!"

The pipe smoked peacefully, steadily on. The béret was motionless. Betweeen the pipe and the cap was a man's profile; it was too much in shadow to be clearly defined.

The next instant the man's face was in full sunlight. The face turned toward me—with the quick instinct of knowing itself watched—and then—

"*Pas—possible!*"

"You—here!"

"Been here a year—but you, when did you arrive? What luck! What luck!"

It was John Renard, the artist; after the first salutations question followed question.

"Are you alone?——"

"No."

"Is she—young?"

"Yes."

"Pretty?"

"Judge for yourself—that is she—in the garden yonder."

The béret dipped itself perilously out into the sky—to take a full view.

"Hem—I'll come in at once."

It was as a trio that the conversation was continued later, in the garden. But Renard was still chief questioner.

"Have you been out on the mussel-beds?"

"Not yet."

"We'll go this afternoon—Have you been to Honfleur? Not yet?—We'll go to-morrow. The tide will be in to-day about four—I'll call for you

—wear heavy boots and old clothes. It's jolly
dirty. Where do you breakfast?"

The breakfast was eaten, as a trio, at our inn, an
hour later. It was so warm a day, it was served
under one of the arbors. Augustine was feeding
and caressing the doves as we entered the inn
garden. At sight of Renard she dropped a quiet
courtesy, smiles and roses struggling for a su-
premacy on her round peasant face. She let the
doves loose at once, saying: "Allez, allez," as if
they quite understood that with Monsieur Renard's advent their hour of success was at an end.

Why does a man's presence always seem to communicate such surprising animation to a woman
—to any woman? Why does his appearance, for
instance, suddenly, miraculously stiffen the sauces,
lure from the cellar bottles incrusted with the
gray of thick cobwebs, give an added drop of the
lemon to the mayonnaise, and make an omelette
to swim in a sea of butter? All these added
touches to our commonly admirable breakfast
were conspicuous that day—it was a breakfast for
a prince and a gourmet.

"The Mère can cook—when she gives her mind
to it," was Renard's meagre masculine comment,
as the last morsel of the golden omelette disappeared behind his mustache.

It was a gay little breakfast, with the circling
above of the birds and the doves. There are duller forms of pleasure than to eat a repast in the
company of an artist. I know not why it is, but it
has always seemed to me that the man who lives
only to copy life appears to get far more out of it

than those who make a point of seeing nothing in
it save themselves.

Renard, meanwhile, was taking pains to assure
us that in less than a month the Villerville beaches
would be crowded; only the artists of the brushes
were here now; the artists of high life would
scarcely be found deserting the Avenue des Aca-
cias before June.

"French people are always coming to the sea-
shore, you know—or trying to come. It's a part
of their emotional religion to worship the sea.
'La mer! la mer!' they cry, with eyes all whites;
then they go into little swoons of rapture—I can
see them now, attitudinizing in salons and at
tables-d'hôte!" To which comment we could find
no more original rejoinder than our laughter.

It was a day when laughter was good; it put one
in closer relations with the universal smiling.
There are certain days when nature seems to laugh
aloud; in this hour of noon the entire universe, all
we could see of it, was on a broad grin. Everything moved, or danced, or sang; the leaves were
each alive, trembling, quivering, shaking; the insect hum was like a Wagnerian chorus, deafening
to the ear; there was a brisk, light breeze stirring
—a breeze that moved the higher branches of the
trees as if it had been an arm; that rippled the
grass; that tossed the wavelets of the sea into
such foam that they seemed over-running with
laughter; and such was still its unspent energy
that it sent the Seine with a bound up through its
shores, its waters clanging like a sheet of mail
armor worn by some lusty warrior. We were

walking in the narrow lane that edged the cliff; it was a lane that was guarded with a sentinel row of osiers, syringas, and laburnums. This was the guard of the cliffs. On the other side was the high garden wall, over which we caught dissolving views of dormer-windows, of gabled roofs, vine-clad walls, and a maze of peach and pear blossoms. This was not precisely the kind of lane through which one hurried. One needed neither to be sixteen nor even in love to find it a delectable path, very agreeable to the eye, very suggestive to the imaginative faculty, exceedingly satisfactory to the most fastidious of all the senses, to that aristocrat of all the five, the sense of smell. Like all entirely perfect experiences in life, the lane ended almost as soon as it began; it ended in a steep pair of steps that dropped, precipitously, on the pebbles of the beach.

For some reason best known to the day and the view, we all, with one accord, proceeded to seat ourselves on the topmost step of this stairway. We were waiting for the tide to fall, to go out to the mussel-bed. Meanwhile the prospect to be seen from this improvised seat was one made to be looked at. There is a certain innate compelling quality in all great beauty. When nature or woman presents a really grandiose appearance, they are singularly reposeful, if you notice; they have the calm which comes with a consciousness of splendor. It is only prettiness which is tormented with the itching for display; and therefore this prospect, which rolled itself out beneath our feet, curling in a half-moon of beach, broaden-

ing into meadows that dropped to the river edge,
lifting its beauty upward till the hills met the sky,
and the river was lost in the clasp of the shore—
this aspect of nature, in this moment of beauty,
was as untroubled as if Châteaubriand had not
found her a lover, and had flattered man by per-
suading him that

" La voix de l'univers, c'est mon intelligence."

CHAPTER IV.

 THAT same afternoon we were out on the mussel-bed.

The tide was at its lowest. Before us, for an acre or more, there lay a wide, wet, stretch of brown mud. Near the beach was a strip of yellow sand; here and there it had contracted into narrow ridges, elsewhere it had expanded into scroll-like patterns. The bed of mud and slime ran out from this yellow sand strip—a surface diversified by puddles of muddy water, by pools, clear, ribbed with wavelets, and by little heaps of stones covered with lichens. The surface of the bed, whether pools or puddles, or rock-heaps or sea-weeds massed, was covered by thousands and thousands of black, lozenge-shaped bivalves. These bivalves were the mussels. Over this bed of shells and slime there moved and toiled a whole villageful of old women. Where the sea met the edges of the mud-flat the throng of women was thickest. The line of the ever-receding shore was marked by the shapes of countless bent figures. The heads of these stooping women were on a level

with their feet, not one stood upright. All that
the eye could seize for outline was the dome made
by the bent hips, and the backs that closed against
the knees as a blade is clasped into a knife handle.
The oblong masses that were lifted now and then,
from the level of the sabots, resolved themselves
into the outlines of women's heads and women's
faces. These heads were tied up in cotton kerchiefs or in cotton nightcaps; these being white,
together with the long, thick, aprons also white,
were in startling contrast to the blue of the sky
and to the changing sea-tones.

Between these women and the incoming tide,
twice daily, was fought a persistent, unrelenting
duel. It was a duel, on the part of the fish-wives,
against time, against the fate of the tides, against
the blind forces of nature. For this combat the
women were armed to the teeth, clad as they were
in their skeleton muscular leanness; helmeted with
their heads of iron; visored in the bronze of their
skin and in wrinkles that laughed at the wind.
In these sinewy, toughened bodies there was a
grim strength that appeared to know neither ache
nor fatigue nor satiety.

High, clear, strong, came their voices. The
tones were the tones that come from deep chests,
and with a prolonged, sustained capacity for en-
during the toil of men. But the high-pitched
laughter proved them women, as did their loud
and unceasing gossip. The battle of the voices
rose above the swash of the waves, above, also,
another sound, as incessant as the women's chatter
and the swish of the water as it hissed along the

A SALE OF MUSSELS—VILLERVILLE.

mud-flat's edges. This was the swift, sharp, saw-like cutting among the stones and the slime, the scrape, scrape of the hundred of knives into the moist earth. This ceaseless scraping, lunging, digging, made a new world of sound—strange, sinister, uncanny. It was neither of the sea nor yet of the land—it was a noise that seemed inseparable from this tongue of mud, that also appeared to be neither of the heavens above nor of the earth, from the bowels out of which it had sprung.

The mussels cling to their slime with extraordinary tenacity; only an expert, who knows the exact point of attachment between the hard shell and its soil, can remove a mussel with dexterity. These women, as they dipped their knives into the thick mud, swept the diminutive black bivalve with a trenchant movement, as a Moor might cleave a human head with one turn of his moon-shaped sword. Into the bronzed, wrinkled old hands the mussels then were slipped as if they had been so many dainty sweets.

New and pungent smells were abroad on this strip of slime. Sea smells, strong and salty; smells of the moist and damp soil, the bitter-sweet of wetted weeds, the aromatic flavor that shell-life yields, and the smells also of rotten and decaying fish—all these were inextricably blended in the air, that was of the keenness of a frost-blight for freshness, and yet was warm with the softness of a June sun.

Meanwhile the voices of the women were nearing. Some of the bent heads were lifted as we approached. Here and there a coif, or cotton cap,

nodded, and the slit of a smile would gape between the nose and the meeting chin. A high
good humor appeared to reign among the groups;
a carnival of merriment laughed itself out in
coarse, cracked laughter; loud was the play of
the jests, hoarse and guttural the gibes that were
abroad on the still air, from old mouths that
uttered strong, deep notes.

"Why should they all be old?" we queried.
We were near enough to see the women face to
face now, since we were far out along the outer
edges of the bed; we were so near the sea that
the tide was beginning to wash us back, along with
the fringe of the diggers.

"They're not—they only look old," replied Renard, stopping a moment to sketch in a group directly in front. "This life makes old women of
them in no time. How old, for instance, should
you think that girl was, over there?"

The girl whom he designated was the only figure of youth we had seen on the bed. She was
working alone and remote from the others. She
wore no coif. Her masses of red, wavy hair shaded
a face already deeply seamed with lines of pre-
mature age. A moment later she passed close to
us. She was bent almost double beneath a huge,
reeking basket, heaped with its pile of wet mussels. She was carrying it to a distant pool. Once
beside the pool, with swift, dexterous movement
the heavy basket was slipped from the bent back,
the load of mussels falling in a shower into the
miniature lake. The next instant she was stamping
on the heap, to plunge them with her sabot still

further into the pool. She was washing her load.
Soon she shouldered the basket again, filling it
with the cleansed mussels. A moment later she
joined the long, toiling line of women that were
perpetually forming and reforming on their way
to the carts. These latter were drawn up near the
beach, their contents guarded by boys and old
men, who received the loads the women had dug,
dragging the whole, later, up the hill.

"She has the Venus de Milo lines, that girl,"
Renard continued, critically, with his eyes on her,
as she now repassed us. The figure was drawn
up at its full height. It had in truth a noble dignity of outline. There was a Spartan vigor and
severity in the lean, uncorseted shape, with the
bust thrown out against the sky—the bust of a
young warrior rather than a woman. There was a
hardy, masculine freedom in the pliable motion
of her straight back, a ripple with muscles that
played easily beneath the close jersey, in her
arms, and her finely turned ankles and legs, that
were bared below the knee. The very simplicity
of her costume helped to mark the Greek severity
of her figure. She wore a short skirt of some
coarse hempen stuff, covered with a thick apron
made of sail-cloth, her feet thrust into black sabots,
while the upper part of her body was covered with
an unbleached chemise, widely open at the throat.

She had the Phidian breadth and the modern
charm—that charm which troubles and disturbs,
haunting the mind with vague, unsatisfied suggestions of something finer than is seen, something
nobler than the gross physical envelope reveals.

"I must have her—for my Salon picture," calmly remarked Renard, after a long moment of scrutiny, his eyes following the lean, stately figure in its grave walk across the weeds and slime. "Yes, I must have her."

"Won't she be hard to get? How can she be made to sit, a stiffened image of clay, after this life of freedom, this athletic struggle out here—with these winds and tides?"

One of us, at least, was stirred at Renard's calm assumption—the assumption so common to artists, who, when they see a good thing at once count on its possessorship, as if the whole world, indeed, were eternally sitting, agape with impatience, awaiting the advent of some painter to sketch in its portrait.

"Oh, it'll be easy enough. She makes two francs a day with her six basketfuls. I'll offer her three, and she'll drop like a shot."

"I'll make it a red picture," he continued, dipping his brushes into a little case of paints he held on his thumb; "the mussel-bed a reddish violet, the sky red in the horizon, and the girl in the foreground, with that torrent of hair as the high light. I've been hunting for that hair all over Europe." And he began sketching her in at once.

"*Bonjour, mère,* how goes it?" He nodded as he sketched at a wrinkled, bent figure, who was smiling out at him from beneath her load of mussels.

"*Pas mal—è' vous, M'sieur Renard?*"

"All right—and the mortgage, how goes that?"

"*Pas si mal*—it'll be paid off next year."

"Who is she ?   One of your models ?"

"Yes, last year's: she was my belle—the belle
of the mussel-bed for me, a year ago.   Now there's
a lesson in patience for you.   She's sixty-five, if
she's a minute ; she's been working here, on this
mussel-bed, for five years, to pay the mortgage off
her farm ; when that is done, her daughter Augustine can marry ; Augustine's *dot* is the farm."

"Augustine—at our inn ?"

"The very same."

"And the blonde—the handsome man at the
creamery, he is the future——— ?"

"I'm sorry to hear such things of Augustine,"
smiled Renard, as he worked; "she must be indulging in an *entr'acte*.   No, the gentleman of
Augustine's—well, perhaps not of her affections,
but of her mother's choice, is a peasant who works
the farm ; the creamery is only an incidental di-
version.   Again, I'm sorry to hear such sad things
of Augustine———"

"Horrors ! "

"Exactly.   That's the way it's done—over here.
Will you join me—over there ?"   Renard blushed
a little.   "I mean I wish to follow that girl—she's
going to dig out yonder.   Will you come ?"

Meanwhile the light was changing, and so was
the tide.   The women were coming inward, washed
up to the shore along with the grasses and sea-
weeds.   A band of diggers suddenly started, with
full basket loads, toward a fishing boat that had
dropped anchor close in to the shore; it was a
Honfleur craft, come to buy mussels for the Paris

market. The women trudged through the water, up to their waists; they clustered about the boats like so many laden beasts. But their shrill bargaining proved them women.

Meanwhile that gentle hissing along the level stretch of brown mud was the tide. It was pushing the women upward, as if it had been a hand—the hand of a relentless fate—instead of a little, liquid kiss.

The sun, as it dipped, made a glory of splendor out of this commonplace bank. It soaked the mud in gold; it was in a royal mood, throwing its largess with reckless abundance to this poor of earth —to the slime and the mud. The long, yellow, lichen leaves massed on the rocks were dyed as if lying in a yellow bath. The sands were richly colored; the ridges were brown in the shadows and burnished at the tops. In the distance the sea-weeds were black, sable furs, covering the velvet robes of earth. The sea out beyond was as rosy as a babe, and the sails were dazzlingly white as they floated past, between the sky and the distant purple line of the horizon.

Meanwhile the tide is coming in.

The procession of the women toward the carts grows in numbers. The thick sabots plunge into the mud, the water squirts out of the wooden shoes as the strong heels press into them. The straw, the universal stocking of these women-diggers, is reeking with dirt. Volumes of slush are splashed on the bared skinny ankles, on the wet skirts, wet to the waists, and on the coarse sail-cloth aprons tied beneath the hanging bosoms. The women

are all drenched now in a bath of filth. The
baskets are reeking with filth also, they rain
showers of dirt along the bent backs. A long line
of the bent figures has formed on their way to the
carts. There is, however, a thick fringe of diggers
left who still dispute their rights with the sea.

But the tide is pushing them inward, upward.
And all the while the light is getting more and
more golden, shimmery, radiant. Under this light,
beneath this golden mantel of color, these creatures appear still more terrible. As they bend
over, their faces tirelessly held downward on a
level with their hands, they seem but gnomes;
surely they are huge, undeveloped embryos of
women, with neither head nor trunk. For this
light is pitiless. It makes them even more a
part of this earth, out of which they seem to have
sprung, a strange amorphous growth. The
bronzed skins are dyed in the gold as if to match
with the hue of the mud; the wet skirts are
shreds, gray and brown tatters, not so good in text-
ure as the lichens, and the ragged jerseys seem
only bits of the more distant weeds woven into
tissues to hide mercifully the lean, sinewy backs.

The tide is almost in.

In the shallows the sunset is fading. Here and
there are brilliant little pools, each pool a mirror,
and each mirror reflects a different picture. Here
is a second sky—faintly blue, with a trailing saffron scarf of cloud; there, the inverted silhouettes
of two fish-wives are conical shapes, their coifs and
wet skirts startlingly distinct in tones; beyond,
sails a fantastic fleet, with polychrome sails, each

spar, masthead, and wrinkled sail as sharply outlined as if chiselled in relief. Presently these miniature pictures fade as the light fades. Blacker
grows the mud, and there is less and less of it;
the silhouetted shapes of the diggers are seen no
more; they are following the carts up the steep
cliffs; even the sky loses its color and fades also.
And the little pools that have been a burning
orange, then a darkening violet, gay with pictured
worlds, in turn pale to gray, and die into the universal blackness.

The tide is in.

It is flowing, rich and full, crested with foam beneath the osier hedges. We hear it break with a
sudden dash and splutter against the cliff parapets. And the mud-bank is no more.

Half an hour later, from our chamber windows
we looked forth through the dusk across at the
mussel-bed. The great mud-bank, all that black
acreage of slime and sea-weed, the eager, struggling band of toiling fish-wives, all was gone; it
was all as if it had not been—would never be
again. The water hissed along the beach; it broke
in rhythmic, sonorous measure against the parapet. Surely there had never been any beds, or
any mussels, or any toiling fish-wives; or if there
had, it was all a world that the sea had washed
up, and then as quietly, as heedlessly, as pitilessly had obliterated.

It was the very epitome of life itself.

CHAPTER V.

 OUR visit to the mussel-bed, as we soon found, had been our formal introduction to the village. Henceforth every door-step held a friend; not a coif or a blouse passed without a greeting. The village, as a village, lived in the open street. Villerville had the true French genius for society; the very houses were neighborly, crowding close upon the narrow sidewalk. Conversation, to be carried on from a dormer-window or from opposite sides of the street, had evidently been the first architectural consideration in the mind of the builders; doors and windows must be as open and accessible as the lives of the inhabitants. The houses themselves appeared to be regarded in the light of pockets, into which the old women and fishermen plunged to drag forth a net or a knife; also as convenient, if rude, little caverns into which the village crawled at night, to take its heavy slumber.

The door-step was the drawing-room, and

the open street was the club of this Villerville world.

The door-way, the yard, or the bit of garden tucked in between two high walls—it was here, under the tent of sky rather than beneath the stuffy roofs, that the village lived, talked, quarrelled, bargained, worked, and more or less openly made love.

To the door-step everything was brought that was portable. There was nothing, from the small boy to the brass kettle, that could not be more satisfactorily polished off, in full view of one's world, than by one's self, in seclusion and solitude. Justice, at least, appeared to gain by this passion for open-air ministration, if one were to judge by the frequency with which the Villerville boy was laid across the parental knee. We were repeatedly called upon to coincide, at the very instant of flagellation, with the verdict pronounced against the youthful offender.

" *S'il est assez méchant, lui ?* Ah, mesdames, what do you think of one who goes forth dry, with clean sabots, that I, myself, have washed, and behold him returned, *après un tout p'tit quart d'heure*, stinking with filth ? Bah ! it's he that will catch it when his father comes home ! " And meanwhile the mother's hand descends, lest justice should cool ere night.

There were other groups that crowded the doorsteps; there were young mothers that sat there, with their babes clasped to the full breasts, in whose eyes was to be read the satisfied passion of recent motherhood; there were gay clusters of

A VILLERVILLE FISH-WIFE.

young Norman maidens, whose glances, brilliant
and restless, were pregnant with all the meaning
of unspent youth. The figures of the fishermen,
toiling up the street with bared legs and hairy
breast, bending beneath their baskets alive with
fish, stopped to have a word or two, seasoned with
a laugh, with these latter groups. There were
also knots of patient old men, wrecks that the sea
had tossed back to earth, to rot and die there, that
came out of the black little houses to rest their
bones in the sun. And everywhere there were
groups of old women, or of women still young to
whom the look of age had come long before its
due time.

The village seemed peopled with women, sexless
creatures for the most part, whom toil and the life
on the mussel-bed or in the field had dried and
hardened into mummy shapes. Only these, the
old and the useless, were left at home to rear the
younger generation and to train them to take up
the same heavy burden of life. The coifs of these
old hags made dazzling spots of brightness against
the gray of the walls and the stuccoed houses;
clustered together, the high caps that nodded in
unison to the chatter were in startling contrast to
the bronzed faces bending over the fish-nets, and
to the blue-veined, leathery hands that flew in and
out of the coarse meshes with the fluent ease of
long practice.

With one of these old women we became friends.
We had made her acquaintance at a poetic moment, under romantic circumstances. We were all
three watching a sunset, under a pink sky; we

were sitting far out on the grasses of the cliff. Her house was in the midst of the grasses, some little distance from the village, attached to it only as a ragged fringe might edge a garment. It was a thatched hut; yet there were circumstances in the life of the owner which had transformed the interior into a luxurious apartment. The owner of the hut was herself hanging on the edge of life; she was a toothless, bent, and withered old remnant; but her vigor and vivacity were those of a witch. Her hands and eyes were ceaselessly active; she was forever busy, fingering a fish-net, or polishing her Normandy brasses, or stirring some dark liquid in an iron pot over the dim fire.

At our first meeting, conversation had immediately engaged itself; it had ended, as all right talk should, in friendship. On this morning of our visit, many a gay one having preceded it, we found our friend arrayed as if for an outing. She had mounted her best coif, and tied across her shrivelled old breast was a vivid purple silk kerchief.

"*Tiens, mes enfants, soyez les bienvenues,*" was her gay greeting, seasoned with a high cackling laugh, as she waved us to two rickety chairs. "No, I'm not going out, not yet; there is plenty of time, plenty of time. It is you who are good, *si aimables*, to come out here to see me. And tired, too, *hein*, with the long walk? *Tiens*, I had nearly forgotten; there's a bottle of wine open below— you must take a glass."

She never forgot. The bottle of wine had always just been opened; the cork was always also

miraculously rebellious for a cork that had been
previously pulled. Although our ancient friend
was a peasant, her cellar was the cellar of a gourmet. Wonderful old wines were hers! Port,
Bordeaux, white wines, of vintages to make the
heart warm; each was produced in turn, a different vintage and wine on each one of our visits, but
no champagne. This was no wine for women—
for the right women. Champagne was a bad, fast
wine, for fast, disreputable people. "*C'est un
vrai poison, qui vous infecte,*" she had declared again
and again, and when she saw her daughter drinking it, it made her shudder; she confessed to having a moment of doubt; had Paris, indeed, really
brought her child no harm? Then the old mère
would shrug her bent shoulders and rub her
hands, and for a moment she would be lost in
thought. Presently the cracked old laugh would
peal forth again, and, as she threw back her head,
she would shake it as if to dispel some dark
vision.

To-day she had dropped, almost as soon as we
entered, into a narrow trap-door, descending a
flight of stone steps. We could hear a clicking of
bottles and a rustling of straw; and then, behold,
a veritable fairy issuing from the bowels of the
earth, with flushes of red suffusing the ribbed, be-
wrinkled face, as the old figure straightens its
crookedness to carry the dusty bottle securely,
steadily, lest the cloudy settling at the bottom
should be disturbed. What a merry little feast
then began! We had learned where the glasses
were kept; we had been busily scouring them while

our hostess was below. Then wine and glasses, along with three chairs, were quickly placed on the pine table at the door of the old house. Here, on the grass of the cliffs, we sat, sipping our wine, enjoying the sea that lay at our feet, and above, the sunlit sky. To our friend both sky and sea were familiar companions; but the fichu was a new friend.

"Yes, it is very beautiful, as you say," she said, in answer to our admiring comments. "It came from Paris, from my daughter. She sent it to me; she is always making me gifts; she is one who remembers her old mother! Figure to yourselves that last year, in midwinter, she sent me no less than three gowns, all wool! What can I do with them? *C'est pour me flatter, c'est sa manière de me dire qu'il faut vivre pour longtemps! Ah, la chère folle!* But she spoils me, the darling!"

This daughter had become the most mysterious of all our Villerville discoveries. Our old friend was a peasant, the child of peasant farmers. She would always remain a peasant; and yet her daughter was a Parisian, and lived in a *bonbonnière.* She was also married; but that only served to thicken the web of mystery enshrouding her How could a daughter of a peasant, brought up as a peasant, who had lived here, a tiller of the fields till her nineteenth year, suddenly be transformed into a woman of the Parisian world, gain the position of a banker's wife, and be dancing, as the old mère kept telling us, at balls at the Elysée? Her mother never answered this riddle for us; and, more amazing still, neither could the village. The village would shrug its shoulders, when we questioned it, with discretion, concerning this enigma. "Ah, dame! It was she—the old mère—who had had chances in life, to marry her daughter like that! Victorine was pretty—yes, there was no gainsaying she was pretty—but not so beautiful as all that, to entrap a banker, *un homme sérieux, qui vit de ses rentes!* and who was generous, too, for the old mère needn't work now, since she was always receiving money." Gifts were perpetually pouring into the low rooms—wines, and Parisian delicacies, and thick garments.

The tie between the two, between the mother and daughter, appeared to be as strong and their relations as complete as if one were not clad in homespun and the other in Worth gowns. There was no shame, that was easily seen, on either side; each apparently was full of pride in the other; their living apart was entirely due to the old mère's preference for a life on the cliffs, alone in the midst of all her old peasant belongings.

" *C'est plus chez-soi, ici!* Victorine feels that, too. She loves the smell of the old wood, and of the peat burning there in the fireplace. When she comes down to see me, I must shut fast all the doors and windows; she wants the whole of the smell, *pour faire le vrai bouquet*, as she says. If she had had children—ah!—I don't say but what I might have consented; but as it is, I love my old fire, and my view out there, and the village, best!"

At this point in the conversation, the old eyes, bright as they were, turned dim and cloudy; the

inward eye was doubtless seeing something other
than the view; it was resting on a youthful figure,
clad in Parisian draperies, and on a face rising
above the draperies, that bent lovingly over the
deep-throated fireplace, basking in its warmth, and
revelling in its homely perfume. We were silent
also, as the picture of that transfigured daughter
of the house flitted across our own mental vision.

"The village?" suddenly broke in the old mère.
" Dieu de Dieu! that reminds me. I must go, my
children, I must go. Loisette is waiting; *la pauvre enfant*—perhaps suffering too—how do I know?
And here am I, playing, like a lazy clout! Did
you know she had had *un nini* this morning? The
little angel came at dawn. That's a good sign!
And what news for Auguste! He was out last
night—fishing; she was at her washing when he
left her. *Tiens*, there they are, looking for him!
They've brought the spy-glass."

The old mère shaded her eyes, as she looked out
into the dazzling sunlight. We followed her finger, that pointed to a projection on the cliffs.
Among the grasses, grouped on top of the highest rock, was a family party. An old fish-wife was
standing far out against the sky; she also was
shading her eyes. A child's round head, crowded
into a white knit cap, was etched against the
wide blue; and, kneeling, holding in both hands a
long seaman's glass, was a girl, sweeping the horizon with long, skilful stretches of arm and hand.
The sun descended in a shower of light on the old
grandam's seamy face, on the red, bulging cheeks
of the chubby child, and on the bent figure of the

girl, whose knees were firmly implanted in the
deep, tall grasses. Beyond the group there was
nothing but sea and sky.

"Yes," the mère went on, garrulously, as she
recorked the bottle of old port, carrying table and
glasses within doors. "Yes, they're looking for
him. It ought to be time, now; he's due about
now. There's a man for you—good—*bon comme le
bon Dieu.* Sober, saving too—good father—in love
with Victorine as on the wedding night—ah, *mes
enfants !*—there are few like him, or this village
would be a paradise ! "

She shut the door of the little cabin. And then
she gave us a broad wink. The wink was entirely
by way of explanation; it was to enlighten us as
to why a certain rare bottle of port—a fresh one—
was being secreted beneath her fichu. It was a
wink that conveyed to us a really valuable number
of facts; chief among them being the very obvious
fact that the French Government was an idiot, and
a tyrant into the bargain, since it imposed stupid
laws no one meant to carry out; least of all a good
Norman. What? pay two *sous octroi* on a bottle
of one's own wine, that one had had in one's cellar
for half a lifetime? To cheat the town out of
those twopence becomes, of course, the true Norman's chief pleasure in life. What is his reputation worth, as a shrewd, sharp man of business, if
a little thing like cheating stops him? It is even
better fun than bargaining, to cheat thus one's
own town, since nothing is to be risked, and one is
so certain of success.

The mère nodded to us gayly, in farewell, as

we all three re-entered the town. She disappeared all at once into a narrow door-way, her arms still clasping her old port, that lay in the folds of her shawl. On her shrewd kindly old face came a light that touched it all at once with a glow of divinity; the mother in her had sprung into life with sharp, sweet suddenness; she had caught the wail of the new-born babe through the open door.

The village itself seemed to have caught something of the same glow. It was not only the splendor of the noon sun that made the faces of the worn fish-wives and the younger women softer and kindlier than common; the groups, as we passed them, were all talking of but one thing—of this babe that had come in the night, of Auguste's absence, and of Victorine's sharp pains and her cries, that had filled the street, so that none could sleep.

CHAPTER VI.

At dusk that evening the same subject, with variations, was the universal topic of the conversational groups. Still Auguste had not come; half the village was out watching for him on the cliffs. The other half was crowding the streets and the door-steps.

Twilight is the classic time, in all French towns and villages, for the *al-fresco* lounge. The cool breath of the dusk is fresh, then, and restful; after the heat and sweat of the long noon the air, as it touches brow and lip, has the charm of a caress. So the door-ways and streets were always crowded at this hour; groups moved, separated, formed and re-formed, and lingered to exchange their budget of gossip, to call out their "*Bonne nuit*," the girls to clasp hands, looking longingly over their shoulders at the younger fishermen and farmers; the latter to nod, carelessly, gayly back at them; and then—as men will—to fling an arm about a

comrade's shoulder as they, in their turn, called
out into the dusk,

"*Allons, mon brave; de l'absinthe, toi?*" as the
cabaret swallowed them up.

Great and mighty were the cries and the oaths
that issued from the cabaret's open doors and
windows. The Villerville fisherman loved Bacchus
only second to Neptune; when he was not out
casting his net into the Channel he was drinking
up his spoils. It was during the sobering process
only that affairs of a purely domestic nature engaged his attention. Some of the streets were
permeated with noxious odors, with the poison of
absinthe and the fumes of cheap brandy. Noisy,
reeling groups came out of the tavern doors, to
shout and sing, or to fight their way homeward.
One such figure was filling a narrow alley, swaying from right to left, with a jeering crowd at his
heels.

"*Est-il assez ridicule, lui?* with his cap over his
nose, and his knees knocking at everyone's door?
Bah! ça pue!" the group of lads following him went
on, shouting about the poor sot, as they pelted him
with their rain of pebbles and paper bullets.

"Ah—h, he will beat her, in his turn, poor
soul; she always gets it when he's full, as full as
that——"

The voice was so close to our ears that we started.
The words appeared addressed to us; they were,
in a way, since they were intended for the street,
as a street, and for the benefit of the groups that
filled it. The voice was gruff yet mellow; despite
its gruffness it had the ring of a latent kindliness

in its deep tones. The man who owned it was
seated on a level with our elbows, at a cobbler's
bench. We stopped to let the crowd push on
beyond us. The man had only lifted his head from
his work, but involuntarily one stopped to salute
the power in it.

"*Bonsoir, mesdames*"—the head gravely bowed
as the great frame of the body below the head
rose from the low seat. The room within seemed
to contain nothing else save this giant figure, now
that it had risen and was moving toward us. The
half-door was courteously opened.

"Will not *ces dames* give themselves the trouble
of entering? The streets are not gay at this
hour."

We went in. A dog and a woman came forth
from a smaller inner room to greet us; of the two
the dog was obviously the personage next in point
of intelligence and importance to the master. The
woman had a snuffed-out air, as of one whose life
had died out of her years ago. She blinked at us
meekly as she dropped a timid courtesy; at a low
word of command she turned a pitifully patient
back on us all. There were years of obedience to
orders written on its submissive curves; and she
bent it once more over her kettles; both she and
the kettles were on the bare floor. It was the
poorest of all the Villerville interiors we had as
yet seen; the house was also, perhaps, the oldest
in the village. It and the old church had been
opposite neighbors for several centuries. The
shop and the living-room were all in one; the low
window was a counter by day and a shutter by

night. Within, the walls were bare as were the
floors. Three chairs with sunken leather covers,
and a bed with a mattress, also sunken—a hollow
in a pine frame, was the equipment in furniture.
The poverty was brutal; it was the naked, unabashed poverty of the middle ages, with no hint
of shame or effort of concealment. The colossus
whom the low roof covered was as unconscious
of the barrenness of his surroundings as were his
own walls. This hovel was his home; he had
made us welcome with the manners of a king.

Meanwhile the dog was sniffing at our skirts.
After a tour of observation and inspection he
wagged his tail, gave a short bark, and seated himself by Charm. The giant's eyes twinkled.

" You see, mesdames, it is a dog with a mind—he
knows in an instant who are the right sort. And
eloquence, also—he is one who can make speeches
with his tail. A dog's tongue is in his tail, and
this one wags his like an orator ! "

Some one else, as well as the dog, possessed the
oratorical gift. The cobbler's voice was the true
speaker's voice—rich, vibrating, sonorous, with a
deep note of melody in it. Pose and gestures
matched with the voice ; they were flexible and
picturesquely suggestive.

"If you care for oratory—" Charm smiled out
upon the huge but mobile face—" you are well
placed. The village lies before you. You can
always see the play going on, and hear the
speeches—of the passers-by."

The large mouth smiled back. But at Charm's
first sentence the keen Norman eyes had fixed

their twinkling glitter on the girl's face. They
seemed to be reading to the very bottom of her
thought and being. The scrutiny was not relaxed
as he answered.

"Yes, yes, it is very amusing. One sees a little
of everything here. *Le monde qui passe*—it makes
life more diverting; it helps to kill the time. I
look out from my perch, like a bird—a very old
one, and caged"—and he shook forth a great
laugh from beneath the wide leather apron.

The woman, hearing the laugh, came out into
the room.

"*E'ben—et toi*—what do you want?"

The giant stopped laughing long enough to
turn tyrant. The woman, at the first of his growl,
smiled feebly, going back with unresisting meekness to her knees, to her pots, and her kettles.
The dog growled in imitation of his master; obviously the soul of the dog was in the wrong
body.

Meanwhile the master of the dog and the
woman had forgotten both now; he was continuing, in a masterful way, to enlighten us about the
peculiarities of his native village. The talk had
now reached the subject of the church.

"Oh, yes, it is fine, very, and old; it and this
old house are the oldest of all the inhabitants
of this village. The church came first, though, it
was built by the English, when they came over,
thinking to conquer us with their Hundred Years'
War. Little they knew France and Frenchmen.
The church was thoroughly French, although the
English did build it; on the ground many times,

but up again, only waiting the hand of the builder
and the restorer."

Again the slim-waisted shape of the old wife
ventured forth into the room.

"Yes, as he says"—in a voice that was but an
echo—"the church has been down many times."

"*Tais-toi—c'est moi qui parle*," grumbled anew
her husband, giving the withered face a terrific
scowl.

"*Ohé, oui, c'est toi*," the echo bleated. The thin
hands meekly folded themselves across her apron.
She stood quite still, as if awaiting more punishment.

"It is our good curé who wishes to pull it down
once more," her terrible husband went on, not
heeding her quiet presence. "Do you know our
curé? Ah, ha, he's a fine one. It's he that rules
us now—he's our king—our emperor. Ugh, he's
a bad one, he is."

"Ah, yes, he's a bad one, he is," his wife echoed,
from the side wall.

"Well, and who asked you to talk?" cried her
husband, with a face as black as when the curé's
name had first been mentioned. The echo shrank
into the wall. "As I was telling these ladies"—
he resumed here his boot work, clamping the last
between his great knees—"as I was saying, we
have not been fortunate in curés, we of our parish.
There are curés and curés, as there are fagots and
fagots—and ours is a bad lot. We've had nothing
but trouble since he came to rule over us. We get
poorer day by day, and he richer. There he is
now, feeding his hens and his doves—look, over

there—with the ladies of his household gathered
about him—his mother, his aunt, and his niece—a
perfect harem. Oh, he keeps them all fat and
sleek, like himself! Bah!"

The grunt of disgust the cobbler gave filled the
room like a thunder-clap. He was peering over
his last, across the open counter, at a little house
adjoining the church green, with a great hatred in
his face. From one of the windows of the house
there was leaning forth a group of three heads;
there was the tonsured head of a priest, round,
pink-tinted, and the figures of two women, one
youthful, with a long, sad-featured face, and the
other ruddy and vigorous in outline. They were
watching the priest as he scattered corn to the
hens and geese in the garden below the window.

The cobbler was still eying them fiercely, as he
continued to give vent to his disgust.

"*Méchaht homme — lui*," he here whipped his
thread, venomously, through the leather he was
sewing. "Figure to yourselves, mesdames, that
besides being wicked, our curé is a very shrewd
man; it is not for the pure good of the parish he
works, not he."

"Not he," the echo repeated, coming forth again
from the wall. This time the whisper passed un-
noticed; her master's hatred of the curé was
greater than his passion for showing his own
power.

"Religion—religion is a very good way of making money, better than most, if one knows how to
work the machine. The soul, it is a fine instrument on which to play if one is skilful. Our

curé has a grand touch on this instrument. You
should see the good man take up a collection, it is
better than a comedy."

Here the cobbler turned actor; he rose, scattering his utensils right and left; he assumed a grand
air and a mincing, softly tread, the tread of a
priest. His flexible voice imitated admirably the
rounded, unctuous, autocratic tone peculiar to the
graduates of St. Sulpice.

"You should hear him, when the collection does
not suit him : ' *Mes frères et mes sœurs*, I see that
le bon Dieu isn't in your minds and your hearts
to-day; you are not listening to his voice; the
Saviour is then speaking in vain?' Then he
prays—" the cobbler folded his hands with a great
parade of reverence, lifting his eyes as he rolled
his lids heavenward hypocritically—"yes, he prays
—and then he passes the plate himself! He holds
it before your very nose, there is no pushing it
aside; he would hold it there till you dropped—
till Doomsday. Ah, he's a hard crust, he is!
There's a tyrant for you—*la monarchie absolue*—
that's what he believes in. He must have this, he
must have that. Now it is a new altar-cloth, or a
fresh Virgin of the modern make, from Paris, with
a robe of real lace ; the old one was black and faded,
too black to pray to. Now it is a *huissier*, forsooth,
that we must have, we, a parish of a few hundred
souls, who know our seats in the church as well as
we know our own noses. One would think a
'suisse' would have done; but we are swells now,
avec ce gaillard-là, only the tiptop is good enough.
So, if you grace our poor old church with your

presence you will be shown to your bench by a
very splendid gentleman in black, in knee-breeches,
with silver chains, with a three-cornered hat, who
strikes with his stick three times as he seats you.
Bah ! ridiculous ! "

" Ridiculous ! " the woman repeated, softly.

" They had the curé once, though. One day in
church he announced a subscription to be taken up
for restorations, from fifty centimes to—to anything; he will take all you give him, avaricious
that he is ! He believes in the greasing of the
palm, he does. Well, think you the subscription
was for restorations, mesdames ? It was for
demolition — that's what it was for — to make
the church level with the ground. To do this
would cost a little matter of twenty thousand
francs, which would pass through his hands,
you understand. Well, that staggered the parish.
Our mayor—a man *pas trop fin*, was terribly upset. He went about saying the curé claimed the
church as his ; he could do as he liked with it, he
said, and he proposed to make it a fine modern
one. All the village was weeping. The church
was the oldest friend of the village, except for
such as I, whom these things have turned pagan. Well, one of our good citizens reminds the
mayor that the church, under the new laws, belongs to the commune. The mayor tells this
timidly to the curé. And the curé retorts, 'Ah,
bien, at least one-half belongs to me.' And the
good citizen answers — he has gone with the
mayor to prop him up—'Which half will you
take ? The cemetery, doubtless, since your charge

is over the souls of the parish.' Ah! ah! he
pricked him well then! he pricked him well!"

The low room rang with the great shout of the
cobbler's laughter. The dog barked furiously in
concert. Our own laughter was drowned in the
thunder of our host's loud guffaws. The poor old
wife shook herself with a laugh so much too vigorous for her frail frame, one feared its after-effects.

The after-effects were a surprise. After the first
of her husband's spasms of glee the old woman
spoke out, but in trembling tones no longer.

" Ah, the cemetery, it is I who forgot to go there
this week."

Her husband stopped, the laugh dying on his
lip as he turned to her.

"*Ah, ma bonne*, how came that? You forgot?"
His own tones trembled at the last word.

" Yes, you had the cramps again, you remember,
and there was no money left for the bouquet."

" Yes, I remember," and the great chest heaved
a deep sigh.

" You have children—you have lost someone?"

" Hélas! no living children, mademoiselle. No,
no—one daughter we had, but she died twenty
years ago. She lies over there—where we can see
her. She would have been thirty-eight years now
—the fourteenth of this very month!"

"Yes, this very month."

Then the old woman, for the first time, left her
refuge along the wall; she crept softly, quietly
near to her husband to put her withered hand in
his. His large paw closed over it. Both of the old
faces turned toward the cemetery; and in the old

eyes a film gathered, as they looked toward all
that was left of the hope that was buried away
from them.

We left them thus, hand in hand, with many
promises to renew the acquaintance.

The village was no longer abroad in the streets.
During our talk in the shop the night had fallen;
it had cast its shadow, as trees cast theirs, in
a long, slow slant. Lights were trembling in the
dim interiors; the shrill cries of the children were
stilled; only a muffled murmur came through the
open doors and windows. The villagers were pattering across the rough floors, talking, as their sabots clattered heavily over the wooden surface, as
they washed the dishes, as they covered their fires,
shoving back the tables and chairs. As we walked
along, through the nearer windows came the sound
of steps on the creaking old stairs, then a rustling
of straw and the heavy fall of weary bodies, as the
villagers flung themselves on the old oaken beds,
that groaned as they received their burden. Presently all was still. Only our steps resounded
through the streets. The stars filled the sky; and
beneath them the waves broke along the beach. In
the closely packed little streets the heavy breathing of the sleeping village broke also in short,
quick gasps.

Only we and the night were awake.

CHAPTER VII.

 QUITE a number of changes came about with our annexation of an artist and his garden. Chief among these changes was the surprising discovery of finding ourselves, at the end of a week, in possession of a villa.

"It's next door," Renard remarked, in the casual way peculiar to artists. "You are to have the whole house to yourselves, all but the top floor; the people who own it keep that to live in. There's a garden of the right sort, with espaliers, also rose-trees, and a tea-house; quite the right sort of thing altogether."

The unforeseen, in its way, is excellent and admirable. *De l'imprévu*, surely this is the dash of seasoning—the caviare we all crave in life's somewhat too monotonous repasts. But as men have been known to admire the still-life in wifely character and then repented their choice, marrying peace only to court dissension, so we, incontinently deserting our humble inn chambers to take possession of a grander state, in the end found the

A DEPARTURE—VILLERVILLE.

capital of experience drained to pay for our little
infidelity.

The owners of the villa Belle Etoile, our friend
announced, he had found greatly depressed; of
this, their passing mood, he had taken such advan-
tage as only comes to the knowing. "They speak
of themselves drearily as 'deux pauvres malheu-
reux' with this villa still on their hands, and here
they are almost 'touching June,' as they put it.
They also gave me to understand that only the
finest flowers of the aristocracy had had the honor
of dwelling in this villa. They have been able, I
should say, more or less successfully to deflower
this 'fine fleur' of some of their gold. But they
are very meek just now—they were willing to listen
to reason."

The "two poor unhappies" were looking surprisingly contented an hour later, when we went
in to inspect our possessions. They received us
with such suave courtesy, that I was quite certain
Renard's skill in transactions had not played its
full gamut of capacity.

Civility is the Frenchman's mask; he wears it
as he does his skin—as a matter of habit. But
courtesy is his *costume de bal ;* he can only afford
to don his bravest attire of smiles and graciousness when his pocket is in holiday mood. Madame
Fouchet we found in full ball-room toilet; she was
wreathed in smiles. Would *ces dames* give themselves the trouble of entering? would they see the
house or the garden first? would they permit their
trunks to be sent for? Monsieur Fouchet, meanwhile, was making a brave second to his wife's

bustling welcome; he was rubbing his hands vigorously, a somewhat suspicious action in a Frenchman, I have had occasion to notice, after the completion of a bargain. Nature had cast this mildeyed individual for the part of accompanyist in the comedy we call life; a *rôle* he sometimes varied as now, with the office of *claqueur*, when an uncommonly clever proof of madame's talent for business drew from him this noiseless tribute of applause. His weak, fat contralto called after us, as we followed madame's quick steps up the waxed stairway; he would be in readiness, he said, to show us the garden, "once the chambers were visited."

"It wasn't a real stroke, mesdames, it was only a warning!" was the explanation conveyed to us in loud tones, with no reserve of whispered delicacy, when we expressed regret at monsieur's detention below stairs; a partially paralyzed leg, dragged painfully after the latter's flabby figure, being the obvious cause of this detention.

The stairway had the line of beauty, describing a pretty curve before its glassy steps led us to a narrow entry; it had also the brevity which is said to be the very soul, *l'anima viva*, of all true wit; but it was quite long and straight enough to serve Madame Fouchet as a stage for a prolonged monologue, enlivened with much affluence of gesture. Fouchet's seizure, his illness, his convalescence, and present physical condition—a condition which appeared to be bristling with the tragedy of danger, "un vrai drame d'anxiété"—was graphically conveyed to us. The horrors of the long winter

also, so sad for a Parisian—"si triste pour la
Parisienne, ces hivers de province"—together with
the miseries of her own home life, between this
paralytic of a husband below stairs, and above, her
mother, an old lady of eighty, nailed to her sofa
with gout. "You may thus figure to yourselves,
mesdames, what a melancholy season is the winter! And now, with this villa still on our hands,
and the season already announcing itself, ruin
stares us in the face, mesdames—ruin!"

It was a moving picture. Yet we remained
strangely unaffected by this tale of woe. Madame
Fouchet herself, the woman, not the actress, was
to blame, I think, for our unfeelingness. Some-
how, to connect woe, ruin, sadness, melancholy, or
distress, in a word, of any kind with our landlady's
opulent figure, we found a difficult acrobatic mental feat. She presented to the eye outlines and
features that could only be likened, in point of
prosperity, to a Dutch landscape. Like certain of
the mediæval saints presented by the earlier de-
lineators of the martyrs as burning above a slow
fire, while wearing smiles of purely animal content, as if in full enjoyment of the temperature,
this lady's sufferings were doubtless an invisible
discipline, the hair shirt which her hardened cuticle felt only to be a pleasurable itching.

"Voilà, mesdames!" It was with a magnificent
gesture that madame opened doors and windows.
The drama of her life was forgotten for the moment in the conscious pride of presenting us with
such a picture as her gay little house offered.

Inside and out, summer and the sun were bloom-

ing and shining with spendthrift luxuriance. The
salon opened directly on the garden; it would
have been difficult to determine just where one
began and the domain of the other ended, with the
pinks and geraniums that nodded in response to
the peach and pear blossoms in the garden. A bit
of faded Aubusson and a print representing Madame Geoffrin's salon in full session, with a poet
of the period transporting the half-moon grouped
listeners about him to the point of tears, were evi-
dences of the refined tastes of our landlady in the
arts; only a sentimentalist would have hung that
picture in her salon. Other decorations further
proved her as belonging to both worlds. The
chintzes gay with garlands of roses, with which
walls, beds, and chairs were covered, revealed the
mundane element, the woman of decorative tastes,
possessed of a hidden passion for effective back-
grounds. Two or three wooden crucifixes, a *prie-
dieu*, and a couple of saints in plaster, went far to
prove that this excellent *bourgeoise* had thriftily
made her peace with Heaven. It was a curious
mixture of the sacred and the profane.

Down below, beneath the windows overlooking
the sea, lay the garden. All the houses fronting
the cliff had similar little gardens, giving, as the
French idiom so prettily puts it, upon the sea.
But compared to these others, ours was as a rose of
Sharon blooming in the midst of little deserts.
Renard had been entirely right about this particular bit of earth attached to our villa. It was a gem
of a garden. It was a French garden, and therefore, entirely as a matter of course, it had walls.

It was as cut off from the rest of the world as if it had been a prison or a fortification.

The Frenchman, above all others, appears to have the true sentiment of seclusion, when the society of trees and flowers is to be enjoyed. Next to woman, nature is his fetich. True to his national taste in dress, he prefers that both should be costumed à la Parisienne; but as poet and lover, it is his instinct to build a wall about his idol, that he may enjoy his moments of expansion unseen and unmolested. This square of earth, for instance, was not much larger than the space covered by the chamber roof above us; and yet, with the high walls towering over the rose-stalks, it was as secluded as a monk's cloister. We found it, indeed, on later acquaintance, as poetic and delicately sensuous a retreat as the romance-writers would wish us to believe did those mediæval connoisseurs of comfort, when, with sandalled feet, they paced their own convent garden-walks. Fouchet was a broken-down shopkeeper; but somewhere hidden within, there lurked the soul of a Mæcenas; he knew how to arrange a feast—of roses. The garden was a bit of greensward, not much larger than a pocket-handkerchief; but the grass had the right emerald hue, and one's feet sank into the rich turf as into the velvet of an oriental rug. Small as was the enclosure, between the espaliers and the flower-beds serpentined minute paths of glistening pebbles. Nothing which belonged to a garden had been forgotten, not even a pine from the tropics, and a bench under the pine that was just large enough for two. This lat-

ter was an ideal little spot in which to bring a
friend or a book. One could sit there and gorge
one's self with sweets; a dance was perpetually
going on—the gold-and-purple butterflies fluttering gayly from morning till night; and the bees
freighted the air with their buzzing. If one tired
of perfumes and dancing, there was always music
to be enjoyed, from a full orchestra. The sea, just
the other side of the wall of osiers, was always in
voice, whether sighing or shouting. The larks and
blackbirds had a predilection for this nest of color,
announcing their preference loudly in a combat
of trills. And once or twice, we were quite certain,
a nightingale with Patti notes had been trying its
liquid scales in the dark.

It was in this garden that our acquaintance with
our landlord deepened into something like friendship. Monsieur Fouchet was always to be found
there, tying up the rose-trees, or mending the
paths, or shearing the bit of turf.

"*Mon jardin, c'est un peu moi, vous savez*—it is my
pride and my consolation." At the latter word,
Fouchet was certain to sigh.

Then we fell to wondering just what grief had
befallen this amiable person which required Hora-
tian consolation. Horace had need of rose-leaves
to embalm his disappointments, for had he not
cooled his passions by plunging into the bath of
literature? Besides, Horace was bitten by the
modern rabies: he was as restless as an American.
When at Rome was he not always sighing for his
Sabine farm, and when at the farm always regret-
ting Rome? But this harmless, innocent-eyed,

benevolent-browed old man, with his passive
brains tied up in a foulard, o' mornings, and his
bourgeois feet adorned with carpet slippers, what
grief in the past had bitten his poor soul and left
its mark still sore ?

"It isn't monsieur—it is madame who has made
the past dark," was Renard's comment, when we
discussed our landlord's probable acquaintance
with regret—or remorse.

Whatever secret of the past may have hovered
over the Fouchet household, the evil bird had not
made its nest in madame's breast, that was clear;
her smooth, white brow was the sign of a rose-leaf
conscience; that dark curtain of hair, looped ma-
donna-wise over each ear, framed a face as unruffled
as her conscience.

She was entirely at peace with her world—and
with heaven as well, that was certain. Whatever
her sins, the confessional had purged her. Like
others, doubtless, she had found a husband and the
provinces excellent remedies for a damaged reputation. She lived now in the very odor of sanctity ;
the curé had a pipe in her kitchen, with something
more sustaining, on certain bright afternoons. Although she was daily announcing to us her approaching dissolution—"I die, mesdames—I die of
ennui "—it seemed to me there were still signs, at
times, of a vigorous resuscitation. The curé's visits
were wont to produce a deeper red in the deep
bloom of her cheek ; the mayor and his wife, who
drank their Sunday coffee in the arbor, brought,
as did Beatrix's advent to Dante, *vita nuova* to this
homesick Parisian.

There were other pleasures in her small world,
also, which made life endurable. Bargaining,
when one teems with talent, may be as exciting
as any other form of conquest. Madame's days
were chiefly passed in imitation of the occupation so dear to an earlier, hardier race, that race
kings have knighted for their powers in dealing
mightily with their weaker neighbors. Madame,
it is true, was only a woman, and Villerville was
somewhat slimly populated. But in imitation of
her remote feudal lords, she also fell upon the
passing stranger, demanding tribute. When the
stranger did not pass, she kept her arm in practice, so to speak, by extracting the last *sou* in a
transaction from a neighbor, or by indulging in a
drama in which the comedy of insult was matched
by the tragedy of contempt.

One of these mortal combats it was my privilege
to witness. The war arose on our announcement
to Mère Mouchard, the lady of the inn by the sea,
of our decision to move next door. To us Mère
Mouchard presented the unruffled plumage of a
dove; her voice also was as the voice of the same,
mellowed by sucking. Ten minutes later the town
was assembled to lend its assistance at the encounter between our two landladies. Each stood
on their respective doorsteps with arms akimbo
and head thrust forward, as geese protrude head
and tongue in moments of combat. And it was
thus, the mère hissed that her boarders were stolen
from her—under her very nose—while her back was
turned, with no more thought of honesty or shame
than a —— (?). The word was never uttered. The

mère's insult was drowned in a storm of voices;
for there came a loud protest from the group of
neighbors. Madame Fouchet, meanwhile, was sustaining her own rôle with great dignity. Her attitude of self-control could only have been learned
in a school where insult was an habitual weapon.
She smiled, an infuriating, exasperating, successful smile. She showed a set of defiant white teeth,
and to her proud white throat she gave a boast-
ful curve. Was it her fault if *ces dames* knew
what comfort and cleanliness were? if they preferred *"des chambres garnies avec goût, vraiment ar-
tistiques"*—to rooms fit only for peasants? *Ces
dames* had just come from Paris; doubtless, they
were not yet accustomed to provincial customs—
aux mœurs provinciales. Then there were exchanged
certain melodious acerbities, which proved that
these ladies had entered the lists on previous occasions, and that each was well practised in the
other's methods of warfare. Opportunely, Renard
appeared on the scene; his announcement that we
proposed still to continue taking our repasts with
the mère, was as oil on the sea of trouble. A rec-
onciliation was immediately effected, and the
street as immediately lost all interest in the play,
the audience melting away as speedily as did the
wrath of the disputants.

"*Le bon Dieu soit loué,*" cried Madame Fouchet,
puffing, as she mounted the stairs a few moments
later—" God be praised "— she hadn't come here
to the provinces to learn her rights—to be taught
her alphabet. Mère Mouchard, forsooth, who
wanted a week's board as indemnity for her loss

of us! A week's board—for lodgings scorned by
peasants!

"Ah, these Normans! what a people, what a
people! They would peel the skin off your back!
They would sell their children! They would cheat
the devil himself!"

"You, madame, I presume, are from Paris."
Madame smiled as she answered, a thin fine smile,
richly seasoned with scorn. "Ah, mesdames! All
the world can't boast of Paris as a birthplace, un-
fortunately. I also, I am a Norman, *mais je ne
m'en fiche pas!* Most of my life, however, I've
lived in Paris, thank God!" She lifted her head
as she spoke, and swept her hands about her
waist to adjust the broad belt, an action pregnant with suggestions. For it was thus conveyed
to us, delicately, that such a figure as hers was not
bred on rustic diet; also, that the Parisian glaze
had not failed of its effect on the coarser provincial clay.

Meanwhile, below in the garden, her husband
was meekly tying up his rose-trees.

Neither of the landladies' husbands had figured
in the street-battle. It had been a purely Amazo-
nian encounter, bloodless but bitter. Both the
husbands of these two belligerent landladies appeared singularly well trained. Mouchard, indeed,
occupied a comparatively humble sphere in his
wife's ménage. He was perpetually to be seen in
the court-yard, at the back of the house, washing
dogs, or dishes, in a costume in which the greatest
economy of cloth compatible with decency had
been triumphantly solved. His wife ran the house,

and he ran the errands, an arrangement which, apparently, worked greatly to the satisfaction of both. But Mouchard was not the first or the second French husband who, on the threshold of his connubial experience, had doubtless had his rôle in life appointed to him, filling the same with patient acquiescence to the very last of the lines.

There is something very touching in the subjection of French husbands. In point of meekness they may well serve, I think, as models to their kind. It is a meekness, however, which does not hint of humiliation; for, after all, what humiliation can there be in being thoroughly understood? The Frenchwoman, by virtue of centuries of activity, in the world and in the field, has become an expert in the art of knowing her man; she has not worked by his side, under the burn of the noon sun, or in the cimmerian darkness of the shop-rear, counting the pennies, for nothing. In exchanging her illusions for the bald front of fact, man himself has had to pay the penalty of this mixed gain. She tests him by purely professional standards, as man tests man, or as he has tested her, when in the ante-matrimonial days he weighed her *dot* in the scale of his need. The Frenchwoman and Shakespeare are entirely of one mind; they perceive the great truth of unity in the scheme of things:

" Woman's test is man's taste."

This is the first among the great truths in the feminine grammar of assent. French masculine taste, as its criterion, has established the excellent

doctrine of utilitarianism. With quick apprehen-
sion the Frenchwoman has mastered this fact;
she has cleverly taken a lesson from ophidian
habits—she can change her skin, quickly shedding
the sentimentalist, when it comes to serious action,
to don the duller raiment of utility. She has accepted her world, in other words, as she finds it,
with a philosopher's shrug. But the philosopher
is lined with the logician; for this system of life
has accomplished the miracle of making its women
logical; they have grasped the subtleties of in-
ductive reasoning. Marriage, for example, they
know is entered into solely on the principle of
mutual benefit; it is therefore a partnership, *bon;*
now, in partnerships sentiments and the emotions
are out of place, they only serve to dim the eye;
those commodities, therefore, are best conveyed
to other markets than the matrimonial one; for in
purely commercial transactions one has need of
perfect clearness of vision, if only to keep one well
practised in that simple game called looking out
for one's own interest. In Frenchwomen, the ra-
tiocinationist is extraordinarily developed; her
logic penetrates to the core of things.

Hence it is that Mouchard washes dishes.

Monsieur Jourdain, in Molière's comedy, who
expressed such surprise at finding that he had
been talking prose for forty years without knowing it, was no more amazed than would Mère Mouchard have been had you announced to her that she
was a logician; or that her husband's daily occu-
pations in the bright little court-yard were the
result of a system. Yet both facts were true.

In that process we now know as the survival of the fittest, the mère's capacity had snuffed out her weaker spouse's incompetency; she had taken her place at the helm, because she belonged there by virtue of natural fitness. There were no tender illusions which would suffer in seeing the husband allotted to her, probably by her parents and the *dot* system, relegated to the ignominy of passing his days washing dishes—dishes which she cooked and served—dishes, it should be added, which she was entirely conscious were cooked by the hand of genius, and which she garnished with a sauce and served with a smile such as only issue from French kitchens.

CHAPTER VIII.

 THE beach, one morning, we found suddenly peopled with artists. It was a little city of tents. Beneath striped awnings and white umbrellas a multitude of flat-capped heads sat immovably still on their three-legged stools, or darted hither and thither. Paris was evidently beginning to empty its studios; the Normandy beaches now furnished the better model.

One morning we were in luck. A certain blonde beard had counted early in the day on having the beach to himself. He had posed his model in the open daylight, that he might paint her in the sun. He had placed her, seated on an edge of seawall; for a background there was the curve of the yellow sands and the flat breadth of the sea, with the droop of the sky meeting the sea miles away. The girl was a slim, fair shape, with long, thin legs and delicately moulded arms; she was dressed in the fillet and chiton of Greece. During her long poses she was as immovable as an antique marble; her natural grace and prettiness were transfigured into positive beauty by the flowing lines and the pink draperies of her Attic costume.

Seated thus, she was a breathing embodiment of
the best Greek period. When the rests came, her
jump from the wall landed her square on her
feet and at the latter end of the nineteenth century. Once free, she bounded from her perch on
the high sea-wall. In an instant she had tucked
her tinted draperies within the slender girdle;
her sandalled feet must be untrammelled, she
was about to take her run on the beach. Soon
she was pelting, irreverently, her painter with a
shower of loose pebbles. Next she had challenged
him to a race; when she reached the goal, her
thin, bare arms were uplifted as she clapped and
shouted for glee; the Quartier Latin in her blood
was having its moment of high revelry in the
morning sun.

This little grisette, running about free and un-
shackled in her loose draperies, quite unabashed
in her state of semi-nudity—gay, reckless, wooing
pleasure on the wing, surely she might have posed
as the embodied archetype of France itself. So has
this pagan among modern nations borrowed something of the antique spirit of wantonness. Along
with its theft of the Attic charm and grace, it has
captured, also, something of its sublime indifference; in the very teeth of the dull modern world,
France has laughed opinion to scorn.

At noon the tents were all deserted. It was at
this hour that the inn garden was full. The gayety and laughter overflowed the walls. Everyone
talked at once; the orders were like a rattle of ar-
tillery—painting for hours in the open air gives a
fine edge to appetite, and patience is never the

true twin of hunger. Everything but the *potage*
was certain to be on time.

Colinette, released from her Greek draperies,
with her Parisian bodice had recovered the *blague*
of the studios.

"Sacré nom de—on reste donc claquemuré ainsi
toute la matinée! And all for an omelette — a
puny, good-for-nothing omelette. And you —
you've lost your tongue, it seems?" And a shrill
voice pierced the air as Colinette gave her painter
the hint of her prodding elbow. With the appearance of the omelette the reign of good humor
would return. Everything then went as merrily
as that marriage-bell which, apparently, is the
only one absent in Bohemia's gay chimes.

These arbors had obviously been built out of
pure charity: they appeared to have been con-
structed on the principle that since man, painting
man, is often forced to live alone, from economic
necessity, it is therefore only the commonest charity to provide him with the proper surroundings
for eating *à deux*. The little tables beneath the
kiosks were strictly *tête-à-tête* tables; even the
chairs, like the visitors, appeared to come only in
couples.

The Frenchman has been reproached with the
sin of ingratitude; has been convicted, indeed, as
possessed of more of that pride that comes late—
the day after the gift of bounty has been given —
than some other of his fellow-mortals. Yet here
were a company of Frenchmen — and Frenchwomen — proving in no ordinary fashion their
equipment in this rare virtue. It was early in

May; up yonder, where the Seine flows beneath the Parisian bridges, the pulse of the gay Paris world was beating in time to the spring in the air. Yet these artists had deserted the asphalt of the boulevards for the cobbles of a village street, the delights of the *café chantant* had been exchanged for the miracle of the moon rising over the sea, and for the song of the thrush in the bush.

The Frenchman, more easily and with simpler art than any of his modern brethren, can change the prose of our dull, practical life into poetry; he can turn lyrical at a moment's notice. He possesses the power of transmuting the commonplace into the idyllic by merely clapping on his cap and turning his back on the haunts of men. He has retained a singular—an almost ideal sensitiveness, of mental cuticle—such acuteness of sensation, that a journey to a field will oftentimes yield him all the flavor of a long voyage, and a sudden introduction to a forest the rapture that commonly comes only with some unwonted aspect of nature. Perhaps it is because of this natural poet one finds in a Frenchman, that makes him content to remain so much at home. Surely the extraordinary is the costly necessity for barren minds; the richly-endowed can see the beauty that lies the other side of their own door-step.

CHAPTER IX.

 THERE were two paths in the village that were well worn. One was that which led the village up into the fields. The other was the one that led the tillers of the soil down into the village, to the door-step of the justice of the peace.

A good Norman is no Norman who has not a lawsuit on hand.

Anything will serve as a pretext for a quarrel. No sum of money is so small as not to warrant a breaking of the closest blood-ties, if thereby one's rights may be secured. Those beautiful stripes of rye, barley, corn, and wheat up yonder in the fields, that melt into one another like sea-tones—down here on the benches before the *juge de paix*—what quarrels, what hatreds, what evil passions these few acres of land have brought their owners, facing each other here like so many demons, ready to spring at the others' throats! Brothers on these benches forget they are brothers, and sisters that they have suckled the same mother.

Two more yards of the soil that should have been
Fillette's instead of Jeanne's, and the grave will
enclose both before the clenched fist of either is
relaxed, and the last *sous* in the stocking will
be spent before the war between their respective
lawyers will end.

Many and many were the tales told us of the
domestic tragedies, born of wills mal-administered,
of the passions of hate, ambition, and despair kept
at a white heat because half the village owned, up
in the fields, what the other half coveted. Many,
also, and fierce were the heated faces we looked in
upon at the justice's door in the very throes of the
great moment of facing justice and their adversary.

Our own way, by preference, took us up into
the fields. Here, in the broad open, the farms lay
scattered like fortifications over a plain. Doubtless, in the earlier warlike days they had served as
such.

Once out of the narrow Villerville streets, and
the pastoral was in full swing.

The sea along this coast was not in the least in-
sistant; it allowed the shore to play its full gamut
of power. There were no tortured shapes of trees
or plants, or barren wastes, to attest the fierce ways
of the sea with the land. Reminders of the sea
and of the life that is lived in ships were conspicuous features everywhere, in the pastoral scenes
that began as soon as the town ended. Women
carrying sails and nets toiled through the green
aisles of the roads and lanes. Fishing-tackle hung
in company with tattered jerseys outside of huts
hidden in grasses and honeysuckle. The shep-

herdesses, as they followed the sheep inland into the heart of the pasture land, were busy netting the coarse cages that trap the finny tribe. Long-limbed, vigorous-faced, these shepherdesses were Biblical figures. In their coarse homespun, with only•a skirt and a shirt, with their bare legs, half-open bosoms, and the fine poise of their blond heads, theirs was a beauty that commanded the homage accorded to a rude virginity.

In some of the fields, in one of our many walks, the grass was being cut. In these fields the groups of men and women were thickest. The long scythes were swung mightily by both; the voices, a gay treble of human speech, rose above the metallic swish of the sharp blades cutting into the succulent grasses.

The fat pasture lands rose and sank in undulations as rounded as the nascent breasts of a young Greek maiden. A medley of color played its charming variations over fields, over acres of poppies, over plains of red clover, over the backs of spotted cattle, mixing, mingling, blending a thousand twists and turns into one exquisite, harmonious whole. There was no discordant note, not one harsh contrast; even the hay-ricks seemed to have been modelled rather than pitched into shape; their sloping sides and finely pointed apexes giving them the dignity of structural intent.

Why should not a peasant, in blouse and sabots, with a grinning idiot face, have put the picture out? But he did not. He was walking, or rather waddling, toward us, between two green walls that rose to be arched by elms that hid the blue of the sky. This lane was the kind of lane one sees only in Devonshire and in Normandy. There are lanes and lanes, as, to quote our friend the cobbler, there are curés and curés. But only in these above-named countries can one count on walking straight into the heart of an emerald, if one turns from the high-road into a lane. The trees, in these Devonshire and Normandy by-paths, have ways of their own of vaulting into space; the hedges are thicker, sweeter, more vocal with insect and song notes than elsewhere; the roadway itself is softer to the foot, and narrower—only two are expected to walk therein.

It was through such a lane as this that the coarse, animal shape of a peasant was walking toward us. His legs and body were horribly twisted; the dangling arms and crooked limbs appeared as if caricaturing the gnarled and tortured boughs and trunks of the apple-trees. The peasant's blouse was filthy; his sabots were reeking with dirty straw; his feet and ankles, bare, were blacker than the earth over which he was painfully crawling; and on his face there was the vacuous, sensuous deformity of the smile idiocy wears. Again I ask, why did he not disfigure this fair scene, and put out something of the beauty of the day? Is it because the French peasant seems now to be an inseparable adjunct of the Frenchman's landscape? That even deformity has been so handled by the realists as to make us see beauty in ugliness? Or is it that, as moderns, we are all bitten by the rabies of the picturesque; that all things serve and are acceptable so long as

we have our necessary note of contrast? Certain
it is that it appears to be the peasant's blouse that
perpetuates the Salon, and perhaps—who knows?
—when over-emigration makes our own American
farmer too poor to wear a boiled shirt when he
ploughs, we also may develop a school of landscape, with figures.

Meanwhile the walk and the talk had made
Charm thirsty. "Why should we not go," she
asked, "across the next field, into that farm-house
yonder, and beg for a glass of milk?"

The farm-house might have been waiting for us,
it was so still. Even the grasses along its sloping
roof nodded, as if in welcome. The house, as we
approached it, together with its out-buildings,
assumed a more imposing aspect than it had from
the road. Its long, low façade, broken here and
there by a miniature window or a narrow doorway,
appeared to stretch out into interminable length
beneath the towering beeches and the snarl of the
peach-tree boughs.

The stillness was ominous—it was so profound.

The only human in sight was a man in a distant
field; he was raking the ploughed ground. He was
too far away to hear the sound of our voices.

"Perhaps the entire establishment is in the
fields," said Charm, as we neared the house.

Just then a succession of blows fell on our ear.

"Someone is beating a mattress within, we shall
have our glass after all."

We knocked. But no one answered our knock.

The beating continued; the sounds of the blows
fell as regularly as if machine-impelled. Then a

cry rose up; it was the cry of a young, strong voice, and it was followed by a low wail of anguish.

The door stood half-open, and this is what we saw: A man—tall, strong, powerful, with a face purple with passion—bending over the crouching form of a girl, whose slender body was quivering, shrinking, and writhing as the man's hand, armed with a short stick, fell, smiting her defenceless back and limbs.

Her wail went on as each blow fell.

In a corner, crouched in a heap, sitting on her heels, was a woman. She was clapping her hands. Her eyes were starting from her head; she clapped as the blows came, and above the girl's wail her strong, exultant voice arose—calling out:

" *Tue-la ! Tue-la !* "

It was the voice of a triumphant fury.

The backs of all these people were turned upon us; they had not seen, much less heard, our entrance.

Someone else had seen us, however. A man with a rake over his shoulder rushed in through the open door; it was the peasant we had seen in the field. He seized Charm by the arm, and then my own hand was grasped as in a grip of iron. Before we had time for resistance he had pushed us out before him into the entry, behind the outer door. This latter he slammed. He put his broad back against it; then he dropped his rake and began to mop his face, violently, with a filthy handkerchief he plucked from beneath his blouse.

" *Què chance ! Nom de Dieu, què chance ! Je v'-avions vue*, I saw you just in time—just in time—"

" But, I must go in—I wish to go back!" But Charm might as well have attempted to move a pillar of stone.

The peasant's coarse, good-humored face broke into a broad laugh.

"Pardon, mam'selle —*j'n bougeons pas. Not' maître e' en colère; c' son jour—faut pas l'irriter—au'-jou'hui.*"

Meantime, during the noise of our forced exit and the ensuing dialogue, the scene within had evidently changed in character, for the blows had ceased. Steps could be heard crossing and re-crossing the wooden floor. A creaking sound succeeded to the beating—it was the creaking and groaning of a wooden staircase bending beneath the weight of a human figure. In an upper chamber there came the sound of a quiet, subdued sobbing now. They were the sobs of the girl. She at least had been released.

A face, cruel, pinched, hardened, with flaming agate eyes and an insolent smile, stood looking out at us through the dulled, dusty window-pane. It was the fury.

Meanwhile the peasant was still defending his post. A moment later the tall frame of the farmer suddenly filled the open doorway. The peasant well-nigh fell into his master's arms. The farmer's face was still terrible to look upon, but the purple stain of passion was now turned to red. There was a mocking insolence in his tone as he addressed us, that matched with the woman's unconcealed glee.

" Will you not come in, mesdames? Will you

not rest a while after your long walk?" On the man's hard face there was still the shadow of a sinister cruelty as he waved his hand toward the room within.

The peasant's good-humored, loutish smile, and his stupid, cow-like eyes, by contrast, were the eyes and smile of a benevolent deity.

The smile told us we were right, as we slunk away toward the open road. The head kept nodding approval as we vanished presently beneath the shade of the protecting trees.

The fields, as we swept rapidly past them, were as bathed in peace as when we had left them; there was even a more voluptuous content abroad: for the twilight was wrapping about the landscape its poppied dusk of gloom and shadow. Above, the birds were swirling in sweeping circles, raining down the ecstasy of their night-song; still above, far beyond them, across a zenith pure, transparent, adorably pink, illumined wisps of clouds were trailing their scarf-like shapes. It was a scene of beatific peace. Across the fields came the sound of a distant bell. It was the *Angelus*. The ploughmen stopped to doff their hats, the women to bend their heads in prayer.

And in our ears, louder than the vibrations of the hamlet bell, louder than the bird-notes and the tumult of the voluptuous insect whirr, there rang the thud, thud of cruel blows falling on quivering human flesh.

The curtain that hid the life of the peasant-farmer had indeed been lifted.

CHAPTER X.

 "Ah, mesdames, what will you have? The French peasant is like that. When he is in a rage nothing stops him—he beats anything, everything; whatever his hand encounters must suffer when he is angry; his wife, his child, his servant, his horse, they are all alike to him when he sees red."

Monsieur Fouchet was tying up his rose-trees; we were watching him from our seat on the green bench. Here in the garden, beneath the blue vault, the roses were drooping from very heaviness of glory; they gave forth a scent that made the head swim. It was a healthy, virile intoxication, however, the salt in the air steadying one's nerves.

Nature, not being mortal and cursed with a conscience, had risen that morning in a mood for carousal; at this hour of noon she had reached the point of ecstatic stupor. No state of trance was ever so exquisite. The air was swooning, but how delicate its gasps, as if it fell away into calm! How adorably blue the sky in its debauch of sun-

lit ether! The sea, too, although it reeled slightly, unsteadily rising only to fall away, what a radiance of color it maintained! Here in the garden
the drowsy air would lift a flower petal, as some
dreamer sunk in hasheesh slumber might touch a
loved hand, only to let it slip away in nerveless
impotence. Never had the charm of this Normandy sea-coast been as compelling; never had
the divine softness of this air, this harmonious
marriage of earth-scents and sea-smells seemed as
perfect; never before had the delicacy of the foliage and color-gradations of the sky as triumphantly proved that nowhere else, save in France,
can nature be at once sensuous and poetic.

We looked for something other than pure enjoyment from this golden moment; we hoped its
beauty would help us to soften our landlord. This
was the moment we had chosen to excite his sympathies, also to gain counsel from him concerning
the tragedy we had witnessed the day before. He
listened to our tale with evident interest, but there
was a disappointing coolness in his eye. As the
narrative proceeded, the brutality of the situation
failed to sting him to even a mild form of indignation. He went on tying his rose-trees, his
ardor expending itself in choice snippings of the
stray stalks and rebellious tendrils.

"This Guichon," he said, after a brief moment,
in the tone that goes with the pursuance of an
occupation that has become a passion. "This
Guichon—I know him. He is a hard man, but no
harder than many others, and he has had his losses,
which don't always soften a man. ' *Qui terre a*

guerre a,' Molière says, and Guichon has had many
lawsuits, losing them all. He has been twice married; that was his daughter by his first wife he
was touching up like that. He married only the
other day Madame Tier, a rich woman, a neighbor,
their lands join. It was a great match for him,
and she, the wife, and his daughter don't hit it
off, it appears. There was some talk of a marriage
for the girl lately; a good match presented itself,
but the girl will have none of it; perhaps that ac-
counts for the beating."

A rose, overblown with its fulness of splendor,
dropped in a shower at Fouchet's feet just then.

"*Tiens, elle est finie, celle-la,*" he cried, with an
accent of regret, and he stooped over the fallen
petals as if they had been the remains of a friend.
Then he sighed as he swept the mass into his
broad palm.

"Come, let us leave him to the funeral of his
roses; he hasn't the sensibilities of an insect;"
and Charm grasped my arm to lead me over the
turf, across the gravel paths, toward the tea-house.

This tottering structure had become one of our
favorite retreats; in the poetic *mise-en-scène* of the
garden it played the part of Ruin. It was ab-
surdly, ridiculously out of repair; its gaping beams
and the sunken, dejected floor could only be due
to intentional neglect. Fouchet evidently had
grasped the secrets of the laws of contrast; the
deflected angle of the tumbling roof made the
clean-cut garden beds doubly true. Nature had
had compassion on the aged little building, however; the clustering, fragrant vines, in their hatred

of nudity, had invested the prose of a wreck with the poetry of drapery. The tip-tilted settee beneath the odorous roof became, in time, our chosen seat; from that perch we could overlook the garden-walls, the beach, the curve of the shore, the grasses and hollyhocks in our neighbor's garden, the latter startlingly distinct against the great arch of the sky.

It was here Renard found us an hour later. To him, likewise, did Charm narrate our extraordinary experience of yesterday, with much adjunct of fiery comment, embellishment of gesture, and imitative pose.

"Ye gods, what a scene to paint! You were in luck—in luck; why wasn't I there ?" was Renard's tribute to human pity.

"Oh, you are all alike, all—nothing moves you—you haven't common human sympathies—you haven't the rudiments of a heart! You are terrible—all of you—terrible!" A moment after she had left us, as if the narrowness of the little house stifled her. With long, swinging steps she passed out, to air her indignation, apparently, beneath the wall of the espaliers.

"Splendid creature, isn't she ?" commented Renard, following the long lines of the girl's fluttering muslin gown, as he plucked at his mustache. "She should always wear white and gold—what is that stuff?—and be lit up like that with a kind of goddess-like anger. She is wrong, however," he went on, a moment later; "those of us who live here aren't really barbarians, only we get used to things. It's the peasants themselves that force us; they wouldn't stand interference. A peasant is a kind of king on his own domain; he does anything he likes, short of murder, and he doesn't always stop at that."

"But surely the Government—at least their Church, ought to teach them——"

"Oh, their Church! they laugh at their curés— till they come to die. He's a heathen, that's what the French peasant is—there's lots of the middle ages abroad up there in the country. Along here, in the coast villages, the nineteenth century has crept in a bit, humanizing them, but the *fonds* is always the same; they're by nature avaricious, sordid, cruel; they'll do anything for money; there isn't anything sacred for them except their pocket."

A few days later, in our friend the cobbler we found a more sympathetic listener. "Dame! I also used to beat my wife," he said, contempla- tively, as he scratched his herculean head, "but that was when I was a Christian, when I went to confession; for the confessional was made for that, *c'est pour laver le linge sale des consciences, ça*" (in- terjecting his epigram). "But now—now that I am a free-thinker, I have ceased all that; I don't beat her," pointing to his old wife, "and neither do I drink or swear."

"It's true, he's good—he is, now," the old wife nodded, with her slit of a smile; "but," she added, quickly, as if even in her husband's religious past there had been some days of glory, "he was al- ways just—even then—when he beat me."

"*C'est très femme, ça—hein, mademoiselle?*" And

the cobbler cocked his head in critical pose, with
a philosopher's smile.

The result of the interview, however, although
not entirely satisfactory, was illuminating, besides
this light which had been thrown on the cobbler's
reformation. For the cobbler was a cousin, distant in point of kinship, but still a cousin, of the
brutal farmer and father. He knew all the points
of the situation, the chief of which was, as Fouchet
had hinted, that the girl had refused to wed the
bon parti, who was a connection of the step-mother.
As for the step-mother's murderous outcry, " Kill
her ! kill her ! " the cobbler refused to take a dramatic view of this outburst.

"In such moments, you understand, one loses
one's head; brutality always intoxicates; she was
a little drunk, you see."

When we proposed our modest little scheme,
that of sending for the girl and taking her, for a
time at least, into our service, merely as a change
of scene, the cobbler had found nothing but admiration for the project. "It will be perfect,
mesdames. They, the parents, will ask nothing
better. To have the girl out at service, away, and
yet not disgracing them by taking a place with
any other farmer; yes, they will like that, for they
are rich, you see, and wealth always respects itself. Ah, yes, it's perfect; I'll arrange all that—
all the details."

Two days later the result of the arrangement
stood before us. She was standing with her arms
crossed, her fingers clasping her elbows—with her
very best peasant manner. She was neatly, and,

for a peasant, almost fashionably attired in her
holiday dress—a short, black skirt, white stockings, a flowery kerchief crossed over her broad
bosom, and on her pretty hair a richly tinted blue
foulard. She was very well dressed for a peasant,
and, from the point of view of two travellers, of
about as much use as a plough.

"It's a beautiful scheme, and it's as dramatic as
the fifth act of a play ; but what.shall we do with
her?"

"Oh," replied Charm, carelessly, "there isn't
anything in particular for her to do. I mean to
buy her a lot of clothes, like those she has on, and
she can walk about in the garden or in the fields."

"Ah, I see ; she's to be a kind of a perambu-
lating figure-piece——"

"Yes, that's about it. I dare say she will be
very useful at sunset, in a dim street ; so few peasants wear anything approaching to costume nowadays."

Ernestine herself, however, as we soon discovered, had an entirely different conception of her
vocation. She was a vigorous, active young
woman, with the sap of twenty summers in her
lusty young veins. Her energies soon found vent
in a continuous round of domestic excitements.
There were windows and floors that cried aloud to
Heaven to be scrubbed ; there were holes in the
sheets to make mam'zelle's lying between them
une honte, une vraie honte. As for Madame Fouchet's
little weekly bill, *Dieu de Dieu,* it was filled with
such extortions as to make the very angels weep.
Madame and Ernestine did valiant battle over

those bills thereafter. Ernestine was possessed of the courage of a true martyr ; she could suffer and submit to the scourge, in the matter of personal persecution, for the religion of her own convictions ; but in the service of her rescuer, she could fight with the fierceness of a common soldier.

" When Norman meets Norman——" Charm began one day, the sound of voices, in a high treble of anger, coming in to us through the windows.

But Ernestine was knocking at the door, with a note in her hand.

" An answer is asked, mesdames," she said, in a voice of honey, as she dropped her low courtesy.

This was the missive :

ALONG AN OLD POST-ROAD TO

HONFLEUR AND TROUVILLE.

CHAPTER XI.

 "WILL *ces dames* join me in a marauding expedition? Like the poet Villon, I am about to turn marauder, house-breaker, thief. I shall hope to end the excursion by one act, at least, of highway robbery. I shall lose courage without the enlivening presence of *ces dames.* We will start when the day is at its best, we will return when the moon smiles. In case of finding none to rob, the coach of the desperadoes will be garrisoned with provisions; Henri will accompany us as counsellor, purveyor, and bearer of arms and costumes. The carriage for *ces dames* will stop the way at the hour of eleven.

"I have the honor to sign myself their humble servant and co-conspirator.

"JOHN RENARD."

"This, in plain English," was Charm's laconic translation of this note, "means that he wishes us to be ready at eleven for the excursion to P——, to spend the day, you may remember, at that old manoir. He wants to paint in a background, he said yesterday, while we stroll about and look at the old place. What shall I wear ? "

In an hour we were on the road.

A jaunty yellow cart, laden with a girl on the front seat; with a man, tawny of mustache, broad of shoulder, and dark of eye, with face shining to match the spring in the air and that fair face beside him ; laden also with another lady on the back seat, beside whom, upright and stiff, with folded arms, sat Henri, costumer, valet, cook, and groom. It was in the latter capacity that Henri was now posing. The rôle of groom was uppermost in his orderly mind, although at intervals, when his foot chanced to touch a huge luncheon-basket with which the cart was also laden, there were betraying signs of anxiety ; it was then that the *chef* crept back to life. This spring in the air was all very well, but how would it affect the sauces ? This great question was written on Henri's brow in a network of anxious wrinkles.

" Henri," I remarked, as we were wheeling down the roadway, " I am quite certain you have put up enough luncheon for a regiment."

" Madame has said it, for a regiment; Monsieur Renard, when he works, eats with the hunger of a wolf."

" Henri, did you get in all the rags ? " This came from Renard on the front seat, as he plied his steed with the whip.

" The costume of Monsieur le Marquis, and also of Madame la Marquise de Pompadour, are be-

neath my feet in the valise, Monsieur Renard. I
have the sword between my legs," replied Henri,
the costumer coming to the surface long enough
to readjust the sword.

"Capital fellow, Henri, never forgets anything,"
said Renard, in English.

"Couldn't we offer a libation or something, on
such a morning——"

"On such a morning," interrupted the painter,
"one should be seated next to a charming young
lady who has the genius to wear Nile green and
white; even a painter with an Honorable Mention
behind him and fame still ahead, in spite of the
Mention, is satisfied. You know a Greek deity
was nothing to a painter, modern, and of the
French school, in point of fastidiousness."

"Nonsense! it's the American woman who is
fastidious, when it comes to clothes."

Meanwhile, there was one of the party who was
looking at the road; that also was arrayed in Nile
green and white; the tall trees also held umbrellas above us, but these coverings were woven of
leaves and sky. This bit of roadway appeared to
have slipped down from the upper country, and to
have carried much of the upper country with it.
It was highway posing as pure rustic. It had
brought all its pastoral paraphernalia along. Nothing had been forgotten: neither the hawthorn
and the osier hedges, nor the tree-trunks, suddenly
grown modest at sight of the sea, burying their
nudity in nests of vines, nor the trick which elms
and beeches have of growing arches in the sky.
Timbered farm-houses were here, also thatched

huts, to make the next villa-gate gain in stateli-
ness; apple orchards were dotted about with such
a knowing air of wearing the long line of the Atlantic girdled about their gnarled trunks, that one
could not believe pure accident had carried them
to the edge of the sea. There were several miles
of this driving along beneath these green aisles.
Through the screen of the hedges and the crowded tree-trunks, picture succeeded picture; bits of
the sea were caught between slits of cliff; farm-
houses, huts, and villas lay smothered in blossoms;
above were heights whereon poplars seemed to
shiver in the sun, as they wrapped about them their
shroud-like foliage; meadows slipped away from
the heights, plunging seaward, as if wearying for
the ocean; and through the whole this line of
green roadway threaded its path with sinuous
grace, serpentining, coiling, braiding in land and
sea in one harmonious, inextricable blending of
incomparable beauty. One could quite compre-
hend, after even a short acquaintance with this
road, that two gentlemen of Paris, as difficult to
please as Daubigny and Isabey, should have seen
points of excellence in it.

There are all sorts of ways of being a painter.
Perhaps as good as any, if one cares at all about a
trifling matter like beauty, is to know a good
thing when one sees it. That poet of the brush,
Daubigny, not only was gifted with this very unusual talent in a painter, but a good thing could
actually be entrusted in his hands after its discovery. And herein, it appears to me, lies all the
difference between good and bad painting; not

only is an artist—any artist—to be judged by what
he sees, but also by what he does with a fact after
he's acquired it—whether he turns it into poetry
or prose.

I might incautiously have sprung these views
on the artist on the front seat, had he not wisely
forestalled my outburst by one of his own.

"By the way," he broke in; "by the way, I'm
not doing my duty as cicerone. There's a church
near here—we're coming to it in a moment—famous
—eleventh or twelfth century, romanesque style
—yes—that's right, although I'm somewhat shaky
when it comes to architecture—and an old manoir,
museum now, with lots of old furniture in it—in
the manoir, I mean."

"There's the church now. Oh, let us stop!"

In point of fact there were two churches before us. There was one of ivy : nave, roof, aisles,
walls, and conic-shaped top, as perfectly defined
in green as if the beautiful mantle had been cut
and fitted to the hidden stone structure. Every
few moments the mantle would be lifted by the
light breeze, as might a priest's vestment; it
would move and waver, as if the building were a
human frame, changing its posture to ease its
long standing. Between this church of stone
and this church of vines there were signs of the
fight that had gone on for ages between them.
The stones were obviously fighting decay, fighting ruin, fighting annihilation; the vines were also
struggling, but both time and the sun were on
their side. The stone edifice was now, it is true,
as Renard told us, protected by the Government

—it was classed as a "monument historique"—
but the church of greens was protected by the
god of nature, and seemed to laugh aloud, as if
with conscious gleeful strength. This gay, triumphant laugh was reflected, as if to emphasize
its mockery of man's work, in the tranquil waters
of a little pond, lily-leaved, garlanded in bushes,
that lay hidden beyond the roadway. Through
the interstices of the vines one solitary window
from the tower, like a sombre eye, looked down
into the pond; it saw there, reflected as in a mirror, the old, the eternal picture of a dead ruin
clasped by the arms of living beauty.

This Criquebœuf church presents the ideal picturesque accessories. It stands at the corner of
two meeting roadways.   It is set in an ideal pastoral frame—a frame of sleeping fields, of waving
tree-tops, of an enchanting, indescribable snarl of
bushes, vines, and wild flowers. In the adjoining
fields, beneath the tree-boughs, ran the long, low
line of the ancient manoir—now turned into a
museum.

We glanced for a few brief moments at the collection of antiquities assembled beneath the old
roof—at the Henry II. chairs, at the Pompadour-
wreathed cabinets, at the long rows of panels on
which are presented the whole history of France—
the latter an amazing record of the industry of a
certain Dr. Le Goupils.

"Criquebœuf doesn't exactly hide its light under a bushel, you know, although it doesn't crown
a hill. No end of people know it; it sits for its
portrait, I should say at least twice a week regu-

larly, on an average, during the season. English
water-colorists go mad over it—they cross over on
purpose to ' do ' it, and they do it extremely badly,
as a rule."

This was Renard's last comment of a biographi-
cal and critical nature, concerning the " historical
monument," as we reseated ourselves to pursue
our way to P——.

" Why don't you show them how it can be
done ? "

" Would," coolly returned Renard, "if it were
worth while, but it isn't in my line. Henri, did
you bring any ice ? "

Henri, I had noticed, when we had reseated ourselves in the cart, had greeted us with an air of
silent sadness; he clearly had not approved of
ruins that interfered with the business of the
day.

" *Oui, monsieur*, I did bring some ice, but as
monsieur can imagine to himself—a two hours'
sun——"

" Nonsense, this sun wouldn't melt a pat of butter ; the ice is all right, and so is the wine."

Then he continued in English : " Now, ladies, as
I should begin if I were a politician, or an auc-
tioneer ; now, ladies, the time for confession has
arrived ; I can no longer conceal from you my bur-
glarious scheme. In the next turn that we shall
make to the right, the park of the P—— manoir
will disclose itself. But, between us and that
Park, there is a gate. That gate is locked. Now,
gates, from the time of the Garden of Eden, I take
it, have been an invention of—of—the other fellow,

to keep people out. I know a way—but it's not
the way you can follow. Henri and I will break
down a few bars, we'll cross a few fields over yonder, and will present ourselves, with all the virtues
written on our faces, to you in the Park. Meanwhile you must enter, as queens should—through
the great gates. Behold, there is a curé yonder, a
great friend of mine. You will step along the roadway; you will ring a door-bell; the curé will appear; you will ask him if it be true that the manoir
of P——- is to rent, you have heard that he has the
keys; he will present you the keys; you will open
the big gate and find me."

"But—but, Mr. Renard, I really don't see how
that scheme will work."

"Work! It will work to a charm. You will
see. Henri, just help the ladies, will you?"

Henri, with decisive gravity, was helping the
ladies to alight; in another instant he had re-
gained his seat, and he and Renard were flying
down the roadway, out of sight.

"Really—it's the coolest proceeding," Charm
began. Then we looked through the bars of the
park gate. The park was as green and as still as
a convent garden; a pink brick mansion, with
closed window-blinds, was standing, surrounded
by a terrace on one side, and by glittering parterres on the other.

"Where did he say the old curé was?" asked
Charm, quite briskly, all at once. Everything had
turned out precisely as Renard had predicted.
Doubtless he had also counted on the efficacy of
the old fable of the Peri at the Gate—one look

had been sufficient to turn us into arrant conspir-
ators; to gain an entrance into that tranquil paradise any ruse would serve.

"Here's a church—he said nothing about a
church, did he?"

Across the avenue, above the branches of a row
of tall trees, rose the ivied façade of a rude hamlet
church; a flight of steep weedy steps led up to its
Norman doorway. The door was wide open;
through the arched aperture came the sounds of
footfalls, of a heavy, vigorous tread; Charm ran
lightly up a few of the lower steps, to peer into
the open door.

"It's the curé dusting the altar—shall I go in?"

"No, we had best ring—this must be his house."
· The clatter of the curé's sabots was the response
that answered to the bell we pulled, a bell attached
to a diminutive brick house lying at the foot of
the churchyard. The tinkling of the cracked-voiced
bell had hardly ceased when the door opened.

But the curé had already taken his first glance
at us over the garden hedges.

CHAPTER XII.

A NORMAN CURE.

"MESDAMES!"

The priest's massive frame filled the narrow door; the tones of his mellow voice seemed also suddenly to fill the air, drowning all other sounds. The grace of his manner, a grace that invested the simple act of his uncovering and the holding of his *calotte* in hand, with an air of homage, made also our own errand the more difficult.

I had already begun to murmur the nature of our errand: we were passing, we had seen the manoir opposite, we had heard it was to rent, also that he, Monsieur le Curé, had the keys.

Yes, the keys were here. Then the velvet in Monsieur le curé's eyes turned to bronze as they looked out at us from beneath the fine dome of brow.

"I have the keys of the garden only, mesdames," he replied, with perfect but somewhat distant courtesy; "the gardener, down the road yonder,

has the keys of the house. Do you really wish to
rent the house?"

He had seen through our ruse with quick Norman penetration. He had not from the first been
in the least deceived.

It became the more difficult to smooth the situation into shape. We had thought perhaps to
rent a villa, we were in one now at Villerville. If
Monsieur le curé would let us look at the garden.
Monsieur Renard, whom perhaps he remembered——

"M. Renard! Oh ho! Oh ho! I see it all now,"
and a deep, mellow laugh smote the air. The keenness in the fine eyes melted into mirth, a mirth
that laid the fine head back on the broad shoulders, that the laugh that shook the powerful frame
might have the fuller play.

"Ah, *mes enfants*, I see it all now—it is that
scoundrel of a boy. I'll warrant he's there, over
yonder, already. He was here yesterday, he was
here the day before, and he is afraid, he is ashamed
to ask again for the keys. But come, *mes enfants*,
come, let us go in search of him." And the little
door was closed with a slam. Down the broad
roadway the next instant fluttered the old curé's
soutane. We followed, but could scarcely keep
pace with the brisk, vigorous strides. The sabots
ploughed into the dust. The cane stamped along
in company with the sabots, all three in a fury of
impatience. The curé's step and his manner might
have been those of a boy burning with haste to
discover a playmate in hiding. All the keenness
and shrewdness on the fine, ruddy face had melted

into sweetness; an exuberance of mirth seemed to
be the sap that fed his rich nature. It was easy to
see he had passed the meridian of his existence in
a realm of high spirits; an irrepressible fountain
within, the fountain of an unquenchable good-
humor, bathed the whole man with the hues of
health. Ripe red lips curved generously over
superb teeth; the cheeks were glowing, as were
the eyes, the crimson below them deepening to
splendor the velvet in the iris. The one severe
line in the face, the thin, straight nose, ended in
wide nostrils—in the quivering, mobile nostrils of
the humorist. The swell of the gourmand's paunch
beneath the soutane was proof that the curé was
a true Norman—he had not passed a lifetime in
these fertile gardens forgetful of the fact that the
fine art of good living is the one indulgence the
Church has left to its celibate sons.

Meanwhile, our guide was peering with quick,
excited gaze, through the thick foliage of the
park; his fine black eyes were sweeping the par-
terre and terrace.

"Ah-h!" his rich voice cried out, mockingly;
and he stopped, suddenly, to plant his cane in the
ground with mock fierceness.

"*Tiens*, Monsieur le Curé!" cried Renard, from
behind a tree, in a beautiful voice. It was a voice
that matched with his well-acted surprise, when
he appeared, confronting us, on the other side of
the tree-trunk.

The curé opened his arms.

"*Ah, mon enfant, viens, viens!* how good it is to
see thee once again!"

They were in each other's arms. The curé was pressing his lips to Renard's cheek, in hearty French fashion. The priest, however, administered his reproof before he released him. Renard's broad shoulders received a series of pats, which turned to blows, dealt by the curé's herculean hand.

"Why didn't you let me know you were here, yesterday, *Hein?* Answer me that. How goes the picture? Is it set up yet? You see, mesdames," turning with a reddened cheek and gleaming eyes, "it is thus I punish him—for he has no heart, no sensibilities—he only understands severities! And he defrauded me yesterday, he cheated me. I didn't even know of his being here till he had gone. And the picture, where is it?"

It was on an easel, sunning itself beneath the park trees. The old priest clattered along the gravelly walk, to take a look at it.

"*Tiens*—it grows—the figures begin to move—they are almost alive. There should be a trifle more shadow under the chin, what do you think?"

Henri raised his chin. Henri had undergone the process of transformation in our absence. He was now M. le Marquis de Pompadour—under the heart-shaped arch of the great trees, he was standing, resplendent in laces, in glistening satins, leaning on a rusty, dull-jewelled sword. Renard had mounted his palette; he was dipping already into the mounds of color that dotted the palette-board, with his long brushes. On the canvas, in colors laid on by the touch of genius, this archway beneath which we were standing reared itself

aloft; the park trees were as tall and noble, trans-
fixed in their image of immutable calm, on that
strip of linen, as they towered now above us; even
the yellow cloud of the laburnum blossoms made
the sunshine of the shaded grass, as it did here,
where else no spot of sun might enter, so dense
was the night of shade. The life of another day
and time lived, however, beneath that shade;
Charm and the curé, as they drooped over the
canvas, confronted a graceful, attenuated courtier,
sickening in a languor of adoration, and a spright-
ly coquette, whose porcelain beauty was as finished as the feathery edges of her lacy sleeves.

" *Très—bien—très—bien,*" said the curé, nodding
his head in critical commendation. " It will be a
little masterpiece. And now," waving his hand
toward us, " what do you propose to do with these
ladies while you are painting ? "

" Oh, they can wander about," Renard replied,
abstractedly. He had already reseated himself
and had begun to ply his brushes; he now saw
only Henri and the hilt of the sword he was painting in.

" I knew it, I could have told you—a painter
hasn't the manners of a peasant when he's painting," cried the priest, lifting cane and hands high
in air, in mock horror. " But all the better, all the
better, I shall have you all to myself. Come, come
with me. You can see the house later. I'll send
for the gardener. It's too fine a day to be indoors.
What a day, *hein ? Le bon Dieu* sends us such days
now and then, to make us ache for paradise. This
way, this way—we'll go through the little door—

my little door; it was made for me, you know,
when the manoir was last inhabited. I and the
children were too impatient—we suffered from
that malady—all of us—we never could wait for
the great gates yonder to be opened. So Mon·
sieur de H——- built us this one."

The little door opened directly on the road, and
on the curé's house. There was a tangle of under-
brush barring the way; but the curé pushed the
briars apart with his strong hands, beating them
down with his cane.

When the door opened, we passed directly be·
yond the roadway, to the steep steps leading to
the church. The curé, before mounting the steps,
swept the road, upward and downward, with his
keen glance. It was the instinctive action of the
provincial, scenting the chance of novelty. Some
distant object, in the meeting of two distant roadways, arrested the darting eyes; this time, at least,
he was to be rewarded for his prudence in looking
about him. The object slowly resolved itself into
two crutches between which hung the limp figure
of a one-legged man.

"*Bonjour, Monsieur le curé.*" The crutches came
to a standstill; the cripple's hand went up to doff
a ragged worsted cap.

"Good-day, good-day, my friend; how goes it?
Not quite so stiff, hein—in such a bath of sunlight
as this? Good-day, good-day."

The crutches and their burden passed on, kick·
ing a little cloud of dust about the lean figure.

"*Un peu cassé, le bonhomme,*" he said, as he nodded
to the cripple in a tone of reflection, as if the

breakage that had befallen his humble friend were
a fresh incident in his experience. "Yes, he's a
little broken, the poor old man; but then," he added, quickly renewing his tone of unquenchable
high spirits—"one doesn't die of it. No, one
doesn't die, fortunately. Why, we're all more or
less cracked, or broken—up here."

He shook another laugh out, as he preceded
us up the stone steps. Then he turned to stop
for a moment to point his cane toward the small
house with whose chimneys we were now on a
level.

"There, mesdames, there is the proof that mere
breaking doesn't signify—in this matter of life
and death. *Tenez*, madame—" and with a charming gesture he laid his richly-veined, strong old
hand on my arm—a hand that ended in beautiful
fingers, each with its rim of moon-shaped dirt;
"*tenez*—figure to yourself, madame, that I myself
have been here twenty years, and I came for two!
I bought out the *bonhomme* who lived over yonder
—I bought him and his furniture out. I said to
myself, 'I'll buy it for eight hundred, and I'll sell
it for four hundred, in a year.'" Here he laid his
finger on his nose—lengthwise, the Norman in him
supplanting the priest in his remembrance of a
good bargain. "And now it is twenty years since
then. Everything creaks and cracks over there; all
of us creak and crack. You should hear my chairs,
elles se cassent les reins—they break their thighs
continually. Ah! there goes another, I cry out, as
I sit down in one in winter and hear them groan.
Poor old things, they are of the Empire, no won-

der they groan. You should see us, when our
brethren come to take a cup of soup with me.
Such a collection of antiquities as we are! I
catch them, my brothers, looking about, slyly
peering into the secrets of my little ménage.
'From his ancestors, doubtless, these old chairs
and tables,' say these good frères, under their
breath. And then I wink slyly at the chairs,
and they never let on."

Again the mellow laugh broke forth. He stopped
again to puff and blow a little, from his toil up
the steep steps. Then all at once, as the rough
music of his clicking sabots and the playful taps
of his cane ceased, the laugh on his mobile lips
melted into seriousness. He lifted his cane, pointing to the cemetery just above us, and to the grave-
stones looking down over the hillsides between a
network of roses.

"We are old, madame—we are old, but, alas! we
never die! It is difficult to people, that cemetery.
There are only sixty of us in the parish, and we
die—we die hard. For example, here is my old
servant"—and he covered a grave with a sweep
of his cane—for we were leisurely sauntering
through the little cemetery now. The grave to
which he pointed was a garden; heliotrope, myo-
sotis, hare-bells and mignonette had made of the
mound a bed of perfume—"see how quietly she
lies—and yet what a restless soul the flowers
cover! She, too, died hard. It took her years to
make up her mind; finally *le bon Dieu* had to de-
cide it for her, when she was eighty-four. She
complained to the last—she was poor, she was in

my way, she was blind. '*Eh bien, tu n'as pas besoin
de me faire les beaux yeux, toi*'—I used to say to
her. Ah, the good soul that she was!" and the
dark eye glistened with moisture. A moment
later the curé was blowing vigorously the note of
his grief, in trumpet-tones, through the organ that
only a Frenchman can render an effective adjunct
to moments of emotion.

"You see, *mes enfants*, I am like that—I weep
over my friends—when they are gone! But see,"
he added quickly, recovering himself— "see,
over yonder there is my predecessor's grave. He
lies well, *hein?*—comfortable, too—looking his old
church in the face and the sun on his old bones
all the blessed day. Soon, in a few years, he will
have company. I, too, am to lie there, I and a
friend." The humorous smile was again curving
his lips, and the laughter-loving nostrils were beginning to quiver. "When my friend and I lie
there, we shall be a little crowded, perhaps. I
said to him, when he proposed it, proposed to lie
there with us, 'but we shall be crunching each
other's bones!' 'No,' he replied, 'only falling into
each other's arms!' So it was settled. He comes
over from Havre, every now and then, to talk our
tombstones over; we drink a glass of wine together, and take a pipe and talk about our future
—in eternity! Ah, how gay we are! It is so good
to be friends with God!"

The voice deepened into seriousness. He went
on in a quieter key:

"But why am I always preaching and talking
about death and eternity to two such ladies—two

such children? Ah—I know, I am really old—I
only deceive myself into pretending I'm young.
You will do the same, both of you, some day.
But come and see my good works. You know
everyone has his little corner of conceit—I have
mine. I like to do good, and then to boast of it.
You shall see—you shall see."

He was hurrying us along the narrow paths
now, past the little company of grave-stones,
graves that were bearing their barbaric burdens
of mortuary wreaths, of beaded crosses, and the
motley assemblage, common to all French grave-
yards, of hideous shrines encasing tin saints and
madonnas in plaster.

Above the sunken graves and the tin effigies of
the martyrs behind the church, arose a fair and
glittering marble tomb. It was strangely out of
keeping with the meagre and paltry surroundings
of the peasant grave-stones. As we approached
the tomb it grew in imposingness. It was a circu-
lar mortuary chapel, with carved pediment and
iron-wrought gateway.

"It's fine, *hein*, and beautiful, *hein?* It is the
Duke's!" The curé, it was easy to see, considered
the chapel in the light of a personal possession.
He stood before it, bare-headed, with a new earnestness on his mobile face. "It is the Duke's.
Yes, the Duke's. I saved his soul, blessed be
God! and he—he rebuilds my cellars for me!
See"—and he pointed to the fine new base of
stone, freshly cemented, on which the church
rested—"see, I save his soul, and he preserves my
buildings for me. It's a fair deal, isn't it? How

does it come about, that he is converted? Ah,
you see, although I am a man without science,
without knowledge, devoid of pretensions and
learning, the good God sometimes makes use of
such humble instruments to work His will. It
came about in the usual way. The Duke came
here carrying his religion lightly, as one may say,
not thinking of his soul. I—I dine with him.
We talk, we argue; he does, that is—I only preach
from my Bible. And behold! one day he is converted. He is devout. And from gratitude, he
repairs my crumbling old stones. And now see
how solid, how strong is my church cellar!"

Again the fountain of his irrepressible merriment
bubbled forth. For all the gayety, however, the
severe line deepened as one grew to know the face
better; the line in profile running from the nose
into the firm upper lip and into the still more
resolute chin, matched the impress of authority
marked on the noble brow. It was the face of one
who might have infinite charity and indulgence
for a sin, and yet would make no compromise
with it.

We had resumed our walk. It led us at last into
the interior of the little church. The gloom and
silence within, after the dazzling brilliancy of the
noon-day sun and the noisy insect hum, invested
the narrow nave and dim altar with an added
charm. The old priest knelt for the briefest instant in reverence to the altar. When he turned
there was surprise as well as a gentle reproach in
the changeable eyes.

"And you, mesdames! How is this? You are

not Catholics? And I was so sure of it! Quite
sure of it, you were so sympathetic, so full of reverence. And you, my child "—turning to Charm—
"you speak our tongue so well, with the very
accent of a good Catholic. What! you are Protestant? La! La! What do I hear?" He shook
his cane over the backs of the straw-bottomed
chairs; the sweet, mellow accents of his voice
melted into loving protest—a protest in which the
fervor was not quenched in spite of the merry key
in which it was pitched.

"Protestants? Pouffe! pouffe! What is that?
What is it to be a Protestant? Heretics, heretics,
that is what you are. So you are *deux affreuses
hérétiques?* Ah, la! la! Horrible! horrible! I
must cure you of all that. I must cure you!"
He dropped his cane in the enthusiasm of his attack; it fell with a clanging sound on the stone
pavement. He let it lie. He had assumed, unconsciously, the orator's, the preacher's attitude.
He crowded past the chairs, throwing back his
head as he advanced, striking into argumentative
gesture:

" *Tenez*, listen, there is so little difference, after
all. As I was saying to M. le comte de Chermont
the other day, no later than Thursday—he has
married an English wife, you know—can't understand that either, how they can marry English
wives. However, that's none of my business—we
have nothing to do with marrying, we priests, except as a sacrament for others. I said to M. le
comte, who, you know, shows tendencies toward
anglicism—astonishing the influence of women—I

said: 'But, my dear M. le comte, why change? You will only exchange certainty for uncertainty, facts for doubts, truth for lies.' 'Yes, yes,' the comte replied, ' but there are so many new truths introduced now into our blessed religion—the infallibility of the pope—the—' ' *Ah, mon cher comte —ne m'en parlez pas.* If that is all that stands in your way—*faites comme le bon Dieu! Lui—il ferme les yeux et tend les bras.* That is all we ask—we his servants—to have you close your eyes and open your arms.' "

The good curé was out of breath; he was panting. After a moment, in a deeper tone, he went on:

" You, too, my children, that is what I say to you—you need only to open your arms and to close your eyes. God is waiting for you."

For a long instant there was a great stillness— a silence during which the narrow spaces of the dim aisles were vibrating with the echoes of the rich voice.

The rustle of a light skirt sweeping the stone flooring broke the moment's silence. Charm was crossing the aisles. She paused before a little wooden box, nailed to the wall. There came suddenly on the ear the sound of coin rattling down into the empty box; she had emptied into it the contents of her purse.

"For your poor, monsieur le curé," she smiled up, a little tremulously, into the burning, glowing eyes. The priest bent over the fair head, laying his hand, as if in benediction, upon it.

" My poor need it sadly, my child, and I thank you for them. God will bless you."

It was a touching little scene, and I preferred, for one, to look out just then at Henri's figure advancing toward us, up the stone steps.

When the priest spoke again, it was in a husky tone, the gold in his voice dusted with moisture; but the bantering spirits in him had reappeared.

"What a pity, that you must burn! For you must—dreadful heretics that you are! And this dear child, she seems to belong to us—I can never sit by, now, in Paradise, happy and secure, and see her burn!" The laugh that followed was a mingled caress and a blessing. Henri came in for a part of the indulgence of the good curé's smile as he came up the steps.

"Ah, Henri, you have come for these ladies?"

"*Oui*, monsieur le curé, luncheon is served."

Our friend followed us to the topmost step, and to the very edge of the step. He stood there, talking down to us, as we continued to press him to return with us.

"No, my children—no—no, I can't join you; don't urge me; I can't, I must not. I must say my prayers instead; besides the children come soon, for their catechism. No, don't beg me, I don't need to be importuned; I know what that dear Renard's wine is. *Au revoir et à bientôt*—and remember," and here he lifted his arms—cane and all, high in the air—"all you need do is to close your eyes and to open your arms. God himself is doing the same."

High up he stood, with uplifted hands, the smile irradiating a face that glowed with a saint's simplicity. Behind the black lines of his robe,

the sunlight lay streaming in noon glory; it aureoled him as never saint was aureoled by mortal
brush. A moment only he lingered there, to raise
his cap in parting salute. Then he turned, the
trail of his gown sweeping the gravel paths, and
presently the low church door swallowed him up.
Through the door, as we crossed the road, there
came out to us the click of sabots striking the
rude flagging. And a moment after, the murmuring echo of a deep, rich voice saying the office of
the hour.

CHAPTER XIII.

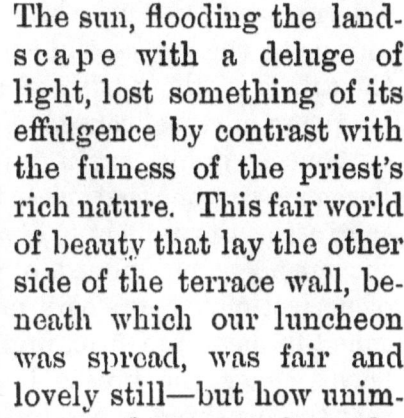

THE stillness of the park trees, as we passed beneath them, was like the silence that comes after a blessing. The sun, flooding the landscape with a deluge of light, lost something of its effulgence by contrast with the fulness of the priest's rich nature. This fair world of beauty that lay the other side of the terrace wall, beneath which our luncheon was spread, was fair and lovely still—but how unimportant the landscape seemed compared to the varied scenery of the curé's soul-lit character! Of all kinds of nature, human nature is assuredly the best; it is at least the most perdurably interesting. When we tire of it, when we weary of our fellow-man and turn the blasé cheek on the fresh pillow of mother-earth, how quickly is the pillow deserted once the mental frame is rested or renewed! The history of all human relations has the same ending—we all of us only fall out of love with man to fall as swiftly in again.

The remainder of the afternoon passed with the rapidity common to all phases of enchantment.

How could one eat seriously, with vulgar, gluttonous hunger, of a feast spread on the parapet of a terrace-wall? The white foam of napkins, the mosaic of the *patties*, the white breasts of chicken, the salads in their bath of dew—these spoke the language of a lost cause. For there was an open-air concert going on in full swing, and the performance was one that made the act of eating seem as gross as the munching of apples at an oratorio—the music being, indeed, of a highly refined order of perfection. One's ears needed to be highly attuned to hear the pricking of the locusts in the leaves; even the breeze kept uncommonly still, that the brushing of the humming-birds' and bees' wings against the flower-petals might be the more distinctly heard.

I never knew which one of the party it was that decided we were to see the day out and the night in; that we were to dine at the Cheval Blanc, on the Honfleur quays, instead of sedately breaking bread at the Mère Mouchard's. Even our steed needed very little urging to see the advantages of such a scheme. Henri alone wore a grim air of disapproval. His aspect was an epitome of rigid protest. As he took his seat in the cart, he held the sword between his legs with the air of one burning with a pent-up anguish of protest. His eye gloomed on the day; his head was held aloft, reared on a column of bristling vertebræ, and on his brow was written the sign of mutiny.

"Henri—you think we should go back; you think going on to Honfleur a mistake?"

"Madame has said it"—Henri was a fatalist —in his speech, at least, he lived up to his creed. "Honfleur is far—Monsieur Renard has not the good digestion—when he is tired—he suffers. *Il passe des nuits d'angoisse. Il souffre des fatigues de l'estomac. Il se fatigue aujourd'hui!*" This, with an air of stern conviction, was accompanied by a glance at his master in which compassion was not the most obvious note to be read. He went on, remorselessly:

"And, as madame knows, the work but begins for me when we are at home. There are the costumes to be dusted and put away, the paint-brushes to clean, the dishes and lunch-basket to be attended to. As madame says, monsieur is sometimes lacking in consideration. *Mais, que voulez-vous? le génie, c'est fait comme ça.*"

Madame had not expressed the feeblest echo of a criticism on the composition of the genius in front; but the short dialogue had helped, perceptibly, to lift the weight of Henri's gloom; he was beginning to accept the fate of the day with a philosopher's phlegm. Already he had readjusted a little difficulty between his feet and the lunch-basket, making his religious care of the latter compatible with the open sin of improved personal comfort.

Meanwhile the two on the front seat were a thousand miles away. Neither we, nor the day, nor the beauty of the drive had power to woo their glances from coming back to the focal point of interest they had found in each other. They were beginning to talk, not about each other but of themselves—the danger-signal of all tête-à-tête adventures.

When two young people have got into the personal-pronoun stage of human intercourse, there is but one thing left for the unfortunate third in the party to do. Yes, now that I think of it, there are two rôles to be played. The usual conception of the part is to turn marplot—to spoil and ruin the others' dialogue—to put an end to it, if possible, by legitimate or illegitimate means; a very successful way, I have observed, of prolonging, as a rule, such a duet indefinitely. The more enlightened actor in any such little human comedy, if he be gifted with insight, will collapse into the wings, and let the two young idiots have the whole stage to themselves. As like as not they'll weary of the play, and of themselves, if left alone. No harm will come of all the sentimental strutting and the romantic attitudinizing other than viewing the scene, later, in perspective, as a rather amusing bit of emotional farce.

Besides being in the very height of the spring fashion, in the matter of the sentiments, these two were also busily treading, at just this particular moment, the most alluring of all the paths leading to what may be termed the outlying territorial domain of the emotions; they were wandering through the land called Mutual Discovery. Now, this, I have always held, is among the most delectable of all the roads of life; for it may lead one—anywhere or nowhere.

Therefore it was from a purely generous impulse
that I continued to look at the view. The surroundings were, in truth, in conspiracy with the
sentimentalists on the front seat; the extreme
beauty of the road would have made any but sentimental egotists oblivious to all else. The road
was a continuation of the one we had followed in
the morning's drive. Again, all the greenness of
field and grass was braided inextricably into the
blue of river and ocean. Above, as before, in that
earlier morning drive, towered the giant aisles
of the beaches and elms. Through those aisles
the radiant Normandy landscape flowed again,
as music from rich organ - piped throats flows
through cathedral arches. Out yonder, on the
Seine's wide mouth, the boats were balancing
themselves, as if they also were half divided between a doubt and a longing; a freshening spurt
of breeze filled their flapping sails, and away they
sped, skipping through the waters with all the
gayety which comes with the vigor of fresh reso-
lutions. The light that fell over the land and
waters was dazzling, and yet of an astonishing
limpidity; only a sun about to drop and end his
reign could be at once so brilliant and so tender
—the diffused light had the sparkle of gold made
soft by usage. Wherever the eye roved, it was fed
as on a banquet of light and color. Nothing could
be more exquisite for depth of green swimming
in a bath of shadow, than the meadows curled
beneath the cliffs; nothing more tempting to the
painter's brush than the arabesque of blossoms
netted across the sky; and would you have the

living eye of nature, bristling with animation, alive with winged sails, and steeped in the very soul of yellow sunshine, look out over the great sheet of the waters, and steep the senses in such a breadth of aqueous splendor as one sees but in one or two of the rare shows of earth.

Then, all at once, all too soon, the great picture seemed to shrink; the quivering pulsation of light and color gave way to staid, commonplace gardens. Instead of hawthorn hedges there was the stench of river smells—we were driving over cobble-paved streets and beneath rows of crooked, crumbling houses. A group of noisy street urchins greeted us in derision. And then we had no doubt whatsoever that we were already in Honfleur town.

"Honfleur is an evil-smelling place," I remarked.

" Oh, well, after all, the smells of antiquity are a part of the show; we should refuse to believe in ancientness, all of us, I fancy, if mustiness wasn't served along with it."

" How can any town have such a stench with all this river and water and verdure to sweeten it ? " I asked, with a ·woman's belief in the morality of environment—a belief much cherished by wives and mothers, I have noticed.

" Wait till you see the inhabitants—they'll enlighten you—the hags and the nautical gentlemen along the basins and quays. They've discovered the secret that if cleanliness is next to godliness, dirt and the devil are likewise near neighbors. Awful set—those Honfleur sailors. The Havre and Seine people call them Chinamen,

they are so unlike the rest of France and Frenchmen."

"Why are they so unlike?" asked Charm.

"They're so low down, so hideously wicked;
they're like the old houses, a rotten, worm-eaten
set—you'll see."

Charm stopped him then, with a gesture. She
stopped the horse also; she brought the whole establishment to a standstill; and then she nodded her head briskly forward. We were in the
midst of the Honfleur streets—streets that were
running away from a wide open space, in all
possible directions. In the centre of the square
rose a curious, an altogether astonishing structure. It was a tower, a belfry doubtless, a house,
a shop, and a warehouse, all in one; such a picturesque medley, in fact, as only modern irreverence,
in its lawless disregard of original purpose and
design, can produce. The low-timbered sub-base
of the structure was pierced by a lovely doorway
with sculptured lintel, and also with two impertinent modern windows, flaunting muslin curtains,
and coquettishly attired with rows of flowering
carnations. Beneath these windows was a shop.
Above the whole rose, in beautiful symmetrical
lines, a wooden belfry, tapering from a square
tower into a delicately modelled spire. To complete and accentuate the note of the picturesque,
the superstructure was held in its place by rude
modern beams, propping the tower with a naïve
disregard of decorative embellishment. We knew
it at once as the quaint and famous Belfry of St.
Catherine.

As we were about to turn away to descend the high street, a Norman maiden, with close-capped face, leaned over the carnations to look down upon us.

" That's the daughter of the bell-ringer, doubtless. Economical idea that," Renard remarked, taking his cap off to the smiling eyes.

" Economical ? "

" Yes, can't you see ? Bell-ringer sends pretty daughter to window, just before vespers or service, and she rings in the worshippers; no need to make the bells ring."

" What nonsense ! "—but we laughed as flatteringly as if his speech had been a genuine coin of wit.

A turn down the street, and the famous Honfleur of the wharves and floating docks lay before us. About us, all at once, was the roar and hubbub of an extraordinary bustle and excitement; all the life of the town, apparently, was centred upon the quays. The latter were swarming with a tattered, ragged, bare-footed, bare-legged assemblage of old women, of gamins, and sailors. The collection, as a collection, was one gifted with the talent of making itself heard. Everyone appeared to be shrieking, or yelling, or crying aloud, if only to keep the others in voice. Sailors lying on the flat parapets shouted hoarsely to their fellows in the rigging of the ships that lay tossing in the docks; fishermen's families tossed their farewells above the hubbub to the captain-fathers launching their fishing-smacks; one shrieking infant was being passed, gayly, from the poop of a distant deck, across the closely lying shipping, to the quay's steps, to be hushed by the generous opening of a peasant mother's bodice. One could hear the straining of cordage, the creak of masts, the flap of the sails, all the noises peculiar to shipping riding at anchor. The shriek of steam-whistles broke out, ever and anon, above all the din and uproar. Along the quay steps and the wharves there were constantly forming and re-forming groups of wretched, tattered human beings; of men with bloated faces and a dull, sodden look, strikingly in contrast with the vivacity common among French people. Even the children and women had a depraved, shameless appearance, as if vice had robbed them of the last vestige of hope and ambition. Along the parapet a half-dozen drunkards sprawled, asleep or dozing. At the legs of one a child was pulling, crying:

" *Viens—mère t' battra, elle est soule aussi.*"

The sailors out yonder, busy in the rigging, and the men on the decks of the smart brigs and steamships, whistled and shouted and sang, as indifferent to this picture of human misery and degradation as if they had no kinship with it.

As a frame to the picture, Honfleur town lay beneath the crown of its hills; on the tops and sides of the latter, villa after villa shot through the trees, a curve of roof-line, with rows of daintily draped windows. At the right, close to the wharves, below the wooded heights, there loomed out a quaint and curious gateway flanked by two watch-towers, grim reminders of the Honfleur of the great days. And above and about the whole, encompassing villa-crowded hills and closely packed

streets, and the forest of masts trembling against
the sky, there lay a heaven of spring and summer.

Renard had driven briskly up to a low, rambling
façade parallel with the quays. It was the "Cheval Blanc." A crowd assembled on the instant, as
if appearing according to command.

"*Allons—n'encombrez pas ces dames !* " cried a
very smart individual, in striking contrast to the
down-at-heel air of the hotel—a personage who
took high-handed possession of us and our traps.
"Will ces dames desire a salon—there is *un vrai
petit bijou* empty just now," murmured a voice in a
purring soprano, through the iron opening of the
cashier's desk.

Another voice was crying out to us, as we wound
our way upward in pursuit of the jewel of a salon.
"And the widow, *La Veuve,* shall she be dry or
sweet ? "

When we entered the low dining-room, a little
later, we found that the artist as well as the epi-
cure has been in active conspiracy to make the
dinner complete; the choice of the table proclaimed one accomplished in massing effects. The
table was parallel with the low window, and
through the latter was such a picture as one travels hundreds of miles to look upon, only to miss
seeing it, as a rule. There was a great breadth of
sky through the windows; against the sky rose
the mastheads; and some red and brown sails curtained the space, bringing into relief the gray line
of the sad-faced old houses fringing the shore-
line.

"Couldn't have chosen better if we'd tried, could

we ? It's just the right hour, and just the right kind of light. Those basins are unendurable— sinks of iniquitous ugliness, unless the tide's in and there's a sunset going on. Just look—now! Who cares whether Honfleur has been done to death by the tourist horde or not ? and been painted until one's art-stomach turns ? I presume I ought to beg your pardon, but I can't stand the abomination of modern repetitions; the hand-organ business in art, I call it. But at this hour, at this time of the year, before this rattle-trap of an inn is as packed with Baedeker attachments as a Siberian prison is with Nihilists—to run out here and look at these quays and basins, and old Honfleur lying here, beneath her green cliffs—well, short of Cairo, I don't know any better bit of color. Look out there, now ! See those sails, dripping with color, and that fellow up there, letting the sail down—there, splash it goes into the water, I knew it would; now tell me where will you get better blues or yellows or browns, with just the right purples in the shore line, than you'll get here ? "

Renard was fairly started; he had the bit of the born monologist between his teeth ; he stopped barely long enough to hear even an echoing assent. We were quite content; we continued to sip our champagne and to feast our eyes. Meanwhile Renard talked on.

"Guide-books—what's the use of guide-books ? What do they teach you, anyway ? Open any one of the cursed clap-trap things. Yes, yes, I know I oughtn't to use vigorous language."

"Do," bleated Charm, smiling sweetly up at him. "Do, it makes you seem manly."

Even Renard had to take time to laugh.

"Thank you! I'm not above making use of any aids to create that illusion. Well, as I was saying, what guide-book ever really helped anyone to *see?*—that's what one travels for, I take it. Here, for instance, Murray or Baedeker would give you this sort of thing: 'Honfleur, an ancient town, with pier, beaches, three floating docks, and a good deal of trade in timber, cod, etc.; exports large quantities of eggs to England.' Good heavens! it makes one boil! Do sane, reasonable mortals travel three thousand miles to read ancient history done up in modern binding, served up à la Murray, à la Baedeker?"

"Oh, you do them injustice, I think—the guides do go in for a little more of the picturesque than that——"

"And how—how do they do it? This is the sort of thing they'll give you: 'Church of St. Catherine is large and remarkable, entirely of timber and plaster, the largest of its kind in France.' Ah! ha! that's the picturesque with a vengeance. No, no, my friends, throw the guide-books into the river, pitch them overboard through the port-holes, along with the flowers, and letters *to be read three days out*, and the nasty novels people send you to make the crossing pleasant. And when you travel, really travel, mind, never make a plan —just go—go anywhere, whenever the impulse seizes you—and you may hope to get there, in the right way, possibly."

Here Renard stopped to finish his glass, draining the last drop of the yellow liquid. Then he went on: "To travel! To start when an impulse seizes one! To go—anywhere! Why not! It was for this, after all, that all of us have come our three thousand miles." Perhaps it was the restless tossing of the shipping out yonder in the basins that awoke an answering impatience within, in response to Renard's outburst. Where did they go, those ships, and, up beyond this mouth of the Seine, how looked the shores, and what life lived itself out beneath the rustling poplars? Is it the mission of all flowing water to create an unrest in men's minds?

Meanwhile, though the talk was not done, the dinner was long since eaten. We rose to take a glimpse of Honfleur and its famous old basin. The quays and the floating docks, in front of which we had been dining, are a part of the nineteenth century; the great ships ride in to them from the sea. But here, in this inner quadrangular dock, beside which we were soon standing, traced by Duquesne when Louis the Great discovered the maritime importance of Honfleur, we found still reminders of the old life. Here were the same old houses that, in the seventeenth century, upright and brave in their brand new carvings, saw the high-decked, picturesquely painted Spanish and Portuguese ships ride in to dip their flag to the French fleur-de-lis. There are but few of the old streets left to crowd about the shipping life that still floats here, as in those bygone days of Honfleur pride;—when Havre was but a yellow

strip of sand; when the Honfleur merchants would
have laughed to scorn any prophet's cry of warning that one day that sand-bar opposite, despised,
disregarded, boasting only a chapel and a tavern,
would grow and grow, and would steal year by year
and inch by inch bustling Honfleur's traffic, till
none was left.

In the old adventurous days, along with the
Spanish ships came others, French trading and
fishing vessels, with the salty crustations of long
voyages on their hulls and masts. The wharves
were alive then with fish-wives, whom Evelyn will
tell you wore "useful habits made of goats' skin."
The captains' daughters were in quaint Normandy
costumes; and the high-peaked coifs and the stiff
woollen skirts, as well as the goat-skin coats,
trembled as the women darted hither and thither
among the sailors—whose high cries filled the air
as they picked out mother and wife. Then were
bronzed beards buried in the deeply-wrinkled old
mères' faces, and young, strong arms clasped
about maidens' waists. The whole town rang with
gayety and with the mad joy of reunion. On the
morrow, coiling its way up the steep hillsides,
wound the long lines of the grateful company, one
composed chiefly of the crews of these vessels
happily come to port. The procession would mount
up to the little church of Notre Dame de Grace
perched on the hill overlooking the harbor. Some
even—so deep was their joy at deliverance from
shipwreck and so fervent their piety—crawled up,
bare-footed, with bared head, wives and children
following, weeping for joy, as the rude *ex-votos*

were laid by the sailors' trembling hands at the
feet of the Virgin Lady.

As reminders of this old life, what is left? Within the stone quadrangle we found clustered a motley fleet of wrecks and fishing-vessels; the nets,
flung out to dry in the night air, hung like shrouds
from the mastheads; here and there a figure be-
strode a deck, a rough shape, that seemed endowed with a double gift of life, so still and
noiseless was the town. Around the silent dock,
grouped in mysterious medley and confusion,
were tottering roof lines, projecting eaves, narrow
windows, all crazily tortured and out of shape.
Here and there, beneath the broad beams of support, a little interior, dimly lighted, showed a
knot of sailors gathered, drinking or lounging.
Up high beneath a chimney perilously overlooking a rude façade, a quaint shape emerged, one
as decrepit and forlorn of life and hope as the
decaying houses it overlooked. Silence, poverty, wretchedness, the dregs of life, to this has
Honfleur fallen. These old houses, in their slow
decay, hiding in their dark bosom the gaunt secrets of this poverty and human misery, seemed to
be dancing a dance of drunken indifference. Some
day the dance will end in a fall, and then the
Honfleur of the past will not even boast of a
ghost as reminder of its days of splendor.

An artist quicker than anyone else, I think, can
be trusted to take one out of history and into the
picturesque. Renard refused to see anything but
beauty in the decay about us; for him the houses
were at just the right drooping angle; the roof

lines were delightful in their irregularity; and
the fluttering tremor of the nets, along the rigging, was the very poetry of motion.

"We'll finish the evening on the pier," he exclaimed, suddenly; "the moon will soon be up
—we can sit it out there and see it begin to
color things."

The pier was more popular than the quaint
old dock. It was crowded with promenaders,
who, doubtless, were taking a bite of the sea-air.
Through the dusk the tripping figures of gentlemen in white flannels and jaunty caps brushed
the provincial Honfleur swells. Some gentle
English voices told us some of the villa residents
had come down to the pier, moved by the beauty
of the night. Groups of sailors, with tanned
faces and punctured ears hooped with gold rings,
sat on the broad stone parapets, talking unintelli-
gible Breton *patois.* The pier ran far out, almost
to the Havre cliffs, it seemed to us, as we walked
along in the dusk of the young night. The sky
was slowly losing its soft flame. A tender, mellow half light was stealing over the waters, making the town a rich mass of shade. Over the top
of the low hills the moon shot out, a large, globular
mass of beaten gold. At first it was only a part
and portion of the universal lighting, of the still
flushed sky, of the red and crimson harbor lights,
of the dim twinkling of lamps and candles in the
rude interiors along the shore. But slowly, triumphantly, the great lamp swung up; it rose
higher and higher into the soft summer sky, and as
it mounted, sky and earth began to pale and fade.

Soon there was only a silver world to look out
upon—a wealth of quivering silver over the breast
of the waters, and a deeper, richer gray on cliffs
and roof tops. Out of this silver world came the
sound of waters, lapping in soft cadence against
the pier; the rise and fall of sails, stirring in the
night wind; the tread of human footsteps moving
in slow, measured beat, in unison with the rhythm
of the waters. Just when the stars were scattering their gold on the bosom of the sea-river, a
voice rang out, a rich, full baritone. Quite near,
two sailors were seated, with their arms about
each other's shoulders. They also were looking
at the moonlight, and one of them was singing to
it:

> " *Te souviens-tu, Marie,*
> *De notre enfance aux champs?*
>
> . . . . .
>
> *Te souviens-tu?——*
> *Le temps que je regrette*
> *C'est le temps qui n'est plus.*"

THE INN AT DIVES—GUILLAUME-LE-CONQUERANT.

DIVES:

AN INN ON A HIGH-ROAD.

CHAPTER XIV.

A COAST DRIVE.

ON our return to Villerville we found that the charm of the place, for us, was a broken one. We had seen the world; the effect of that experience was to produce the common result—there was a fine deposit of discontent in the cup of our pleasure.

Madame Fouchet had made use of our absence to settle our destiny; she had rented her villa. This was one of the bitter dregs. Another was to find that the life of the village seemed to pass us by; it gave us to understand, with unflattering frankness, that for strangers who made no bargains for the season, it had little or no civility to squander. For the Villerville beach, the inn, and the villas were crowded. Mère Mouchard was tossing omelettes from morning till night; even Augustine was far too hurried to pay her usual visit to the creamery. A detachment of Parisian costumes and be-ribboned nursery maids was crowding out the fish-wives and old hags from their stations on the low door-steps and the grasses on the cliffs.

Even Fouchet was no longer a familiar figure in the foreground of his garden; his roses were blooming now for the present owners of his villa. He and madame had betaken themselves to a box of a hut on the very outskirts of the village—a miserable little hovel with two rooms and a bit of pasture land being the substitute, as a dwelling, for the gay villa and its garden along the sea-cliffs. Pity, however, would have been entirely wasted on the Fouchet household and their change of habitation. Tucked in, cramped, and uncomfortable beneath the low eaves of their cabin ceilings, they could now wear away the summer in blissful contentment: Were they not living on nothing—on less than nothing in this dark pocket of a *chaumière*, while their fine house yonder was paying for itself handsomely, week after week? The heart beats high, in a Norman breast, when the pocket bulges; gold— that is better than bread to feel in one's hand.

The whole village wore this triumphant expression—now that the season was beginning. Paris had come down to them, at last, to be shorn of its strength; angling for pennies in a Parisian pocket was better, far, than casting nets into the sea. There was also more contentment in such fishing —for true Norman wit.

Only once did the village change its look of triumph to one of polite regret; for though it was Norman, it was also French. It remembered, on the morning of our departure, that the civility of the farewell costs nothing, and like bread prodigally scattered on the waters, may perchance bring back a tenfold recompense.

Even the morning arose with a flattering pallor. It was a gray day. The low houses were like so many rows of pale faces; the caps of the fish-wives, as they nodded a farewell, seemed to put the village in half-mourning.

"You will have a perfect day for your drive—there's nothing better than these grays in the French landscape," Renard was saying, at our carriage wheels; "they bring out every tone. And the sea is wonderful. Pity you're going. Grand day for the mussel-bed. However, I shall see you, I shall see you. Remember me to Monsieur Paul; tell him to save me a bottle of his famous old wine. Good-by, good-by."

There was a shower of rose-leaves flung out upon us; a great sweep of the now familiar béret; a sonorous "Hui!" from our driver, with an accompaniment of vigorous whip-snapping, and we were off.

The grayness of the closely-packed houses was soon exchanged for the farms lying beneath the elms. With the widening of the distance between our carriage-wheels and Villerville, there was soon a great expanse of mouse-colored sky and the breath of a silver sea. The fields and foliage were softly brilliant; when the light wind stirred the grain, the poppies and bluets were as vivid as flowers seen in dreams.

It is easy to understand, I think, why French painters are so enamoured of their gray skies—such a background makes even the commonplace wear an air of importance. All the tones of the land-scape were astonishingly serious; the features of

the coast and the inland country were as signifi-
cant as if they were meditating an outbreak into
speech. It was the kind of day that bred reflection; one could put anything one liked into the
picture with a certainty of its fitting the frame.
We were putting a certain amount of regret into
it; for though Villerville has seen us depart with
civilized indifference or the stolidity of the barbarian—for they are one, we found our own attain-
ments in the science of unfeelingness deficient: to
look down upon the village from the next hill-top
was like facing a lost joy.

Once on the highroad, however, the life along
the shore gave us little time for the futility of regret. Regret, at best, is a barren thing: like the
mule, it is incapable of perpetuating its own mis-
takes; it appears to apologize, indeed, for its stu-
pidity by making its exit as speedily as possible.
With the next turn of the road we were in fitting
condition to greet the wildest form of adventure.

Pedlars' carts and the lumbering Normandy farm
wagons were, at first, our chief companions along
the roadway. Here and there a head would peep
forth from a villa window, or a hand be stretched
out into the air to see if any rain was falling from
the moist sky. The farms were quieter than usual;
there was an air of patient waiting in the courtyards, among the blouses and standing cattle, as
though both man and beast were there in attendance on the day and the weather, till the latter
could come to the point of a final decision in regard to the rain.

Finally, as we were nearing Trouville, the big

drops fell. The grain-fields were soon bent double
beneath the spasmodic shower. The poppies were
drenched, so were the cobble-paved courtyards;
only the geese and the regiment of the ducks came
abroad to revel in the downpour. The villas were
hermetically sealed now—their summer finery was
not made for a wetting. The landscape had no
such reserves; it gave itself up to the light summer
shower as if it knew that its raiment, like Rachel's,
when dampered the better to take her plastic outlines, only gained in tone and loveliness the closer
it fitted the recumbent figure of mother earth.

Our coachman could never have been mistaken
for any other than a good Norman. He was endowed with the gift of oratory peculiar to the
country; and his profanity was enriched with all
the flavor of the provincial's elation in the com-
mitting of sin. From the earliest moment of our
starting, the stream of his talk had been unending.
His vocabulary was such as to have excited the
envy and despair of a French realist, impassioned
in the pursuit of " the word."

" *Hui !—bougré !* "—This was the most common
of his salutations to his horse. It was the Norman coachman's familiar apostrophe, impossible
of imitation; it was also one no Norman horse who
respects himself moves an inch without first hearing. Chat noir was a horse of purest Norman an-
cestry; his Percheron blood was as untainted as
his intelligence was unclouded by having no
mixtures of tongues with which to deal. His
owner's " *Hui !* " lifted him with arrowy lightness to the top of a hill. The deeper " *Bougré* "

steadied his nerve for a good mile of unbroken trotting. Any toil is pleasant in the gray of a cool morning, with a friend holding the reins who is a gifted monologist; even imprecations, rightly administered, are only lively punctuations to really talented speech.

" Come, my beauty, take in thy breath—courage ! The hill is before thee ! Curse thy withered legs, and is it thus thou stumbleth ? On—up with thee and that mountain of flesh thou carriest about with thee." And the mountain of flesh would be lifted— it was carried as lightly by the finely-feathered legs and the broad haunches as if the firm avoir- dupois were so much gossamer tissue. On and on the neat, strong hoofs rang their metallic click, clack along the smooth macadam. They had car- ried us past the farm-houses, the cliffs, the mead- ows, and the Norman-roofed manoirs buried in their apple-orchards. These same hoofs were now care- fully, dexterously picking their way down the steep hill that leads directly into the city of the Trouville villas.

Presently, the hoofs came to a sudden halt, from sheer amazement. What was this order, this com- mand the quick Percheron hearing had overheard ? Not to go any farther into this summer city—not to go down to its sand-beach — not to wander through the labyrinth of its gay little streets ?— Verily, it is the fate of a good horse, how often !— to carry fools, and the destiny of intelligence to serve those deficient in mind and sense.

The criticism on our choice of direction was an- nounced by the hoofs turning resignedly, with the

patient assent of the fatigue that is bred of disgust, into one of the upper Trouville by-streets.
Our coachman contented himself with a commiser-
ating shrug and a prolonged flow of explanation.
Perhaps *ces dames*, being strangers, did not know
that Trouville was now beginning its real season
—its season of baths? The Casino, in truth, was
only opened a week since; but we could hear the
band even now playing above the noise of the
waves. And behold, the villas were filling; each
day some *grande dame* came down to take possession of her house by the sea.

How could we hope to make a Frenchman com-
prehend an instinctive impulse to turn our backs
on the Trouville world? What, pray, had we just
now to do with fashion—with the purring accents
of boudoirs, with all the life we had run away
from? Surely the romance—the charm of our
present experiences would be put to flight once
we exchanged salutations with the *beau monde*—
with that world that is so sceptical of any pleasure
save that which blooms in its own hot-houses, and
so disdainful of all forms of life save those that are
modelled on fashion's types. We had fled from
cities to escape all this; were we, forsooth, to be
pushed into the motley crowd of commonplace
pleasure-seekers because of the scorn of a human
creature, and the mute criticism of a beast that
was hired to do the bidding of his betters? The
world of fashion was one to be looked out upon as
a part of the general *mise-en-scène*—as a bit of the
universal decoration of this vast amphitheatre of
the Normandy beaches.

Chat noir had little reverence for philosophic reflections; he turned a sharp corner just then; he stopped short, directly in front of the broad windows of a confectioner's shop. This time he did not appeal in vain to the strangers with a barbarian's contempt for the great world. The brisk drive and the salt in the air were stimulants to appetite to be respected; it is not every day the palate has so fine an edge.

"*Du thé, mesdames—à l'Anglaise?*" a neatly-corsetted shape, in black, to set off a pair of dazzling pink cheeks, shone out behind rows of apricot tarts. There was also a cap that conveyed to one, through the medium of pink bows, the capacities of coquetry that lay in the depths of the rich brown eyes beneath them. The attractive shape emerged at once from behind the counter, to set chairs about the little table. We were bidden to be seated with an air of smiling grace, one that invested the act with the emphasis of genuine hospitality. Soon a great clatter arose in the rear of the shop; opinions and counter-opinions were being volubly exchanged in shrill French, as to whether the water should or should not come to a boil; also as to whether the leaves of oolong or of green should be chosen for our beverage. The cap fluttered in several times to ask, with exquisite politeness — a politeness which could not wholly veil the hidden anxiety—our own tastes and preferences. When the cap returned to the battling forces behind the screen, armed with the authority of our confessed prejudices, a new war of tongues arose. The fate of nations, trembling on the turn of a battle, might have been settled before that pot of water, so watched and guarded over, was brought to a boil. When, finally, the little tea service was brought in, every detail was perfect in taste and appointment, except the tea; the faction that had held out valiantly, that the water should not boil, had prevailed, as the half-soaked tea-leaves floating on top of our full cups triumphantly proclaimed.

We sipped the beverage, agreeing Balzac had well named it *ce boisson fade et mélancolique;* the novelist's disdain being the better understood as we reflected he had doubtless only tasted it as concocted by French ineptitude. We were very merry over the liver-colored liquid, as we sipped it and quoted Balzac. But not for a moment had our merriment deceived the brown eyes and the fluttering cap-ribbons. A little drama of remorse was soon played for our benefit. It was she, her very self, the cap protested—as she pointed a tragic finger at the swelling, rounded line of her firm bodice—it was she who had insisted that the water should *not* boil; there had been ladies—*des vraies anglaises*—here, only last summer, who would not that the water should boil, when their tea was made. And now, it appears that they were wrong, "*c'était probablement une fantaisie de la part de ces dames.*" Would we wait for another cup? It would take but an instant, it was a little mistake, so easy to remedy. But this mistake, like many another, like crime, for instance, could never be remedied, we smilingly told her;

a smile that changed her solicitous remorse to a
humorist's view of the situation.

Another humorist, one accustomed to view the
world from heights known as trapeze elevations,
we met a little later on our way out of the narrow
upper streets; he was also looking down over
Trouville. It was a motley figure in a Pierrot garb,
with a smaller striped body, both in the stage
pallor of their trade. These were somewhat startling objects to confront on a Normandy high-road.
For clowns, however, taken by surprise, they were
astonishingly civil. They passed their "*bonjour*"
to us and to the coachman as glibly as though ac-
costing us from the commoner circus distance.

"They have come to taste of the fresh air, they
have," laconically remarked our driver, as his
round Norman eyes ran over the muscled bodies
of the two athletes. "I had a brother who was
one—I had; he was a famous one—he was; he
broke his neck once, when the net had been forgotten. They all do it—*ils se cassent le cou tous, tôt
ou tard! Allons — toi — t'as peur, toi?*" Chat
noir's great back was quivering with fear; he
had no taste, himself, for shapes like these, spectral and wan as ghosts, walking about in the sun.
He took us as far away as possible, and as quickly, from these reminders of the thing men call
pleasure.

We, meanwhile, were asking Pierre for a certain promised château, one famous for its beauty,
between Trouville and Cabourg.

"It is here, madame—the château," he said, at
last.

Two lions couchant, seated on wide pedestals
beneath a company of noble trees, were the only
visible inhabitants of the dwelling. There was a
sweep of gardens; terraces that picked their way
daintily down the cliffs toward the sea, a mansard
roof that covered a large mansion—these were the
sole aspects of château life to keep the trees company. In spite of Pierre's urgent insistance that
the view was even more beautiful than the one
from the hill, we refused to exchange our first experiences of the beauty of the prospect for a second
which would be certain to invite criticism; for it is
ever the critic in us that plays the part of Blue-
beard to our many-wived illusions.

We passed between the hedgerows with not even
a sigh of regret. We were presently rewarded by
something better than an illusion — by reality,
which, at its best, can afford to laugh at the spectral shadow of itself. Near the château there lived
on the remnant of a hamlet. It was a hamlet, apparently, that boasted only one farm-house; and the
farm-house could show but a single hayrick. Beneath the sloping roof, modelled into shape by a
pitchfork and whose symmetrical lines put Mansard's clumsy creation yonder to the blush, sat
an old couple—a man and a woman. Both were
old, with the rounded backs of the laborer; the
woman's hand was lying in the man's open palm,
while his free arm was clasped about her neck
with all the tenderness of young love. Both of
the old heads were laid back on the pillow made
by the freshly-piled grasses. They had done a long
day's work already, before the sun had reached its

meridian; they were weary and resting here before they went back to their toil.

This was better than the view; it made life seem finer than nature; how rich these two poor old things looked, with only their poverty about them!

Meanwhile Pierre had quickly changed the rural *mise-en-scène;* instead of pink hawthorn hedges we were in the midst of young forest trees. Why is it that a forest is always a surprise in France? Is it that we have such a respect for French thrift, that a real forest seems a waste of timber? There are forests and forests; this one seemed almost a stripling in its tentative delicacy, compared to the mature splendor of Fontainebleau, for example. This forest had the virility of a young savage; it was neither dense nor vast; and yet, in contrast to the ribbony grain-fields, and to the finish of the villa parks, was as refreshing to the eye as the right cord that strikes upon the ear after a succession of trills.

In all this fair Normandy sea-coast, with its wonderful inland contrasts, there was but one disappointing note. One looked in vain for the old Normandy costumes. The blouse and the close white cap—this is all that is left of the wondrous headgear, the short brilliant petticoats, the embroidered stomacher and the Caen and Rouen jewels abroad in the fields only a decade ago.

Pierre shrugged his shoulders when asked a question concerning these now pre-historic costumes.

"Ah! mademoiselle, you must see for yourself, that the peasant who doesn't despise himself dresses now in the fields as he would in Paris."

As if in confirmation of Pierre's news of the fashions, there stepped forth from an avenue of trees, fringing a near farm-house, a wedding-party. The bride was in the traditional white of brides; the little cortège following the trail of her white gown, was dressed in costumes modelled on Bon Marché styles. The coarse peasant faces flamed from bonnets more flowery than the fields into which they were passing. The men seemed choked in their high collars; the agony of new boots was written on faces not used to concealing such form of torture. Even the groom was suffering; his bliss was something the gay little bride hanging on his arm must take entirely for granted. It was enough greatness for the moment to wear broadcloth and a white vest in the face of men.

" *Laissez, laissez, Marguerite,* it is clean here; it will look fine on the green!" cried the bride to an improvised train-bearer, who had been holding up the white alpaca. Then the full splendor of the bridal skirt trailed across the freshly mown grasses. An irrepressible murmur of admiration welled up from the wedding guests; even Pierre made part of the chorus. The bridegroom stopped to mop his face, and to look forth proudly, through starting eyeballs, on the splendor of his possessions.

"Ah! Lizette, thou art pretty like that, thou knowest. *Faut t'embrasser, tu sais.*"

He gave her a kiss full on the lips. The little bride returned the kiss with unabashed fervor. Then she burst into a loud fit of laughter.

"How silly you look, Jean, with your collar burst open."

The groom's enthusiasm had been too much for his toilet; the noon sun and the excitements of the marriage service had dealt hardly with his celluloid fastenings. All the wedding cortège rushed to the rescue. Pins, shouts of advice, pieces of twine, rubber fastenings, even knives, were offered to the now exploding bridegroom; everyone was helping him repair the ravages of his moment of bliss; everyone excepting the bride. She sat down upon her train and wept from pure rapture of laughter.

Pierre shook his head gravely, as he whipped up his steed.

"Jean will repent it; he'll lose worse things than a button, with Lizette. A woman who laughs like that on the threshold of marriage will cry before the cradle is rocked, and will make others weep. However, Jean won't be thinking of that—to-night."

"Where are they going—along the highroad?"

"Only a short distance. They turn in there," and he pointed with his whip to a near lane; "they go to the farm-house now—for the wedding dinner. Ah! there'll be some heavy heads to-morrow. For you know, a Norman peasant only really eats and drinks well twice in his life—when he marries himself and when his daughter marries. Lizette's father is rich—the meat and the wines will be good to-night."

Our coachman sighed, as if the thought of the excellence of the coming banquet had disturbed his own digestion.

CHAPTER XV.

THE wedding party was lost in a thicket. Pierre gave his whip so resounding a snap, it was no surprise to find ourselves rolling over the cobbles of a village street.

"This is Dives, mesdames, this is the inn!"

Pierre drew up, as he spoke, before a long, low façade.

Now, no one, I take it, in this world enjoys being duped. Surely disappointment is only a civil term for the varying degrees of fraud practised on the imagination. This inn, apparently, was to be classed among such frauds. It did not in the least, externally at least, fulfil Renard's promises. He had told us to expect the marvellous and the mediæval in their most approved period. Yet here we were, facing a featureless exterior! The façade was built yesterday—that was writ large, all over the low, rambling structure. One end, it is true, had a gabled end; there was also an old shrine niched in glass beneath the gable, and a low Norman gateway with rude letters carved over the arch. June was in its glory, and the barrenness of the commonplace structure was mercifully hidden by a wreath of pink and amber roses. But one scarcely drives twenty miles in the sun to look upon a façade of roses!

Chat noir, meanwhile, was becoming restless. Pierre had managed to keep his own patience well in hand. Now, however, he broke forth:

" Shall we enter, my ladies? "

Pierre drove us straight into paradise; for here, at last, within the courtyard, was the inn we had come to seek.

A group of low-gabled buildings surrounded an open court. All of the buildings were timbered, the diagonal beams of oak so old they were black in the sun, and the snowy whiteness of fresh plaster made them seem blacker still. The gabled roofs were of varying tones and tints; some were red, some mossy green, some as gray as the skin of a mouse; all were deeply, plentifully furrowed with the washings of countless rains, and they were bearded with moss. There were outside galleries, beginning somewhere and ending anywhere. There were open and covered outer stairways so laden with vines they could scarce totter to the low heights of the chamber doors on which they opened; and there were open sheds where huge farm-wagons were rolled close to the most modern of Parisian dog-carts. That not a note of contrast might be lacking, across the courtyard, in one of the windows beneath a stairway, there flashed the gleam of some rich stained glass, spots of color that were repeated, with quite a different lustre, in the dappled haunches of rows of sturdy Percherons munching their meal in the adjacent stalls. Add to such an ensemble a vagrant multitude of rose, honeysuckle, clematis, and wistaria vines, all blooming in full rivalry of perfume and color; insert in some of the corners and beneath some of the older casements archæic bits of sculpture—strange barbaric features with beards of Assyrian correctness and forms clad in the rigid draperies of the early Jumièges period of the sculptor's art; lance above the roof-ridges the quaint polychrome finials of the earlier Palissy models; and crowd the rough cobble-paved courtyard with a rare and distinguished assemblage of flamingoes, peacocks, herons, cockatoos swinging from gabled windows, and game-cocks that strut about in company with pink doves— and you have the famous inn of Guillaume le Conquérant!

Meanwhile an individual, with fine deep-gray eyes, and a face grave, yet kindly, over which a smile was humorously breaking, was patiently waiting at our carriage door. He could be no other than Monsieur Paul, owner and inn-keeper, also artist, sculptor, carver, restorer, to whom, in truth, this miracle of an inn owed its present perfection and picturesqueness.

"We have been long expecting you, mesdames," Monsieur Paul's grave voice was saying. "Monsieur Renard had written to announce your coming. You took the trouble to drive along the coast this fine day? It is idyllically lovely, is it not—under such a sun?"

Evidently the moment of enchantment was not to be broken by the worker of the spell. Monsieur Paul and his inn were one; if one was a poem the other was a poet. The poet was also lined with the man of the practical moment. He had quickly summoned a host of serving-people to take charge of us and our luggage.

"Lizette, show these ladies to the room of Madame de Sévigné. If they desire a sitting-room—to the Marmousets."

The inn-keeper gave his commands in the quiet, well-bred tone of a man of the world, to a woman in peasant's dress. She led us past the open court to an inner one, where we were confronted with a building still older, apparently, than those grouped about the outer quadrangle. The peasant passed quickly beneath an overhanging gallery, draped in vines. She was next preceding us up a spiral turret stairway; the adjacent walls were hung here and there with faded bits of tapestry. Once more she turned to lead us along an open gallery; on this several rooms appeared to open. On each door a different sign was painted in rude Gothic letters. The first was " Chambre de l' Officier; " the second, " Chambre du Curé," and the next was flung widely open. It was the room of the famous lady of the incomparable Letters. The room might have been left, in the two centuries of a yesterday, by the lady whose name it bore. There was a beautiful Seventeenth century bedstead, a couple of wide arm-chairs, with down pillows for seats, and a clothes press with the carvings and brass work peculiar to the epoch of Louis XIV. The chintz hangings and draperies were in keeping, being copies of the brocades of that day. There were portraits in miniature of the courtiers and the ladies

of the Great Reign on the very ewers and basins.
On the flounced dressing-table, with its antique
glass and a diminutive patch-box, now the recep-
tacle of Lubin's power, a sprig of the lovely Rose
Thè was exhaling a faint, far-away century perfume.
It was surely a stage set for a real comedy; some
of these high-coiffed ladies, who knows? perhaps
Madame de Sévigné herself would come to life and
give to the room the only thing it lacked—the living presence of that old world grace and speech.

Presently, we sallied forth on a further voyage
of discovery. We had reached the courtyard when
Monsieur Paul crossed it; it was to ask if, while
waiting for the noon breakfast, we would care to
see the kitchen; it was, perhaps, different to those
now commonly seen in modern taverns.

The kitchen which was thus modestly described
as unlike those of our own century might easily,
except for the appetizing smell of the cooking
fowls and the meats, have been put under lock and
key and turned over to a care-taker as a full-fledged
culinary museum of antiquities. One entire side
of the crowded but orderly little room was taken up
by a huge open fireplace. The logs resting on the
great andirons were the trunks of full-grown
trees. On two of the spits were long rows of fowl
and legs of mutton roasting; the great chains were
being slowly turned by a *chef* in the paper cap of
his profession. In deep burnished brass bowls lay
water-cresses; in Caen dishes of an age to make a
bric-à-brac collector turn green with envy, a *Béar-
naise* sauce was being beaten by another gallic mas-
ter-hand. Along the beams hung old Rouen plates

and platters; in the numberless carved Normandy cupboards gleamed rare bits of Delft and Limoges; the walls may be said to have been hung with Normandy brasses, each as burnished as a jewel. The floor was sanded and the tables had attained that satiny finish which comes only with long usage and tireless use of the brush. There was also a shrine and a clock, the latter of antique Norman make and design.

The smell of the roasting fowls and the herbs used by the maker of the sauces, a hungry palate found even more exciting than this most original of kitchens. There was a wine that went with the sauce; this fact Monsieur Paul explained, on our sitting down to the noonday meal; one which, in remembrance of Monsieur Renard's injunctions, he would suggest our trying. He crossed the courtyard and disappeared into the bowels of the earth, beneath one of the inn buildings, to bring forth a bottle incrusted with layers of moist sod. This Sauterne was by some, Monsieur Paul smilingly explained, considered as among the real treasures of the inn. Both it and the sauce, we were enabled to assure him a moment later, had that golden softness which make French wines and French sauces at their best the rapture of the palate.

In the courtyard, as our breakfast proceeded, a variety of incidents was happening. We were facing the open archway; through it one looked out upon the high-road. A wheelbarrow passed, trundled by a peasant-girl; the barrow stopped, the girl leaving it for an instant to cross the court.

" *Bonjour, mère——*"

" *Bonjour, ma fille—*it goes well ? " a deep guttural voice responded, just outside of the window.

" *Justement—*I came to tell you the mare has foaled and Jean will be late to-night."

" *Bien.*"

"And Barbarine is still angry——"

" Make up with her, my child—anger is an evil bird to take to one's heart," the deep voice went on.

"It is my mother," explained Monsieur Paul. " It is her favorite seat, out yonder, on the green bench in the courtyard. I call it her judge's bench," he smiled, indulgently, as he went on. " She dispenses justice with more authority than any other magistrate in town. I am Mayor, as it happens, just now; but madame my mother is far above me, in real power. She rules the town and the country about, for miles. Everyone comes to her sooner or later for counsel and command. You will soon see for yourselves."

A murmur of assent from all the table accompanied Monsieur Paul's prophecy.

" *Femme vraiment remarquable,*" hoarsely whispered a stout breakfaster, behind his napkin, between two spoonsful of his soup.

" Not two in a century like her," said my neighbor.

"No—nor two in all France—*non plus,*" retorted the stout man.

" She could rule a kingdom—hey, Paul ? "

" She rules me—as you see—and a man is harder to govern than a province, they say," smiled Monsieur Paul with a humorous relish, obviously the offspring of experience. " In France, mesdames," he added, a sweeter look of feeling coming into the deep eyes, " you see we are always children— *toujours enfants*—as long as the mother lives. We are never really old till she dies. May the good God preserve her!" and he lifted his glass toward the green bench. The table drank the toast, in silence.

CHAMBRE DE LA PUCELLE—DIVES.

CHAPTER XVI.

THE GREEN BENCH.

In the course of the first few days we learned what all Dives had known for the past fifty years or so—that the focal point of interest in the inn was centred in Madame Le Mois. She drew us, as she had the country around for miles, to circle close about her green bench.

The bench was placed at the best possible point for one who, between dawn and darkness, made it the business of her life to keep her eye on her world. Not the tiniest mouse nor the most spectral shade could enter or slip away beneath the open archway without undergoing inspection from that omniscient eye, that seemed never to blink nor to grow weary. This same eye could keep its watch, also, over the entire establishment, with no need of the huge body to which it was attached moving a hair's-breadth. Was it Nitouche, the head-cook, who was grumbling because the kitchen-wench had not scoured the brass saucepans to the last point of mirrory brightness? Behold both Nitouche and the trembling peasant-girl, together with the brasses as evidence, all could be brought at an instant's call, into the open court. Were the maids—were Marianne or Lizette neglecting their work to flirt with the coachmen in the sheds yonder?

"*Allons, mes filles—doucement, là-bas—et vos lits? qui les fait—les bons saints du paradis, peut-être?*" And Marianne and Lizette would slink away to the waiting beds. Nothing escaped this eye. If the *poule sultane* was gone lame, limping in the inner quadrangle, madame's eye saw the trouble—a thorn in the left claw, before the feathered cripple had had time to reach her objective point, her mistress's capacious lap and the healing touch of her skilful surgeon's fingers. Neither were the cockatoes nor the white parrots given license to make all the noise in the court-yard. When madame had an unusually loquacious moment, these more strictly professional conversationists were taught their place.

"*E'ben, toi*—and thou wishest to proclaim to the world what a gymnast thou art—swinging on thy perch? Quietly, quietly, there are also others who wish to praise themselves! And now, my

child, you were telling me how good you had
been to your old grandmother, and how she scolded
you. Well, and how about obedience to our parents, *hein*—how about that?" This, as the old
face bent to the maiden beside her.

There was one, assuredly, who had not failed
in his duty to his parents. Monsieur Paul's
whole life, as we learned later, had been a willing
sacrifice to the unconscious tyranny of his mother's affection. The son was gifted with those gifts
which, in a Parisian atelier, would easily have made
him successful, if not famous. He had the artistic endowment in an unusual degree; it was all
one to him whether he modelled in clay or carved
in wood or stone, or built a house, or restored old
bric-à-brac. He had inherited the old world round-
ness of artistic ability—his was the plastic renas-
cent touch that might have developed into that of
a Giotto or a Benvenuto.

It was such a sacrifice as this that he had lain
at his mother's feet.

Think you for an instant the clever, witty, canny
woman in Madame Le Mois looked upon her son's
renouncing the world of Paris, and holding to the
glories of Dives and their famous inn in the light
of a sacrifice? "*Parbleu!*" she would explode,
when the subject was touched on, "it was a lucky
thing for him that Paul had had an old mother to
keep him from burning his fingers. Paris! What
did the provinces want with Paris? Paris had
need enough of them, the great, idle, shiftless, dis-
sipated, cruel old city, that ground all their sons
to powder, and then scattered their ashes abroad

like so many cinders. Oh, yes, Paris couldn't get
along without the provinces, to plunder and rob,
to seduce their sons away from living good, pure
lives, and to suck these lives as a pig would a
trough of fresh water! But the provinces, if they
valued their souls, shunned Paris as they would the
devil. And as for artists—when it came to the
young of the provinces, who thought they could
paint or model——

"*Tenez, madame*—this is what Paris does for our
young. My neighbor yonder," and she pointed,
as only Frenchwomen point, sticking her thumb
into the air to designate a point back of her
bench, "my neighbor had a son like Paul. He
too was always niggling at something. He nig-
gled so well a rich cousin sent him up to Paris.
Well, in ten years he comes back, famous, rich,
too, with a wife and even a child. The establishment is complete. Well, they come here to breakfast one fine morning, with his mother, whom he
put at a side table, with his nurse—he is ashamed
of his mother, you see. Well, then his wife talks
and I hear her. '*Mais, mon Charles, c'est toi qui
est le plus fameux—il n'y a que toi! Tu es un dieu,
tu sais—il n'y a pas deux comme toi!*' The famous one deigns to smile then, and to eat of his
breakfast. His digestion had gone wrong, it appears. The *Figaro* had placed his name second
on a certain list *after* a rival's! He alone must be
great—there must not be another god of painting
save him! Hé! Hé! that's fine, that's greatness
—to lose one's appetite because another is praised,
and to be ashamed of one's old mother!"

Madame Le Mois's face, for a moment, was terrible to look upon. Even in her kindliest moments hers was a severe countenance, in spite of the true Norman curves in mouth and nostril—the laughter-loving curves. Presently, however, the fierceness of her severity melted; she had caught sight of her son. He was passing her, now, with the wine bottles for dinner piled up in his arms.

"You see," croaked the mother, in an exultant whisper, "I've saved him from all that—he's happy, for he still works. In the winter he can amuse himself, when he likes, with his carving and paintbrushes. Ah, *tiens, du monde qui arrive !*" And the old woman seated herself, with an air of great dignity, to receive the new-comers.

The world that came in under the low archway was of an altogether different character from any we had as yet seen. In a satin-lined victoria, amid the cushions, lay a young and lovely-eyed Anonyma. Seated beside her was a weak-featured man, with a huge flower decorating his coat lappel. This latter individual divided the seat with an army of small dogs who leaped forth as the carriage stopped.

Madame Le Mois remained immovable on her bench. Her face was as enigmatic as her voice as it gave Suzette the order to show the lady to the salon bleu. The high Louis XV. slipper, as it picked its way carefully after Suzette, never seemed more distinctly astray than when its fair wearer confided her safety to the insecure footing of the rough, uneven cobbles. In a brief half-hour the frou-frou of her silken skirts was once more

sweeping the court-yard. She and her companion
and the dogs chose the open air and a tent of sky
for their banqueting - hall. Soon all were seated
at one of the many tables placed near the kitchen,
beneath the rose-vines.

Madame gave the pair a keen, dissecting glance.
Her verdict was delivered more in the emphasis
of her shrug and the humor of her broad wink
than in the loud-whispered—" *Comme vous voyez,
chère dame, de toutes sortes ici, chez nous—mais—
toujours bon genre!* "

The laughter of one who could not choose her
world was stopped, suddenly, by the dipping of
the thick fingers into an old snuff-box. That very
afternoon the court-yard saw another arrival; this
one was treated in quite a different spirit.

A dog-cart was briskly driven into the yard by
a gentleman who did not appear to be in the best
of humor. He drew his horse up with a sudden
fierceness; he as fiercely called out for the hostler.
Monsieur Paul bit his lip; but he composedly
confronted the disturbed countenance perched on
the driver's seat. The gentleman wished——

"I want indemnity—that is what I want. Indemnity for my horse," cried out a thick, coarse
voice, with insolent authority.

"For your horse? I do not think I understand——"

" O—h, I presume not," retorted the man, still
more insolently; "people don't usually understand
when they have to pay. I came here a week ago,
and stayed two days; and you starved my horse—
and he died—that is what happened—he died!"

The whole court-yard now rang with the cries of the assembled household. The high, angry tones had called together the last serving-man and scullery-maid; the cooks had come out from their kitchens; they were brandishing their long-handled saucepans. The peasant-women were shrieking in concert with the hostlers, who were raising their arms to heaven in proof of their innocence. Dogs, cats, cockatoes swinging on their perches, peacocks, parrots, pelicans, and every one of the cocks swarmed from the barnyards and garden and cellars, to add their shrill cries and shrieks to the universal babel.

Meanwhile, calm and unruffled as a Hindoo goddess, and strikingly similar in general massiveness of structure and proportion to the common reproduction of such deities, sat Madame Le Mois. She went on with her usual occupation; she was dipping fresh-cut salad leaves into great bowls of water as quietly as if only her own little family were assembled before her. Once only she lifted her heavily-moulded, sagacious eyebrow at the irate dog-cart driver, as if to measure his pitiful strength. She allowed the fellow, however, to touch the point of abuse before she crushed him.

Her first sentence reduced him to the ignominy of silence. All her people were also silent. What, the deep sarcastic voice chanted on the still air—what, this gentleman's horse had died—and yet he had waited a whole week to tell them of the great news? He was, of a truth, altogether too considerate. His own memory, perhaps, was also a short one, since it told him nothing of the condition in which the poor beast had arrived, dropping with fatigue, wet with sweat, his mouth all blood, and an eye as of one who already was past the consciousness of his suffering? Ah no, monsieur should go to those who also had short memories.

"For we use our eyes—we do. We are used to deal with gentlemen—with Christians" (the Hebrew nose of the owner of the dead horse even more plainly abused the privilege of its pedigree in proving its race by turning downward, at this onslaught of the mère's satire), "as I said, with Christians," continued the mère, pitilessly. "And do those gentlemen complain and put upon us the death of their horses? No, my fine sir, they return—*ils reviennent, et sont revenus depuis la Conquête!*"

With this fine climax madame announced the court as closed. She bowed disdainfully, with a grand and magisterial air, to the defeated claimant, who crept away, sulkily, through the low archway.

"That is the way to deal with such vermin, Paul; whip them, and they turn tail." And the mère shook out a great laugh from her broad bosom, as she regaled her wide nostrils with a fresh pinch of snuff. The assembled household echoed the laugh, seasoning it with the glee of scorn, as each went to his allotted place.

CHAPTER XVII.

THE WORLD THAT CAME TO DIVES.

 It was a world of many mixtures, of various ranks and habits of life that found its way under the old archway, and sat down at the table d'hôte breakfasts and dinners. Madame and her gifted son were far too clever to attempt to play the mistaken part of Providence; there was no pointed assortment made of the sheep and the goats; at least, not in a way to suggest the most remote intention of any such separation being premeditated. Such separation as there was came about in the most natural and in the pleasantest possible fashion. When Petitjean, the pedler, and his wife drove in under the Gothic sign, the huge lumbering vehicle was as quickly surrounded as when any of the neighboring notabilities arrived in emblazoned chariots. Madame was the first to waddle forward, nodding up toward the open hood as, with a short, brisk, business " *Bonjour*," she welcomed the head of Petitjean and his sharp-eyed spouse looking over the aprons.

The pedler is always popular with his world; and Dives knew Petitjean to be as honest as a pedler can ever hope to be in a world where small pence are only made large by some one being sacrificed on the altar of duplicity. Therefore it was that Petitjean's hearse-like cart was always a welcome visitor;—one could at least be as sure of a just return for one's money in trading with a pedler as from any other source in this thieving world. In the end, one always got something else besides the bargain to carry away with one. For Petitjean knew all the gossip of the province; after dinner, when the stiff cider was working in his veins, he would be certain to tell all one wanted to know. Even Madame Le Mois, whose days were too busy in summer to include the daily reading of her newspaper, had grown dependent, in these her later years, on such sources of information as the pedler's garrulous tongue supplied. In the end she had found his talent for fiction quite as reliable as that of the journalists, besides being infinitely more entertaining, abounding in personalities which were the more racy as the pedler felt himself to be exempt from that curse of responsibility which, in French journalism, is so often a barrier to the full play of one's talent.

Therefore it was that Petitjean and his bright-eyed spouse were always made welcome at Dives.

"It goes well, Madame Jean? Ah, there you are. Well, *hein*, also? It is long since we saw you."

"Ah, madame, centuries, it is centuries since we were here. But what will you have? with the bad season, the rains, the banks failing, the—but you, madame, are well ? And Monsieur Paul ?"

"*Ah, ça va tout doucement*—Paul is well, the good God be praised, but I—I perish day by day——"

At which the entire court-yard was certain to burst into laughing protest. For the whole house-hold of Guillaume le Conquérant was quite sure to be assembled about the great wheels of the ped-ler's wagon—only to look, not to buy, not yet. Petitjean and his wife had not dined yet, and a pedler's hunger is something to be respected—one made money by waiting for the hour of digestion. The little crowd of maids, hostlers, cooks, and scullery wenches, were only here to whet their ap-petite and to greet Petitjean. Nitouche, the head *chef*, put a little extra garlic in his sauces that day. But in spite of this compliment to their palate, the pedler and his wife dined in the smaller room off the kitchen;—Madame was desolated, but the *salle-à-manger* was crowded just now. One was really suffocated in there these days ! Therefore it was that the two ate the herbaceous sauces with an extra relish, as those conscious of having a larger space for the play of vagrant elbows than their less fortunate brethren.

The gossip and trading came later.

On the edge of the fading daylight there was still time to see; the chosen articles could easily be taken into the brightly lit kitchen to be passed before the lamps. After the buying and bargain-ing came the talking. All the household could find time to spend the evening on the old benches; these latter lined the sidewalk just beneath the low

kitchen casements.   They had been here for many
a long year.

What a history of Dives these old benches could
have told!   What troopers, and beggars, and
cowled monks, and wayfarers had sat there!—each
sitter helping to wear away the wood till it had
come to have the depressions of a drinking-trough.
Night after night in the long centuries, as the darkness fell upon the hamlet—what tales and confidences, and what murmured anguish of remorse,
what cries for help, what gay talk and light song
must have welled up into the dome of sky!

Once, as we sat within the court-yard, under the
stars, a young voice sang out.   It was so still and
quiet every word the youth phrased was as clear
as his fresh young voice.

" *Tiens*—it is Mathieu—he is singing *Les Oreil-
lers !* " cried Monsieur Paul, with an accent of
pride in his own tone.

The young voice sang on:

> " *J'arrive en ce pays*
> *De Basse Normandie,*
> *Vous dire une chanson,*
> *S'il plait la compagnie !* "

"It is an old Norman bridal song," Monsieur
Paul went on, lowering his voice.   " One I taught
a lot of young boys and lads last winter—for a
wedding held here—in the inn."

Still the fresh notes filled the air:

> " *Les amours sont partis*
> *Dans un bateau de verre ;*
> *Le bateau a cassé*
> *a cassé—*
> *Les amours sont parterre.*"

"How the old women laughed—and cried—at once! It was years since they had heard it—the old song. And when these boys—their sons and grandsons—sang it, and I had trained them well— they wept for pure delight."

Again the song went on:

. . . . .

> *" Ouvrez la porte, ouvrez !*
> *Nouvelle mariée,*
> *Car si vous ne l'ouvrez*
> *Vous serez accusée."*

. . . . .

"I dressed all the young girls in old costumes," our friend continued, still in a whisper. "I ransacked all the old chests and closets about here. I got the ladies of the châteaus near by to aid me; they were so interested that many came down from Paris to see the wedding. It was a pretty sight, each in a different dress! Every century since the thirteenth was represented."

> *" Attendez à demain,*
> *La fraîche matinée,*
> *Quand mon oiseau privé*
> *Aura pris sa volée ! "*

Clear, strong, free rang the young tenor's voice —and then it broke into " *Comment—tu dis que Claire est là ? "* whereat Monsieur Paul smiled.

"That will be the next wedding—what shall I devise for that? That will also be the ending of a long lawsuit. But he should have sung the last verse—the prettiest of all. Mathieu!" Paul lifted his voice, calling into the dark.

"Oui, Monsieur Léon ! "
" Sing us the last verse——"

> *" Dans se jardin du Roi*
> *A pris sa reposée,*
> *Cueillant le romarin*
> *La—vande—bouton—née——"*

The last notes were but faint vibrations, coming from a lengthening distance.

"Ah!" and Monsieur Paul breathed a sigh. " They don't care about singing. They are doing it all the time—they are so much in love. The fathers' lawsuit ended only last month. They've waited three years—happy Claire—happy Mathieu ! "

CHAPTER XVIII.

THE world that found its way to the mayor's table at this early period of the summer season was largely composed of the class that travels chiefly to amuse others. The commercial gentlemen in France, however, have the outward bearing of those who travel to amuse themselves. The selling of other people's goods—it is surely as good an excuse as any other for seeing the world! Such an occupation offers an orator, one gifted in conversational talents—talents it would be a pity to see buried in the domestic napkin—a fine arena for display.

The French commercial traveller is indeed a genus apart; he makes a fetich of his trade; he preaches his propaganda. The fat and the lean, the tall and the little, the well or meanly dressed representatives of the great French houses who sat down to dine, as our neighbors or *vis-à-vis*, night after night, were, on the whole, a great credit to their country. Their manners might have been mistaken for those of a higher rank; their gifts as talkers were of such an order as to make listening the better part of discretion.

Dining is always a serious act in France. At this inn the sauces of the *chef*, with their reputation behind them and the proof of their real excellence before one, the dinner-hour was elevated to the importance of a ceremony. How the petty merchants and the commercial gentlemen ate, at first in silence, as if respecting the appeal imposed by a great hunger, and then warming into talk as the acid cider was passed again and again! What crunching of the sturdy, dark-colored bread between the great knuckles! What huge helps of the famous sauces! What insatiable appetites! What nice appreciation of the right touch of the tricksy garlic! What nodding of heads, clinking of glasses, and warmth of friendship established over the wine-cups! At dessert everyone talked at once. On one occasion the subject of Gambetta's death was touched on; all the table, as one man, broke out into an effervescence of political babble.

"What a loss! What a death-blow to France was his death!" exclaimed a heavy young man in a pink cravat.

"If Gambetta had lived, Alsace and Lorraine would be ours now, without the firing of a gun!" added an elderly merchant at the foot of the table.

"Ah—h! without the firing of a gun they will come to us yet. I tell you, without the firing of a gun—unless we insist on a battle," explosively rejoined a fiery-hued little man sitting next to Monsieur Paul; "but you will see—we shall insist.

There is between us and Germany an inextinguishable hate—and we must kill, kill, right and left!"

"*Allons—allons!*" protested the table, in chorus.

"Yes, yes, a general massacre, that is what we want; that is what we must have. Men, women, and children—all must fall. I am a married man —but not a woman or a child shall escape—when the time comes," continued the fiery-eyed man, getting more and more ferocious as he warmed with the thought of his revenge.

"What a monster!" broke in Madame Le Mois, her deep base notes unruffled by the spectacle of her bloodthirsty neighbor's violence; "you—to bayonet a woman with a child in her arms!"

"I would—I would——"

"Then you would be more cruel than they were. They treated our women with respect."

There was a murmur of assenting applause, at this sentiment of justice, from the table. But the fiery-eyed man was not to be put down.

"Oh, yes, they were generous enough in '71, but I should remember their insults of 1815!"

"*Ancienne histoire—ça,*" said the mère, dismissing the subject, with a humorous wink at the table.

"As you see," was Monsieur Paul's comment on the conversation, as we were taking our after-dinner stroll in the garden—"as you see, that sort of person is the bad element in our country— the dangerous element—unreasoning, revengeful, and ignorant. It is such men as he who still uphold hatreds and keep the flame alive. It is better to have no talent at all for politics—to be harmless like me, for instance, whose worst vice is to buy up old laces and carvings."

"And roses——"

"Yes—that is another of my vices—to perpetuate the old varieties. They call me along our coast—the millionnaire—of roses ! Will you have a 'Marie Louise,' mademoiselle ? "

The garden was as complete in its old-time aspect as the rest of the inn belongings. Only the older, rarer varieties of flowers and rose-stalks had been chosen to bloom within the beautifully arranged inclosure. *Citronnelle,* purple irises, fringed asters, sage, lavender, *rose-pêche,* bachelor's - button, *thè d'Horace,* and the wonderful electric fraxinelle, these and many other shrubs and plants of the older centuries were massed here with the taste of one difficult to please in horticultural arrangements. Our after-dinner walks became an event in our day. At that hour the press of the day's work was over, and Madame Mère or Monsieur Paul were always ready to join us for a stroll.

"For myself, I do not like large gardens," Monsieur Paul remarked, during one of these after-dinner saunters. "The monks, in the old days, knew just the right size a garden should be—small and sheltered, with walls—like a strong arm about a pretty woman—to protect the shrubs and flowers. One should enter the garden, also, by a gate which must click as it closes—the click tickles the imagination—it is the sound henceforth connected with silence, with perfumes and seclusion. How far away we seem now, do we not ?—from the bustle of the inn court-yard—and yet I could throw a stone into it."

The only saunterers besides ourselves were the flamingo, who, cautiously, timorously picked his way—as if he were conscious he was only a bunch of feathers hoisted on stilts; the white parrot, who was wabbling across the lawn to a favorite perch in the leaves of a tropical palm; and the peacock, whose train had been spread with a due regard to effect across a bed of purple irises, with a view to annihilating the brilliancy of their rival hues.

The bit of sky framed by these four garden walls always seemed more delicate in tone than that which covered the open court-yard. The birds in the bushes had moments of melodious outbursts they did not, apparently, indulge in along the high-road. And what with the fading lights, the stars pricking their way among the palms, the scents of flowers, and the talk of a poet, it is little wonder that this twilight hour in the old garden was certain to be the most lyrical of the twenty-four.

CHAPTER XIX.

"IT is the winters, mesdames, that are hard to bear. They are long—they are dull. No one passes along the high-road. It is then, when sometimes the snow is piled knee-deep in the court-yard, it is then I try to amuse myself a little. Last year I did the Jumièges sculptures; they fit in well, do they not?"

It was raining; and Monsieur Paul was paying us an evening call. A great fire was burning in the beautiful François I. fireplace of our sitting-room, the famous Chambre des Marmousets. We had not consented that any of the lights should be lit, although the lovely little Louis XIV. chandelier and the antique brass sconces were temptingly filled with fresh candles. The flames of the great logs would suffer no rival illuminations; if the trunks of full-grown trees could not suffice to light up an old room, with low-raftered ceilings, and a mass of bric-à-brac, what could a few thin waxen candles hope to do?

On many other occasions we had thought our marvellous sitting-room had had exceptional mo-

ments of beauty. To turn in from the sunlit,
open court-yard ; to pass beneath the vine-hung
gallery ; to lift the great latch of the low Gothic
door and to enter the rich and sumptuous interior, where the light came, as in cathedral aisles,
only through the jewels of fourteenth - century
glass; to close the door; to sit beneath the prismatic shower ensconced in a nest of old tapestried
cushions, and to let the eye wander over the
wealth of carvings, of ceramics, of Spanish and
Normandy trousseaux chests, on the collection of
antique chairs, Dutch porcelains, and priceless embroideries—all the riches of a museum in a living-
room—such a moment in the Marmousets we had
tested again and again with delectable results.
At twilight, also, when the garden was submerged
in dew, this old seigneurial chamber was a retreat fit for a sybarite or a modern æsthete. The
stillness, the soft luxurious cushions, the rich dusk
thickening in the corners, the complete isolation
of the old room from the noise and tumult of the
inn life, its curious, its delightful unmodernness,
made this Marmouset room an ideal setting for
any mediæval picture. Even a sentiment tinct-
ured with modern cynicism would, I think, have
borrowed a little antique fervor, if, like the pho-
tographic negative our nineteenth-century emo-
tionalism somewhat too closely resembles in its
colorless indefiniteness, the sentiment were sufficiently exposed, in point of time and degree of
sensitiveness, to the charm of these old surround-
; ings.   •
   On this particular evening, however, the patter-

ing of the rain without on the cobbles and the
great blaze of the fire within, made the old room
seem more beautiful than we had yet seen it.
Perhaps the capture of our host as a guest was
the added treasure needed to complete our collection. Monsieur Paul himself was in a mood of
prodigal liberality; he was, as he himself neatly
termed the phrase, ripe for confession; not a secret should escape revelation; all the inn mys-
teries should yield up the fiction of their frauds;
the full nakedness of fact should be given to us.

"You see, *chères dames*, it is not so difficult to
create the beautiful, if one has a little taste and
great patience. My inn — it has become my
hobby, my pride, my wife, my children. Some
men marry their art, I espoused my inn. I found
her poor, tattered, broken-down in health, if you
will; verily, as your Shakespeare says of some
country wench: 'a poor thing but mine own.'"
Monsieur Paul's possession of the English language was scarcely as complete as the storehouse
of his memory. He would have been surprised,
doubtless, to learn he had called poor Audrey, "a
pure ting, buttaire my noon!"

"She was, however," he continued, securely, in
his own richer Norman, "though a wench, a beautiful one. And I vowed to make her glorious.
'She shall be famous,' I vowed, and—and—better than most men I have kept my vow. All
France now has heard of Guillaume le Conqué-
ant!"

The pride Monsieur Paul took in his inn was
indeed a fine thing to see. The years of toil he

had spent on its walls and in its embellishment
had brought him the recompense much giving
always brings; it had enriched him quite as
much as the wealth of his taste and talent had
bequeathed to the inn. Latterly, he said, he had
travelled much, his collection of curios and antiquities having called him farther afield than many
Frenchmen care to wander. His love of Delft
had taken him to Holland; his passion for Spanish leather to the country of Velasquez; he must
have a Virgin, a genuine fifteenth-century Virgin,
all his own; behold her there, in her stiff wooden
skirts, a Neapolitan captive. The brass braziers
yonder, at which the courtiers of the Henris had
warmed their feet, stamping the night out in cold
ante-chambers, had been secured at Blois; and
his collection of tapestries, of stained glass, of
Normandy brasses, and Breton carvings had made
his own coast as familiar as the Dives streets.

"The priests who sold me these, madame," he
went on, as he picked up a priest's chasuble, now
doing duty as a table covering" would sell their
fathers and their mothers. It is all a question of
price."

After a review of the curios came the history of
the human collection of antiquities who had peopled the inn and this old room.

Many and various had been the visitors who
had slept and dined here and gone forth on their
travels along the high-road.

The inn had had a noble origin; it had been
built by no less a personage than the great William himself. He had deemed the spot a fitting

one in which to build his boats to start forth for
his modest project of conquering England. He
could watch their construction in the waters of
Dives River—that flows still, out yonder, among
the grasses of the sea-meadows. For some years
the Norman dukes held to the inn, in memory of
the success of that clever boat-building. Then
for five centuries the inn became a manoir—the
seigneurial residence of a certain Sieur de Sem-
illy. It was his arms we saw yonder, joined to
those of Savoy, in the door panel, one of the
family having married into a branch of that great
house.

Of the famous ones of the world who had travelled along this Caen post-road and stopped the
night here, humanly tired, like any other humble
wayfarer, was a hurried visit from that king who
loved his trade—Louis XI. He and his suite
crowded into the low rooms, grateful for a bed
and a fire, after the weary pilgrimage to the
heights of Mont St. Michel. Louis's piety, however, was not as lasting in its physically exhaust-
ive effects, as were the fleshly excesses of a
certain óther king—one Henri IV., whose over-ap-
preciation of the oysters served him here caused
a royal attack of colic, as you may read at your
pleasure in the State Archives in Paris—since,
quite rightly, the royal secretary must write the
court physician every detail of so important an
event. What with these kingly travellers and
such modern uncrowned kings as Puvis de Cha-
vannes, Dumas, George Sand, Daubigny, and Troy-
on, together with a goodly number of lesser great

ones, the famous little inn has had no reason to
feel itself slighted by the great of any century.
Of all this motley company of notabilities there
were two whose visits seemed to have been indefinitely prolonged. There was nothing, in this
present flowery, picturesque assemblage of buildings to suggest a certain wild drama enacted here
centuries ago. Nothing either in yonder tender
sky, nor in the silvery foliage on a fair day, which
should conjure up the image of William as he
must have stood again and again beside the little
river; nor of the fury of his impatience as the
boats were building all too slowly for his hot
hopes; nor of the strange and motley crew he had
summoned there from all corners of Europe to cut
the trees; to build and launch boats ; to sail them,
finally, across the strip of water to that England
he was to meet at last, to grapple with, and over-
throw, even as the English huscarles in their turn
bore down on that gay Minstrel Taillefer, who
rode so insolently forth to meet them with a song
in his throat, tossing his sword in English eyes,
still chanting the song of Roland as he fell.
None of the inn features were in the least informed
with this great, impressive picture of its past.
Yet does William seem by far the most realizable
of all the personages who have inhabited the old
house.

There was another visitor whose presence Monsieur Paul declared was as entirely real as if she,
also, had only just passed within the court-yard.

"I know not why it is, but of all these great, *ces
fameux,* Madame de Sévigné seems to me the

nearest, in point of time. Her visit appears to
have happened only yesterday. I never enter her
room but I seem to see her moving about, talking, laughing, speaking in epigrams. She men-
tions the inn, you know, in her letters. She gives
the details of her journey in full."

I, also, knew not why; but, later, after Monsieur Paul had left us, when he had shut himself
out, along with the pattering raindrops, and had
closed us in with the warmth and the flickering
fire-light, there came, with astonishing clearness,
a vision of that lady's visit here. She and her
company of friends might have been stopping,
that very instant, without, in the open court. I,
also, seemed to hear the very tones of their voices;
their talk was as audible as the wind rustling in
the vines. In the growing stillness the vision
grew and grew, till this was what I saw and heard:

CHAMBRE DES MARMOUSETS—DIVES.

TWO BANQUETS AT DIVES.

CHAPTER XX.

OUTSIDE the inn, some two hundred years ago, there was a great noise and confusion; the cries of outriders, of mounted guardsmen and halberdiers, made the quiet village as noisy as a camp. An imposing cavalcade was being brought to a sharp stop; for the outriders had suddenly perceived the open inn entrance, with its raised portcullis, and they were shouting to the coachmen to turn in, beneath the archway, to the paved court-yard within.

In an incredibly short space of time the open quadrangle presented a brilliant picture; the dashing guardsmen were dismounting; the maids and lackeys had quickly descended from their perches in the calèches and coaches; and the gentlemen of the household were dusting their wide hats and lace-trimmed coats. The halberdiers, ranging themselves in line, made a prismatic grouping beneath the low eaves of the picturesque old inn. In the very middle of the

court-yard stood a coach, resplendent in painted
panels and emblazoned with ducal arms. About
this coach, as soon as the four horses which drew
the vehicle were brought to a standstill, cavaliers,
footmen, and maids swarmed with effusive zeal.
One of the footmen made a rush for the door;
another let down the steps; one cavalier was
already presenting an outstretched, deferential
hand, while still another held forth an arm, as
rigid as a post, for the use of the occupants of the
ducal carriage.

Three ladies were seated within. Large and
roomy as was the vehicle, their voluminous draperies and the paraphernalia of their belongings
seemed completely to fill the wide, deep seats.
The ladies were the Duchesse de Chaulnes, Madame de Kerman, and Madame de Sévigné. The
faces of the Duchesse and of Madame de Kerman
were invisible, being still covered with their
masks, which, both as a matter of habit and as
precautions against the sun's rays, they had religiously worn during the long day's journey.
But Madame de Sévigné had ripped hers off; she
was holding it in her hand, as if glad to be relieved from its confinement.

All three ladies were in the highest possible
spirits, Madame de Sévigné obviously being the
leader of the jests and the laughter.

They were in a mood to find everything amusing and delightful. Even after they had left the
coach and were carefully picking their way over
the rough stones—walking on their high-heeled
"mules," at best, was always a dangerous per-

formance—their laughter and gayety continued in undiminished exuberance. Madame de Sévigné's keen sense of humor found so many things to ridicule. Could anything, for example, be more comical than the spectacle they presented as they walked, in state, with their long trains and high-heeled slippers, up these absurd little turret steps, feeling their way as carefully as if they were each a pickpocket or an assassin? The long line behind of maids carrying their muffs, and of lackeys with the muff-dogs, and of pages holding their trains, and the grinning innkeeper, bursting with pride and courtesying as if he had St. Vitus's dance, all this crowd coiling round the rude spiral stairway—it was enough to make one die of laughter. Such state in such savage surroundings !—they and their patch-boxes, and towering head-gears and trains, and dogs and fans, all crowded into a place fit only for peasants!

When they reached their bedchambers the ridicule was turned into a condescending admiration ; they found their rooms unexpectedly clean and airy. The furniture was all antique, of interesting design, and though rude, really astonishingly comfortable. Beds and dressing-tables, mostly of Henry III.'s time, were elaborately canopied in the hideous crude draperies of that primitive epoch. How different were the elegant shapes and brocades of their own time! Fortunately their women had suitable hangings and draperies with them, as well, of course, as any amount of linen and any number of mattresses. The settees and benches would do very well, with the aid of their own hassocks and cushions, and, after all, it was only for a night, they reminded the other.

The toilet, after the heat and exposure of the day, was necessarily a long one. The Duchesse and Madame de Kerman had their faces to make up—all the paint had run, and not a patch was in its place. Hair, also, of this later de Maintenon period, with its elaborate artistic ranges of curls, to say nothing of the care that must be given to the coif and the "follette," these were matters that demanded the utmost nicety of arrangement.

In an hour, however, the three ladies reassembled, in the panelled lower room—in "la Chambre de la Pucelle." In spite of the care her two companions had given to repairing the damages caused by their journey, of the three Madame de Sévigné looked by far the freshest and youngest. She still wore her hair in the loosely flowing de Montespan fashion; a style which, though now out of date, was one that exactly suited her fair skin, her candid brow, and her brilliant eyes. These latter, when one examined them closely, were found to be of different colors; but this peculiarity, which might have been a serious defect in any other countenance, in Madame de Sévigné's brilliant face was perhaps one cause of its extraordinarily luminous quality. Not one feature was perfect in that fascinatingly mobile face : the chin was a trifle too long for a woman's chin ; the lips, that broke into such delicious curves when she laughed, when at rest betrayed the firmness of her wit and the almost masculine quality of her reasoning judgment. Even her arms and hands

and her shoulders were "*mal taillés*," as her con-
temporaries would have told you. But what a
charm in those irregular features! What a seduc-
tiveness in the ensemble of that not too-well-pro-
portioned figure! What an indescribable radiance
seemed to emanate from the entire personality of
this most captivating of women!

As she moved about the low room, dark with
the trembling shadows of light that flowed from
the bunches of candles in the sconces, Madame
de Sévigné's clear complexion and her unpow-
dered chestnut curls seemed to spot the room with
light. Her companions, though dressed in the
very height of the fashion, were yet not half as
catching to the eye. Neither their minute waists,
nor their elaborate underskirts and trains, nor
their tall goffered coifs (the duchesse's was not unlike a bishop's mitre, studded as it was with ruby-
headed pins), nor the correctness of these ladies'
carefully placed patches, nor yet their painted
necks and tinted eyebrows, could charm as did the
unstylish figure of Madame de Sévigné—a figure
so indifferently clad, and yet one so replete with
its distinction of innate elegance and the subtle
charm of her individuality.

With the entrance of these ladies dinner was
served at once. The talk flowed on; it was, however, more or less restrained by the presence of the
always too curious lackeys, of the bustling inn-
keeper, and the gentlemen of the household in attendance on the party. As a spectacle, the little
room had never boasted before of such an assemblage of fashion and greatness. Never before had

the air under the rafters been so loaded with
scents and perfumes—these ladies seeming, indeed,
to breathe out odors. Never before had there
been grouped there such splendor of toilet, nor
had such courtly accents been heard, nor such
finished laughter. The fire and the candlelight
were in competition which should best light up
the tall transparent caps, the lace fichus, the bro-
cade bodices, and the long trains. The little muff-
dogs, released from their prisons, since the muffs
were laid aside at dinner-time, blinked at the fire,
curling their minute bodies—clipped lion-fashion
—about the huge andirons, as they snored to kill
time, knowing their own dinner would come only
when their mistresses had done.

After the dessert had been served the ladies
withdrew; they were preceded by the ever-bowing
innkeeper, who assured them, in his most rever-
ential tones, that they would find the room opening on the other court-yard even warmer and more
comfortable than the one they were in. In spite
of the walk across the paved court-yard and the
enormous height of their heels, always a fact to be
remembered, the ladies voted to make the change,
since by that means they could be assured the
more entire seclusion. Mild as was the May air,
Madame de Kerman's hand-glass hanging at her
side was quickly lifted in the very middle of the
open court-yard; she had scarcely passed the door
when she had felt one of her patches blowing
off.

"I caught it just in time, dear duchesse," she
cried, as she stood quite still, replacing it with a

fresh one picked from her patch-box, as the others passed her.

"The very best patch-maker I have found lives in the rue St. Denis, at the sign of La Perle des Mouches; have you discovered him, dear friend?" said the duchesse, as they walked on toward the low door beneath the galleries.

"No, dear duchesse, I fear I have not even looked for him—the science of patches I have always found so much harder than the science of living!" gayly answered Madame de Sévigné.

Madame de Kerman had now rejoined them, and all three passed into la Chambre des Marmousets.

CHAPTER XXI.

 THE three ladies grouped themselves about the fire, which they found already lighted. The duchesse chose a Henry II. carved arm-chair, one, she laughingly remarked, quite large enough to have held both the King and Diana. A lackey carrying the inevitable muff-dogs, their fans, and scent-bottles, had followed the ladies; he placed a hassock at the duchesse's feet, two beneath the slender feet of Madame de Kerman, and, after having been bidden to open one of the casements, since it was still so light without, withdrew, leaving the ladies alone.

Although Madame de Sévigné had comfortably ensconced herself in one of the deep window-seats, piling the cushions behind her, no sooner was the window opened than with characteristic impetuosity she jumped up to look out into the country that lay beyond the leaded glass. In spite of the long day's drive in the open air, her appetite for blowing roses and sweet earth smells had not been sated. Madame de Sévigné all her life had been the victim of two loves and a passion; she adored society and she loved nature; these were her

MADAME DE SÉVIGNÉ.

lesser delights, that gave way before the chief
idolatry of her soul, her adoration for her daughter.

As she stood by the open window, her charming
face, always a mirror of her emotions, was suf-
fused with a glow and a bloom that made it seem
young again. Her eyes grew to twice their common size under the "wandering" eyelids, as her
gaze roved over the meadows and across the tall
grasses to the sea. A part of her youth was being, indeed, vividly brought back to her; the sight
of this marine landscape recalled many memories;
and with the recollection her whole face and figure seemed to irradiate something of the inward
ardor that consumed her. She had passed this
very road, through this same country before, long
ago, in her youth, with her children. She half
smiled at the remembrance of a description given
of the impression produced by her appearance on
the journey by her friend the Abbé Arnauld; he
had ecstatically compared her to Latona seated in
an open coach, between a youthful Apollo and a
young Diana. In spite of the abbé's poetical extravagance, Madame de Sévigné recognized, in
this moment of retrospect, the truth of the picture. That, indeed, had been a radiant moment!
Her life at that time had been so full, and the
rapture so complete—the rapture of possessing
her children—that she could remember to have
had the sense of fairly evaporating happiness.
And now, the sigh came, how scattered was this
gay group! her son in Brittany, her daughter in
Provence, two hundred leagues away! And she,

an elderly Latona, mourning her Apollo and her
divine huntress, her incomparable Diana.

The inextinguishable flame of youth was burning still, however, in Madame de Sévigné's rich
nature. This adventure, this amazing adventure
of three ladies of the court having to pass the
night in a rude little Normandy inn, she, for one,
was finding richly seasoned with the spice of the
unforeseen; it would be something to talk of and
write about for a month hence at Chaulnes and at
Paris. Their entire journey, in point of fact, had
been a series of the most delightful episodes. It
was now nearly a month since they had started from
Picardy, from the castle of Chaulnes, going into
Normandy *via* Rouen. They had been on a driving
tour, their destination being Rennes, which they
would reach in a week or so. They had been travelling in great state, with the very best coach, the
very best horses; and they had been guarded by a
whole regiment of cavaliers and halberdiers. Every possible precaution had been taken against
their being disagreeably surprised on their route.
Their chief fear on the journey had been, of course,
the cry common in their day of "*Au voleur !*" and
the meeting of brigands and assassins; for, once
outside of Paris and the police reforms of that
dear Colbert, and one must be prepared to take
one's life in one's hand. Happily, no such misad-
ventures had befallen them. The roads, it is true,
they had found for the most part in a horrible
condition; they had been pitched about from one
end of their coach to the other; they might easily
have imagined themselves at sea. The dust also

had nearly blinded them, in spite of their masks. The other nuisances most difficult to put up with had been the swarm of beggars that infested the roadsides; and worst of all had been the army of crippled, deformed, and mangy soldiers. These latter they had encountered everywhere; their whines and cries, their armless, legless bodies, their hideous filth, and their insolent importunities, they had found a veritable pest.

Another annoyance had been the over-zealous courtesy of some of the upper middle-class. Only yesterday, in the very midst of the dust and under the burning noon sun, they had all been forced to alight, to receive the homage tendered the duchesse, of some thirty women and as many men. Each one of the sixty must, of course, kiss the duchesse's hand. It was really an outrage to have exposed them to such a form of torture! Poor Madame de Kerman, the delicate one of the party, had entirely collapsed after the ceremony. The duchesse also had been prostrated; it had wearied her more than all the rest of the journey. Madame de Sévigné alone had not suffered. She was possessed of a degree of physical fortitude which made her equal to any demand. The other two ladies, as well as she herself, were now experiencing the pleasant exhilaration which comes with the hour of rest after an excellent dinner. They were in a condition to remember nothing except the agreeable. Madame de Sévigné was the first to break the silence.

She turned, with a brisk yet graceful abruptness, to the two ladies still seated before the low

fire. With a charming outburst of enthusiasm
she exclaimed aloud:

"What a beauty, and youth, and tenderness this
spring has, has it not?"

"Yes," answered the duchesse, smiling graciously into Madame de Sévigné's brilliantly lit
face; "yes, the weather in truth has been perfect."

"What an adorable journey we have had!" continued Madame de Sévigné, in the same tone, her
ardor undampened by the cooler accent of her
friend—she was used to having her enthusiasm
greeted with consideration rather than response.
"What a journey!—only meeting with the most
agreeable of adventures; not the slightest incon-
venience anywhere; eating the very best of everything; and driving through the heart of this enchanting springtime!"

Her listeners laughed quietly, with an accent
of indulgence. It was the habit of her world to
find everything Madame de Sévigné did or said
charming. Even her frankness was forgiven her,
her tact was so perfect; and her spontaneity had
always been accounted as her chief excellence; in
the stifled air of the court and the *ruelles* it had
been frequently likened to the blowing in of a
fresh May breeze. Her present mood was one
well known to both ladies.

"Always 'pretty pagan,' dear madame," smiled
Madame de Kerman, indulgently. "How well
named—and what a happy hit of our friend Arnauld d'Audilly! You are in truth a delicious—
an adorable pagan! You have such a sense of the
joy of living! Why, even living in the country

has, it appears, no terrors for you. We hear of your walking about in the moonlight—you make your very trees talk, they tell us, in Italian—in Latin; you actually pass whole hours alone with the hamadryads!" There was just a suspicion of irony in Madame de Kerman's tone, in spite of its caressing softness; it was so impossible to conceive of anyone really finding nature endurable, much less pretending to discover in trees and flowers anything amusing or suggestive of sentiment!

But Madame de Sévigné was quite impervious to her friend's raillery. She responded, with perfect good humor:

"Why not?—why not try to discover beauties in nature? One can be so happy in a wood! What a charming thing to hear a leaf sing! I know few things more delightful than to watch the triumph of the month of May when the nightingale, the cuckoo, and the lark open the spring in our forests! And then, later, come those beautiful crystal days of autumn—days that are neither warm, nor yet are they really cold! And then the trees—how eloquent they can be made; with a little teaching they may be made to converse so charmingly. *Bella cosa far niente,* says one of my trees; and another answers, *Amor odit inertes.* Ah, when I had to bid farewell to all my leaves and trees; when my son had to dispose of the forest of Buron, to pay for some of his follies, you remember how I wept! It seemed to me I could actually feel the grief of those dispossessed sylvans and of all those homeless dryads!"

"It is this, dear friend—this life you lead at Les Rochers—and your enthusiasm which keep you so young. Yes, I am sure of it. How inconceivably young, for instance, you are looking this very evening! You and the glow out yonder make youth seem no longer a legend."

The duchesse delivered her flattering little speech with a caressing tone. She moved gently forward in her chair, as if to gain a better view of the twilight and her friend. At the sound of the duchesse's voice Madame de Sévigné again turned, with the same charming smile and the quick impulsiveness of movement common to her. During her long monologue she had remained standing; but she left the window now to regain her seat amid the cushions of the window. There was something better than the twilight and the spring in the air; here, within, were two delightful friends—and listeners; there was before her, also, the prospect of one of those endless conversations that were the chief delight of her life.

She laughed as she seated herself—a gay, frank, hearty little laugh — and she spread out her hands with the opening of her fan, as, with her usual vivacious spontaneity, her mood changed.

"Fancy, dear duchesse, the punishment that comes to one who commits the crime of looking young—younger than one ought! My son-in-law, M. de Grignan, actually avows he is in daily terror lest I should give him a father-in-law ; "

All three ladies laughed gayly at this absurdity; the subject of Madame de Sévigné's remarrying had come to be a venerable joke now It had been talked of at court and in society for nearly forty years; but such was the conquering power of her charms that these two friends, her listeners, saw nothing really extravagant in her son-in-law's fear; she was one of those rare women who, even at sixty, continue to suggest the altar rather than the grave. Madame de Kerman was the first to re-cover her breath after the laughter.

"Dear friend, you might assure him that after a youth and the golden meridian of your years passed in smiling indifference to the sighs of a Prince de Conti, of a Turenne, of a Fouquet, of a Bussy de Rabutin, at sixty it is scarcely likely that——"

"Ah, dear lady! at sixty, when one has the complexion and the curls, to say nothing of the eyes of our dear enchantress, a woman is as dangerous as at thirty!" The duchesse's flattery was charmingly put, with just enough vivacity of tone to save it from the charge of insipidity. Madame de Sévigné bowed her curls to her waist.

"Ah, dear duchesse, it isn't age," she retorted, quickly, "that could make me commit follies. It is the fact that that son-in-law of mine actually surrounds me with spies—he keeps me in perpetual surveillance. Such a state of captivity is capable of making me forget everything; I am beginning to develop a positive rage for follies. You know that has been my chief fault—always; discretion has been left out of my composition. But I say now, as I have always said, that if I could manage to live two hundred years, I should become the most delightful person in the world!"

She herself was the first to lead in the laughter that followed her outburst; and then the duchesse broke in:

"You talk of defects, dear friend; but reflect what a life yours has been. So surrounded and courted, and yet you were always so guarded; so free, and yet so wise! So gay, and yet so chaste!"

"If you rubbed out all those flattering colors, dear duchesse, and wrote only, 'She worshipped her children, and preferred friends to lovers,' the portrait would be far nearer to the truth. It is easy to be chaste if one has only known one passion in one's life, and that the maternal one!"

Again a change passed over Madame de Sévigné's mobile face; the bantering tone was lost in a note of deep feeling. This gift of sensibility had always been accounted as one of Madame de Sévigné's chief charms; and now, at sixty, she was as completely the victim of her moods as in her earlier youth.

"Where is your daughter, and how is she?" sympathetically queried the duchesse.

"Oh, she is still at Grignan, as usual; she is well, thank God. But, dear duchesse, after all these years of separation I suffer still, cruelly." The tears sprang to Madame de Sévigné's eyes, as she added, with passion and a force one would scarcely have expected in one whose manners were so finished, "the truth is, dear friends, I cannot live without her. I do not find I have made the least progress in that career. But, dear friends, believe me, these tears are sweeter than all else

in life—more enrapturing than the most transporting joy!"

Madame de Kerman smiled tenderly into the
rapturous mother's face; but the duchesse moved,
as if a little restless and uneasy under this shower
of maternal feeling. For thirty years her friends
had had to listen to Madame de Sévigné's rhap-
sodies over the perfections of her incomparable
daughter. Although sensibility was not the emotional fashion of the day, maternity, in the person
of Madame de Sévigné, had been apotheosized
into the queen of the passions, if only because of
its rarity; still, even this lady's most intimate
friends sometimes wearied of banqueting off the
feast of Madame de Grignan's virtues.

"Have you heard from Madame de La Fayette
recently?" asked the duchesse, allowing just time
enough to elapse, before putting the question, for
Madame de Sévigné's emotion to subside into composure. The duchesse was too exquisitely bred to
allow her impatience to take the form of even the
appearance of haste.

"Oh, yes," was Madame de Sévigné's quiet re-
ply; the turn in the conversation had been instantly understood, in spite of the delicacy of the
duchesse's methods. "Oh, yes—I have had a line
—only a line. You know how she detests writing,
above all things. Her letters are all the same—
two lines to say that she has no time in which to
say it!"

"Did she not once write you a pretty little series
of epigrams about not writing?"

"Oh, yes—some time ago, when I was with my

daughter. I've quoted them so often, they have
become famous. 'You are in Provence, my
beauty; your hours are free, and your mind still
more so. Your love for corresponding with everyone still endures within you, it appears; as for me,
the desire to write to any human being has long
since passed away—forever; and if I had a lover
who insisted on a letter every morning, I should
certainly break with him!'"

"What a curious compound she is! And how
well her soubriquet becomes her!"

"Yes, it is perfect—'*Le Brouillard*'—the fog.
It is indeed a fog that has always enveloped her,
and what charming horizons are disclosed once it
is lifted!"

"And her sensibilities—of what an exquisite
quality; and what a rare, precious type, indeed, is
the whole of her nature! Do you remember how
alarmed she would become when listening to
music?"

"And yet, with all this sensibility and delicacy
of organization there was another side to her
nature." Madame de Kerman paused a moment
before she went on; she was not quite sure how
far she dared go in her criticism; Madame de La
Fayette was such an intimate friend of Madame
de Sévigné's.

"You mean," that lady broke out, with unhesi-
tating candor, "that she is also a very selfish person. You know that is my daughter's theory of
her—she is always telling me how Madame de La
Fayette is making use of me; that while her sensitiveness is such that she cannot sustain the

tragedy of a farewell visit—if I am going to Les
Rochers or to Provence, when I go to pay my last
visit I must pretend it is only an ordinary run-
ning-in; yet her delicacy does not prevent her
from making very indelicate proposals, to suit her
own convenience. You remember what one of her
commands was, don't you ? "

" No," answered the duchesse, for both herself
and her companion. "Pray tell us."

Madame de Sévigné went on to narrate that
once, when at Les Rochers, Madame de La Fayette
was quite certain that she, Madame de Sévigné,
was losing her mind, for no one could live in the
provinces and remain sane, poring over stupid
books and sitting over fires.

"She was certain I should sicken and die, besides losing the tone of my mind," laughed Madame de Sévigné, as she called up the picture of
her dissolution and rapid disintegration; "and
therefore it was necessary at once that I should
come up to Paris. This latter command was delivered in the tone of a judge of the Supreme
Court. The penalty of my disobedience was to be
her ceasing to love me. I was to come up to Paris
directly—on the minute; I was to live with you,
dear duchesse; I was not to buy any horses until
spring; and, best of all, I was to find on my arrival a purse of a thousand crowns which would be
lent me without interest! What a proposition,
mon Dieu, what a proposition! To have no house
of my own, to be dependent, to have no carriage,
and to be in debt a thousand crowns! "

As Madame de Sévigné lifted her hands the

laces of her sleeves were fairly trembling with the
force of her indignation. There were certain
things that always put her in a passion, and Madame de La Fayette's peculiarities she had found
at times unendurable. Her listeners had followed
her narration with the utmost intensity and absorption. When she stopped, their eyes met in a
look of assenting comment.

"It was perfectly characteristic, all of it! She
judged you, doubtless, by herself. She always
seems to me, even now, to keep one eye on her
comfort and the other on her purse!"

"Ah, dear duchesse, how keen you are!" laugh-
ingly acquiesced Madame de Sévigné, as with a
shrug she accepted the verdict—her indignation
melting with the shrug. "And how right! No
woman ever drives better bargains, without moving
a finger. From her invalid's chair she can conduct
a dozen lawsuits. She spends half her existence
in courting death; she caresses her maladies; she
positively hugs them; but she can always be miraculously resuscitated at the word money!"

"Yes," added with a certain relish Madame de
Kerman. "And this is the same woman who
must be forever running away from Paris because
she can no longer endure the exertion of talking,
or of replying, or of listening; because she is
wearied to extinction, as she herself admits, of
saying good-morning and good-evening. She
must hide herself in some pastoral retreat, where
simply, as she says, 'to exist is enough;' where
she can remain, as it were, miraculously suspended
between heaven and earth!"

A ripple of amused laughter went round the little group; there was nothing these ladies enjoyed so keenly as a delicate dish of gossip, seasoned with wit, and stuffed with epigrams. This talk was exactly to their taste. The silence and seclusion of their surroundings were an added stimulus to confidence and to a freer interchange of opinions about their world. Paris and Versailles seemed so very far away; it would appear safe to say almost anything about one's dearest friends. There was nothing to remind them of the restraints of levees, or the penalty indiscretion must pay for folly breathed in that whispering gallery—the *ruelle*. It was indeed a delightful hour; altogether an ideal situation.

The fire had burned so low only a few embers were alive now, and the candles were beginning to flicker and droop in the sconces. But the three ladies refused to find the little room either cold or dark; their talk was not half done yet, and their muffs would keep them warm. The shadow of the deepening gloom they found delightfully provocative of confidences.

After a short pause, while Madame de Kerman busied herself with the tongs and the fagots, trying to reinvigorate the dying flames, the duchesse asked, in a somewhat more intimate tone than she had used yet:

"And the duke—do you really think she loved the Duke de La Rochefoucauld?"

"She reformed him, dear duchesse; at least she always proclaims his reform as the justification of her love."

"You—you esteemed him yourself very highly, did you not?"

"Oh, I loved him tenderly; how could one help it? He was the best as well as the most brilliant of men! I never knew a tenderer heart; domestic joys and sorrows affected him in a way to render him incomparable. I have seen him weep over the death of his mother, who only died eight years before him, you know, with a depth of sincerity that made me adore him."

"He must in truth have been a very sincere person."

"Sincere!" cried Madame de Sévigné, her eyes flaming. "Had you but seen his deathbed! His bearing was sublime! Believe me, dear friend, it was not in vain that M. de La Rochefoucauld had written philosophic reflections all his life; he had already anticipated his last moments in such a way that there was nothing either new or strange in death when it came to him."

"Madame de La Fayette truly mourned him—don't you think so? You were with her a great deal, were you not, after his death?"

"I never left her. It was the most pitiable sight to see her in her loneliness and her misery. You see their common ill-health and their sedentary habits had made them so necessary to each other! It was, as it were, two souls in a single body. Nothing could exceed the confidence and charm of their friendship; it was incomparable. To Madame de La Fayette his loss came as her death-blow; life seems at an end for her; for where, indeed, can she find another such friend, or such intercourse, such sweetness and charm—such confidence and consideration ? "

There was a moment's silence after Madame de Sévigné's eloquent outburst. The eyes of the three friends were lost for a moment in the twinkling flames. The duchesse and Madame de Kerman exchanged meaning glances.

"Since the duke's death her thoughts are more and more turned toward religion. I hear she has been fortunate in her choice of directors, has she not ? Du Guet is said to be an ideal confessor for the authoress of 'La Princesse de Clèves.'" There was just a suspicion of malice in the duchesse's tones.

"Oh, he was born to take her in hand. He knew just when to speak with authority, and when to make use of the arts of persuasion. He wrote to her once, you remember: 'You, who have passed your life in dreaming—cease to dream ! You, who have taken such pride unto yourself for being so true in all things, were very far, indeed, from the truth—you were only half true—falsely true. Your godless wisdom was in reality purely a matter of good taste!'"

"What audacity! Bossuet himself could not have put the truth more nakedly." The duchesse was one of those to whom truths were novelties, and unpleasant ones.

"Bossuet, if I remember rightly, was with the Duke de La Rochefoucauld at the last, was he not ? "

" Yes," responded Madame de Sévigné ; " he was with him ; he administered the supreme unction.

The duke was in a beautiful state of grace. M. Vinet, you remember, said of him that he died with ' perfect decorum.' "

" Speaking of dying reminds me "—cried suddenly Madame de Sévigné—" how are the duke's hangings getting on ? "

"They begin, the duke writes me, to hang again to-morrow," answered the duchesse, with a certain air of disdain, the first appearance of this weapon of the great now coming to the *grande dame's* aid. Her husband, the Duke de Chaulnes' trouble with his revolutionary citizens at Rennes was a subject that never failed to arouse a feeling of angry contempt in her. It was too preposterous, the idea of those insolent creatures rising against him, their rightful duke and master !

The duchesse's feeling in the matter was fully shared by her friends. In all the court there was but one opinion in the matter—hanging was really far too good for the wretched creatures.

"Monsieur de Chaulnes," the duchesse went on, with ironical contempt in her voice, " still goes on punishing Rennes ! "

" This province and the duke's treatment of it will serve as a capital example to all others. It will teach those rascals," Madame de Kerman continued, in lower tones, " to respect their governors, and not to throw stones into their gardens ! "

" Fancy that—the audacity of throwing stones into their duke's garden ! Why, did you know, they actually—those insolent creatures actually called him—called the duke—' *gros cochon ?* ' "

All three ladies gasped in horror at this unpar-

alleled instance of audacity; they threw up their
hands as they groaned over the picture in low
tones of finished elegance.

"It is little wonder the duke hangs right and
left! The dear duke—what a model governor!
How I should like to have seen him sack that street
at Rennes, with all the ridiculous old men, and the
women in childbirth, and the children, turned out
pêle-mêle! And the hanging, too—why, hanging
now seems to me a positively refreshing performance!" And Madame de Sévigné laughed with
unstinted gayety as at an excellent joke.

The picture of Rennes and the cruelty dealt its
inhabitants was a pleasant picture, in the contem-
plation of which these ladies evidently found
much delectation. They were quiet for a longer
period of time than usual; they continued silent,
as they looked into the fire, smiling; the flames
there made them think of other flames as forms of
merited punishment.

"A curious people those Bas Bretons," finally
ejaculated Madame de Sévigné. "I never could
understand how Bertrand Duguesclin made them
the best soldiers of his day in France!"

"You know Lower Brittany very well, do you
not, dear friend?"

"Not so well as the coast. Les Rochers is in
Upper Brittany, you know. I know the south
better still. Ah, what a charming journey I
once took along the Loire with my friend *Bien-
Bon*, the Abbé de Coulanges. We found it the
most enchanting country in the world—the country of feasts and of famine; feasts for us and fam-

ine for the people. I remember we had to cross
the river; our coach was placed on the barge, and
we were rowed along by stout peasants. Through
the glass windows of the coach we looked out at
a series of changing pictures — the views were
charming. We sat, of course, entirely at our
ease, on our soft cushions. The country people,
crowded together below, were—ugh!—like pigs in
straw."

"Was Bien-Bon with you when you made that
little excursion to St. Germain?" queried the
duchesse.

"Ah, that was a gay night," joyously responded
Madame de Sévigné. "How well we amused ourselves on that little visit that we paid Madame
de Maintenon—when she was only Madame Scarron."

"Was she so handsome then as they say she
was—at that time?"

"Very handsome; she was good, too, and amiable, and easy to talk to; one talked well and
readily with her. She was then only the governess of the king's bastards, you know—of the
children he had had by Madame de Montespan.
That was the first step toward governing the
king. Well, one night—the night to which you
refer—I remember we were all supping with
Madame de La Fayette. We had been talking
endlessly! Suddenly it occurred to us it would be
a most amusing adventure to take Madame Scarron home, to the very last end of the Faubourg
Saint Germain, far beyond where Madame de La
Fayette lived—near Vaugirard, out into the Bois,

in the country. The Abbé came too. It was midnight when we started. The house, when at last we reached it, we found large and beautiful, with large and fine rooms and a beautiful garden ; for Madame Scarron, as governess of the king's children, had a coach and a lot of servants and horses. She herself dressed then modestly and yet magnificently, as a woman should who spent her life among people of the highest rank. We had a merry outing, returning in high spirits, blessed in having no end of lanterns, and thus assured against robbers."

"She and Madame de La Fayette were very close friends, I remember, during that time," mused the duchesse, "when they were such near neighbors."

" Yes," Madame de Sévigné went on, as unwearied now, although it was nearly midnight, as in the beginning of the long evening. "Yes; I always thought Madame de Maintenon's satirical little joke about Madame de La Fayette's bed festooned with gold—'I might have fifty thousand pounds income, and never should I live in the style of a great lady; never should I have a bed festooned with gold like Madame de La Fayette'—was the beginning of their rupture."

" All the same, Madame de La Fayette, lying on that bed, beneath the gold hangings, was a much more simple person than ever was Madame de Maintenon ! "

"Your speaking of bed reminds me, dear ladies ours must be quite cold by this time. How we have chatted ! What a delightful gossip ! But we must not forget that our journey to-morrow is to be a long one!"

The duchesse rose, the other two ladies rising instantly, observing, in spite of the intimate relations in which they stood toward the duchesse, the deference due to her more exalted rank. The latter clapped her hands; outside the door a shuffling and a low groan were heard—the groan came from the sleepy lackey, roused from his deep slumber, as he uncoiled himself from the close knot into which his legs and body were knit in the curve of the narrow stairs.

The ladies, a few seconds later, were wending their way up the steep turret steps. They were preceded by torches and followed by quite a long train of maids and lackeys. For a long hour, at least, the little inn resounded with the sound of hurrying feet, of doors closing and shutting; with the echo of voices giving commands and of others purring in sleepy accents of obedience. Then one by one the sounds died away; the lights went out in the bedchambers; faint flickerings stole through the chinks of doors and windows. The watchman cried out the hour, and the gleam of a lantern flashed here and there, illuminating the open court-yard. The cocks crowed shrilly into the night air. A halberdier turned in his sleep where he lay, on some straw beneath the coach-shed, his halberd rattling as it struck the cobbles. And over the whole—over the gentle slumber of the great ladies and the sleep of beast and man—there fell the peace and the stillness of the midnight—of that midnight of long ago.

CHAMBRE DE LA PUCELLE—DIVES.

CHAPTER XXII.

THE very next morning, after the rain and the vision I had had of Madame de Sévigné, conjured up by my surroundings and the reading of her letters, Monsieur Paul paid us an early call. He came to beg the loan of our sitting-room, he said. He had had a despatch from a coaching-party from Trouville; they were to arrive for breakfast. The whip and owner of the coach was a great friend of his, he proffered by way of explanation—a certain count who had a genius for friendship—one who also had an artist's talent for admiring the beautiful. He was among those who were in a state of perpetual adoration before the inn's perfections. He made yearly pilgrimages from his château above Rouen to eat a noon breakfast in the Chambre des Marmousets. Now, a breakfast served elsewhere than in this chamber would be, from his point of view, to have journeyed to a shrine to find the niche empty. The gift that was begged of us, therefore, was the loan for a few hours of the famous little room.

In less than a half-hour we were watching the

entrance of the coach by the side of Madame Le
Mois. We were all three seated on the green
bench.

Faintly at first, and presently gaining in dis-
tinctness, came the fall of horses' hoofs and the
rumble of wheels along the highway. A little
cavalcade was soon passing beneath the archway.
First there dashed in two horsemen, who had
sprung to the ground almost as soon as their
steeds' hoofs struck the paved court-yard. Then
there swept by a jaunty dog-cart, driven by a mannish figure radiantly robed in white. Swiftly following came the dash and jingle of four coach-
horses, bathed in sweat, rolling the vehicle into
the court as if its weight were a thing of air. All
save one among the gay party seated on the high
seats were too busy with themselves and their
chatter to take heed of their surroundings. A
lady beneath her deep parasol was busily engaged in a gay traffic of talk with the groups of
men peopling the back seats of the coach. One
of the men, however, was craning his neck beyond
the heads of his companions; he was running his
eye rapidly up and down the long inn façade.
Finally his glance rested on us ; and then, with a
rush, a deep red mounted the man's cheek, as he
tore off his derby to wave it, as if in a triumph of
discovery. Renard had been true to his promise.
He had come to see his friends and to test the
famous Santerne. He flung himself down from
his lofty perch to take his seat, entirely as a matter of course, beside us on the green bench.

"What luck, hey ?—greatest luck in the world,

finding you in like this. I've been in no end of a
tremble, fearing you'd gone to Caen, or Falaise, or
somewhere, and that I shouldn't see you after all.
Well, how are you? How goes it? What do you
think of old Dives and Monsieur Paul, and the
rest of it? I see you're settled; you took the
palace chamber. Trust American women—they
know the best, and get it."

"But these people, who are they, and how did
you—?" We were unfeignedly glad to see him,
but curiosity is a passion not to be trifled with—
after a month in the provinces.

"Oh—the De Troisacs? Old friends of mine
—known them years. Jolly lot. Charming fellow, De Troisac—only good Frenchman I've ever
known. They're just off their yacht; saw them
all yesterday at the Trouville Casino. Said they
were running down here for breakfast to-day,
asked me, and I came, of course." He laughed as
he added: "I said I should come, you remember,
to get some of that Sauterne. A man will go any
distance for a good bottle of wine, you know."

Meanwhile, in the court-yard, the party on the
coach, by means of ladders and the helping of the
grooms, were scrambling down from their seats.
Renard's friend, the Comte de Troisac, was easily picked out from the group of men. He was
the elder of the party—stoutish, with frank eyes
and a smiling mouth; he was bustling about from
the gaunt grooms to the ladder, and from ladder
to the coach-seat, giving his commands right and
left, and executing most of them himself. A tall,
slim woman, with drooping eyelids, and an air of

extreme elegance and of cultivated fatigue, was also easily recognizable as the countess. It took two grooms, two of the gentlemen guests, and her husband to assist her to the ground. Her passage down the steps of the ladder had been long enough, however, to enable her to display a series of pretty poses, each one more effective than the others. When one has an instep of ideal elevation, what is the use of being born a Frenchwoman unless one knows how to make use of opportunity?

From the dog-cart, that had rattled in across the cobbles with a dash and a spurt, there came quite a different accent and pose. The whitish personage, whom we had mistakenly supposed to be a man, wore petticoats; the male attire only held as far as the waist of the lady. The stiff white shirt-front, the knotted tie—a faultless male knot—the loose driving-jacket, with its sprig of white geranium, and the round straw-hat worn in mannish fashion, close to the level brows, was a costume that would have deceived either sex. Below the jacket flowed the straight lines of a straight skirt, that no further conjectures should be rendered necessary. This lady had a high-bred air of singular distinction, accentuated by a tremendously knowing look. She was at once elegant and rakish; the *gamin* in her was obvi-ously the touch of *caviare* to season the woman of fashion. The mixture made an extraordinarily at-tractive ensemble. As she jumped to the ground, throwing her reins to a groom, her jump was a master-stroke; it landed her squarely on her feet; even as she struck the ground her hands were thrust deeply into her pockets. The man seated beside her, who now leaped out after her, seemed timid and awkward by contrast with her alert precision. This couple moved at once toward the bench on which madame was seated. With the coming in of the coach and the cart she had risen, waddling forward to meet the party. Monsieur Paul was at the coach-wheels before the grooms had shot themselves down; De Troisac, with eager friendliness, stretched forth a hand from the top of his seat, exclaiming, with gay heartiness,

"*Ah, mon bon—comment ça va?*"

The mère was as eagerly greeted. Even the countess dismissed her indifference for the moment, as she held out her hand to Madame Le Mois.

"Dear Madame Le Mois—and it goes well with you? And the gout and the rheumatism, they have ceased to torment you? *Quelle bonne nouvelle!* And here are the dear old cocks and the wounded bantam. The cockatoos—ah, there they are, still swinging in the air! *Comme c'est joli—et frais—et que ça sent bon!*"

Madame and Monsieur Paul were equally effusive in their inquiries and exclamations—it was clearly a meeting of old friends. Madame Le Mois' face was meanwhile a study. The huge surface was glistening with pleasure; she was unfeignedly glad to see these Parisians:—but there was no elation at this meeting on such easy terms with greatness. Her shrewdness was as alive as ever; she was about to make money out of the

visit—they were to have of her best, but they
must pay for it. Between her rapid fire of ques-
tionings as to the countess's health and the history of her travels, there was as rapid a shower
of commands, sometimes shouted out, above all
the hubbub, to the cooks standing gaping in the
kitchen doorway, or whispered hoarsely to Ernestine and Marianne, who were flying about like
wild pigeons, a little drunk with the novelty of
this first breakfast of the season.

" *Allons, mon enfant—cours—cours—*get thy linen,
my child, and the silver candelabres. It is to be
laid in the Marmousets, thou knowest. Paul will
come presently. And the salads, pluck them and
bring them in to me—*cours—cours.*"

The great world was all very well, and it was
well to be on friendly, even intimate terms, with it ;
but, *Dieu !* one's own bread is of importance too !
And the countess, for all her delicacy, was a *bonne
fourchette.*

The countess and her friend, after a moment
of standing in the court-yard, of patting the peli-
can, of trying their blandishments on the flamingo, of catching up the bantam, and filling the
air with their purring, and caressing, and incessant chatter, passed beneath the low door to
the inner sanctum of madame. The two ladies
were clearly bent on a few moments of unre-
served gossip and that repairing of the toilet
which is a religious act to women of fashion the
world over.

In the court-yard the scene was still a brilliant
one. The gayly painted coach was now deserted.

It stood, a chariot of state, as it were, awaiting royalty; its yellow sides gleamed like topaz in the sun. The grooms were unharnessing the leaders, that were still bathed in the white of their sweat. The count's dove-colored flannels were a soft mass against the snow of the *chef's* apron and cap; the two were in deep consultation at the kitchen door. Monsieur Paul was showing, with all the absorption of the artist, his latest Jumièges carvings to the taller, more awkward of the gentlemen, to the one driven in by the mannish beauty.

The cockatoos had not ceased shrieking from the very beginning of the hubbub; nor had the squirrels stopped running along the bars of their cage, a-flutter with excitement. The peacocks trailed their trains between the coach-wheels, announcing, squawkingly, their delight at the advent of a larger audience. Above the cries of the fowls and the shrieks of the cocks, the chatter of human tongues, the subdued murmur of the ladies' voices coming through the open lattice, and the stamp of horses' hoofs, there swept above it all the light June breeze, rustling in the vines, shaking the thick branches against the wooden façades.

The two ladies soon made their appearance in the sunlit court-yard. The murmur of their talk and their laughter reached us along with the froufrou of their silken petticoats.

"You were not bored, *chère enfant,* driving Monsieur d'Agreste all that long distance?"

The countess was smiling tenderly into her companion's face. She had stopped her to readjust the geranium sprig that was drooping in her

friend's cover-coat. The smile was the smile of a
sympathizing angel, but what a touch of hidden
malice there was in the notes of her caressing
voice! As she repinned the *boutonnière* she gave
the dancing eyes that were brimming with the
mirth of the coming retort, the searching inquest
of her glance.

"Bored! *Dieu, que non!*" The black little
beauty threw back her throat, laughing, as she
rolled her great eyes. "Bored—with all the tricks
I was playing? Fernande! pity me, there was
such a little time, and so much to do!"

"So little time—only fourteen kilos!" The
countess compressed her lips; they were smiling
no longer.

"Ah, but you see, I had so much to combat.
You had a whole season, last summer, in which to
play your game, your solemn game." Here the
gay young widow rippled forth a pearly scale of
treble laughter. "And I have had only a week,
thus far!"

"Yes, but what time you make!"

And this time both ladies laughed, although,
still, only one laughed well.

"Ah! those women—how they love each other,"
commented Renard, as he sat on the bench,
swinging his legs, with his eyes following the
two vanishing figures. "Only women who are
intimate—Parisian intimates—can cut to the bone
like that, with a surgeon's dexterity."

He explained then that the handsome brunette
was a widow, a certain Baronne d'Autun, noted for
her hunting and her conquests; the last on the

latter list was Monsieur d'Agreste, a former ad-
mirer of the countess; he was somewhat famous
as a scientist and socialist, so good a socialist
as to refuse to wear his title of duke. The other
two gentlemen of the party, who had joined them
now, the two horsemen, were the Comtes de Mirant
and de Fonbriant. These latter were two typical
young swells of the Jockey Club model; their
vacant, well-bred faces wore the correct degree of
fashionable pallor, and their manners appeared
to be also as perfect as their glances were insolent.

Into these vacant faces the languid countess
was breathing the inspiration of her smile. Enigmatic as was the latter, it was as simple as an infant's compared to the occult character of her
glance. A wealth of complexities lay enfolded in
the deep eyes, rimmed with their mystic darkened
circlet—that circle in which the Parisienne frames
her experience, and through which she pleads to
have it enlarged!

A Frenchwoman and cosmetics! Is there any
other combination on this round earth more suggestive of the comedy of high life, of its elegance
and of its perfidy, of its finish and of its emptiness ?

The men of the party wore costumes perilously
suggestive of Opera Bouffe models. Their fingers
were richly begemmed; their watch-chains were
laden with seals and charms. Any one of the costumes was such as might have been chosen by a
tenor in which to warble effectively to a *soubrette*
on the boards of a provincial theatre; and it was

worn by these fops of the Jockey Club with the
air of its being the last word in nautical fashions.
Better than their costumes were their voices; for
what speech from human lips pearls itself off with
such crispness and finish as the delicate French
idiom from a Parisian tongue ?

I never quite knew how it came about that we
were added to this gay party of breakfasters.
We found ourselves, however, after a high skir-
mish of preliminary presentations, among the
number to take our places at the table.

In the Chambre des Marmousets, Monsieur
Paul, we found, had set the feast with the taste of
an artist and the science of an archæologist. The
table itself was long and narrow, a genuine fifteenth-century table. Down the centre ran a strip
of antique altar-lace; the sides were left bare, that
the lustre of the dark wood might be seen. In the
centre was a deep old Caen bowl, with grapes and
fuchsias to make a mound of soft color. A pair
of seventeenth-century candelabres twisted and
coiled their silver branches about their rich *re-
poussé* columns; here and there on the yellow strip
of lace were laid bunches of June roses, those only
of the rarer and older varieties having been chosen,
and each was tied with a Louis XV. love-knot.
Monsieur Paul was himself an omniscient figure
at the feast; he was by turns officiating as butler,
carving, or serving from the side-tables; or he
was crossing the court-yard with his careful, cat-
like tread, a bottle under each arm. He was also
constantly appealed to by Monsieur d'Agreste or
the count, to settle a dispute about the age of the

china, or the original home of the various old
chests scattered about the room.

"Paul, your stained glass shows up well in this
light," the count called out, wiping his mustache
over his soup-plate.

"Yes," answered Monsieur Paul, as he went on
serving the sherry, pausing for a moment at the
count's glass. "They always look well in full
sunlight. It was a piece of pure luck, getting
them. One can always count on getting hold of
tapestries and carvings, but old glass is as rare
as——"

"A pretty woman," interpolated the gay young
widow, with the air of a connoisseur."

"Outside of Paris—you should have added,"
gallantly contributed the count. Everyone went
on eating after the light laughter had died away.

The countess had not assisted at this brief conversation; she was devoting her attention to receiving the devotion of the two young counts;
one was on either side of her, both of whom gave
every outward and visible sign of wearing her
chains, and of wearing them with insistance. The
real contest between them appeared to be, not so
much which should make the conquest of the languid countess, as which should outflank the other
in his compromising demeanor. The countess,
beneath her drooping lids, watched them with the
indulgent indolence of a lioness, too luxuriously
lazy to spring.

The countess, clearly, was not made for sunlight. In the courtyard her face had seemed
chiefly remarkable as a triumph of cosmetic treat-

ment; here, under this rich glow, the purity and
delicacy of the features easily placed her among
the beauties of the Parisian world. Her eyes,
now that the languor of the lids was disappearing
with the advent of the wines, were magnificent;
her use of them was an open avowal of her own
knowledge of their splendor. The young widow
across the table was also using her eyes, but in a
very different fashion. She had now taken off her
straw hat; the curly crop of a brown mane gave the
brilliant face an added accent of vigor. The *chien
de race* was the dominant note now in the muscular, supple body, the keen-edged nostrils, and the
intent gaze of the liquid eyes. These latter were
fixed with the fixity of a savage on Charm. She
was giving, in a sweet sibilant murmur, the man
seated next her—Monsieur d'Agreste, the man who
refused to bear his title—her views of the girl.

"Those Americans, the Americans of the best
type, are a race apart, I tell you; we have nothing
like them; we condemn them because we don't understand them. They understand us—they read
us——"

"Oh, they read our books—the worst of them."

"Yes, but they read the best too; and the worst
don't seem to hurt them. I'll warrant that Mees
Gay—that is her name, is it not?—has read Zola,
for instance; and yet, see how simple and innocent—yes—innocent, she looks."

"Yes, the innocence of experience—which knows
how to hide," said Monsieur d'Agreste, with a slight
shrug.

"Mees Gay!" the countess cried out across the

table, suddenly waking from her somnolence ; she
had overheard the baroness in spite of the low
tone in which the dialogue had been carried on;
her voice was so mellifluously sweet, one instinct-
ively scented a touch of hidden poison in it—" Mees
Gay, there is a question being put at this side of
the table you alone can answer. Pray pardon the
impertinence of a personal question—but we hear
that American young ladies read Zola; is it
true ?"

"I am afraid that we do read him," was Charm's
frank answer. "I have read him—but my reading
is all in the past tense now."

"Ah—you found him too highly seasoned?"
one of the young counts asked, eagerly, with his
nose in the air, as if scenting an indiscretion.

"No, I did not go far enough to get a taste of
his horrors ; I stopped at his first period."

"And what do you call his first period, dear
mademoiselle?" The countess's voice was still
freighted with honey. Her husband coughed and
gave her a warning glance, and Renard was moving uneasily in his chair.

"Oh," Charm answered lightly, "his best period—when he didn't sell."

Everyone laughed. The little widow cried beneath her breath :

"*Elle a de l'esprit, celle-là*——"

"*Elle en a de trop,*" retorted the countess.

"Did you ever read Zola's ' Quatre Saisons?' "
Renard asked, turning to the count, at the other
end of the table.

No, the count had not read it—but he could

read the story of a beautiful nature when he encountered one, and presently he allowed Charm to see how absorbing he found its perusal.

"*Ah, bien—et tout de même*—Zola, yes, he writes terrible books; but he is a good man—a model husband and father," continued Monsieur d'Agreste, addressing the table.

"And Daudet—he adores his wife and children," added the count, as if with a determination to find only goodness in the world.

"I wonder how posterity will treat them? They'll judge their lives by their books, I presume."

"Yes, as we judge Rabelais or Voltaire——"

"Or the English Shakespeare by his 'Hamlet.'"

"Ah! what would not Voltaire have done with Hamlet!" The countess was beginning to wake again.

"And Molière? What of *his* 'Misanthrope?' There is a finished, a human, a possible Hamlet! a Hamlet with flesh and blood," cried out the younger count on her right. "Even Mounet-Sully could do nothing with the English Hamlet."

"Ah, well, Mounet-Sully did all that was possible with the part. He made Hamlet at least a lover!"

"Ah, love! as if, even on the stage, one believed in that absurdity any longer!" was the countess's malicious comment.

"Then, if you have ceased to believe in love, why did you go so religiously to Monsieur Carot's lectures?" cried the baroness.

"Oh, that dear Carot! He treated the passions so delicately, he handled them as if they were curiosities. One went to hear his lecture on Love

as one might go to hear a treatise on the peculiarities of an extinct species," was the countess's
quiet rejoinder.

"One should believe in love, if only to prove
one's unbelief in it," murmured the young count
on her left.

"Ah, my dear comte, love, nowadays, like nature, should only be used for decoration, as a bit
of stage setting, or as stage scenery."

"A moonlight night can be made endurable,
sometimes," whispered the count.

"A *clair de lune* that ends in *lune de miel*, that is
the true use to which to put the charms of Diana."
It was Monsieur d'Agreste's turn now to murmur
in the baroness's ear.

"Oh, honey, it becomes so cloying in time," interpolated the countess, who had overheard; she
overheard everything. She gave a wearied glance
at her husband, who was still talking vigorously
to Charm and Renard. She went on softly : "It's
like trying to do good. All goodness, even one's
own, bores one in the end. At Basniege, for
example, lovely as it is, ideally feudal, and with
all its towers as erect as you please, I find this
modern virtue, this craze for charity, as tiresome
as all the rest of it. Once you've seen that all
the old women have woollen stockings, and that
each cottage has fagots enough for the winter,
and your *rôle* of benefactress is at an end. In
Paris, at least, charity is sometimes picturesque;
poverty there is tainted with vice. If one believed in anything, it might be worth while to
begin a mission ; but as it is——"

"The gospel of life, according to you, dear comtesse, is that in modern life there is no real excitement except in studying the very best way to be rid of it," cried out Renard, from the bottom of the table.

"True; but suicide is such a coarse weapon," the lady answered, quite seriously; "so vulgar now, since the common people have begun to use it. Besides, it puts your adversary, the world, in possession of your secret of discontent. No, no. Suicide, the invention of the nineteenth century, goes out with it. The only refined form of suicide is to bore one's self to death," and she smiled sweetly into the young man's eyes nearest her.

"Ah, comtesse, you should not have parted so early in life with all your illusions," was Monsieur d'Agreste's protest across the table.

"And, Monsieur d'Agreste, it isn't given to us all to go to the ends of the earth, as you do, in search of new ones! This friction of living doesn't wear on you as it does on the rest of us."

"Ah, the ends of the earth, they are very much like the middle and the beginning of things. Man is not so very different, wherever you find him. The only real difference lies in the manner of approaching him. The scientist, for example, finds him eternally fresh, novel, inspiring; he is a mine only as yet half-worked." Monsieur d'Agreste was beginning to wake up; his eyes, hitherto, alone had been alive; his hands had been busy, crunching his bread; but his tongue had been silent.

"Ah—h science! Science is only another

anæsthetic—it merely helps to kill time. It is a hobby, like any other," was the countess's rejoinder.

"Perhaps," courteously returned Monsieur d'Agreste, with perfect sweetness of temper. "But at least, it is a hobby that kills no one else. And if of a hobby you can make a principle——"

"A principle?" The countess contracted her brows, as if she had heard a word that did not please her.

"Yes, dear lady; the wise man lays out his life as a gardener does a garden, on the principle of selection, of order, and with a view to the succession of the seasons. You all bemoan the dulness of life; you, in Paris, the torpor of ennui stifles you, you cry. On the contrary, I would wish the days were weeks, and the weeks months. And why? Simply because I have discovered the philosopher's stone. I have grasped the secret of my era. The comedy of rank is played out; the life of the trifler is at an end; all that went out with the Bourbons. Individualism is the new order. To-day a man exists simply by virtue of his own effort—he stands on his own feet. It is the era of the republican, of the individual—science is the true republic. For us who are displaced from the elevation our rank gave us, work is the watchword, and it is the only battle-cry left us now. He only is strong, and therefore happy, who perceives this truth, and who marches in step with the modern movement."

The serious turn given to the conversation had silenced all save the baroness. She had listened

even more intently than the others to her friend's
eloquence, nodding her head assentingly to all
that he said. His philosophic reflections produced as much effect on her vivacious excitability
as they might on a restless Skye-terrier.

"Yes, yes—he's entirely right, is Monsieur
d'Agreste; he has got to the bottom of things.
One must keep in step with modernity—one must
be *fin de siècle*. Comtesse, you should hunt; there
is nothing like a fox or a boar to make life worth
living. It's better, infinitely better, than a pursuit of hearts; a boar's more troublesome than a
man."

"Unless you marry him," the countess interrupted, ending with a thrush-like laugh. When
she laughed she seemed to have a bird in her
throat.

"Oh, a man's heart, it's like the flag of a defenceless country—anyone may capture it."

The countess smiled with ineffable grace into
the vacant, amorous-eyed faces on either side of
her, rising as she smiled. We had reached dessert now; the coffee was being handed round.
Everyone rose; but the countess made no move
to pass out from the room. Both she and the baroness took from their pockets dainty cigarette-
cases.

"*Vous permettez?*" asked the baroness, leaning
over coquettishly to Monsieur d'Agreste's cigar.
She accompanied her action with a charming
glance, one in which all the woman in her was
uppermost, and one which made Monsieur
d'Agreste's pale cheeks flush like a boy's. He

was a philosopher and a scientist; but all his science and philosophy had not saved him from the barbed shafts of a certain mischievous little god. He, also, was visibly hugging his chains.

The party had settled themselves in the low divans and in the Henri IV. arm-chairs; a few here and there remained, still grouped about the table, with the freedom of pose and in the comfort of attitude smoking and coffee bring with them.

It was destined, however, that the hour was to be a short one. One of the grooms obsequiously knocked at the door; he whispered in the count's ear, who advanced quickly toward him, the news that the coach was waiting; one of the leaders——

"Desolated, my dear ladies—but my man tells me the coach is in readiness, and I have an impertinent leader who refuses to stand, when he is waiting, on anything more solid than his hind legs. Fernande, my dear, we must be on the move. Desolated, dear ladies—desolated—but it's only *au revoir*. We must arrange a meeting later, in Paris——"

The scene in the court-yard was once again gay with life and bristling with color. The coach and the dog-cart shone resplendent in the slanting sun's rays. In the brighter sunlight the added glow in the eyes and the cheeks of the brilliantly costumed group made both men and women seem younger and fresher than when they had appeared, two hours since. All were in high good humor—the wines and the talk had warmed the quick French blood. There was a merry scramble for the top coach-seats; the two young counts exchanged their seat in their saddles for the privilege of holding, one the countess's vinaigrette, and the other her long-handled parasol. Renard was beside his friend De Troisac; the horn rang out, the horses started as if stung, dashing at their bits, and in another moment the great coach was being whirled beneath the archway.

"*Au revoir—au revoir !*" was cried down to us from the throne-like elevation. There was a pretty waving of hands—for even the countess's dislike melted into sweetness as she bade us farewell. There were answering cries from the shrieking cockatoos, from the peacocks who trailed their tails sadly in the dust, from the cooks and the peasant serving-women who had assembled to bid the distinguished guests adieu. There was also a sweeping bow from Monsieur Paul, and a grunt of contented dismissal from Madame Le Mois.

A moment after the departure of the coach the court-yard was as still as a convent cloister.

It was still enough to hear the click of madame's fingers, as she tapped her snuff-box.

"The count doesn't see any better than he did —*toujours myope, lui,*" the old woman murmured to her son, with a pregnant wink, as she took her snuff.

"*C'est sa façon de tout voir, au contraire, ma mère,*" significantly returned Monsieur Paul, with his knowing smile.

The mother's shrug answered the smile, as both mother and son walked in different directions—across the sunlit court.

A LITTLE JOURNEY ALONG
THE COAST.

CAEN, BAYEUX, ST. LO, COUTANCES.

CHAPTER XXIII.

 I HAVE always found the act of going away contagious. Who really enjoys being left behind, to mope in a corner of the world others have abandoned? The gay company atop of the coach, as they were whirled beneath the old archway, had left discontent behind; the music of the horn, like that played by the Pied Piper, had the magic of making the feet ache to follow after.

Monsieur Paul was so used to see his world go and come—to greeting it with civility, and to assist at its departure with smiling indifference—that the announcement of our own intention to desert the inn within a day or so, was received with unflattering impassivity. We had decided to take a flight along the coast—the month and the weather were at their best as aids to such adventure. We hoped to see the Fête-Dieu at Caen. Why not push on to Coutances, where the Fête was still celebrated with a mediæval splendor?

From thence to the great Mont, the Mont St. Michel, it was but the distance of a good steed's galloping—we could cover the stretch of country between in a day's driving, and catch, who knows?—perhaps the June pilgrims climbing the Mont.

"Ah, mesdames! there are duller things in the world to endure than a glimpse of the Normandy coast and the scent of June roses! *Idylliquement belle, la côte à ce moment-ci!* "

This was all the regret that seasoned Monsieur Paul's otherwise gracious and most graceful of farewells. Why cannot we all attain to an innkeeper's altitude, as a point of view from which to look out upon the world? Why not emulate his calm, when people who have done with us turn their backs and stalk away? Why not, like him, count the pennies as not all the payment received when a pleasure has come which cannot be footed up in the bill?

The entire company of the inn household was assembled to see us start. Not a white mouse but was on duty. The cockatoos performed the most perilous of their trapeze accomplishments as a last tribute; the doves cooed mournfully; the monkeys ran like frenzied spirits along their gratings to see the very last of us. Madame Le Mois considerately carried the bantam to the archway, that the lost joy of strutting might be replaced by the pride of preferment above its fellows.

" *Adieu,* mesdames."

" *Au revoir*—you will return—*tout le monde revient*—Guillaume le Conquérant, like Cæsar, conquers once to hold forever—remember——"

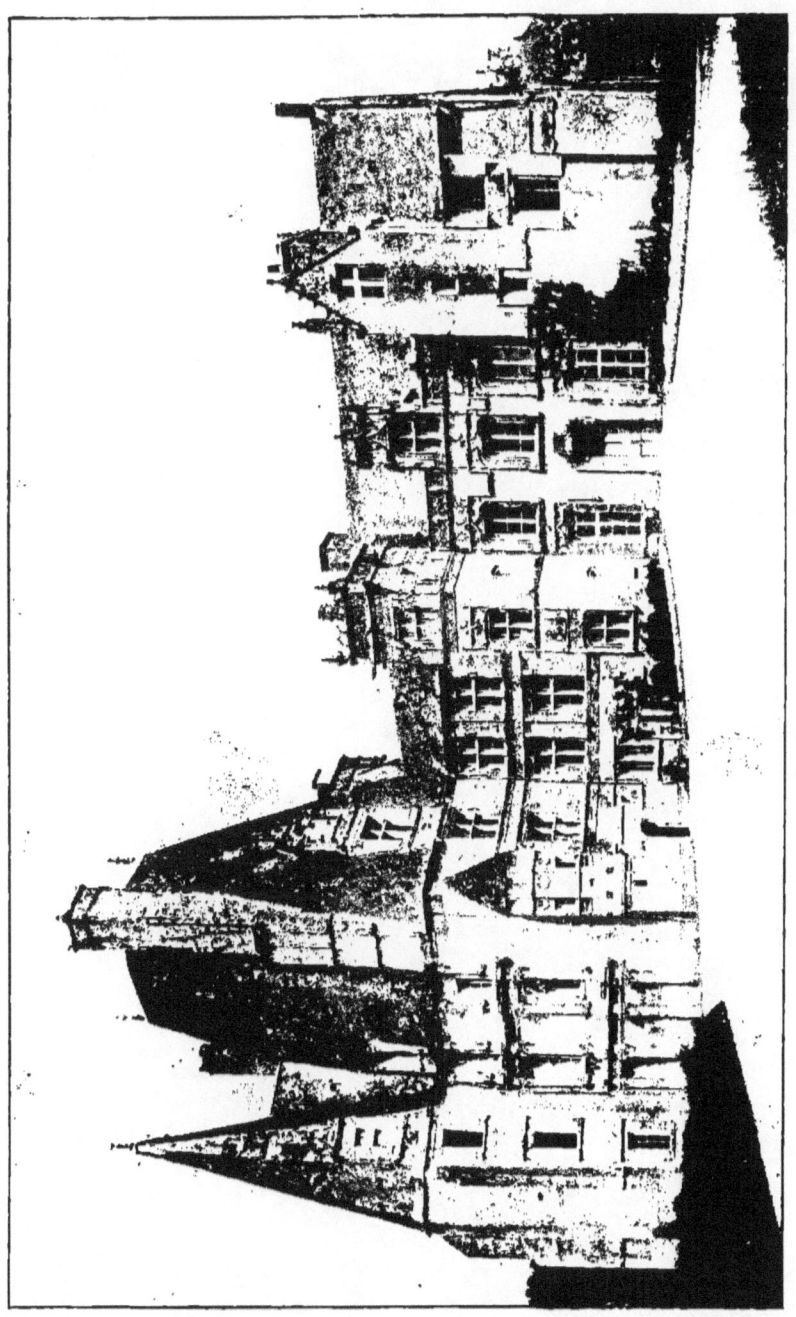

CHÂTEAU FONTAINE LE HENRI, NEAR CAEN.

From Monsieur Paul, in quieter, richer tones, came his true farewell, the one we had looked for:

"The evenings in the Marmousets will seem lonely when it rains—you must give us the hope of a quick return. Hope is the food of those who remain behind, as we Normans say!"

The archway darkened the sod for an instant; the next we had passed out into the broad highway. Jean, in his blouse, with Suzette beside him, both jolting along in the lumbering *char-à-banc*, stared out at us with a vacant-eyed curiosity. We were only two travellers like themselves, along a dusty roadway, on our way to Caen; we were of no particular importance in the landscape, we and our rickety little phaeton. Yet only a moment before, in the inn court-yard, we had felt ourselves to be the pivotal centre of a world wholly peopled with friends! This is what comes to all men who live under the modern curse—the double curse of restlessness and that itching for novelty which made the old Greek longing for the unknown deity—which is also the only honest prayer of so many *fin de siècle* souls!

Besides the dust, there were other things abroad on the high-road. What a lot of June had got into the air! The meadows and the orchards were exuding perfumes; the hedge-rows were so many yards of roses and wild grape-vines in blossom. The sea-smells, aromatic, pungent, floated inland to be married, in hot haste, to a perfect harem of clover and locust scents. The charm of the coast was enriched by the homely, familiar scenes of farm-house life. All the country between Dives and Caen seemed one vast farm, beautifully tilled, with its meadow-lands dipping seaward. For several miles, perhaps, the agricultural note alone would be the dominant one, with the fields full of the old, the eternal surprise—the dawn of young summer rising over them. Down the sides of the low hills, the polychrome grain waved beneath the touch of the breeze like a moving sea. Many and vast were the flat-lands; they were wide vistas of color: there were fields that were scarlet with the pomp of poppies, others tinged to the yellow of a Celestial by the feathery mustard; and still others blue as a sapphire's heart from the dye of millions of bluets. A dozen small rivers—or perhaps it was only one—coiled and twisted like a cobra in sinuous action, in and out among the pasture and sea-meadows.

As we passed the low, bushy banks, we heard the babel of the washerwomen's voices as they gossiped and beat their clothes on the stones. A fisherman or two gave one a hint that idling was understood here, as elsewhere, as being a fine art for those who possess the talent of never being pressed for time. A peasant had brought his horse to the bank; the river, to both peasant and Percheron, was evidently considered as a personal possession—as are all rivers to those who live near them. There was a naturalness in all the life abroad in the fields that gave this Normandy highroad an incomparable charm. An Arcadian calm, a certain patriarchal simplicity reigned beneath the trees. Children trudged to the river bank with pails and pitchers to be filled; women, with rakes

and scythes in hand, crept down from the upper
fields to season their mid-day meal with the cooling
whiff of the river and sea air. Children tugged at
their skirts. In two feet of human life, with kerchief tied under chin, the small hands carrying
a huge bunch of cornflowers, how much of great
gravity there may be! One such rustic sketch
of the future peasant was seriously carrying its
bouquet to another small edition seated in a grove
of poppies; it might have been a votive offering.
Both the children seated themselves, a very earnest conversation ensuing. On the hill-top, near
by, the father and mother were also conversing,
as they bent over their scythes. Another picture
was wheeling itself along the river bank; it was a
farmer behind a huge load of green grass; atop
of the grasses two moon-faced children had laps
and hands crowded with field flowers. Behind
them the mother walked, with a rake slung over
her shoulder, her short skirts and scant draperies
giving to her step a noble freedom. The brush
of Vollon or of Breton would have seized upon
her to embody the type of one of their rustic
beauties, that type whose mingled fierceness and
grace make their peasants the rude goddesses of
the plough.

Even a rustic river wearies at last of wandering,
as an occupation. Miles back we had left the
sea; even the hills had stopped a full hour ago,
as if they had no taste for the rivalry of cathedral
spires. Behold the river now, coursing as sedately as the high-road between two interminable lines of poplars. Far as the eye could reach

stretched a wide, great plain. It was flat as an old woman's palm; it was also as fertile as the city sitting in the midst of its luxuriance has been rich in history.

"*Ce pays est très beau, et Caen la plus jolie ville, la plus avenante, la plus gaie, la mieux située, les plus belles rues, les plus beaux bâtiments, les plus belles églises——*"

There was no doubt, Charm added, as she repeated the lady's verdict, of the opinion Madame de Sévigné had formed of the town. As we drove, some two hundred years later, through the Caen streets, the charm we found had been perpetuated, but alas! not all of the beauty. At first we were entirely certain that Caen had retained its old loveliness; the outskirts were tricked out with the bloom of gardens and with old houses brave in their armor of vines. The meadows and the great trees of the plain were partly to blame for this illusion; they yielded their place grudgingly to the cobble-stoned streets and the height of dormer windows.

To come back to the world, even to a provincial world, after having lived for a time in a corner, is certain to evoke a pleasurable feeling of elation. The streets of Caen were by no means the liveliest we had driven into; nor did the inhabitants, as at Villerville, turn out *en masse* to welcome us. The streets, to be quite truthful, were as sedately quiet as any thoroughfares could well be, and proudly call themselves boulevards. The stony-faced gray houses presented a singularly chill front, considering their nationality. But neither the pallor of

the streets nor their aspect of provincial calm had
power to dampen the sense of our having returned
to the world of cities. A girl issuing from a doorway with a netted veil drawn tightly over her rosy
cheeks, and the curve of a Parisian bodice, immediately invested Caen with a metropolitan importance.

The most courteous of innkeepers was bending
over our carriage-door. He was desolated, but
his inn was already full; it was crowded to reple-
tion with people ; surely these ladies knew it was
the week of the races ? Caen was as crowded as
the inn; at night many made of the open street
their bed; his own court-yard was as filled with
men as with farm-wagons. It was altogether
hopeless as a situation; as a welcome into a
strange city, I have experienced none more arctic.
I had, however, forgotten that I was travelling
with a conqueror; that when Charm smiled she
did as she pleased with her world. The innkeeper
was only a man ; and since Adam, when has any
member of that sex been known to say "No" to a
pretty woman ? This French Adam, when Charm
parted her lips, showing the snow of her teeth,
found himself suddenly, miraculously, endowed
with a fragment of memory. *Tiens,* he had forgotten! that very morning a corner of the attic—
un bout du toît—had been vacated. If these ladies
did not mind mounting to a *grenier*—an attic, comfortable, although still only an attic !

The one dormer window was on a level with the
roof-tops. We had a whole company of "belles
voisines," a trick of neighborliness in windows the

quick French wit, years ago, was swift to name.
These "neighbors" were of every order and pat-
tern. All the world and his mother-in-law were
gone to the race-course, and yet every window was
playing a different scene in the comedy of this life
in the sky. Who does not know—and love—a
French window, the higher up in the world of air
the better? There are certain to be plants, rows
of them in pots, along the wide sill; one can
count on a bullfinch or a parrot, as one can on the
bébés that appear to be born on purpose to poke
their fingers in the cages; there is certain also
to be another cage hanging above the flowers—
one filled with a fresh lettuce or a cabbage-leaf.
There is usually a snowy curtain, fringed; just at
the parting of the draperies an old woman is
always seated, with chin and nose-tip meeting,
her bent figure rounding over the square of her
knitting-needles.

It was such a window as this that made us feel,
before our bonnets were laid aside, that Caen was
glad to see us. The window directly opposite
was wide open. Instead of one there were half a
dozen songsters aloft; we were so near their cages
that the cat-bird whistled, to call his master and
mistress to witness the intrusion of these strangers. The master brought a hot iron along—he
was a tailor and was just in the act of pressing a
seam. His wife was scraping carrots, and she
tucked her bowl between her knees as she came to
stand and gaze across. A cry rose up within the
low room. Some one else wished to see the new-
comers. The tailor laid aside his iron to lift

proudly, far out beyond the cages, the fattest, rosiest offspring that ever was born in an attic. The babe smote its hands for pure joy. We were better than a broken doll—we were alive. The family as a family accepted us as one among them. The man smiled, and so did his wife. Presently both nodded graciously, as if, understanding the cause of our intrusion on their aërial privacy, they wished to present us with the compliment of their welcome. The manners among these garret-windows, we murmured, were really uncommonly good.

"*Bonjour, mesdames!*" It was the third time the woman had passed, and we were still at the window. Her husband left his seam to join her.

"*Ces dames* are not accustomed to such heights —*à ces hauteurs—peut-être?*"

The ladies in truth were not, unhappily, always so well lodged; from this height at least one could hope to see a city.

"Ah! ha! *c'est gai par ici, n'est-ce pas?* One has the sun all to one's self, and air! Ah! for freshness one must climb to an attic in these days, it appears."

It was impossible to be more contented on a height than was this family of tailors; for when not cooking, or washing, or tossing the "*bébé*" to the birds, the wife stitched and stitched all her husband cut, besides taking a turn at the family socks. Part of this contentment came, no doubt, from the variety of shows and amusements with which the family, as a family, were perpetually supplied. For workers, there were really too many so-

cial distractions abroad in the streets; it was almost
impossible for the two to meet all the demands
on their time. Now it was the jingle of a horse's
bell-collar; the tailor, between two snips at a collar, must see who was stopping at the hotel door.
Later a horn sounded; this was only the fish-ven-
der, the wife merely bent her head over the flowers to be quite sure. Next a trumpet, clear and
strong, rang its notes up into the roof-eaves; this
was something *bébé* must see and hear—all three
were bending at the first throbbing touch of that
music on the still air, to see whence it came. Thus
you see, even in the provinces, in a French street,
something is quite certain to happen; it all de-
pends on the choice one makes in life of a window
—of being rightly placed—whether or not one
finds life dull or amusing. This tailor had the
talent of knowing where to stand, at life's corner—
for him there was a ceaseless procession of excitements.

It may be that our neighbor's talent for seeing
was catching. It is certain that no city we had
ever before looked out upon had seemed as crowded
with sights. The whole history of Caen was writ
in stone against the blue of the sky. Here, below
us, sat the lovely old town, seated in the grasses of
her plain. Yonder was her canal, as an artery to
keep her pulse bounding in response to the sea;
the ship-masts and the drooping sails seemed
strange companions for the great trees and the
old garden walls. Those other walls William built
to cincture the city, Froissart found three centuries later so amazingly " strong, full of drapery and

merchandise, rich citizens, noble dames, damsels,
and fine churches," for this girdle of the Conqueror's great bastions the eye looks in vain. But William's vow still proclaims its fulfilment; the spire
of l'Abbaye aux Hommes, and the Romanesque
towers of its twin, l'Abbaye aux Dames, face each
other, as did William and Mathilde at the altar—
that union that had to be expiated by the penance
of building these stones in the air.

Commend me to an attic window to put one in
sympathetic relations with cathedral spires! At
this height we and they, for a part of their flight
upward, at least, were on a common level—and
we all know what confidences come about from the
accident of propinquity. They seemed to assure
us as never before when sitting at their feet, the
difficulties they had overcome in climbing heavenward. Every stone that looked down upon the
city wore this look of triumph.

In the end it was this Caen in the air—it was this
aërial city of finials, of towers, of peaked spires, of
carved chimneys, of tree-tops over which the clouds
rode; of a plain melting—like a sea—into the
mists of the horizon; this high, bright region
peopled with birds and pigeons; of a sky tender,
translucent, and as variable as human emotions;
of an air that was rapture to breathe, and of nights
in which the stars were so close they might almost
be handled; it was this free, hilly city of the roofs
that is still the Caen I remember best.

There were other features of Caen that were
good to see, I also remember. Her street expression, on the whole, was very pleasing. It was

singularly calm and composed, even for a city in a
plain. But the quiet came, doubtless, from its population being away at the races. The few townspeople who, for obvious reasons, were stay-at-
homes, were uncommonly civil; Caen had evidently
preserved the tradition of good manners. An
army of cripples was in waiting to point the way
to the church doors; a regiment of beggars was
within them, with nets cast already for the catching of the small fry of our pennies. In the gay,
geranium-lit garden circling the side walls of St.
Pierre there were many legless soldiers; the old
houses we went to see later on in the high street
seemed, by contrast, to have survived other wars,
those of the Directory and the Mountain, with a
really scandalous degree of good fortune. On our
way to a still greater church than St. Pierre, to
the Abbaye aux Dames, that, like the queen who
built her, sits on the throne of a hill—on our way
thither we passed innumerable other ancient mansions. None of these were down in the guide-
books; they were, therefore, invested with the
deeper charm of personal discovery. Once away
from the little city of the shops, the real Caen
came out to greet us. It was now a gray, sad,
walled town; behind the walls, level-browed Francis I. windows looked gravely over the tufts of verdure; here was an old gateway; there what might
once have been a portcullis, now only an arched
wreath of vines; still beyond, a group of severe-
looking mansions with great iron bound windows
presented the front of miniature fortresses.

And everywhere gardens and gardens.

Turn where you would, you would only turn to
face verdure, foliage, and masses of flowers. The
high walls could neither keep back the odors nor
hide the luxuriance of these Caen gardens. These
must have been the streets that bewitched Madame
de Sévigné. Through just such a maze of foliage
Charlotte Corday has also walked, again and again,
with her wonderful face aflame with her great purpose, before the purpose ripened into the dagger
thrust at Marat's bared breast—that avenging Angel
of Beauty stabbing the Beast in his bath. Auber,
with his Anacreontic ballads in his young head,
would seem more fittingly framed in this old Caen
that runs up a hill-side. But women as beautiful
as Marie Stuart and the Corday can deal safely in
the business of assassination, the world will always continue to aureole their pictures with a gar-
land of roses.

The Abbaye on its hill was reached at last. All
Caen lay below us; from the hillside it flowed
as a sea rolls away from a great ship's sides.
Down below, far below, as if buttressing the town
that seemed rushing away recklessly to the waste
of the plains, stands the Abbaye's twin-brother,
the Aux Hommes. Plains, houses, roof-tops,
spires, all were swimming in a sea of golden light;
nothing seemed quite real or solid, so vast was the
prospect and so ethereal was the medium through
which we saw it. Perhaps it was the great contrast between that shimmering, unstable city below, that rocked and balanced itself like some human creature whose dazzled vision had made its
footing insecure—it may be that it was this note

of contrast which invested this vast structure bestriding the hill with such astonishing grandeur. I have known few, if any, other churches produce so instantaneous an effect of a beauty that was one with austerity. This great Norman is more Puritan than French; it is Norman Gothic with a Puritan severity.

The sound of a deep sonorous music took us quickly within. It was as mysterious a music as ever haunted a church aisle. The vast and snowy interior was as deserted as a Presbyterian church on a week-day. Yet the sound of the rich, strong voices filled all the place. There was no sound of tingling accompaniment: there was no organ pipe, even, to add its sensuous note of color. There was only the sound of the voices, as they swelled, and broke, and began afresh.

The singing went on.

It was a slow "plain chant." Into the great arches the sonorous chanting beat upon the ear with a rhythmic perfection that, even without the lovely flavor of its sweetness, would have made a beauty of its own. In this still and holy place, with the company of the stately Norman arches soaring aloft—beneath the sombre glory of the giant aisles—the austere simplicity of this chant made the heart beat, one knew not why, and the eyes moisten, one also knew not why.

We had followed the voices. They came, we found, from within the choir. A pattering of steps proclaimed we were to go no farther.

"Not there, my ladies—step this way, one only enters the choir by going into the hospital."

The voice was low and sweet; the smile, a spark of divinity set in a woman's face; and the whole was clothed in a nun's garb.

We followed the fluttering robes; we passed out once more into the sunlit parvis. We spoke to the smile and it answered: yes, the choir was reserved for the Sisters—they must be able to approach it from the convent and the hospital; it had always, since the time of Mathilde, been reserved for the nuns; would we pass this way? The way took us into an open vaulted passage, past a grating where sat a white-capped Sister, past a group of girls and boys carrying wreaths and garlands—they were making ready for the *Fête-Dieu,* our nun explained—past, at the last, a series of corridors through which, faintly at first, and then sweeter and fuller, there struck once more upon our ears the sounds of the deep and resonant chanting.

The black gown stopped all at once. The nun was standing in front of a green curtain. She lifted it. This was what we saw. The semicircle of a wide apse. Behind, rows upon rows of round arches. Below the arches, in the choir-stalls, a long half-circle of stately figures. The figures were draped from head to foot. When they bent their heads not an inch of flesh was visible, except a few hands here and there that had escaped the long, wide sleeves. All these figures were motionless; they were as immobile as statues; occasionally, at the end of a " Gloria," all turned to face the high altar. At the end of the " Amen " a cloud of black veils swept the ground. Then for several measures of the chant the figures were again as marble. In each of the low, round arches, a stately woman, tall and nobly planned, draped like a goddess turned saint, stood and chanted to her Lord. Had the Norman builders carved these women, ages ago, standing about Mathilde's tomb, those ancient sculptures could not have embodied, in more ideal image, the type of womanly renunciation and of a saint's fervor of exaltation.

We left them, with the rich chant still full upon their lips, with heads bent low, calm as graven images. It was only the bloom on a cheek, here and there, that made one certain of the youth entombed within these nuns' garb.

"Happy, *mesdames ? Oh, mais très heureuses, toutes*—there are no women so happy as we. See how they come to us, from all the country around. *En voilà une*—did you remark the pretty one, with the book, seated, all in white ? She is to be a full Sister in a month. She comes from a noble family in the south. She was here one day, she saw the life of the Sisters, of us all working here, among the poor soldiers—*elle a vu ça, et pour tout de bon, s'est donnée à Dieu !* "

The smile of our nun was rapturous. She was proving its source. Once more we saw the young countess who had given herself to her God. An hour later, when we had reached the hospital wards, her novice's robes were trailing the ground. She was on her knees in the very middle of the great bare room. She was repeating the office of the hour, aloud, with clasped hands and uplifted head. On her lovely young face there was the glow of a divine ecstasy. All the white faces from the long rows of the white beds were bending toward her; to one even in all fulness of strength and health that girlish figure, praying beside the great vase of the snowy daisies, with the glow that irradiated the sweet, pure face, might easily enough have seemed an angel's.

As companions for our tour of the grounds we had two young Englishmen. Both eyed the nuns in the distance of the corridors and the gardens with the sharpened glances all men level at the women who have renounced them. It is a mystery no man ever satisfactorily fathoms.

"Queer notion, this, a lot of women shutting themselves up," remarked the younger of the two. "In England, now, they'd all go in for being old maids, drinking tea and coddling cats, you know."

"I wonder which are the happier, your countrywomen or these Sisters, who, in renouncing the world devote their lives to serving it. See, over yonder!" and I nodded to a scene beneath the wide avenue of the limes. Two tall Augustines were supporting a crippled old man; they were showing him some fresh garden-beds. Beyond was a gayer group. Some of the lay sisters were tugging at a huge basket of clothes, fresh from the laundry. Running across the grass, with flying draperies, two nuns, laughing as they ran, each striving to outfoot the other, were hastening to their rescue.

"They keep their bloom, running about like that; only healthy nuns I ever saw."

"That's because they have something better than cats to coddle."

"Ah, ha! that's not bad. It's a slow suicide, all the same. But here we are, at the top; it's a fine outlook, is it not?"

The young man panted as he reached the top of the Maze, one of the chief glories of the old Abbaye grounds. He had a fair and sensitive face; a weak product on the whole, he seemed, compared with the nobly-built, vigorous-bodied nuns crowding the choir-stalls yonder. Instead of that long, slow suicide, surely these women should be doing their greater work of reproducing a race. Even an open-air cell seems to me out of place in our century. It will be entirely out of fashion in time, doubtless, as the mediæval cell has gone along with the old castle life, whose princely mode of doing things made a nunnery the only respectable hiding-place for the undowered daughters.

As we crept down into Caen, it was to find it thick with the dust of twilight. The streets were dense with other things besides the thickened light. The Caen world was crowding homeward; all the boulevards and side-streets were alive with a moving throng of dusty, noisy, weary holiday-makers. The town was abroad in the streets to hear the news of the horses, and to learn the history of the betting.

Although we had gone to church instead of doing the races, many of those who had peopled the gay course-track came back to us. The table d'hôte at our inn that night was as noisy as a

Parisian café. It was scarcely as discreet, I should say. On our way to our attic that night the little corridors made us a really amazing number of confidences.

It was strange, but all the shoes appeared to have come in pairs of twos. Never was there such a collection of boots in couples. Strange it was, also, to see how many little secrets these rows of candid shoe-leather disclosed. Here a pert, coquettish pair of ties were having as little in common as possible with the stout, somewhat clumsy walking-boots next them. In the two just beyond, at the next door, how the delicate, slender buttoned kids leaned over, floppingly, to rest on the coarse, yet strong, hobnailed clumpers!

Shabbier and shabbier grew the shoes as we climbed upward. With each pair of stairs we seemed to have left a rung in the ladder of fortune behind. But even the very poorest in pocket had brought his little extravagance with him to the races.

The only genuine family party had taken refuge, like ourselves, in the attic.

At the very next door to our own, Monsieur, Madame, et Bébé proclaimed, by the casting of their dusty shoes, that they also, like the rest of the world, had come to Caen to see the horses run.

CHAPTER XXIV.

 CAEN seated in its plain, wearing its crown of steeples—this was our last glimpse of the beautiful city. Our way to Bayeux was strewn thick with these Normandy jewels; with towns smaller than Caen; with Gothic belfries; with ruined priories, and with castles, stately even when tottering in decay. When the last castle was lost in a thicket, we discovered that our iron horse was stopping in the very middle of a field. If the guard had shouted out the name of any American city, built overnight, on a Western prairie, we should have felt entirely at home in this meadow; we should have known any clearing, with grass and daisies, was a very finished evidence of civilization at high pressure.

But a lane as the beginning of a cathedral town!

Evidently Bayeux has had a Ruskinian dread of steam-whistles, for this ancient seat of bishops has succeeded in retaining the charms of

its old rustic approaches, whatever else it may
have sacrificed on the altar of modernness.

An harangue at the door of the quaint old
Normandy omnibus, by the driver of the same,
was proof that the lesson of good oratory administered by generations of bishops had not
been lost on the Bayeuxnaise minds. Two rebellious English tourists furnished the text for
the driver's sermon; they were showing, with all
the naïve pride of pedestrians, their intention of
footing the distance between the station and the
cathedral. This was an independence of spirit no
Norman could endure to see. What? these gentlemen proposed to walk, in the sun, through
clouds of dust, when here was a carriage, with
ladies for companions, at their command? The
coach had come down the hill on purpose to conduct *Messieurs les voyageurs;* how did these gentlemen suppose a *père de famille* was to make his
living if the fashion of walking came in? And
the rusty red vest was thumbed by the gnarled
hand of the father, who was also an orator; and
a high-peaked hat swept the ground before the
hard-hearted gentlemen. All the tragedy of the
situation had come about from the fact that the
tourists, also, had gotten themselves up in costume. When two fine youths have risen early in
the day to put on checked stockings, leggings,
russet walking-shoes, and a plaited coat with a
belt, such attire is one to be lived up to. Once
in knickerbockers and a man's getting into an
omnibus is really too ignominious! With such
a road before two sets of such well-shaped calves—

a road all shaped and graded—this, indeed, would
be flying in the face of a veritable providence of
bishop-builders intent on maintaining pastoral
effects.

The knickerbockers relentlessly strode onward;
the driver had addressed himself to hearts of
stone. But he had not yet exhausted his quiver
of appeal. Englishmen walk, well! there's no
accounting for the taste of Britons who are also
still half savages; but even a barbarian must eat.
Half-way up the hill, the rattle of the loose-
jointed vehicle came to a dead stop. With great
gravity the guard descended from his seat; this
latter he lifted to take from the entrails of the old
vehicle a handful of hand-bills. He, the horse,
the omnibus, and we, all waited for, what do you
suppose? To besprinkle the walking Englishmen as they came within range with a shower of
circulars announcing that at "*midi, chez Nigaud,
il y aura un déjeuner chaud.*"

The driver turned to look in at the window—
and to nod as he turned—he felt so certain of
our sympathy; had he not made sure of them at
last?

A group of gossamer caps beneath a row of sad,
gray-faced houses was our Bayeux welcome. The
faces beneath the caps watched our approach with
the same sobriety as did the old houses—they had
the antique Norman seriousness of aspect. The
noise we made with the clatter and rattle of our
broken-down vehicle seemed an impertinence, in
the face of such severe countenances. We might
have been entering a deserted city, except for

the presence of these motionless Normandy figures. The cathedral met us at the threshold of
the city: magnificent, majestic, a huge gray
mountain of stone, but severe in outline, as if the
Norman builders had carved on the vast surface
of its façade an imprint of their own grave
earnestness.

We were somewhat early for the hot breakfast
at Nigaud's. There was, however, the appetizing
smell of soup, with a flourishing pervasiveness of
onion in the pot, to sustain the vigor of an appetite whetted by a start at dawn. The knickerbockers came in with the omelette. But one is
not a Briton on his travels for nothing; one does
not leave one's own island to be the dupe of
French inn-keepers. The smell of the soup had
not departed with our empty plates, and the
voice of the walkers was not of the softest when
they demanded their rights to be as odorous as
we. There is always a curiously agreeable sensation, to an American, in seeing an Englishman
angry; to get angry in public is one thing we
do badly; and in his cup of wrath our British
brother is sublime—he is so superbly unconscious
—and so contemptuous—of the fact that the
world sometimes finds anger ridiculous.

At the other end of the long and narrow table
two other travellers were seated, a man and a
woman. But food, to them, it was made mani-
festly evident, was a matter of the most supreme
indifference. They were at that radiant moment
of life when eating is altogether too gross a form
of indulgence. For these two were at the most

interesting period of French courtship—just *after*
the wedding ceremony, when, with the priest's
blessing, had come the consent of their world and
of tradition to their making the other's acquaintance. This provincial bride and her husband
of a day were beginning, as all rustic courting
begins, by a furtive holding of hands; this
particular couple, in view of our proximity and
their own mutual embarrassment, had recourse to
the subterfuge of desperate lunges at the other's
fingers, beneath the table-cloth. The screen, as a
screen, did not work. It deceived no one—as the
bride's pale-gray dress and her flowery bonnet
also deceived no one—save herself. This latter,
in certain ranks of life, is the bride's travelling
costume, the world over. And the world over, it
is worn by the recently wedded with the profound
conviction that in donning it they have discovered
the most complete of all disguises.

This bride and groom were obviously in the
first rapture of mutual discovery. The honey in
their moon was not fresher than their views of the
other's tastes and predilections.

"Ah—ah—you like to travel quickly—to see
everything, to take it all in in a gulp—so do I,
and then to digest at one's leisure."

The bride was entirely of this mind. Only, she
murmured, there were other things one must not
do too quickly—one must go slow in matters of
the heart—to make quite sure of all the stages.

But her husband was at her throat, that is, his
eyes and lips were, as he answered, so that all the
table might partake of his emotion—"No, no, the

quicker the heart feels the quicker love comes. *Tiens, voyons, mon amie, toi-même, tu m'as confié"—* and the rest was lost in the bride's ear.

Apparently we were to have them, these brides, for the rest of our journey, in all stages and of all ages! Thus far none others had appeared as determined as were these two honey-mooners, that all the world should share their bliss. They were cracking filberts with their disengaged fingers, the other two being closely interlocked, in quite scandalous openness, when we left them.

That was the only form of excitement that greeted us in the quiet Bayeux streets. The very street urchins invited repose; the few we saw were seated sedately on the threshold of their own door - steps, frequent sallies abroad into this quiet city having doubtless convinced them of the futility of all sorties. The old houses wore their carved façades as old ladies wear rich lace— they had reached the age when the vanity of personal adornment has ceased to inflate. The great cathedral towers above the tranquil town wore a more conscious air; its significance was too great a contrast to the quiet city asleep at its feet. In these long, slow centuries the towers had grown to have the air of protectors.

The famous tapestries we went to see later, might easily enough have been worked yesterday, in any one of the old mediæval houses; Mathilde and her hand-maidens would find no more—not so much—to distract and disturb them now in this still and tranquil town, with its sad gray streets and its moss-grown door-steps, as they must in

those earlier bustling centuries of the Conqueror.
Even then, when Normandy was only beginning
its career of importance among the great French
provinces, Bayeux was already old. She was
far more Norse then than Norman; she was
Scandinavian to the core; even her nobles spoke
in harsh Norse syllables; they were as little
French as it was possible to be, and yet govern a
people.

Mathilde, when she toiled over her frame, like
all great writers, was doubtless quite unconscious
she was producing a masterpiece. She was, however, in point of fact, the very first among the
great French realists. No other French writer has
written as graphically as she did with her needle,
of the life and customs of their day. That long
scroll of tapestry, for truth and a naïve perfection
of sincerity—where will you find it equalled or
even approached? It is a rude Homeric epic;
and I am not quite certain that it ought not to
rank higher than even some of the more famous
epics of the world—since Mathilde had to create
the mould of art into which she poured her story.
For who had thought before her of making wom-
en's stitches write or paint a great historical
event, crowded with homely details which now are
dubbed archæological veracities?

Bayeux and its tapestry; its grave company of
antique houses; its glorious cathedral dominating the whole—what a lovely old background
against which poses the eternal modernness of the
young noon sun! The history of Bayeux is commonly given in a paragraph. Our morning's walk

had proved to us it was the kind of town that does more to re-create the historic past than all the pages of a Guizot or a Challamel.

The bells that were ringing out the hour of high-noon from the cathedral towers at Bayeux were making the heights of St. Lô, two hours later, as noisy as a village fair. The bells, for rivals, had the clatter of women's tongues. I think I never, before or since, have beheld so lively a company of washerwomen as were beating their clothes in Vire River. The river bends prettily just below the St. Lô heights, as if it had gone out of its way to courtesy to a hill. But even the waters, in their haste to be polite, could not course beneath the great bridge as swiftly as ran those women's tongues. There were a good hundred of them at work beneath the washing - sheds. Now, these sheds, anywhere in France, are really the open-air club - room of the French peasant woman; the whole dish of the village gossip is hung out to dry, having previously been well soused and aired, along with the blouses and the coarse che-mises. The town of St. Lô had evidently fur-nished these club members of the washing-stones with some fat dish of gossip.—the heads were as close as currants on a stem, as they bent in groups over the bright waters. They had told it all to the stream ; and the stream rolled the vol-ume of the talk along as it carried along also the gay, sparkling reflections of the life and the toil that bent over it—of the myriad reflections of those moving, bare-armed figures, of the brilliant kerchiefs, of the wet blue and gray jerseys, and of the long prismatic line of the damp, motley-hued clothes that were fluttering in the wind.

The bells' clangor was an assurance that something was happening on top of the hill. Just what happened was as altogether pleasing a spectacle, after a long and arduous climb up a hillside, as it has often been my good fortune to encounter.

The portals of the church of Notre-Dame were wide open. Within, as we looked over the shoulders of the townspeople who, like us, had come to see what the bells meant by their ringing, within the church there was a rich and sombre dusk; out of this dusk, indistinctly at first, lit by the tremulous flicker of a myriad of candles, came a line of white-veiled heads; then another of young boys, with faces as pale as the nosegays adorning their brand-new black coats; next the scarlet-robed choristers, singing, and behind them still others swinging incense that thickened the dusk. Suddenly, like a vision, the white veils passed out into the sunlight, and we saw that the faces beneath the veils were young and comely. The faces were still alternately lighted by the flare of the burning tapers and the glare of the noon sun. The long procession ended at last in a straggling group of old peasants with fine tremulous mouths, a-tremble with pride and with feeling; for here they were walking in full sight of their town, in their holiday coats, with their knees treacherously unsteady from the thrill of the organ's thunder and the sweetness of the choir-boys' singing.

Whether it was a pardon, or a *fête*, or a first communion, we never knew. But the town of St.

Lô is ever gloriously lighted, for us, with a nimbus of young heads, such as encircled the earlier madonnas.

After such a goodly spectacle, the rest of the town was a tame morsel. We took a parting sniff of the incense still left in the eastern end of the church's nave; there was a bit of good glass in a window to reward us. Outside the church, on the west from the Petite Place, was a wide outlook over the lovely vale of the Vire, with St. Lô itself twisting and turning in graceful postures down the hillside.

On the same prospect two kings have looked, and before the kings a saint. St. Lô or St. Laudus himself, who gave his name to the town, must, in the sixth century, have gazed on virgin forests stretching away from the hill far as the eye could reach. Charlemagne, three hundred years later, in his turn, found the site a goodly one, one to tempt men to worship the Creator of such beauty, for here he founded the great Abbey of St. Croix, long since gone with the monks who peopled it. Louis XI., that mystic wearing the warrior's helmet, set his seal of approval on the hill, by sending the famous glass yonder in the cathedral, when the hill and the St. Lô people beat the Bretons who had come to capture both.

Like saint, and kings, and monks, and warriors, we in our turn crept down the hill. For we also were done with the town.

CHAPTER XXV.

A DINNER AT COUTANCES.

 THE way from St. Lô to Coutances is a pleasant way. There is no map of the country that will give you even a hint of its true character, any more than from a photograph you can hope to gain an insight into the moral qualities of a pretty woman.

Here, at last, was the ideal Normandy landscape. It was a country with a savage look—a savage that had been trained to follow the plough. Even in its color it had retained the true barbarians' instinct for a good primary. Here were no melting-yellow mustard-fields, nor flame-lit poppied meadows, nor mignonettes lifting their baby-blue eyes out of the grain. All the land was green. Fields, meadows, forests, plains—all were green, green, green. The features of the landscape had changed with this change in coloring. The slim, fragile grace of slim trees and fragile cliffs had been replaced by trees of heroic proportions, and by outlines nobly rounded and full—like the breasts of a mother. The whole country had an astonishing

look of vigor—of the vigor which comes with rude
strength; and it had that charm which goes with
all untamed beauty—the power to sting one into a
sense of agitated enjoyment.

Even the farm-houses had been suddenly transformed into fortresses. Each one of the groups of
the farm enclosures had its outer walls, its miniature turrets, and here and there its rounded bastions. Each farm, apparently, in the olden days
had been a citadel unto itself. The Breton had
been a very troublesome neighbor for many a
long century; every ploughman, until a few hundred years ago, was quite likely to turn soldier at
a second's notice—every true Norman must look
to his own sword to defend his hearth-stone. Such
is the story those stone turrets that cap the farm
walls tell you—each one of these turrets was an
open lid through which the farmer could keep his
eye on Brittany.

Meanwhile, along the roads as we rushed swiftly
by, a quieter life was passing. The farm wagons
were jogging peacefully along on a high-road as
smooth as a fine lady's palm—and as white. The
horses were harnessed one before the other, in interminable length of line. Sometimes six, sometimes eight, even so many as ten marched with great
gravity, and with that majestic dignity only possible to full-blooded Percherons, one after the
other. They each wore a saddle-cloth of blue sheepskin. On their mottled haunches this bit of color
made their polished coats to gleam like unto a liz-
ards' skin.

Meanwhile, also, we were nearing Coutances.

The farm-houses were fortresses no longer; the thatched roofs were one once more with the green of the high-roads; for even in the old days there was a great walled city set up on a hill, to which refuge all the people about for miles could turn for protection.

A city that is set on a hill! That for me is commonly recommendation enough. Such a city, so set, promises at the very least the dual distinction of looking up as well as looking down; it is the nearer heaven, and just so much the farther removed from earth.

Coutances, for a city with its head in the air, was surprisingly friendly. It went out of its way to make us at home. At the very station, down below in the plain, it had sent the most loquacious of coach-drivers to put us in immediate touch with its present interests. All the city, as the coarse blue blouse, flourishing its whip, took pains to explain, was abroad in the fields; the forests, *tiens*, down yonder through the trees, we could see for ourselves how the young people were making the woods as crowded as a ball-room. The city, as a city, was stripping the land and the trees bare—it would be as bald as a new-born babe by the morrow. But then, of a certainty, we also had come for the *fête*—or, and here a puzzled look of doubt beclouded the provincial's eyes— might we, perchance, instead, have come for the trial? *Mais non, pas ça*, these ladies had never come for that, since they did not even know the court was sitting, now, this very instant, at Coutances. And—*sapristi!* but there was a trial go-

ing on—one to make the blood curdle; he himself
had not slept, the rustic coachman added, as he
shivered beneath his blouse, all the night before—
the blood had run so cold in his veins.

The horse and the road were all the while going
up the hill. The road was easily one that might
have been the path of warriors; the walls, still
lofty on the side nearest the town, bristled with a
turret or a bastion to remind us Coutances had
not been set on a hill for mere purposes of beauty.
The ramparts of the old fortifications had been
turned into a broad promenade. Even as we
jolted past, beneath the great breadth of the
trees' verdure we could see how gloriously the
prospect widened—the country below reaching
out to the horizon like the waters of a sea that
end only in indefiniteness.

The city itself seemed to grow out of the walls
and the trees. Here and there a few scattered
houses grouped themselves as if meaning to start
a street; but a maze of foliage made a straight
line impossible. Finally a large group of buildings, with severe stone faces, took a more serious
plunge away from the vines; they had shaken
themselves free and were soon soberly ranging
themselves into the parallel lines of narrow city
streets.

It was a pleasant surprise to find that, for once,
a Norman blouse had told the truth; for here
were the people of Coutances coming up from the
fields to prove it. In all these narrow streets a
great multitude of people were passing us; some
were laden with vines, others with young forest

trees, and still others with rude garlands of flowers. The peasant women's faces, as the bent figures staggered beneath a young fir-tree, were purple, but their smiles were as gay as the wild
flowers with which the stones were thickly strewn.
Their words also were as rough:

"*Diantre—mais c'é lourd !*"

"*E-ben, é toi, tu n' bougeons point, toi !*"

And the nearest fir-tree carrier to our carriage-
wheels cracked a swift blow over the head of a
vine-bearer, who being but an infant of two, could
not make time with the swift foot of its mother.

The smell of the flowers was everywhere. Fir-
trees perfumed the air. Every doorstep was a
garden. The courtyards were alive with the
squat figures of capped maidens, wreathing and
twisting greens and garlands. And in the streets
there was such a noise as was never before heard
in a city on a hill-top.

For Coutances was to hold its great *fête* on the
morrow.

It was a relief to turn in from the noise and
hubbub to the bright courtyard of our inn. The
brightness thereof, and of the entire establishment, indeed, appeared to find its central source
in the brilliant eyes of our·hostess. Never was
an inn-keeper gifted with a vision at once so omniscient and so effulgent. Those eyes were everywhere; on us, on our bags, our bonnets, our boots;
they divined our wants, and answered beforehand
our unuttered longings. We had come far? the
eyes asked, burning a hole through our gossamer
evasions; from Paris, perhaps—a glance at our

bonnets proclaimed the eyes knew all; we were
here for the *fête*, to see the bishop on the morrow; that was well; we were going on to the
Mont; and the eyes scented the shortness of our
stay by a swift glance at our luggage.

" *Numéro quatre, au troisième !* "

There was no appeal possible. The eyes had
penetrated the disguise of our courtesy; we were
but travellers of a night; the top story was built
for such as we.

But such a top story, and such a chamber
therein! A great, wide, low room; beams deep
and black, with here and there a brass bit hanging; waxed floors, polished to mirrory perfection;
a great bed clad in snowy draperies, with a snow-
white *duvet* of gigantic proportions. The walls
were gray with lovely bunches of faded rosebuds
flung abroad on the soft surface; and to give a
quaint and antique note to the whole, over the
chimney was a bit of worn tapestry with formid-
able dungeon, a Norman keep in the background,
and well up in front, a stalwart young master of
the hounds, with dogs in leash, of the heavy Norman type of bulging muscle and high cheek-
bones.

Altogether, there were worse fates in the world
than to be travellers of a night, with the destiny
of such a room as part of the fate.

When we descended the steep, narrow spiral of
steps to the dining-room, it was to find the eyes
of our hostess brighter than ever. The noise in
the streets had subsided. It was long after dusk,
and Coutances was evidently a good provincial.

But in the gay little dining-room there was an astonishing bustle and excitement.

The *fête* and the court had brought a crowd of
diners to the inn-table; when we were all seated
we made quite a company at the long, narrow
board. The candles and lamps lit up any number
of Vandyke-pointed beards, of bald heads, of
loosely-tied cravats, and a few matronly bosoms
straining at the buttons of silk holiday gowns.
For the *Fête-Dieu* had brought visitors besides
ourselves from all the country round; and then
" a first communion is like a marriage, all the rela-
tives must come, as doubtless we knew," was a
bald-head's friendly beginning of his soup and
his talk, as we took our seats beside him.

With the appearance of the *potage* conversation,
like a battle between foes eager for contest, had
immediately engaged itself. The setting of the
table and the air of companionship pervading the
establishment were aiders and abettors to immediate intercourse. Nothing could be prettier than
the Caen bowls with their bunches of purple
flocks and spiked blossoms. Even a metropolitan
table might have taken a lesson from the perfection of the lighting of the long board. In order
that her guests should feel the more entirely at
home, our brilliant-eyed hostess came in with
the soup; she took her place behind it at the
head of the table.

It was evident the merchants from Cherbourg
who had come as witnesses to the trial, had had
many a conversational bout before now with madame's ready wit. So had two of the town lawyers.

Even the commercial gentlemen, for once, were
experiencing a brief moment of armed suspense,
before they flung themselves into the arena of
talk. At first, or it would never have been in the
provinces, this talk at the long table, everyone
broke into speech at once. There was a flood of
words; one's sense of hearing was stunned by the
noise. Gradually, as the cider and the thin red
wine were passed, our neighbors gave digestion a
chance; the din became less thick with words;
each listened when the other talked. But, as the
volume of speech lessened, the interest thickened.
It finally became concentrated, this interest, into
true French fervor when the question of the trial
was touched on.

"They say D'Alençon is very clever. He
pleads for Filon, the culprit, to-night, does he
not ? "

" Yes, poor Filon—it will go hard with him.
His crime is a black one."

"I should think it was—implicating *le petit !* "

"Dame! the judge doesn't seem to be of your
mind."

" Ah—h ! " cried a florid Vandyke-bearded man,
the dynamite bomb of the table, exploding with
a roar of rage. " *Ah—h, cré nom de Dieu !—Messieurs les présidents* are all like that; they are
always on the side of the innocent——"

" Till they prove them guilty."

" Guilty ! guilty ! " the bomb exploded in earnest now. " How many times in the annals of
crime is a man guilty—really guilty ? They
should search for the cause—and punish that.

That is true justice. The instigator, the instigator—he is the true culprit. Inheritances—*voilà les vrais coupables.* But when are such things investigated? It is ever the innocent who are punished. I know something of that—I do."

"*Allons—allons !*" cried the table, laughing at the beard's vehemence. "When were you ever under sentence ? "

"When I was doing my duty," the beard hurled back with both arms in the air; "when I was doing my three years—I and my comrade; we were convicted—punished—for an act of insubordination we never committed. Without a trial, without a chance of defending ourselves, we were put on two crumbs of bread and a glass of water for two months. And we were innocent—as innocent as babes, I tell you."

The table was as still as death. The beard had proved himself worthy of this compliment; his voice was the voice of drama, and his gestures such as every Frenchman delights in beholding and executing. Every ear was his, now.

"I have no rancor. I am, by nature, what God made me, a peaceable man, but "—here the voice made a wild *crescendo*—" if I ever meet my colonel —*gare à lui !* I told him so. I waited two years, two long years, till I was released ; then I walked up to him " (the beard rose here, putting his hand to his forehead), "I saluted "(the hand made the salute), "and I said to him, 'Mon colonel, you convicted me, on false evidence, of a crime I never committed. You punished me. It is two years since then. But I have never forgotten. Pray to

God we may never meet in civil life, for then yours
would end!"

"*Allons, allons!* A man after all must do his
duty. A colonel—he can't go into details!" re-
monstrated the hostess, with her knife in the air.

"I would stick him, I tell you, as I would a pig
—or a Prussian! I live but for that!"

"*Monstre!*" cried the table in chorus, with a
laugh, as it took its wine. And each turned to his
neighbor to prove the beard in the wrong.

"Of what crime is the defendant guilty—he who
is to be tried to-night?" Charm asked of a silent
man, with sweet serious eyes and a rough gray
beard, seated next her. Of all the beards at the
table this one alone had been content with listening.

"Of fraud—mademoiselle—of fraud and for-
gery." The man had a voice as sweet as a church
bell, and as deep. Every word he said rang out
slowly, sonorously. The attention of the table was
fixed in an instant. "It is the case of a Monsieur
Filon, of Cherbourg. He is a cider merchant. He
has cheated the state, making false entries, etc.
But his worst crime is that he has used as his accomplice *un tout petit jeune homme*—a lad of barely
fifteen——"

"It is that that will make it go hard for him
with the jury——"

"Hard!" cried the ex-soldier, getting red at
once with the passion of his protest—"hard—it
ought to condemn him, to guillotine him. What
are juries for if they don't kill such rascals as
he?"

"*Doucement, doucement, monsieur*," interrupted the bell-note of the merchant. " One doesn't condemn people without hearing both sides. There may be extenuating circumstances ! "

"Yes—there are. He is a merchant. All merchants are thieves. He does as all others do— *only* he was found out."

A protesting murmur now rose from the table, above which rang once more, in clear vibrations, the deep notes of the merchant.

"*Ah—h, mais—tous voleurs—non*, not all are thieves. Commerce conducted on such principles as that could not exist. Credit is not founded on fraud, but on trust."

" *Très bien, très bien*," assented the table. Some knives were thumped to emphasize the assent.

"As for stealing"—the rich voice continued, with calm judicial slowness—"I can understand a man's cheating the state once, perhaps—yielding to an impulse of cupidity. But to do as *ce* Monsieur Filon has done—he must be a consummate master of his art—for his processes are organized robbery."

"Ah—h, but robbery against the state isn't the same thing as robbing an individual," cried the explosive, driven into a corner.

"It is quite the same—morally, only worse. For a man who robs the state robs everyone—including himself."

"That's true—perfectly true—and very well put." All the heads about the table nodded admiringly ; their hostess had expressed the views of them all. The company was looking now at the gray beard with glistening eyes; he had proved himself master of the argument, and all were desirous of proving their homage. Not one of the nice ethical points touched on had been missed; even the women had been eagerly listening, following, criticising. Here was a little company of people gathered together from rustic France, meeting, perhaps, for the first time at this board. And the conversation had, from the very beginning, been such as one commonly expects to hear only among the upper ranks of metropolitan circles. Who would have looked to see a company of Norman provincials talking morality and handling ethics with the skill of rhetoricians?

Most of our fellow-diners, meanwhile, were taking their coffee in the street. Little tables were ranged close to the house-wall. There was just room for a bench beside the table, and then the sidewalk ended.

"Shall you be going to the trial to-night?" courteously asked the merchant who had proven himself a master in debate, of Charm. He had lifted his hat before he sat down, bowing to her as if he had been in a ball-room.

"It will be fine to-night—it is the opening of the defence," he added, as he placed carefully two lumps of sugar in his cup.

"It's always finer at night—what with the lights and the people," interpolated the landlady, from her perch on the door-sill. "If *ces dames* wish to go, I can show them the way to the galleries. Only," she added, with a warning tone, her growing excitement obvious at the sense of the com-

ing pleasure, "it is like the theatre. The earlier
we get there the better the seat. I go to get my
hat." And thé door swallowed her up.

"She is right—it is like a theatre," soliloquized
the merchant—"and so is life. Poor Filon!"

We should have been very content to remain
where we . were. The night had fallen; the
streets, as they lost themselves in dim turnings,
in mysterious alleyways, and arches that seemed
grotesquely high in the vague blur of things,
were filled for us with the charm of a new and
lovely beauty. At one end the street ended in a
towering mass of stone; that doubtless was the
cathedral. At the right, the narrow houses
dipped suddenly; their roof-lines were lost in
vagueness. Between the slit made by the street
a deep, vast chasm opened; it was the night filling the great width of sky, and the mists that
shrouded the hill, rising out of the sleeping earth.
There was only one single line of light; a long
deep glow was banding the horizon; it was a bit
of flame the dusk held up, like a fading torch, to
show where the sun had reigned.

In and out of this dusk the townspeople came
and went. Away from the mellow lights, streaming past the open inn doors, the shapes were
only a part of the blur; they were vague, phantasmal masses, clad in coarse draperies. As they
passed into the circle of light, the faces showed
features we had grown to know—the high cheek-
bones, the ruddy tones, the deep-set, serious
eyes, and mouths firm-set with lips close together. The air on this hill-top must be of ex-

cellent quality; the life up here could scarcely be so hard as in the field villages. For the women looked less worn, and less hideously old, and in the men's eyes there was not so hard and miserly a glittering.

Almost all, young or old, were bearing strange burdens. Some of the men were carrying huge floral crosses; the women were laden with every conceivable variety of object—with candlesticks, vases, urns, linen sheets, rugs, with chairs even.

"They are helping to dress the reposoirs, they must all be in readiness for the morning," answered our friend, still beside us, when we asked the cause of this astonishing spectacle.

Everywhere garlands and firs, leaves, flowers, and wreaths; people moving rapidly; the carriers of the crosses stopping to chat for an instant with groups working at some mysterious scaffolding— all shapes in darkness. Everywhere, also, there was the sweet, aromatic scent of the greens and the pines abroad in the still, clear air of the summer night.

This was the perfume and these the dim pictures that were our company along the narrow Coutances streets.

CHAPTER XXVI.

 THE court-room was brightly
lighted; the yellow radi-
ance on the white walls
made the eyes blink. We
had turned, following our
guide, from the gloom of
the dim streets into the
roomy corridors of the
Préfecture. Even the gar-
dens about the building
were swarming with townspeople and peasants
waiting for the court to open. When we entered
it was to find the hallways and stairs blocked with
a struggling mass of people, all eager to get seats.
A voice that was softened to a purring note, the
voice that goes with the pursuit of the five-franc
piece, spoke to our landlady. "The seats to be
reserved in the tribune were for these ladies ? "

No time had been lost, you perceive. We were
strangers; the courtesies of the town were to be
extended to us. We were to have of their best,
here in Coutances; and their best, just now, was
this *mise-en-scène* in their court-room.

The stage was well set. The Frenchman's instinctive sense of fitness was obvious in the ar-

rangements. Long lines of blue drapery from
the tall windows brought the groups below into
high relief; the scarlet of the judges' robes was
doubly impressive against this background. The
lawyers, in their flowing black gowns and white
ties, gained added dignity from the marine note
behind them. The bluish pallor of the walls made
the accused and the group about him pathetically
sombre. Each one of this little group was in black.
The accused himself, a sharp, shrewd, too keen-eyed
man of thirty or so, might have been following a
corpse—so black was his raiment. Even the youth
beside him, a dull, sodden-eyed lad, with an air of
being here not on his own account, but because
he had been forced to come, was clad in deepest
mourning. By the side of the culprit sat the one
really tragic figure in all the court—the culprit's
wife. She also was in black. In happier times
she must have been a fair, fresh-colored blonde.
Now all the color was gone from her cheek. She
was as pale as death, and in her sweet downcast
eyes there were the tell-tale vigils of long nights
of weeping. Beside her sat an elderly man who
bent over her, talking, whispering, commenting as
the trial went on.

Every eye in the tribune was fixed on the slim
young figure. A passing glance sufficed, as a rule,
for the culprit and his accomplice; but it was
on the wife that all the quick French sympathy,
that volubly spoke itself out, was lavished. The
blouses and peasants' caps, the tradesmen and their
wives crowded close about the railing to pass their
comment.

"She looks far more guilty than he," muttered a wizened old man next to us, very crooked on his three-legged stool.

"Yes," warmly added a stout capped peasant, with a basket once on her arm, now serving as a pedestal to raise the higher above the others her own curiosity. "Yes—she has her modesty—too —to speak for her——"

"Bah—all put on—to soften the jury." It was our fiery one of the table d'hôte who had wedged his way toward us.

"And why not? A woman must make use of what weapons she has at hand——"

"*Silence ! Silence ! messieurs !*" The *huissier* brought down his staff of office with a ring. The clatter of sabots over the wooden floor of the tribune and the loud talking were disturbing the court.

This French court, as a court, sat in strange fashion, it seemed to us. The bench was on wonderfully friendly terms with the table about which the clerks sat, with the lawyers, with the foreman of the jury, with even the *huissiers.* Monsieur le Président was in his robes, but he wore them as negligently as he did the dignity of his office. He and the lawyer for the defence, a noted Coutances orator, openly wrangled; the latter, indeed, took little or no pains to show him respect; now they joked together, next a retort flashed forth which began a quarrel, and the court and the trial looked on as both struggled for a mastery in the art of personal abuse. The lawyer made nothing of raising his finger, to shake it in open

menace in the very teeth of the scarlet robes. And
the robes clad a purple-faced figure that retorted
angrily, like a fighting school-boy.

But to Coutances, this, it appears, was a proper
way for a court to sit.

"*Ah, D'Alençon—il est fort, lui. C'est lui qui agace
toujours monsieur le président——*"

"He'll win—he'll make a great speech—he is
never really fine unless it's a question of life or
death——" Such were the criticisms that were
poured out from the quick-speaking lips about us.

Presently a simultaneous movement on the part
of the jury brought the proceedings to confusion.
A witness in the act of giving evidence stopped
short in his sentence; he twisted his head; looking upward, he asked a question of the foreman,
and the latter nodded, as if assenting. The judge
then looked up. All the court looked up. All
the heads were twisted. Something obviously
was wrong. Then, presently the *concierge* appeared with a huge bunch of keys.

And all the court waited in perfect stillness—
while the windows were being closed!

"*Il y avait un courant d'air*—there was a
draught,"—gravely announced the crooked man,
as he rose to let the *concierge* pass. This latter
had her views of a court so susceptible to whiffs
of night air.

"*Ces messieurs* are delicate—pity they have to be
out at night!"—whereat the tribune snickered.

All went on bravely for a good half-hour. More
witnesses were called; each answered with wonderful aptness, ease, and clearness; none were

confused or timid; these were not men to be the playthings of others who made tortuous cross-questionings their trade. They, also, were Frenchmen; they knew how to speak. The judge and the Coutances lawyer continued their jokes and their squabblings. And still only the poor wife hung her head

Then all at once the judge began to mop his brow. The jury, to a man, mopped theirs. The witnesses and lawyers each brought forth their big silk handkerchiefs. All the court was wiping its brow.

"It's the heat," cried the judge. "*Huissier*, call the *concierge*; tell her to open the windows."

The *concierge* reappeared. Flushed this time, and with anger in her eye. She pushed her way through the crowd; she took not the least pains in the world to conceal her opinion of a court as variable as this one.

"*Ah mais*, this is too much! if the jury doesn't know its mind better than this!"—and in the fury of her wrath she well-nigh upset the crooked little old gentleman and his three-legged stool.

"That's right—that's right. I'm not a fine lady, tip me over. You open and shut me as if I were a bureau drawer ; *continuez—continuez——*"

The *concierge* had reached the windows now. She was opening and slamming them in the face of the judge, the jury, and *messieurs les huissiers*, with unabashed violence. The court, except for that one figure in sombre draperies, being men, suffered this violence as only men bear with a woman in a temper. With the letting in of the

fresh air, fresh energy in the prosecution mani-
fested itself. The witnesses were being sub-
jected to inquisitorial torture; their answers
were still glib, but the faces were studies of the
passions held in the leash of self-control. Not
twenty minutes had ticked their beat of time
when once more the jury, to a man, showed signs
of shivering. Half a dozen gravely took out their
pocket-handkerchiefs, and as gravely covered their
heads. Others knotted the square of linen, thus
making a closer head-gear. The judge turned uneasily in his own chair; he gave a furtive glance
at the still open windows; as he did so he caught
sight of his jury thus patiently suffering. The
spectacle went to his heart; these gentlemen were
again in a draught? Where was the *concierge?*
Then the *huissier* whispered in the judge's ear;
no one heard, but everyone divined the whisper.
It was to remind monsieur le président that the
concierge was in a temper; would it not be better for him, the *huissier*, to close the windows?
Without a smile the judge bent his head, assenting. And once more all proceedings were at a
standstill; the court was patiently waiting, once
more, for the windows to be closed.

Now, in all this, no one, not even the wizened
old man who was obviously the humorist of the
tribune, had seen anything farcical. To be too
hot—to be too cold! this is a serious matter in
France. A jury surely has a right to protect itself
against cold, against *la migraine*, and the devils of
rheumatism and pleurisy. There is nothing ridiculous in twelve men sitting in judgment on a fel-

low-man, with their handkerchiefs covering their
bare heads. Nor of a judge who gallantly remembers the temper of a *concierge.* Nor of a whole
court sitting in silence, while the windows are
opened and closed. There was nothing in all this
to tickle the play of French humor. But then, we
remembered, France is not the land of humorists,
but of wits. Monsieur d'Alençon down yonder, as
he rises from his chair to address the judge and
jury, will prove to you and me, in the next two
hours, how great an orator a Frenchman can be
without trenching an inch on the humorist's
ground.

The court-room was so still now that you could
have heard the fall of a pin.

At last the great moment had come—the moment and the man. There is nothing in life
Frenchmen love better than a good speech—*un
discours;* and to have the same pitched in the
dramatic key, with a tragic result hanging on the
effects of the pleading, this is the very climax of
enjoyment. To a Norman, oratory is not second,
but first, nature; all the men of this province have
inherited the gift of a facile eloquence. But this
Monsieur d'Alençon, the crooked man whispered,
in hurried explanation, he was *un fameux*—even
the Paris courts had to send for him when they
wanted a great orator.

The famous lawyer understood the alphabet of
his calling. He knew the value of effect. He
threw himself at once into the orator's pose. His
gown took sculptural lines; his arms were waved
majestically, as arms that were conscious of hav-

ing great sleeves to accentuate the lines of gesture.

Then he began to speak. The voice was soft; at first one was chiefly conscious of the music in its cadences. But as it warmed and grew with the ardor of the words, the room was filled with such vibrations as usually come only with the sounding of rich wind-instruments. With such a voice a man could do anything. D'Alençon played with it as a man plays with a power he has both trained and conquered. It was firmly modulated, with no accent of sympathy when he opened his plea for his client. It warmed slightly when he indignantly repelled the charges brought against the latter. It took the cadence of a lover when he pointed to the young wife's figure and asked if it were likely a husband could be guilty of such crimes, year after year, with such a woman as that beside him? It was tenderly explanatory as he went on enlarging on the young wife's perfections, on her character, so well known to them all here in Coutances, on the influence she had given the home-life yonder in Cherbourg. Even the children were not forgotten, as an aid to incidental testimony. Was it even conceivable a father of a young family would lead an innocent lad into error, fraud, and theft?

"It is he who knows how to touch the heart!"

" *Quel beau moment !* " cried the wizened man, in a transport.

"See—the jury weep!"

All the court was in tears, even monsieur le président sniffled, and yet there was no draught.

As for the peasant women and the shop-keepers, they could not have been more moved if the culprit had been a blood-relation. How they enjoyed their tears! What a delight it was to thus thrill and shiver! The wife was sobbing now, with her head on her uncle's shoulder. And the culprit was acting his part, also, to perfection. He had been firmly stoical until now. But at this parade of his wife's virtues he broke down, his head was bowed at last. It was all the tribune could do to keep its applause from breaking forth. It was such a perfect performance! it was as good as the theatre—far better—for this was real—this play—with a man's whole future at stake!

Until midnight the lawyer held all in the town in a trance. He ended at last with a Ciceronian, declamatory outburst. A great buzz of applause welled up from the court. The tribune was in transports; such a magnificent harangue he had not given them in years. It was one of his greatest victories.

"And his victories, madame, they are the victories of all Coutances."

The crooked man almost stood upright in the excitement of his enthusiasm. Great drops of sweat were on his wrinkled old brow. The evening had been a great event in his life, as his twisted frame, all a-tremble with pleasurable elation, exultingly proved. The women's caps were closer together than ever; they were pressing in a solid mass close to the railing of the tribune to gain one last look at the figure of the wife.

"It is she who will not sleep——"

"Poor soul, are her children with her?"

"No—and no women either. There is only the uncle."

"He is a good man, he will comfort her!"

"*Faut prier le bon Dieu!*"

At the court-room door there was a last glimpse of the stricken figure. She disappeared into the blackness of the night, bent and feeble, leaning with pitiful attempt at dignity on the uncle's arm. With the dawn she would learn her husband's fate. The jury would be out all night.

"You see, madame, it is she who must really suffer in the end." We were also walking into the night, through the bushes of the garden, to the dark of the streets. Our landlady was guiding us, and talking volubly. She was still under the influence of the past hour's excitement. Her voice trembled audibly, and she was walking with brisk strides through the dim streets.

"If Filon is condemned, what would happen to them?"

"Oh, he would pass a few years in prison—not many. The jury is always easy on the rich. But his future is ruined. They—the family—would have to go away. But even then, rumor would follow them. It travels far nowadays—it has a thousand legs, as they say here. Wherever they go they will be known. But Monsieur d'Alençon, what did you think of him, *hein?* There's a great man—what an orator! One must go as far as Paris—to the theatre; one must hear a great play —and even there, when does an actor make you weep as he did? Henri, he was superb. I tell

you, superb! *d'une éloquence!*" And to her husband, when we reached the inn door, our vivacious landlady was still narrating the chief points
of the speech as we crawled wearily up to our
beds.

It was early the next morning when we descended into the inn dining-room. The lawyer's eloquence had interfered with our rest. Coffee and
a bite of fresh air were best taken together, we
agreed. Before the coffee came the news of the
culprit's fate. Most of the inn establishment had
been sent to court to learn the jury's verdict.
Madame confessed to a sleepless night. The
thought of that poor wife had haunted her pillow.
She had deemed it best—but just to us all, in a
word, to despatch Auguste—the one inn waiter, to
hear the verdict. *Tiens*, there he was now, turning the street corner.

" *Il est acquitté!* " rang through the streets.

"He is acquitted—he is acquitted! *Le bon Dieu
soit loué!* Henri—Ernest—Monsieur Terier, he
is acquitted—he is acquitted! I tell you!"

The cry rang through the house. Our landlady
was shouting the news out of doors, through windows, to the passers-by, to the very dogs as they
ran. But the townspeople needed no summon-
ing. The windows were crowded full of eager
heads, all asking the same question at once. A
company of peasants coming up from the fields
for breakfast stopped to hear the glad tidings.
The shop-keepers all the length of the street
gathered to join them. Everyone was talking at
once. Every shade of opinion was aired in the

morning sun. On one subject alone there was a universal agreement.

" What good news for the poor wife ! "

"And what a night she must have passed ! "

All this sympathy and interest, be it remembered, was for one they barely knew. To be the niece of a Coutances uncle—this was enough, it appears, for the good people of this cathedral city, to insure the flow of their tears and the gift of their prayers.

CHAPTER XXVII.

THE FETE-DIEU—A JUNE CHRISTMAS.

 WHEN we stepped forth into the streets, it was to find a flower-strewn city. The paving-stones were covered with the needles of pines, with fir-boughs, with rose-leaves, lily stocks, and with the petals of flock and clematis. One's feet sank into the odorous carpet as in the thick wool of an Oriental prayer-rug. To tread upon this verdure was to crush out perfume. Yet the fragrance had a solemn flavor. There was a touch of consecration in the very aroma of the fir-sap.

Never was there a town so given over to its festival. Everything else—all trade, commerce, occupation, work, or pleasure even, was at a dead standstill. In all the city there was but one thought, one object, one end in view. This was the great day of the *Fête-Dieu*. To this blessed feast of the Sacrament the townspeople had been looking forward for weeks.

It is their June Christmas. The great day brings families together.

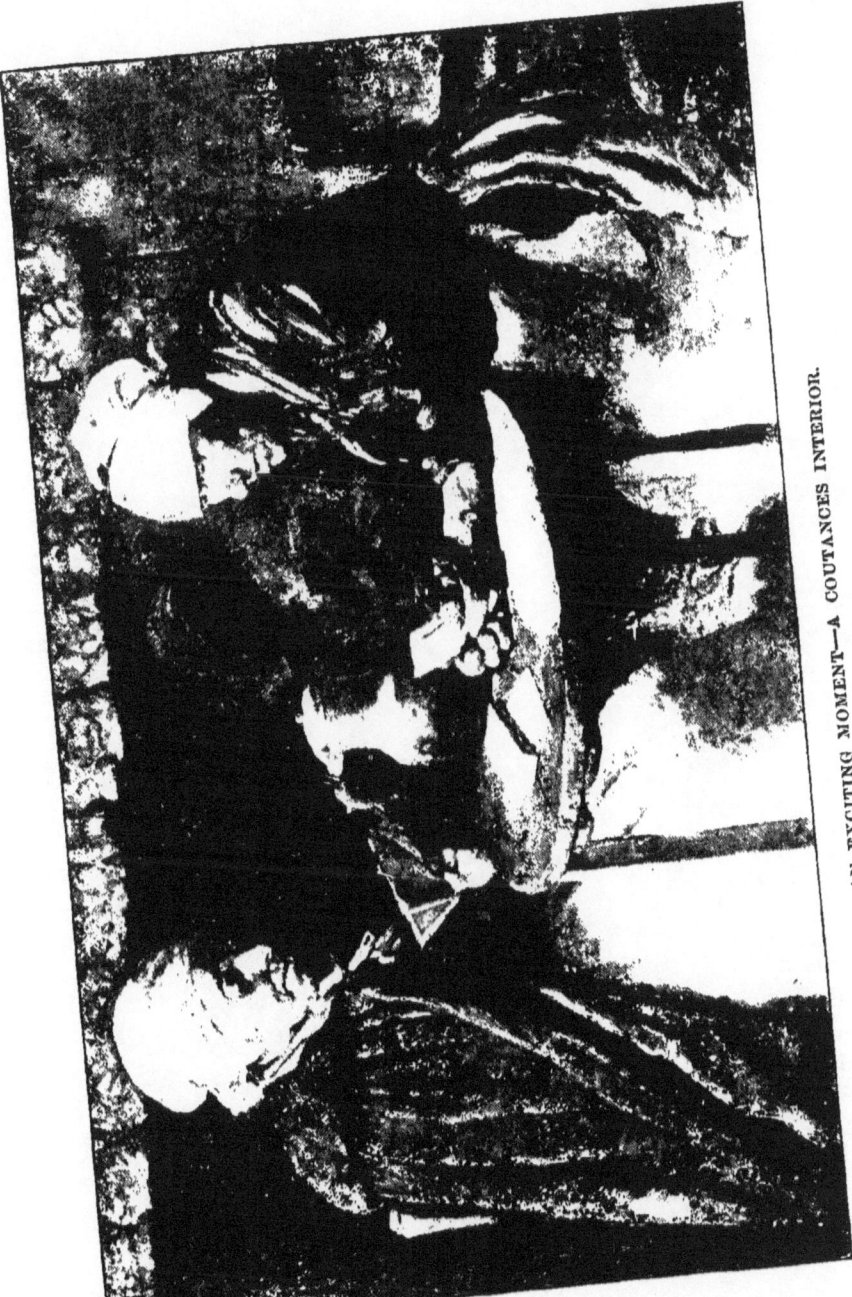

AN EXCITING MOMENT—A COUTANCES INTERIOR.

From all the country round the farm wagons had been climbing the hill for hours. The peasants were in holiday dress. Gold crosses and amber beads encircled leathery old necks; the gossamer caps, real Normandy caps at last, crowned heads held erect to-day, with the pride of those who had come to town clad in their best. Even the younger women were in true peasant garb; there was a touch of a ribbon, brilliant red and blue stockings, and the sparkle of silver shoe-buckles and gold necklaces to prove they had donned their finery in honor of the *fête*. The men wore their blue and purple blouses over their holiday suits; but almost all had pinned a sprig of bright geranium or honeysuckle to brighten up the shiny cotton of the preservative blouse. Even the children carried bouquets; and thus many of the farm wagons were as gay as the streets.

No, gay is not the word. Neither the city nor the streets were really gay. The city, as a city, was too dead in earnest, too absorbed, too intent, to indulge in gayety. It was the greatest of all the days of the year in Coutances. In the climaxic moments of life, one is solemn, not gay. It was not only the greatest, but the busiest, day of the year for this cathedral town. Here was a whole city to deck; every street, every alleyway must be as beautiful as a church on a feast-day. The city, in truth, must be changed from a bustling, trading, commercial entrepôt into an altar. And this altar must be beautiful—as beautiful, as ingeniously picturesque as only the French instinct for beauty could make it.

Think you, with such a task on hand, this city-ful of artists had time for frivolous idling? Since dawn these artists had been scrubbing their doors, washing windows, and sluicing the gutters. One is not a provincial for nothing; one is honest in the provinces; one does not drape finery over a filthy frame. The city was washed first, before it was adorned.

Opposite, across from our inn door-sill, where we lingered a moment before we began our journey through the streets, we could see for ourselves how thorough was this cleansing. A shop-keeper and his wife were each mounted on a step-ladder. One washed the inside and the other the outside of the low shop-windows. They were in the greatest possible haste, for they were late in their preparations. In two hours the procession was to pass. Their neighbors stopped to cry up to them :

" *Tendez-vous, aujourd'hui ?* " It is the universal question, heard everywhere.

"*Mais oui,*" croaked out the man, his voice sounding like the croak of a rook, from the height from which he spoke. "Only we are late, you see."

It was his wife who was taking the question to heart. She saw in it just cause for affront.

" Ah, those Espergnous, they're always on time, they are; they had their hangings out a week ago, and now they are as filthy as wash-rags. No wonder they have time to walk the streets! " and the indignant dame gave her window-pane an extra polish.

"Here, Léon, catch hold, I'm ready now!"

The woman was holding out one end of a long, snowy sheet. Léon meekly took his end; both hooked the stuff to some rings ready to secure the hanging; the façade of the little house was soon hidden behind the white fall of the family linen; and presently Léon and his wife began very gravely to pin tiny sprigs of purple clematis across the white surface. This latter decoration was performed with the sure touch of artists. No mediæval designer of tapestry could have chosen with more secure selection the precise points of distance at which to place the bouquets, nor could the tones and tints of the greens and purples, and the velvet of the occasional heartsease, sparsely used, been more correctly combined. When the task was ended, the commonplace house was a palace wall, hung with the sheen of fine linen, on which bloomed geometric figures beautifully spaced.

All the city was thus draped. One walked through long walls of snow, in which flowers grew. Sometimes the floral decorations expanded from the more common sprig into wreaths and garlands. Here and there the Coutances fancy worked itself out in *fleur-de-lis* emblems or in armorial bearings. But everywhere an astonishing, instinctive sense of beauty, a knowledge of proportion, and a natural sense for color were obvious. There was not, in all the town, a single offence committed against taste. Is it any wonder, with such an heredity at their fingers' ends, that the provinces feed Paris, and that Paris sets the fashions in beauty for the rest of the world?

Come with us, and look upon this open-air chapel. It stands in the open street, in front of an old house of imposing aspect. The two commonplace-looking women who are putting the finishing touches to this beautiful creation tell us it is the reposoir of Madame la Baronne. They have been working on it since the day before. In the night the miracle was finished—nearly—they were so weary they had gone to bed at dawn. They do not tell you it is a miracle. They think it fine, oh, yes—"*c'est beau*—Madame la Baronne always has the most beautiful of all the reposoirs," but then they have decked these altars since they were born; their grandmothers built them before ever they saw the light. For always in Coutances "*on la fête beaucoup;*" this feast of the Sacrament has been a great day in Coutances for centuries past. But although they are so used to it, these natural architects love the day. "It's so fine to see—*si beau à voir*—all the reposoirs, and the children and the fine ladies walking through the streets, and then, all kneeling when Monseigneur l'Archevêque prays. Ah yes, it is a fine sight." They nod, and smile, and then they turn to light a taper, and to consult about the placing of a certain vase from out of which an Easter lily towers.

At the foot of these miniature altars trees had been planted. Gardens had also been laid out; the parterres were as gravely watered as if they were to remain in the middle of a bustling high street in perpetuity. Steps lead up to the altar. These were covered with rugs and carpets; for the feet of the bishop must tread only on velvet and

flowers. Candelabra, vases, banners, crosses, crucifixes, flowers, and tall thin tapers—all the altars
were crowded with such adornments. Human
vanity and the love of surpassing one's neighbors,
these also figured conspicuously among the things
the fitfully shining sun looks down upon. But
what a charm there is in such a contest! Surely
the desire to beautify the spot on which the
Blessed Sacrament rests—this is only another
way of professing one's adoration.

As we passed through the streets a multitude of
pictures crowded upon the eyes. In an archway
groups of young first communicants were forming:
they were on their way to the cathedral. Their
white veils against the gloom of the recessed
archways were like sunlit clouds caught in an
abyss. Priests in gorgeous vestments were walking quickly through the streets. All the peasants
were going also toward the cathedral. A group
stopped, as did we, to turn into a side-street. For
there was a picture we should not see later on.
Between some lovely old turrets, down from convent walls a group of nuns fluttered tremulously:
they were putting the last touches to the reposoir
of their own Sacré Cœur. Some were carrying
huge gilt crosses, staggering as they walked;
others were on tiptoes filling the tall vases;
others were on their knees, patting into perfect
smoothness the turf laid about the altar steps.
There was an old curé among them and a young
carpenter whom the curé was directing. Everyone of the nuns had her black skirts tucked up:
their stout shoes must be free to fly over the

ground with the swiftness of hounds. How pretty
the faces were, under the great caps, in that
moment of unwonted excitement! The cheeks,
even of the older nuns, were pink; it was a pink
that made their habitual pallor have a dazzling
beauty. The eyes were lighted into a fresh flame
of life, and the lips were temptingly crimson:
they were only women, after all, these nuns, and
once a year at least this feast of the Sacrament
brings all their feminine activities into play.

Still we moved on, for within the cathedral
the procession had not yet formed. There was
still time to make a tour of the town.

To plunge into the side-streets away from the
wide cathedral parvis was to be confronted with a
strange calm. These narrow thoroughfares had
the stillness which broods over all ancient cities'
by-ways. Here was no festival bustle; all was
grave and sad. The only dwellers left in the antique fifteenth century houses were those who
must remain at home till a still smaller house
holds them. We passed several aged Coutançais
couples. By twos they were seated at the low
windows; they had been dressed and then left;
they were sitting here, in the pathetic patience of
old age; they were hoping something of the *fête*
might come their way. Two women, in one of
the low interiors, were more philosophic than
their neighbors; if their stiffened knees would not
carry them to the *fête*, at least their gnarled old
hands could hold a pack of cards. They were
seated close to the open casement, facing each
other across a small round table; along the win-
dow-sill there were rows of flower-pots; a pewter

A STREET IN COUTANCES—ÉGLISE SAINT-PIERRE.

tankard was set between them: and out of the
shadowy interior came the topaz gleam of the
Normandy brasses, the huge bed, with its snowy
draperies, the great chests, and the flowery chintz-
frill defining the width of the yawning fireplace.
The two old faces, with the strong features, deep
wrinkles, sunken mouths, and bald heads tied up
in dazzling white coifs, were in full relief against
the dim background. They were as motionless as
statues; neither looked up as our footfall struck
along the cobbles: it was an exciting moment in
the game.

Below these old houses stretched the public
gardens. Here also there was a great stillness.
For us alone the rose gardens bloomed, the tropical trees were shivering, and the palms were
making a night of shade for wide acres of turf.
Rarely does a city boast of such a garden. It was
no surprise to learn, later, that these lovely paths
and noble terraces had been the slow achievement
of a lover of landscape gardening, one who, dying, had given this, his master-piece, to his native
town.

There is no better place from which to view the
beautiful city. From the horizontal lines of the
broad terraces flows the great sweep of the hillside; it takes a swift precipitous plunge, and rests
below in wide stretches of meadow. The garden
itself seemed, by virtue of this encompassing circle of green, to be only a more exquisitely cultivated portion of the lovely outlying hills and
wooded depths. The cows, grazing below in the
valleys, were whisking their tails, and from the
farm-yards came the crow of the chanticleer.

One turned to look upward—to follow heavenward the soaring glory of the cathedral towers. From the plane of the streets their geometric perfection had made their lines seem cold. Through this aërial perspective the eye followed, enraptured, the perfect Gothic of the spires and the lower central tower. The great nave roof and the choir lifted themselves above the turrets and the tiled house-tops of the city as gray mountains of stone rise above the huts of pygmies. Coutances does well to be proud of its cathedral.

The sound of a footstep, crunching the gravel of the garden-walk, caused us to turn. It was to find, face to face, the hero of the night before; the celebrated Coutances lawyer was also taking his constitutional. But not alone, some friends were with him, come up to town doubtless for the *fête* or the trial. He was showing them his city. He stretched a hand forth, with the same magisterial gesture of the night before, to point out the glory of the prospect lying below the terrace. He faced the cathedral towers, explaining the points of their perfection. And then, for he was a Frenchman, he perceived the presence of two ladies. In an instant his hat was raised, and as quickly his eyes told us he had seen us before, in the court-room. The bow was the lower because of this recognition, and the salute was accompanied by a grave smile.

Manners in the provinces are still good, you perceive—if only you are far enough away from Paris.

Someone else also bestowed on us the courtesy of a passing greeting. It was a curé who was saying his Ave, as he paced slowly, in the sun, up and down the yew path. He was old; one leg was already tired of life—it must be dragged painfully along, when one walked in the sun. The curé himself was not in the least tired of life. His smile was as warm as the sun as he lifted his *calotte.*

"Surely, mesdames, you will not miss the *fête?* It must be forming now."

He had taken an old man's, and a priest's, privilege. We were all three looking down into the valley, which lay below, a pool of freshness. He had spoken, first of the beauty of the prospect, and then of the great day. To be young and still strong, to be able to follow the procession from street to street, and yet to be lingering here among the roses!—this passed the simple curé's comprehension. The reproach in his mild old eyes was quickly changed to approval, however; for upon the announcement that the procession was already in motion we started, bidding him a hurried adieu.

The huge cathedral portals yawned at the top of the hill; they were like a gaping chasm. The great place of the cathedral square was half filled; a part of the procession had passed already beyond the gloom of the vast aisles into the frank openness of day. Winding in and out of the white-hung streets a long line of figures was marching; part of the line had reached the first reposoir and gradually the swaying of the heads was slackening, as, by twos and twos, the figures stopped.

Still, from between the cathedral doors an un-ending multitude of people kept pouring forth upon the cathedral square. Now it was an inter-minable line of young girls, first communicants, in their white veils and gowns; against the grays and browns of the cathedral façade this mass of snow was of startling purity — a great white rose of light. Closely following the dazzling line marched a grave company of nuns; with their black robes sweeping the flower-strewn streets, the pallor of their faces, and the white wings of their huge coifs they might have been so many marble statues moving with slow, automatic step, repeating in life the statues in stone above their heads, incarnations of meek renunciation. With the free and joyous step of a vigorous youth not yet tamed to complete self-obliteration, next there stepped forth into the sun a group of seminarists. In the lace and scarlet of their bright robes they were like unto so many young kings. High in the summer air they swung their golden censers; from huge baskets, heaped with flowers, they scattered flowers as they swayed, in the grace of their youth, from side to side, with priestly rhythmic motion.

In the days of Greece, under the Attic tent of sky, it was Jove that was thus worshipped; here in Coutances, under the paler, less ardent blue of France, it was the Christian God these youths were honoring. So men have continued to scat-ter flowers; to swing incense; to bend the knee; surely in all ages the long homage of men, like the

procession here before us, has been but this—the
longing to worship the Invisible, and to make the
act one with beauty.

Is it Greek, is it Christian, this festival? If it
be Catholic, it is also pagan. It is as composite a
union of religious ceremonials as man is himself
an aggregate of lost types, for there is a subtle
law of repetition which governs both men and
ceremonials.

How pagan was the color! how Greek the sense
of beauty that lies in contrasts! how Jewish the
splendor of the priestly vestments as the gold and
silver tissues gleamed in the sun! How mediæval
this survival of an old miracle play!

See this group of children, half-frightened,
half-proud, wandering from side to side as children unused to walking soberly ever march. They
were following the leadership of a huge Suisse.
This latter was magnificently apparelled. He
carried a great mace, and this he swung high in
the air. The children, little John the Baptist,
Christ, Mary the Mother, and Magdalen, were
magnetized by his mighty skill. They were
looking at the golden stick; they were thinking
only of how high he, this splendid giant who ter-
rified them so, would throw it the next time, and
if he would always surely catch it. The small
Virgin, in her long brown robes, tripped as she
walked. The cherubic John the Baptist, with
only his sheepskin and his cross, shivered as he
stumbled after her.

"At least they might have covered his arms, *le
pauvre petit*," one stout peasant among the bystand-

ers was Christian enough to mutter, "Poor little
John!" Even in summer the sun is none too hot
on this hill-top; and a sheepskin is a garment one
must be used to, it appears. Christ, himself, was
no better off. He was wearing his crown of thorns,
but he had only his night-dress, bound with a
girdle, to keep his naked little body warm. An
angel, in gossamer wings and a huge rose-wreath,
being of the other sex, had her innate woman's
love of finery to make her oblivious to the light
sting of the wind, as it passed through her draperies. As this group in the procession moved
slowly along, the city took on a curiously antique
aspect. In every lattice window a head was
framed. The lines of the townspeople pressed
closer and closer; they made a serried mass of
blouses and caps, of shiny coats and bared heads.
The very houses seemed to recognize that a part
of their own youth was passing them by; these
were the figures they had looked out upon, time
after time, in the old fourteenth and fifteenth century days, when the great miracle plays drew the
country around, for miles and miles, to this Coutances square.

Across the square, in the long gray distance of
the streets, the archbishop's canopy was motionless. A sweet groaning murmur rippled from lip
to lip.

Then a swift and mighty rustling filled the air,
for the bones of thousands of knees were striking
the stones of the street;—even heretic knees were
bent when the Host was lifted. It was the moment
of silent prayer. It was also, perhaps, the most

beautiful, it was assuredly the most consum-
mately picturesque moment of the day. The bent
heads; the long vistas of kneeling figures : the
lovely contrasts of the flowing draperies ; the
trailing splendor of the priests' robes dying into
the black note made by the nuns' sombre skirts :
the gossamer brilliance of the hundreds of white
veils, through which the young rapture of religious awe on lips and brow made even commonplace features beautiful : the choristers' scarlet
petticoats ; the culminating note of splendor, the
Archbishop, throned like some antique scriptural
king under the feathers and velvets of his crimson
canopy ; then the long lines of the townspeople with
the groups of peasants beside them, whose well-
sunned skins made even their complexion seem
pale by the side of cheeks that brought the burn
of noon-suns in the valleys to mind ; and behind
this wall of kneeling figures, those other walls,
the long white-hung house façades, with their
pendent sprigs and wreaths and garlands above
which hung the frieze of human heads beneath
the carved cornices : surely this was indeed the
culminating moment, both in point of beauty and
in impressiveness, of the great day's festival.

Thus was reposoir after reposoir visited. Again
and again the multitude was on its knees. Again
and again the Host was lifted. And still we
followed. Sometimes all the line was in full
light, a long perspective of color and of prismatic radiance. And then the line would be lost ;
some part of it was still in a side-street ; and
the rest were singing along the edges of the

city's ramparts, under the great branches of the
trees. Here, in the gray of the narrow streets.
the choristers' gowns were startling in their richness. Yonder, in full sunlight, the brightness on
the maidens' robes made the shadows in their
white skirts as blue as light caught in a grotto's
depth.

Still they sang. In the dim streets or under
the trees, where the gay banners were still fluttering, and the white veils, like airy sails, were
bulging in the wind, the hymn went on. It was
thin and pathetically weak in the mouths of the
babes that walked. It was clear, as fresh and pure
as a brooklet's ripple, from the mouths of the
young communicants. It was of firm contralto
strength from the throats of the grave nuns. The
notes gained and gained in richness; the hymn
was almost a chant with the priests; and in the
mouths of the people it was as a ringing chorus.
Together with the swelling music swung the incense into high air; and to the Host the rose-
leaves were flung.

Still we followed. Still the long line moved
on from altar to altar.

Then, when the noon was long past, wearily we
climbed upward to our inn.

In the high streets there was much going to
and fro. The shop-keepers already were taking
down their linen. Pouffe! Pouffe! there was
much blowing through mouths and a great standing on tiptoes to reach the tall tapers on the
reposoirs.

Coutances was pious. Coutances was proud of

its *fête*. But Coutances was also a thrifty city.
Once the *cortège* had passed, it was high time to
snuff out the tapers. Who could stand by and see
good candles blowing uselessly in the wind, and
one's money going along with the dripping?

CHAPTER XXVIII.

 Two hours later the usual collection of forces was assembled in our inn court-yard: for a question of importance was to be decided. Madame was there—chief of the council: her husband was also present, because he might be useful in case any dispute as to madame's word came up; Auguste, the one inn waiter, was an important figure of the group; for he, of them all, was the really travelled one: he had seen the world—he was to be counted on as to distances and routes: and above, from the upper windows, the two ladies of the bed-chamber looked down, to act as chorus to the brisk dialogue going on between madame and the owner of a certain victoria for which we were in treaty.

"*Ces dames,*" madame said, with a shrug which was meant for the coachman, and a smile which was her gift to us—"these ladies wish to go to Mont St. Michel, to drive there. Have you your little victoria and Poulette?"

Now, by the shrug madame had conveyed to the man and the assembled household generally, her

own great scorn of us, and of our plans. What a
whim this, of driving, forsooth, to the Mont!
Dieu sait—French people were not given to any
such follies; they were serious-minded, *always*, in
matters of travel. To travel at all, was no light
thing; one made one's will and took an honest
and tearful farewell of one's family, when one
went on a journey. But these English, these
Americans, there's no foretelling to what point
their folly will make them tempt fate! However,
madame was one who knew on which side her
bread was buttered, if ever a woman did, and the
continuance of these mad follies helped to butter
her own French roll. And so her shrug and wink
conveyed to the tall Norman just how much these
particular lunatics before them would be willing
to pay for this their whim.

"Have you Poulette?"

"Yes—yes—Poulette is at home. I have made
her repose herself all day—hearing these ladies
had spoken of driving to the Mont——"

Chorus from the upper window-sills. "The
poor beast! it is *joliment longue—la distance.*"

"As these ladies observe," continued the owner
of the doomed animal, not raising his head, but
quickly acting on the hint, "it is long, the distance—one does not go for nothing." And though
the man kept his mouth from betraying him, his
keen eyes glittered with avarice.

"And then—*ces dames* must descend at Genets,
to cross the *grève, tu sais,*" interpolated the waiter,
excitedly changing his napkin, his wand of office,
from one armpit to the other. The thought of

travel stirred his blood. It was fine—to start off
thus, without having to make the necessary arrangements for a winter's service or a summer's
season. And to drive, that would be new—yes
that would be a change indeed from the stuffy
third-class compartments. For Auguste, you see,
approved of us and of the foolishness of our plans.
His sympathy being *gratis*, was allied to the pro-
tective instinct—he would see the cheating was at
least as honestly done as was compatible with
French methods.

"Another carriage—and why ?" we meekly queried, warned by this friendly hint. A chorus now
arose from the entire audience.

"*Mais, madame !*—it is as much as five or six
kilos over the sands to the Mont from Genets !"
was cried out in a tone of universal reproach.

"Through rivers, madame, through rivers as
high as that !" and Auguste, striking in after the
chorus, measured himself off at the breast.

"Yes—the water comes to there, on the horse,"
added the driver, sweeping an imaginary horse's
head, with a fine gesture, in the air.

"Dame, that must be fine to see," cried down
Léontine and Marie, gasping with little sighs of
envy.

"And so it is !" cried back Auguste, nodding
upward with dramatic gesture. " One can get as
wet as a duck—splashing through those rivers.
Dieu ! que c'est beau !" And he clasped his hands
as his eye, rolling heavenward, caught the blue
and the velvet of the four feminine orbs on its upward way. Seeing which ecstasy, the courtyard

visibly relented; Auguste's rapture and his envy
had worked the common human miracle of turning
contempt for a folly into belief in it.

This quick firing of French people to a pleasurable elation in others' adventure is, I think we
must all agree, one of the great charms of this ex-
citable race : anything will serve as a pretext for
setting this sympathetic vibration in motion.
What they all crave as a nation is a daily, hourly
diet of the unusual, the unforeseen.

It is this passion for incident which makes a
Frenchman's life not unlike his soups, since in the
case of both, how often does he make something
out of nothing !

An hour later we were picking our way through
the city's streets. Sweeter than the crushed flowers was the free air of the valley.

There is no way of looking back so agreeable, on
the whole, I think, as to look back upon a city.

From the near distance of the first turn in the
road, Coutances and its cathedral were at their
very best. The hill on which both stood was only
one of the many hills we now saw growing out of
the green valley; among the dozen hill-tops, this
one we were leaving was only more crowded than
the others, and more gloriously crowned. In giant
height uprose, above the city's roofs and the lesser
towers, the spires and the lovely lantern tower.
This vast mass of stone, pricked into lacy apertures and with its mighty lines of grace—for how
many a long century has it been in the eye of the
valley ? Tancrède de Hauteville saw it before
William was born—before he, the Conqueror, rode

in his turn through the green lanes to consecrate
the church to One greater than he. From Tancrède
to Boileau, what a succession of bishops, each in
their turn, have had their eye on the great cathedral. There was a sort of viking bishop, one
Geoffrey de Montbray, of the Conqueror's day, who,
having a greater taste for men's blood than their
purification, found Coutances a dull city; there
was more war of the kind his stout arm rejoiced
in across the Channel; and so he travelled a bit
to do a little pleasant killing. From Geoffrey to
Boileau and the latter's lacy ruffles—how many a
rude Norman epic was acted out, here in the valley, beneath the soaring spires, before the Homeric
combat was turned into the verse of a *chanson de
geste*, a *Roman de Rou*, or a *Lutrin !*

As Poulette rolled the wheels along, instead of
visored bishop or mail rustling on strong breasts,
there was the open face of the landscape, and the
tremble of the grasses beneath the touch of the
wind. Coming down the hill was a very peaceable
company; doubtless, between wars in those hot
fighting centuries, just such travellers went up and
down the hill-road as unconcernedly as did these
peasants. There was quite a variety among the
present groups: some were strictly family parties;
these talked little, giving their mind to stiff walking—the smell of the soup in the farmyard kitchen
was in their nostrils. The women's ages were
more legibly read in their caps than in their faces—
the older the women the prettier the caps. Among
these groups, queens of the party, were some first
communicants. Their white kid slippers were

brown now, from the long walk in the city streets
and the dust of the highway. They held their
veils with a maiden's awkwardness; with bent
heads they leaned gravely on their fathers' arms.
In this, their first supreme experience of self-
consciousness, they had the self-absorption of
young brides. The trail of their muslin gowns
and the light cloud of their veils made dazzling
spots of brightness in the delicate frame of the
June landscape. Each of these white-clad figures
was followed by a long train of friends and rela-
tives.

"*C'est joli à voir*—it's a pretty sight, *hein*, my ladies?—these young girls are beautiful like that!"
Our coachman took his eye off Poulette to turn in
his seat, looking backward at the groups as they
followed in our wake. "Ah—it was hard to leave
my own—I had two like that, myself, in the procession to-day." And the full Norman eye filled
with a sudden moisture. This was a more attractive glitter than the avarice of a moment before.

"You see, mesdames," he went on, as if wishing
to excuse the moistened eyelids, "you see—it's a
great day in the family when our children take
their first communion. It is the day the child dies
and the man, the woman is born. When our children kneel at our feet, before the priest, before
their comrades, and beg us to forgive them all the
sin they have done since they were born—it is too
much—the heart grows so big it is near to bursting. Ah—it is then we all weep!"

Charm settled herself in her seat with a satis-

fied smile. " We are in luck—an emotional coachman who weeps and talks! The five hours will
fly," she murmured. Then aloud, to Jacques—as
we learned the now sniffling father was called—she
presently asked, with the oil of encouragement in
her tone :

"You say your two were in the procession ? "

"Two! there were five in all. Even the babies
walked. Did you see Jesu and the Magdalen?
They were mine—*C'était à moi, ça !* For the priests
will have them—as many as they can get."

"They are right. If the children didn't walk,
how could the procession be so fine ? "

"Fine — *beau* — *ça ?* " And there was a deep
scorn in Jacques's voice. "You should have seen
the *fête* twenty years ago! Now, its glory is as
nothing. It's the priests themselves who are to
blame. They've spoiled it all. Years ago, the
whole town walked. *Dieu*—what a spectacle! The
mayor, the mairie, all the firemen, municipal officers—yes, even the soldiers walked. And as for
the singing—*dame*, all the young men were choristers then—we were trained for months. When we
walked and sang in the open streets the singing
filled all the town. It was like a great thunder."

"And the change—why has it come ? " persisted
Charm.

"Oh," Jacques replied, caressing Poulette's
haunches with his whip-lash. "It's the priests;
they were too grasping. They are avaricious,
that's what they are. They want everything for
themselves. And a *fête*—*ça coûte, vous savez.* Besides, the spirit of the times has changed. People

aren't so devout now. *Libres penseurs*—that's the
fashion now. *Holà*, Poulette! "

Poulette responded. She dashed into the valley
below us now as if this rolling along of a heavy
victoria, a lot of luggage, and three travellers,
was an agreeable episode in her career of toil.
But on the mind of her owner, the spectre of the
free-thinkers was still hovering like an evil spirit.
During the next hour he gave us a long and exhaust-
ive exposition of the changes wrought by *ces messieurs qui nient le bon Dieu.* Among their crimes was
to be numbered that of having disintegrated the
morale of the peasantry. They—the peasants—no
longer believed in miracles, and as for sorcery, for
the good old superstitions, bah! they were looked
upon as old wives' tales. Even here, in the heart
of this rural country, you would have to walk far
before you could find *une vraie sorcière*, one who,
by looking into a glass of water, for instance, could
read the future as in a book, or one who, if your cow
dried up, could name the evil spirit, the demon,
who, among the peasants was exercising the curse.
All this science was lost. A peasant would now
be ashamed to bring his cow to a fortune-teller;
all the village would laugh. Even the shepherds
had lost the power of communing with the planets
at night; and all the valley read the *Petit Journal*
instead of consulting the *vieilles mères.* One must
go as far as Brittany to see a real peasant with the
superstitions of a peasant. As for Normandy, it
went in step with the rest of the world, *que diable!*
And again the whip lash descended. Poulette
must suffer for Jacques's disgust.

If the Norman peasant was a modern, his country, at least, had retained the charm of its ancient beauty. The road was as Norman a highway as one could wish to see. It had the most capricious of natures, turning and perversely twisting among the farms and uplands. The land was ribboned with growing grain, and the June grass was being cut. The farms stood close upon the roadway, as if longing for its companionship; and then, having done so much toward the establishment of neighborly gossip, promptly turned their backs upon it—true Normans, all of them, with this their appearance of frankness and their real reserves of secrecy.

For a last time we caught a distant glimpse of the great cathedral. As we looked back across the bright-roofed villages, we saw the stately pile, gray, glorious, superb, dominating the scene, the hills, river, and fields, as in the old days the great city walls and the cathedral towers had dominated all the human life that played helplessly about them.

We were out once more among the green and yellow broadlands; between our carriage-wheels and the horizon there was now spread a wide amphitheatre of wooded hills. The windings of the poplar-lined road serpentined in sinuous grace in and out of forests, meadows, hills, and islands. The afternoon lights were deepening; the shadows on the grain-fields cast by the oaks and beeches were a part of our company. The blue bloom of the distant hills was strengthening into purple. As the light was intensifying in color, the human

life in the fields was relaxing its tension; the bent
backs were straightening, the ploughmen were
whipping their steeds toward the open road; for
although it was Sunday, and a *fête* day, the farmer
must work. The women were gathering up some
of the grasses, tying them into bundles, and tossing them on their heads as they moved slowly
across the blackening earth.

One field near us was peopled with a group of
girls resting on their scythes. One or two among
them were mopping their faces with their coarse
blue aprons; the faces of all were aflame with
the red of rude health. As we came upon them,
some had flung away their scythes, the tallest
among the group grasping a near companion,
playfully, in the pose of a wrestler. In an instant
the company was turned into a group of wrestlers.
There was a great shout of laughter, as maiden after maiden was tumbled over on her back or face
amid the grasses. Sabots, short skirts, kerchiefs,
scarlet arms rose and fell to earth in the mad
whirl of their gayety.

"Stop, Jacques, I must see the end," cried
Charm. "Will they fight or dance, I wonder!"

"Oh, it is a pure Georgic—they'll dance."
They were dancing already. The line, with dis-
hevelled hair, aprons and kerchiefs askew, had
formed into the square of a quadrille. A rude
measure was tripped; a snatch of song, shouted
amid the laughter, gave rhythm to the measure,
and then the whole band, singing in chorus,
linked arms and swept with a furious dash beneath the thatched roof of a low farm-house.

"As you see, my ladies, sometimes the fields are gay — even now," was Jacques's comment. "But they should be getting their grasses in—for it'll rain before night. It's time to sing when the scythe sleeps—as we say here."

To our eyes there were no signs of rain. The clouds rolling in the blue sea above us were only gloriously lighted. But the birds and the peasants knew their sky; there was a great fluttering of wings among the branches; and the peasants, as we rattled in and out of the hamlets, were pulling the *reposoirs* to pieces in the haste that predicts bad weather. They had been "celebrating" all along the road; and besides the piety, the Norman thrift was abroad upon the highway. Women were tearing sheets off the house façades; the lads and girls were bearing crosses, china vases, and highly-colored Virgins from the wooden altars into the low houses.

Presently the great drops fell; they beat upon the smooth roadway like so many hard bits of coin. In less than two ticks of the clock, the world was a wet world; there were masses of soft gray clouds that were like so much cotton dripping with moisture. The earth was as drenched as if, half an hour ago, it had not been a jewel gleaming in the sun; and the very farm-houses had quickly assumed an air of having been caught out in the rain without an umbrella. The farm gardens alone seemed to rejoice in the suddenness of the shower. Flowers have a way of shining, when it rains, that proves flower-petals have a woman's love of solitaires.

There were other dashes of color that made the gray landscape astonishingly brilliant. Some of the peasants on their way to the village *fêtes* were also caught in the passing shower. They had opened their wide blue and purple umbrellas : these latter made huge disks of color reflected in the glass of the wet macadam. The women had turned their black alpaca and cashmere skirts inside out, tucking the edges about their stout hips; beneath the wide vivid circles of the dripping umbrellas these brilliantly colored under-petticoats showed a liberal revelation of scarlet hose and thick ankles sunk in the freshly polished black sabots. The men's cobalt-blue blouses and their peaked felt hats spotted the landscape with contrasting notes and outlines.

After the last peaked hat had disappeared into the farm enclosures, we and the wet landscape had the rain to ourselves. The trees now were spectral shapes ; they could not be relied on as companions. Even the gardens and grain lands were mysteriously veiled, so close rolled the mists to our carriage-wheels. Beyond, at the farthest end of the road, these mists had formed themselves into a solid, compact mass.

The clouds out yonder, far ahead, seemed to be enwrapping some part of earth that had lanced itself into the sky.

After a little the eyes unconsciously watched those distant woolly masses. There was a something beyond, faint, vague, impalpable as yet, which the rolling mists begirt as sometimes they cincture an Alpine needle. Even as the thought

came, a sudden lifting of the gray mass showed
the point of a high uplifted pinnacle. The point
thereof pricked the sky. Then the wind, like a
strong hand, swept the clouds into a mantle, and
we saw the strange spectacle no more.

For several miles our way led us through a
dim, phantasmal landscape. All the outlines were
blurred. Even the rain was a veil; it fell between
us and the nearest hedgerows as if it had been a
curtain. The jingling of Poulette's bell-collar and
the gurgle of the water rushing in the gulleys—
these were the only sounds that fell upon the ear.

Still the clouds about that distant mass curled
and rolled; they were now breaking, now re-forming—as if some strange and wondrous thing were
hanging there—between heaven and earth.

It was still far out, the mass; even the lower
mists were not resting on any plain of earth. They
also were moved by something that moved beneath
them, as a thick cloak takes the shape and motion of the body it covers. Still we advanced,
and still the great mountain of cloud grew and
grew. And then there came a little lisping, hissing sound. It was the kiss of the sea as it met
some unseen shore. And on our cheeks the sea-
wind blew, soft and salty to the lips.

The mass was taking shape and outline. The
mists rolled along some wide, broad base that
rested beneath the sea, and skyward they clasped
the apexal point of a pyramid.

This pyramid in the sky was Mont St. Michel.

With its feet in the sea, and its head vanishing
into infinity—here, at last, was this rock of rocks,

caught, phantom-like, up into the very heavens
above.

It loomed out of the spectral landscape—itself
the superlative spectre; it took its flight upward
as might some genius of beauty enrobed in a
shroud of mystery.

Such has it been to generations of men. Beautiful, remote, mysterious! With its altars and its
shrines, its miracle of stone carved by man on
those other stones hewn by the wind and the tem-
pest, Mont St. Michel has ever been far more a
part of heaven than a thing of earth.

Then, for us, the clouds suddenly lifted, as, for
modern generations of men, the mists of superstition have also rolled themselves away.

MONT S·T. MICHEL:

AN INN ON A ROCK:

MONT SAINT MICHEL.

CHAPTER XXIX.

WE were being tossed in the air like so many balls. A Normandy *char-à-banc* was proving itself no respecter of nice distinctions in conditions in life. It phlipped, dashed, and rolled us about with no more concern than if it were taking us to market to be sold by the pound.

For we were on the *grève*. The promised rivers were before us.

So was the Mont, spectral no longer, but nearing with every plunge forward of our sturdy young Percheron. Locomotion through any new or untried medium is certain to bring with the experiment a dash of elation. Now, driving through water appears to be no longer the fashion in our fastidious century; someone might get a wetting, possibly, has been the conclusion of the prudent. And thus a very innocent and exciting bit of fun has been gradually relegated among the lost arts of pleasure.

We were taking water as we had never taken it before, and liking the method. We were as wet as ducks, but what cared we? We were being deluged with spray; the spume of the sea was spurting in our faces with the force of a strong wet breeze, and still we liked it. Besides, driving thus into the white foam of the waters, over the sand ridges, across the downs, into the wide plains of wet mud, this was the old classical way of going up to the Mont. Surely, what had been found good enough as a pathway for kings and saints and pilgrims should be good enough for two lovers of old-time methods. The dike yonder was built for those who believe in the devil of haste, and for those who also serve him faithfully.

Someone else besides ourselves was enjoying our drive through the waves. Our gay young Normandy driver seemed to find an exquisite relish in the spectacle of our wet faces and unstable figures. He could not keep his eyes off us; they fairly glistened with the dew of his enjoyment. Two ladies pitched and rolled about, exactly as if they were peasants, and laughing as if they were children—this was a spectacle and a keen appreciation of a joke that brought joy to a rustic blouse.

" Ah—ah! mesdames!" he cried, exultingly, between the gasps of his own laughter, as he tossed his own fine head in the air, sitting on his rude bench, covered with sheepskin, as if it had been

an armchair. "Ah, ah! mesdames, you didn't expect this, *hein?* You hoped for a landau, and
feathers and cushions, perhaps? But soft feathers and springs are not for the *grève.*"

"Is it dangerous? are there deep holes?"

"Oh, the holes, they are as nothing. It is the
quicksands we fear. But it is only a little danger, and danger makes the charm of travel, is it
not so, my ladies? Adventure, that is what one
travels for! *Hui!* Fend l'Air!"

It had occurred to us before that we had been
uncommonly lucky in our coachmen, as well as
in the names of the horses, that had brightened
our journey. In spite of Juliet, whose disdain of
the virtue or the charm that lies in a name is no
more worthy of respect than is any lover's opinion
when in the full-orbed foolishness of his lunacy,
I believe names to be a very effective adjunct to
life's scenic setting. Most of the horses we had
had along these Normandy high-roads, had answered to names that had helped to italicize the
features of the country. Could Poulette, the sturdy
little mare, with whom only an hour ago we had
parted forever, have been given a better sobri-
quet by which to have identified for us the fat
landscape? And now here was Fend l'Air proving
good his talent for cleaving through space, whatever of land or sea lay in his path.

"And he merits his name, my lady," his driver
announced with grave pride, as he looked at the
huge haunches with a loving eye. "He can go,
oh, but as the wind! It is he who makes of the
crossing but as if it were nothing!"

The crossing! That was the key-note of the
way the coast spoke of the Mont. The rock out
yonder was a country apart, a bit of land or stone
the shore claimed not, had no part in, felt to be as
remote as if it were a foreign province. At Genets the village spoke of the Mont as one talks of
a distant land. Even the journey over the sands
was looked upon with a certain seriousness. A
starting forth was the signal for the village to as-
semble about the *char-à-banc's* wheels. Quite a
large company for a small village to muster was
grouped about our own vehicle, to look on gravely
as we mounted to the rude seat within. The villagers gave us their "*bonjours*" with as much fervor as if we were starting forth on a sea voyage.

"You will have a good crossing!" cackled one
of the old men, nodding toward the peak in the
sky.

"The sands may be wet, but they are firm already!" added a huge peasant—the fattest man in
all the canton, whisperingly confided the landlady,
as one proud of possessing a village curiosity.

"*Hui*, Fend l'Air! *attention, toi!*" Fend l'Air
tossed his fine mane, and struck out with a will
over the cobbles. But his driver was only posing for the assembled village. He was in no real
haste; there was a fresh voice singing yonder in
his mother's tavern; the sentimentalist in him
was on edge to hear the end of the song.

"Do you hear that, mesdames? There's no such
singing as that out of Paris. One must go to a
café——"

"*Allons, toi!*" shrieked his mother's voice, as

her face darkened. "Do you think these ladies want to spend the night on the *grève? Dépêches-toi, vaurien!*" And she gave the wheels a shove with her strong hand, whereat all the village laughed. But the good-for-nothing son made no haste as the song went on—

> " *Le bon vin me fait dormir,*
> *L'amour me réveil——*"

He continued to cock his head on one side and to let his eyes dream a bit.

Within, a group of peasants was gathered about the inn table. There were some young girls seated among the blouses; one of them, for the hour that we had sat waiting for Fend l'Air to be captured and harnessed, had been singing songs of questionable taste in a voice of such contralto sweetness as to have touched the heart of a bishop. "Some young girls from the factories at Avranches, mesdames, who come here Sundays to get a bit of fresh air; *Dieu sait si elles en ont besoin, pauvres enfants!*" was the landlady's charitable explanation. It appeared to us that the young ladies from Avranches were more in need of a moral than a climatic change. But then, we also charitably reflected, it makes all the difference in the world, in these nice questions of taste and morality, whether one has had as an inheritance a past of Francis I. and a Rabelais, or of Calvin and a Puritan conscience.

The geese on the green downs, just below the village, had clearly never even heard of Calvin;

they were luxuriating in a series of plunges into
the deep pools in a way to prove complete igno-
rance of nice sabbatarian laws.

With our first toss upon the downs, a world of
new and fresh experiences began. Genets was
quite right; the Mont over yonder was another
country; even at the very beginning of the
journey we learned so much. This breeze blowing in from the sea, that had swept the ramparts
of the famous rock, was a double extract of the
sea-essence; it had all the salt of the sea and the
aroma of firs and wild flowers; its lips had not
kissed a garden in high air without the perfume
lingering, if only to betray them. Even this strip
of meadow marsh had a character peculiar to itself;
half of it belonged to earth and half to the sea.
You might have thought it an inland pasture,
with its herds of cattle, its flocks of sheep, and its
colonies of geese—patrolled by ragged urchins.
But behold, somewhere out yonder the pasture was
lost in high sea-waves; ships with bulging sails
replaced the curve of the cattle's sides, and instead of bending necks of sheep, there were sea-
gulls swooping down upon the foamy waves.

As the incarnation of this dual life of sea and
land, the rock stands. It also is both of the sea
and the land. Its feet are of the waters—rocks
and stones the sea-waves have used as playthings
these millions of years. But earth regains possession as the rocks pile themselves into a mountain. Even from this distance, one can see the
moving arms of great trees, the masses of yellow
flower-tips that dye the sides of the stony hill,

and the strips of green grass here and there. So
much has nature done for this wonderful pyramid
in the sea. Then man came and fashioned it to
his liking. He piled the stones at its base into
titanic walls; he carved about its sides the rounded breasts of bastions; he piled higher and higher
up the dizzy heights a medley of palaces, con-
vents, abbeys, cloisters, to lay at the very top the
fitting crown of all, a jewelled Norman-Gothic
cathedral.

Earth and man have thrown their gauntlet down
to the sea—this rock is theirs, they cry to the
waves and the might of oceans. And the sea
laughs—as strong men laugh when boys are
angry or insistent. She has let them build and
toil, and pray and fight; it is all one to her what
is done on the rock — whether men carve its
stones into lace, or rot and die in its dungeons;
it is all the same to her whether each spring the
daffodils creep up within the crevices and the
irises nod to them from the gardens.

It is all one to her. For twice a day she re-
captures the Mont. She encircles it with the
strong arm of her tides; with the might of her
waters she makes it once more a thing of the sea.

The tide was rising now.

The fringe of the downs had dabbled in the
shoals till they had become one. We had left
behind the last of the shepherd lads, come out to
the edge of the land to search for a wandering
kid. We were all at once plunging into high
water. Our road was sunk out of sight; we were
driving through waves as high as our cart-wheels.

Fend l'Air was shivering; he was as a-tremble as
a woman. The height of the rivers was not to his
liking.

"*Sacré fainéant!*" yelled his owner, treating
the tremor to a mighty crack of the whip.

"Is he afraid?"

"Yes—when the water is as high as that, he is
always afraid. Ah, there he is—*diantre*, but he took
his time!" he growled, but the growl was set in
the key of relief. He was pointing toward a figure that was leaping toward us through the water.
"It is the guide!" he added, in explanation.

The guide was at Fend l'Air's shoulder. Very
little of him was above water, but that little was
as brown as an Egyptian. He was puffing and
blowing like unto a porpoise. In one hand he
held a huge pitchfork—the trident of this watery
Mercury.

"Shall I conduct you?" he asked, dipping the
trident as if in salute, into the water, as he still
puffed and gasped.

"If you please," as gravely responded our driver. For though up to our cart-wheels and breasts
in deep water, the formalities were not to be dis-
pensed with, you understand. The guide placed
himself at once in front of Fend l'Air, whose
shivers as quickly disappeared.

"You see, mesdames—the guide gives him courage—and he now knows no fear," cried out with
pride our whip on the outer bench. "And what
news, Victor—is there any?" It was of the Mont
he was asking. And the guide replied, taking an
extra plunge into deep water:

"Oh, not much. There's to be a wedding to-
morrow and a pilgrimage the next day. Madame
Poulard has only a handful as yet. *Ces dames*
descend doubtless at Madame Poulard's—*celle qui
fait les omelettes ?* " The ladies were ignorant as
yet of the accomplishments of the said landlady ;
they had only heard of her beauty.

" *C'est elle,*" gravely chorussed the guide and
the driver, both nodding their heads as their
eyes met. " *Fameuse, sa beauté, comme son omelette,*"
as gravely added our driver.

The beauty of this lady and the fame of her omelette were very sobering, apparently, in their effects on the mind ; for neither guide nor driver
had another word to say.

Still the guide plunged into the rivers, and Fend
l'Air followed him. Our cart still pitched and
tossed—we were still rocked about in our rough
cradle. But the sun, now freed from the banks of
clouds, was lighting our way with a great and sudden glory. And for the rest of our watery journey we were conscious only of that lighting. Behind the Mont, lay a vast sea of saffron. But it
was in the sky ; against it the great rock was as
black as if the night were upon it. Here and
there, through the curve of a flying buttress, or the
apertures of a pierced parapet, gay bits of this
yellow world were caught and framed. The sea
lay beneath like a quiet carpet ; and over this carpet ships and sloops swam with easy gliding
motion, with sails and cordage dipped in gold.
The smaller craft, moored close to shore, seemed
transfigured as in a fog of gold. And nearer still

were the brown walls of the Mont making a great
shadow, and in the shadow the waters were as
black as the skin of an African. In the shoals
there were lovely masses of turquoise and pal-
est green; for here and there a cloudlet passed,
to mirror their complexions in the translucent
pools.

But Fend l'Air's hoofs had struck a familiar
note. His iron shoes were clicking along the
macadam of the dike. There was a rapid dashing
beneath the great walls; a sudden night of darkness as we plunged through an open archway
into a narrow village street; a confused impression of houses built into side-walls; of machicolated gateways; of rocks and roof-tops tumbling
about our ears; and within the street was sounding the babel of a shrieking troop of men and
women. Porters, peasants, lads, and children were
clamoring about our cart-wheels like unto so many
jackals. The bedlam did not cease as we stopped
before a wide, brightly-lit open doorway.

Then through the doorway there came a tall,
finely - featured brunette. She made her way
through the yelling crowd as a duchess might
cleave a path through a rabble. She was at the
side of the cart in an instant. She gave us a bow
and smile that were both a welcome and an act of
appropriation. She held out a firm, soft, brown
hand. When it closed on our own, we knew it to
be the grasp of a friend, and the clasp of one who
knew how to hold her world. But when she
spoke the words were all of velvet, and her voice
had the cadence of a caress.

"I have been watching you, *chères dames*—crossing the *grève*, but how wet and weary you must be! Come in by the fire, it is ablaze now—I have been feeding it for you!" And once more the beautifully curved lips parted over the fine teeth, and the exceeding brightness of the dark eyes smiled and glittered in our own. The caressing voice still led us forward, into the great gay kitchen; the touch of skilful, discreet fingers undid wet cloaks and wraps; the soft charm of a lovely and gracious woman made even the penetrating warmth of the huge fire-logs a secondary feature of our welcome. To those who have never crossed a *grève;* who have had no jolting in a Normandy *char-à-banc;* who, for hours, have not known the mixed pleasures and discomfort of being a part of sea-rivers; and who have not been met at the threshold of an Inn on a Rock by the smiling welcome of Madame Poulard—all such have yet a pleasant page to read in the book of travelled experience.

Meanwhile somewhere, in an inner room, things sweet to the nostrils were cooking. Maids were tripping up and down stairs with covered dishes; there was the pleasant clicking in the ear of the lids of things; dishes or pans or jars were being lifted. And more delicious to the ear than even the promise to starving mouths of food and of red wine to the lip, was the continuing music of madame's voice, as she stood over us purring with content at seeing her travellers drying and being thoroughly warmed. "The dinner-bell must soon be rung, dear ladies; I delayed it as long as I

dared—I gauged your progress across from the
terrace—I have kept all my people waiting; for
your first dinner here must be hot! But now it
rings! Shall I conduct you to your rooms?"

I have no doubt that, even without this brunette
beauty, with her olive cheek and her comely figure as guides, we should have gone the way she
took us in a sort of daze. One cannot pass under machicolated gateways; rustle between the
walls of fourteenth century fortifications; climb a
stone stairway that begins in a watch-tower and
ends in a rampart, with a great sea view, and with
the breadth of all the land shoreward; walk calmly
over the top of a king's gate, with the arms of a
bishop and the shrine of the Virgin beneath one's
feet; and then, presently, begin to climb the side
of a rock in which rude stone steps have been cut,
till one lands on a miniature terrace, to find a pre-
posterously sturdy-looking house affixed to a ridiculous ledge of rock that has the presumption
to give shelter to a hundred or more travellers—
ground enough, also, for rows of plane-trees, for
honeysuckles, and rose-vine, with a full coquettish equipment of little tables and iron chairs—
no such journey as that up a rock was ever taken
with entirely sober eyes.

Although her people were waiting below, and
the dinner was on its way to the cloth, Madame
Poulard had plenty of time to give to the beauty
about her. How fine was the outlook from the top
of the ramparts! What a fresh sensation, this
of standing on a terrace in mid-air and looking
down on the sea and across to the level shores!

The rose-vines—we found them sweet—*tiens*—one of the branches had fallen—she had full time to re-adjust the loosened support. And "Marianne, give these ladies their hot water, and see to their bags—" even this order was given with courtesy. It was only when the supple, agile figure had left us to fly down the steep rock-cut steps; when it shot over the top of the gateway and slid with the grace of a lizard into the street far below us, that we were made sensible of there having been any especial need of madame's being in haste.

That night, some three hours later, a picturesque group was assembled about this same supple figure. A pretty and somewhat unique ceremony was about to take place.

It was the ceremony of the lighting of the lanterns.

In the great kitchen, in the dance of the firelight and the glow of the lamps, some seven or eight of us were being equipped with Chinese lanterns. This of itself was an engaging sight. Madame Poulard was always gay at this performance—for it meant much innocent merriment among her guests, and with the lighting of the last lantern her own day was done. So the brilliant eyes flashed with a fresh fire, and the olive cheek glowed anew. All the men and women laughed as children sputter laughter, when they are both pleased and yet a little ashamed to show their pleasure. It was so very ridiculous, this journey up a rock with a Chinese lantern! But just because it was ridiculous, it was also delightful. One—two—three—seven—eight—they were

all lit. The last male guest had touched his cap
to madame, exchanging the "*bonne nuit*" a man
only gives to a pretty woman, and that which a
woman returns who feels that her beauty has received its just meed of homage; madame's figure
stood, still smiling, a radiant benedictory presence, in the doorway, with the great glow of the
firelight behind her; the last laugh echoed down
the street—and behold, darkness was upon us!

The street was as black as a cavern. The strip
of sky and the stars above seemed almost day, by
contrast. The great arch of the Porte du Roi en-
gulphed us, and then, slowly groping our way, we
toiled up the steps to the open ramparts. Here
the keen night air swept rudely through our
cloaks and garments; the sea tossed beneath the
bastions like some restless tethered creature, that
showed now a gray and now a purple coat, and
the stars were gold balls that might drop at any
instant, so near they were.

The men shivered and buttoned their coats,
and the women laughed, a trifle shrilly, as they
grasped the floating burnous closer about their
faces and shoulders.

And the lanterns' beams danced a strange dance
on the stone flagging.

Once more we were lost in darkness. We were
passing through the old guard-house. And then
slowly, more slowly than ever, the lanterns were
climbing the steps cut in the rock. Hands groped
in the blackness to catch hold of the iron railing;
the laughter had turned into little shouts and
gasps for help. And then one of the lanterns

played a treacherous trick; it showed the backs of two figures groping upward together—about one of the girlish figures a man's arm was flung. As suddenly the noise of the cries was stilled.

The lanterns played their fitful light on still other objects. They illumined now a vivid yellow shrub; they danced upon a roof-top; they flooded, with a sudden circlet of brilliance, the awful depths below of the swirling waters and of rocks that were black as a bottomless pit.

Then the terrace was reached. And the lanterns danced a last gay little dance among the roses and the vines before, Pouffe! Pouffe! and behold! they were all blown out.

Thus it was we went to bed on the Mont.

CHAPTER XXX.

To awake on a hill-top at sea.
This was what morning
brought.

Crowd this hill with
houses plastered to the sides
of rocks, with great walls
girdling it, with tiny gardens
lodged in crevices, and with
a forest tumbling seaward.
Let this hill yield you a
town in which to walk, with a street of many-
storied houses; with other promenades along ramparts as broad as church aisles; with dungeons,
cloisters, halls, guard-rooms, abbatial gateways,
and a cathedral whose flying buttresses seemed
to spring from mid-air and to end in a cloud—
such was the world into which we awoke on the
heights of Mont St. Michel.

The verdict of the shore on the hill had been a
just one; this world on a rock was a world apart.
This hill in the sea had a detached air—as if,
though French, at heart a true Gaul, it had had
from the beginning of things a life of adventure
peculiar to itself. The shore, at best, had been

only a foster-mother; the hill was the true child
of the sea. Since its birth it has had a more or
less enforced separateness, in experience, from the
country to which it belonged. Whether temple
or fortress, whether forest-clad in virginal fierceness of aspect, or subdued into beauty by the
touch of man's chisel, its destiny has ever been
the same—to suffice unto itself—to be, in a word,
a world in miniature.

The Mont proved by its appearance its history
in adventure; it had the grim, grave, battered
look that comes only to features, whether of rock
or of more plastic human mould—that have been
carved by the rough handling of experience.

It is the common habit of hills and mountains,
as we all know, to turn disdainful as they grow
skyward; they only too eagerly drop, one by one,
the things by which man has marked the earth for
his own. To stand on a mountain top and to go
down to your grave are alike, at least in this—
that you have left everything, except yourself, behind you. But it is both the charm and the triumph of Mont St. Michel, that it carries so much
of man's handiwork up into the blue fields of air;
this achievement alone would mark it as unique
among hills. It appears as if for once man and
nature had agreed to work in concert to produce a
masterpiece in stone. The hill and the archi-
tectural beauties it carries aloft, are like a taunt
flung out to sea and to the upper heights of air;
for centuries they appear to have been crying
aloud, "See what we can do, against your tempests
and your futile tides—when we try."

On that particular morning, the taunt seemed more like an epithalamium—such marriage-lines did sea and sky appear to be reading over the glistening face of the rock. June had pitched its tent of blue across the seas ; all the world was blue, except where the sun smote it into gold. To eyes in love with beauty, what a world at one's feet ! Beneath that azure roof, toward the west, was the world of water, curling, dimpling, like some human thing charged with the conscious joy of dancing in the sun. Shoreward, the more stable earth was in the Moslem's ideal posture—that of perpetual prostration. The Brittany coast was a long, flat, green band; the rocks of Cancale were brown, but scarcely higher in point of elevation than the sand-hills ; the Normandy forests and orchards were rippling lines that focussed into the spiral of the Avranches cathedral spires ; floating between the two blues, hung the aerial shapes of the Chaunsey and the Channel Islands ; and nearer, along the coast-line, were the fringing edges of the shore, broken with shoals and shallows—earth's fingers, as it were, touching the sea —playing, as Coleridge's Abyssinian maid fingered the dulcimer, that music that haunts the poet's ear.

We were seated at the little iron tables, on the terrace. We were sipping our morning coffee, beneath the plane-trees. The terrace, a foot beyond our coffee-cups instantly began its true career as a precipice. We, ourselves, seemed to have begun as suddenly our own flight heavenward—on such astonishing terms of intimacy were we with the sky. The clapping close to our ears

of large-winged birds; the swirling of the circling
sea-gulls; the amazing nearness of the cloud
drapery—all this gave us the sense of being in a
new world, and of its being a strangely pleasant
one.

Suddenly a cock's crow, shrill and clear, made
us start from the luxurious languor of our contentment; for we had scarcely looked to find poultry
on this Hill of Surprises. Turning in the direction
of the homely, familiar note, we beheld a garden.
In this garden walked the cock—a two-legged
gentleman of gorgeous plumage. If abroad for
purely constitutional purposes, the crowing chanticleer must be forced to pass the same objects
many times in review. Of all infinitesimal, micro-
scopic gardens, this one, surely, was a model in
minuteness. Yet it was an entirely self-respect-
ing little garden. It was not much larger than a
generous-sized pocket-handkerchief; yet how much
talent—for growing—may be hidden in a yard of
soil—if the soil have the right virtue in it. Here
were two rocks forming, with a fringe of cliff, a tri-
angle : in that tri-cornered bit of earth a lively
crop of growing vegetables was offering flattering signs of promise to the owner's eye. Where
all land runs aslant, as all land does on this Mont,
not an inch was to be wasted ; up the rocks peach
and pear-split trees were made to climb—and why
should they not, since everything else—since man
himself must climb from the moment he touches
the base of the hill ?

Following the cock's call, came the droning
sweetness of bees; the rose and the honeysuckle

vines were loading the morning air with the perfume of their invitations. Then a human voice
drowned the bees' whirring, and a face as fresh
and as smiling as the day stood beside us. It was
the voice and the face of Madame Poulard, on the
round of her morning inspections. Our table and
the radiant world at her feet were included in this,
her line of observations.

"*Ah, mesdames, comme vous savez bien vous
placer !*—how admirably you understand how to
place yourselves ! Under such a sky as this—before such a spectacle—one should be in the front
row, as at a theatre !"

And that was the beginning of our deeds finding
favor in the eyes of Madame Poulard.

It was our happy fate to drink many a morning
cup of coffee at those little iron tables; to have
many a prolonged chat with the charming landlady of the famous inn; to become as familiar
with the glories and splendors of the historical
hill as with the habits and customs of the world
that came up to view them.

For here our journey was to end.

The comedy of life, as it had played itself out
in Normandy inns, was here, in this Inn on a Rock,
to give us a series of farewell performances. On
no other stage, we were agreed, could the versatile
French character have had as admirable and picturesque a setting; and surely, on no other bit of
French soil could such an astonishing and amazing variety of types be assembled for a final appearance, as came up, day after day, to make the
tour of the Mont.

To the shore, and for the whole of the near-lying Breton and Norman rustic world, the Mont is still the Hill of Delight. It is their Alp, their shrine, the tenth wonder of the world, a prison, a palace, and a temple still. In spite of Parisian changes in religious fashions, the blouse is still devout; for curiosity is the true religion of the provincial, and all love of adventure did not die out with the Crusades.

Therefore it is that rustic France along this coast still makes pilgrimages to the shrine of the Archangel St. Michael. No marriage is rightly arranged which does not include a wedding-journey across the *grève;* no nuptial breakfast is aureoled with the true halo of romance which is eaten elsewhere than on these heights in mid-air. The young come to drink deep of wonders; the old, to refresh the depleted fountains of memory; and the tourist, behold, he is as a plague of locusts let loose upon the defenceless hill!

After a fortnight's sojourn, Charm and I held many a grave consultation; close observation of this world that climbed the heights had bred certain strange misgivings. What was it this world of sight-seers came up to the Mont for to see? Was it to behold the great glories thereof, or was it, oh, human eye of man! to look on the face of a charming woman? It was impossible, after sojourning a certain time upon the hill, not to concede that there were two equally strong centres of attractions, that drew the world hitherward. One remained, indeed, gravely suspended between the doubt and the fear, as to which of

these potential units had the greater pull, in
point of actual attraction. The impartial histo-
rian, given to a just weighing of evidence, would
have been startled to find how invariably the
scales tipped; how lightly an historical Mont,
born of a miracle, crowned by the noblest buildings, a pious Mecca for saints and kings innumerable, shot up like feathers in lightness
when over-weighted by the modern realities of
a perfectly appointed inn, the cooking and eating of an omelette of omelettes, and the all-con-
quering charms of Madame Poulard. The fog of
doubt thickened as, day after day, the same scenes
were enacted; when one beheld all sorts and con-
ditions of men similarly affected; when, again
and again, the potentiality in the human magnet
was proved true. Doubt turned to conviction, at
the last, that the holy shrine of St. Michael had,
in truth, been violated; that the Mont had been
desecrated; that the latter exists now solely as a
setting for a pearl of an inn; and that within the
shrine—it is Madame Poulard herself who fills
the niche!

The pilgrims come from darkest Africa and the
sunlit Yosemite, but they remain to pray at the
Inn of the Omelette. Yonder, on the *grèves*, as
we ourselves had proved, one crosses the far seas
and one is wet to the skin, only to hear the
praises sung of madame's skill in the handling of
eggs in a pan; it was for this the lean guide
strides before the pilgrim tourist, and that he
dippeth his trident in the waters. At the great
gates of the fortifications the pilgrim descends,

and behold, a howling chorus of serving-people
take up the chant of : " *Chez Madame Poulard, à
gauche, à la renommée de l'omelette !* " The inner
walls of the town lend themselves to their last
and best estate, that of proclaiming the glory of
" *L'Omelette.*" Placards, rich in indicative illus-
trations of hands all forefingers, point, with a
directness never vouchsafed the sinner eager to
find the way to right and duty, to the inn of
" *L'Incomparable, la Fameuse Omelette !* " The pilgrims meekly descend at that shrine. They bow
low to the worker of the modern miracle ; they
pass with eager, trembling foot, into the inner
sanctorum, to the kitchen, where the presiding
deity receives them with the grace of a queen and
the simplicity of a saint.

Life on the Mont, as we soon found, resolved
itself into this—into so arranging one's day as to
be on hand for the great, the eventful hour. In
point of fact there were two such hours in the Mont
St. Michel day. There was the hour of the cooking of the omelette. There was always the other
really more tragic hour of the coming across the
dike of the huge lumbering omnibuses. For you
see, that although one may be beautiful enough
to compete successfully against dead-and-gone
saints, against worn-out miracles, and wonders
in stone, human nature, when it is alive, is human nature still. It is the curse of success, the
world over, to arouse jealousy ; and we all have
lived long enough to know that jealousy's evil-
browed offspring are named Hate and Competition. Up yonder, beyond the Porte du Roi, ri-

valry has set up a counter-shrine, with a competing saint, with all the hateful accessories of a pretty face, a younger figure, and a graceful if less skilled aptitude in the making of omelettes in public.

The hour of the coming in of the coaches was therefore a tragic hour.

On the arrival of the coaches Madame was at her post long before the pilgrims came up to her door. Being entirely without personal vanity— since she felt her beauty, her cleverness, her grace, and her charm to be only a part of the capital of the inn trade—a higher order of the stock in trade, as it were—she made it a point to look handsomer on the arrival of coaches than at any other time. Her cheeks were certain to be rosier; her bird's head was always carried a trifle more takingly, perched coquettishly sideways, that the caressing smile of welcome might be the more personal; and as the woman of business, lining the saint, so to speak, was also present, into the deep pockets of the blue-checked apron, the calculating fingers were thrust, that the quick counting of the incoming guests might not be made too obvious an action.

After such a pose, to see a pilgrim escape! To see him pass by, unmoved by that smile, turning his feelingless back on the true shrine! It was enough to melt the stoutest heart. Madame's welcome of the captured, after such an affront, was set in the minor key; and her smile was the smile of a suffering angel.

"*Cours, mon enfant*, run, see if he descends or if

he pushes on; tell him *I* am Madame Poulard!"
This, a low command murmured between a hundred orders, still in the minor key, would be
purred to Clémentine, a peasant in a cap, exceeding fleet of foot, and skilled in the capture of
wandering sheep.

And Clémentine would follow that stray pilgrim; she would attack him in the open street;
would even climb after him, if need be, up the
steep rock-steps, till, proved to be following
strange gods, he would be brought triumphantly
back to the kitchen-shrine, by Clémentine, puffing, but exultant.

"Ah, monsieur, how could you pass us by?"
madame's soft voice would murmur reproachfully
in the pilgrim's ear. And the pilgrim, abashed,
ashamed, would quickly make answer, if he were
born of the right parents: "*Chère* madame, how
was I to believe my eyes? It is ten years since I
was here, and you are younger, more beautiful
than ever! I was going in search of your mother!" at which needless truism all the kitchen
would laugh. Madame Poulard herself would find
time for one of her choicest smiles, although this
was the great moment of the working of the
miracle. She was beginning to cook the omelette.

The head-cook was beating the eggs in a great
yellow bowl. Madame had already taken her
stand at the yawning Louis XV. fireplace; she
was beginning gently to balance the huge *casserole*
over the glowing logs. And all the pilgrims were
standing about, watching the process. Now, the

group circling about the great fireplace was
scarcely ever the same: the pilgrims presented a
different face and garb day after day—but in point
of hunger they were as one man; they were each
and all as unvaryingly hungry as only tourists
could be, who, clamoring for food have the smell
of it in their nostrils, with the added ache of
emptiness gnawing within. But besides hunger,
each one of the pilgrims had brought with him a
pair of eyes; and what eyes of man can be pure
savage before the spectacle of a pretty woman
cooking, *for him*, before an open fire? Therefore
it was that still another miracle was wrought, that
of turning a famished mob into a buzzing swarm
of admirers.

"*Mais si, monsieur*, in this pan I can cook an
omelette large enough for you all: you will see.
Ah, madame, you are off already? Célestine!
Madame's bill, in the desk yonder. And you,
monsieur, you too leave us? *Deux cognacs?* Victor — *deux cognacs et une demi-tasse pour monsieur!*"

These and a hundred other answers and questions and orders, were uttered in a fluted voice or
in a tone of sharp command, by the miracle-worker,
as the pan was kept gently turning, and the eggs
were poured in at just the right moment—not one
of the pretty poses of head and wrist being forgotten. Madame Poulard, like all clever women who
are also pretty, had two voices: one was dedicated
solely to the working of her charms; this one was
soft, melodious, caressing, the voice of dove when
cooing; the other, used for strictly business pur-

poses, was set in the quick, metallic *staccato* tones
proper for such occasions.

The dove's voice was trolling its sweetness, as
she went on——

"Eggs, monsieur? How many I use? Ah, it
is in the season that counting the dozens becomes
difficult — seventy dozen I used one day last
year!"

"Seventy dozen!" the pilgrim - chorus ejaculated, their eyes growing the wider as their lips
moistened. For behold, the eggs were now cooked
to a turn; the long-handled pan was being lifted
with the effortless skill of long practice, the omelette was rolled out at just the right instant of
consistency, and was being as quickly turned into
its great flat dish.

There was a scurrying and scampering up
the wide steps to the dining-room, and a hasty
settling into the long rows of chairs. Presently
madame herself would appear, bearing the huge
dish. And the omelette—the omelette, unlike the
pilgrims, would be found to be always the same—
melting, juicy, golden, luscious, and above all
hot!

The noon-day table d'hôte was always a sight to
see. Many of the pilgrim-tourists came up to the
Mont merely to pass the day, or to stop the night;
the midday meal was therefore certain to be the
liveliest of all the repasts.

The cloth was spread in a high, white, sunlit
room. It was a trifle bare, this room, in spite of
the walls being covered with pictures, the windows with pretty draperies, and the spotless linen

that covered the long table. But all temples, however richly adorned, have a more or less unfurnished aspect; and this room served not only as the dining-table, but also as a foreshadowing of the apotheosis of Madame Poulard. Here were grouped together all the trophies and tributes of a grateful world; there were portraits of her charming brunette face signed by famous admirers; there were sonnets to her culinary skill and her charms as hostess, framed; these alternated with gifts of horned beasts that had been slain in her honor, and of stuffed birds who, in life, had beguiled the long winters for her with their songs. About the wide table, the snow of the linen reflected always the same picture; there were rows of little palms in flower-pots, interspersed with fruit dishes, with the butter pats, the almonds, and raisins, in their flat plates.

The rows of faces above the cloth were more varied. The four corners of the earth were sometimes to be seen gathered together about the breakfast-table. Frenchmen of the Midi, with the skin of Spaniards and the buzz of Tartarin's *ze ze* in their speech ; priests, lean and fat ; Germans who came to see a French stronghold as defenceless as a woman's palm ; the Italian, a rarer type, whose shoes, sufficiently pointed to prick, and whose choice for décolleté collars betrayed his nationality before his lisping French accent could place him indisputably beyond the Alps ; herds of English—of all types—from the aristocrat, whose open-air life had colored his face with the hues of a butcher, to the pale, ascetic clerk off on a two

weeks' holiday, whose bending at his desk had
given him the stoop of a scholar; with all these
were mixed hordes of French provincials, chiefly
of the *bourgeois* type, who singly, or in family
parties, or in the nuptial train of sons or daughters, came up to the shrine of St. Michel.

To listen to the chatter of these tourists was to
learn the last word of the world's news. As in the
days before men spoke to each other across conti-
nents, and the medium of cold type had made the
event of to-day the history of to-morrow, so these
pilgrims talked through the one medium that
alone can give a fact the real essence of freshness
—the ever young, the perdurably charming human voice. It was as good as sitting out a play
to watch the ever-recurring characteristics which
made certain national traits as marked as the
noses on the faces of the tourists. The question,
for example, on which side the Channel a pilgrim
was born, was settled five seconds after he was
seated at table. The way in which the butter was
passed was one test; the manner of the eating of
the famous omelette was another. If the tourist
were a Frenchman, the neat glass butter-dish was
turned into a visiting-card—a letter of introduction, a pontoon-bridge, in a word, hastily improvised to throw across the stream of conversation.
" *Madame* " (this to the lady at the tourist's left),
me permet-elle de lui offrir le beurre ? " Whereat madame bowed, smiled, accepted the golden balls as
if it were a bouquet, returning the gift, a few seconds later, by the proffer of the gravy dish. Between the little ceremony of the two bows and the

smiling *mercis* a tentative outbreak of speech ensued, which at the end of a half-hour, had spread
from *bourgeois* to countess, from curé to Parisian
boulevardier, till the entire side of the table was
in a buzz of talk. These genial people of a genial
land finding themselves all in search of the same
adventure, on top of a hill, away from the petty
world of conventionality, remembered that speech
was given to man to communicate with his fellows. And though neighbors for a brief hour,
how charming such an hour can be made when
into it are crowded the effervescence of personal
experience, the witty exchange of comment and
observation, and the agreeable conflict of thought
and opinion!

On the opposite side of the table, what a contrast! There the English were seated. There
was the silence of the grave. All the rigid figures sat as upright as posts. In front of these
severe countenances, the butter-plates remained
as fixtures; the passing of them to a neighbor
would be a frightful breach of good form—besides being dangerous. Such practices, in public
places, had been known to lead to things—to un-
speakable things—to knowing the wrong people,
to walks afterward with cads one couldn't shake
off, even to marriages with the impossible! Therefore it was that the butter remained a fixture.
Even between those who formed the same tourist-
party, there was rarely such an act of self-forget-
fulness committed as an indulgence in talk—in
public. The eye is the only active organ the
Englishman carries abroad with him; his talking

MONT SAINT MICHEL SNAIL-GATHERERS.

is done by staring. What fierce scowls, what dark
looks of disapproval, contempt, and dislike were
levelled at the chattering Frenchmen opposite.

Across the table, the national hate perpetuated
itself. It appears to be a test of patriotism,
this hatred between Frenchmen and Englishmen.
That strip of linen might easily have been the
Channel itself; it could scarcely more effectually
have separated the two nations. A whole comedy
of bitterness, a drama of rivalry, and a five-act
tragedy of scorn were daily played between the
Briton who sat facing the south, and the Frenchman who faced north. Both, as they eyed their
neighbor over the foam of their napkins, had the
Island in their eye!—the Englishman to flaunt its
might and glory in the teeth of the hated Gaul,
and the Frenchman to return his contempt for a
nation of moist barbarians.

Meanwhile, the omelette was going its rounds.
It was being passed at that moment to Monsieur
le Curé. He had been watching its progress with
glistening eye and moistening lips. Madame
Poulard, as she slipped the melting morsel beneath his elbow, had suddenly assumed the rôle
of the penitent. Her tone was a reminder of the
confessional, as of one who passed her masterpiece apologetically. She, forsooth, a sinner, to
have the honor of ministering to the carnal needs
of a son of the Church!

The son of the Church took two heaping spoonsful. His eye gave her, with his smile, the benediction of his gratitude, even before he had tasted of
the luscious compound.

"*Ah, chère madame! il n'y a que vous*—it is only you who can make the ideal omelette! I have tried, but Suzette has no art in her fingers; your receipt doesn't work away from the Mont!" And the good man sighed as he chuckled forth his praises.

He had come up to the hill in company with the two excellent ladies beside him, of his flock, to make a little visit to his brethren yonder, to the priests who were still here, wrecks of the once former flourishing monastery. He had come to see them, and also to gaze on La Merveille. It was a good five years since he had looked upon its dungeons and its lace-work. But after all, in his secret soul of souls, he had longed to eat of the omelette. *Dieu!* how often during those slow, quiet years in the little hamlet yonder on the plain, had its sweetness and lightness mocked his tongue with illusive tasting! Little wonder, therefore, that the good curé's praises were sweet in madame's ear, for they had the ring of truth— and of envy! And madame herself was only mortal, for what woman lives but feels herself uplifted by the sense of having found favor in the eyes of her priest?

The omelette next came to a halt between the two ladies of the curé's flock. These were two *bourgeoises* with the deprecating, mistrustful air peculiar to commonplace the world over. The walk up the steep stairs was still quickening their breath—their compressed bosoms were straining the hooks of their holiday woollen bodices—cut when they were of slenderer build. Their bon-

nets proclaimed the antique fashions of a past
decade; but the edge of their tongues had the
keenness that comes with daily practice—than
which none has been found surer than adoration
of one's pastor, and the invigorating gossip of
small towns.

These ladies eyed the omelette with a chilled
glance. Naturally, they could not see as much to
admire in Madame Poulard or in her dish as did
their curé. There was nothing so wonderful after
all in the turning of eggs over a hot fire. The
omelette!—after all, an omelette is an omelette!
Some are better—some are worse; one has one's
luck in cooking as in anything else. They had
come up to the Mont with their good curé to see
its wonders and for a day's outing; admiration of
other women had not been anticipated as a part of
the programme. *Tiens*—who was he talking to
now? To that tall blonde—a foreigner, a young
girl—*tiens*—who knows?—possibly an American—
those Americans are terrible, they say—bold, im-
modest, irreverant. And the two ladies' necks
were screwed about their over-tight collars, to
give Charm the verdict of their disapproval.

"Monsieur le Curé, they are passing you the
fish!" cried the stouter, more aggressive parish-
ioner, who boasted a truculent mustache.

"Monsieur le Curé, the roast is at your elbow!"
interpolated the second, with the more timid
voice of a second in action; this protector of the
good curé had no mustache, but her face was
mercifully protected by nature from a too-disturb-
ing combination of attractions by being plenti-

fully punctuated with moles from which sprouted
little tufts of hair. The rain of these ladies' interruption was incessant; but the curé was a man of
firm mind; their efforts to recapture his attention
were futile. For the music of Charm's foreign
voice was in his ear.

Worship of the cloth is not a national, it is a
more or less universal culte, I take it. It is in
the blood of certain women. Opposite the two
fussy, jealous *bourgeoises*, were others as importun-
ate and aggressive. They were of fair, lean, lank
English build, with the shifting eyes and the persistent courage which come to certain maidens in
whose lives there is but one fixed and certain fact
—that of having missed the matrimonial market.
The shrine of their devotions, and the present
citadel of their attack, was seated between them—
he also being lean, pale, high-arched of brow,
high anglican by choice and noticeably weak of
chin, in whose sable garments there was framed
the classical clerical tie.

To this curate Madame was now passing her
dish. She still wore her fine sweet smile, but
there was always a discriminating reserve in its
edge when she touched the English elbow. The
curate took his spoonful with the indifference of a
man who had never known the religion of good
eating. He put up his one eye-glass; it swept
Madame's bending face, its smile, and the yellow
glory floating beneath both. "Ah—h—ya—as—
an omelette!" The glass was dropped; he took a
meagre spoonful which he cut, presently, with his
knife. He turned then to his neighbors—to both

his neighbors! They had been talking of the
parish church on the hill.

"Ah-h-h, ya-as—lovely porch—isn't it ?"

" Oh, lovely—lovely ! " chorussed the two maidens, with assenting fervor. " *Were* you there this
morning ?" and they lifted eyes swimming with
the rapture of their admiration.

" Ya-as."

" Only fancy—our missing you! We were *both*
there ! "

" De-ar me! Really, were you?"

" *Could* you go this afternoon? I do want so to
hear your criticism of my drawing—I'm working
on the arch now."

"So sorry—can't—possibly, I promised what's
his name to go over to Tombelaine, don't you
know ! "

"Oh-h! We do so want to go to Tombelaine ! "

"Ah-h—do you, really? One ought to start a
little before the tide drops—they tell me!" and
the clerical eye, through its correctly adjusted
glass, looked into those four pleading eyes with
no hint of softening. The dish that was the masterpiece of the house, meanwhile, had been de-
spatched as if it were so much leather.

The omelette fared no better with the brides,
as a rule, than with the English curates. Such a
variety of brides as came up to the Mont! You
could have your choice, at the midday meal, of
almost any nationality, age, or color. The attempt among these bridal couples to maintain the
distant air of a finished indifference only made
their secret the more open. The British phlegm,

on such a journey, did not always serve as a con-
venient mask; the flattering, timid glance, the ripple of the tender whispers, and the furtive touching of fingers beneath the table, made even these
English couples a part of the great human marrying family; their superiority to their fellows would
return, doubtless, when the honey had dried out of
their moon. The best of our adventures into this
tender country were with the French bridal tourists; they were certain to be delightfully human.
As we had had occasion to remark before, they
were off, like ourselves, on a little voyage of discovery; they had come to make acquaintance with
the being to whom they were mated for life.
Various degrees of progress could be read in the
air and manner of the hearty young *bourgeoises*
and their paler or even ruddier partners, as they
crunched their bread or sipped their thin wine.
Some had only entered as yet upon the path of
inquiry; others had already passed the mile-stone
of criticism; and still others had left the earth
and were floating in full azure of intoxication.
Of the many wedding parties that sat down to
breakfast, we soon made the commonplace discovery that the more plebeian the company, the more
certain-orbed appeared to be the promise of happiness.

Some of the peasant weddings were noisy,
boisterous performances; but how gay were the
brides, and how bloated with joy the hardy,
knotty-handied grooms! These peasant wedding
guests all bore a striking family likeness; they
might easily all have been brothers and sisters,

whether they had come from the fields near Pontorson, or Cancale, or Dol, or St. Malo. The older the women, the prettier and the more gossamer were the caps; but the younger maidens were always delightful to look upon, such was the ripe vigor of their frames, and the liquid softness of eyes that, like animals, were used to wide sunlit fields and to great skies full of light. The bride, in her brand-new stuff gown, with a bonnet that recalled the bridal wreath only just laid aside, was also certain to be of a general universal type—with the broad hips, wide waist, muscular limbs, and the melting sweetness of lips and eyes that only abundant health and a rich animalism of nature bring to maidenhood.

Madame Poulard's air with this, her world, was as full of tact as with the tourists. Many of the older women would give her the Norman kiss, solemnly, as if the salute were a part of the ceremony attendant on the eating of a wedding breakfast at Mont St. Michel. There would be a three times' clapping of the wrinkled or the ruddy peasant cheeks against the sides of Madame Poulard's daintier, more delicately modelled face. Then all would take their seats noisily at table. It was Madame Poulard who then would bring us news of the party ; at the end of a fortnight, Charm and I felt ourselves to be in possession of the hidden and secret reasons for all the marrying that had been done along the coast that year. " *Tiens, ce n'est pas gai, la noce !* I must learn the reason ! " Madame would then flutter over the bridal breakfasters as a delicate-plumaged bird hovers over a

mass of stuff out of which it hopes to make a respectable meal. She presently would return to
murmur in a whisper, "it is a *mariage de raison.*
They, the bride and groom, love elsewhere, but
they are marrying to make a good partnership;
they are both hair-dressers at Caen. They have
bought a new and fine shop with their earnings."
Or it would be, "Look, madame, at that *jolie per-
sonne;* see how sad she looks. She is in love with
her cousin who sits opposite, but the groom is the
old one. He has a large farm and a hundred cows."
To look on such a trio would only be to make the
acquaintance anew of Sidonie and Risler and of
Froment Jeune. Such brides always had the wandering gaze of those in search of fresh horizons,
or of those looking already for the chance of escape. For such "unhappies," *ces malheureuses,* Madame's manner had an added softness and tenderness; she passed the frosted bridal cake as if it
were a propitiatory offering to the God of Hymen.
However melancholy the bride, the cake and Madame's caressing smiles wrought ever the same
spell; for an instant, at least, the newly-made
wife was in love with matrimony and with the
cake, accepting the latter with the pleased surprise of one who realizes that, at least, on one's
wedding day, one is a person of importance; that
even so far as Mont St. Michel the news of their
marriage had turned the ovens into a baking of
wedding-cakes. This was destined to be the first
among the deceptions that greeted such brides; for
there were hundreds of such cakes, alas! kept constantly on hand. They were the same—a glory of

sugar-mouldings and devices covering a mountain
of richness—that were sent up yearly at Christmas
time to certain mansard studios in the Latin quar-
ter, where the artist recipients, like the brides, eat
of the cake as did Adam when partaking of the
apple, believing all the woman told them!

There were other visitors who came up to the
Mont, not as welcome as were these tourist parties.

One morning, as we looked toward Pontorson,
a small black cloud appeared to be advancing
across the bay. The day was windy; the sky was
crowded with huge white mountains — round,
luminous clouds that moved in stately sweeps.
And the sea was the color one loves to see in an
earnest woman's eye, the dark-blue sapphire that
turns to blue-gray. This was a setting that made
that particular cloud, making such slow progress
across from the shore, all the more conspicuous.
Gradually, as the black mass neared the dike, it
began to break and separate; and we saw plainly
enough that the scattering particles were human
beings.

It was, in point of fact, a band of pilgrims; a
peasant pilgrimage was coming up to the Mont. In
wagons, in market carts, in *char-à-bancs*, in don-
key-carts, on the backs of monster percherons—
the pilgrimage moved in slow processional dignity across the dike. Some of the younger black
gowns and blue blouses attempted to walk across
over the sands; we could see the girls sitting
down on the edge of the shore, to take off their
shoes and stockings and to tuck up their thick

skirts. When they finally started they were like
unto so many huge cheeses hoisted on stilts. The
bare legs plunged boldly forward, keeping ahead
of the slower-moving peasant-lads; the girls'
bravery served them till they reached the fringe
of the incoming tide; not until their knees went
under water did they forego their venture. A
higher wave came in deluging the ones farthest
out; and then ensued a scampering toward the
dike and a climbing up of the stone embank-
ment. The old route across the sands, that had
been the only one known to kings and barons,
was not good enough for a modern Norman peasant. The religion of personal comfort has spread
even as far as the fields.

At the entrance gate a tremendous hubbub and
noise announced the arrival of the pilgrimage.
Wagons, carts, horses, and peasants were crowded
together as only such a throng is mixed in pilgrimages, wars, and fairs. Women were taking
down hoods, unharnessing the horses, fitting slats
into outsides of wagons, rolling up blankets, un-
packing from the *char-à-bancs* cooking utensils,
children, grain-bags, long columns of bread, and
hard-boiled eggs. For the women, darting hither
and thither in their blue petticoats, their pink
and red kerchiefs, and the stiff white Norman caps,
were doing all the work. The men appeared to
be decorative adjuncts, plying the Norman's gift
of tongue across wagon-wheels and over the back
of their vigorous wives and daughters. For them
the battle of the day was over; the hour of relax-
ation had come. The bargains they had made

along the route were now to be rehearsed, seasoned with a joke.

"*Allons, toi, on ne fait pas de la monnaie blanche
comme ça!*"

"*Je t'ai offert huit sous, tu sais, lapin!*"

"*Farceur, va-t'en——*"

"Come, are you never going to have done fool-
ing?" cried a tan-colored, wide-hipped peasant to
her husband, who was lounging against the wagon
pole, sporting a sprig of gentian pinned to his
blouse. He was fat and handsome; and his eye
proclaimed, as he was making it do heavy work at
long range at a cluster of girls descending from
an antique gig, that the knowledge of the same
was known unto him.

"That's right, growl ahead, thou, *tes beaux jours
sont passés*, but for me *l'amour, l'amour—que c'est
gai, que c'est frais!*" he half sung, half shouted.

The moving mass of color, the Breton caps, and
the Norman faces, the gold crosses that fell from
dented bead necklaces, the worn hooped earrings,
the clean bodices and home-spun skirts, streamed
out past our windows as we looked down upon
them. How pretty were some of the faces, of the
younger women particularly! and with what gay
spirits they were beginning their day! It had
begun the night before, almost; many of the
carts had been driven in from the forests beyond
Avranches; some of the Brittany groups had started the day before. But what can quench the fountain of French vivacity? To see one's world, surely,
there is nothing in that to tire one; it only excites
and exhilarates; and so a fair or market day, and

above all a pilgrimage, are better than balls, since they come more regularly; they are the peasant's opera, his Piccadilly and Broadway, club, drawing-room, Exchange, and parade, all in one.

A half-hour after a landing of the pilgrims at the outer gates of the fortifications, the hill was swarming with them. The single street of the town was choked with the black gowns and the cobalt-blue blouses. Before these latter took a turn at their devotions they did homage to Bacchus. Crowds of peasants were to be seen seated about the long, narrow inn-tables, lifting huge pewter tankards to bristling beards. Some of these taverns were the same that had fed and sheltered bands of pilgrims that are now mere handfuls of dust in country churchyards. Those sixteenth century pilgrims, how many of them, had found this same arched doorway of La Licorne as cool as the shade of great trees after the long hot climb up to the hill! What a pleasant face has the timbered façade of the Tête d'Or, and the Mouton Blanc, been to the weary-limbed! and how sweet to the dead lips has been the first taste of the acid cider!

Other aspects of the hill, on this day of the pilgrimage, made those older dead-and-gone bands of pilgrims astonishingly real. On the tops of bastions, in the clefts of the rocks, beneath the glorious walls of La Merveille, or perilously lodged on the crumbling cornice of a tourelle, numerous rude altars had been hastily erected. The crude blues and scarlets of banners were fluttering, like so many pennants, in the light breeze. Beneath

the improvised altar-roofs—strips of gay cloth
stretched across poles stuck into the ground—were
groups not often seen in these less fervent centuries. High up, mounted on the natural pulpit,
formed of a bit of rock, with the rude altar before
him with its bit of scarlet cloth covered with cheap
lace, stood or knelt the priest. Against the wide
blue of the open heaven his figure took on an imposing splendor of mien and an unmodern impressiveness of action. Beneath him knelt, with bowed
heads, the groups of the peasant-pilgrims; the
women, with murmuring lips and clasped hands,
their strong, deeply-seamed faces outlined with
the precision of a Francesco painting against the
gray background of a giant mass of wall or the
amazing breadth of a vast sea-view; children,
squat and chubby, with bulging cheeks starting
from the close-fitting French *bonnet;* and the peas-
ant-farmers, mostly of the older varieties, whose
stiffened or rheumatic knees and knotty hands
made their kneeling real acts of devotional zeal.
There were a dozen such altars and groups scattered over the perpendicular slant of the hill.
The singing of the choir-boys, rising like skylark
notes into the clear space of heaven, would be
floating from one rocky-nested chapel, while below, in the one beneath which we, for a moment,
were resting, there would be the groaning murmur
of the peasant groups in prayer.

All day little processions were going up and
down the steep stone steps that lead from fortified rock to parish church, and from the town to
the abbatial gateway. The banners and the choir-

boys, the priests in their embroideries and lace,
the peasants in cap and blouse, were incessantly
mounting and descending, standing on rock edges,
caught for an instant between a medley of perpendicular roofs, of giant gateways, and a long perspective of fortified walls, only to be lost in the
curve of a bastion, or a flying buttress, that, in
their turn, would be found melting into a distant
sea-view.

All the hours of a pilgrimage, we discovered, were
not given to prayer; nor yet is an incessant bowing at the shrine of St. Michel the sole other di-
version in a true pilgrim's round of pious devotions. Later on in this eventful day, we stumbled
on a somewhat startling variation to the peniten-
tial order of the performances. In a side alley,
beneath a friendly overhanging rock and two protecting roof-eaves, an acrobat was making her professional toilet. When she emerged to lay a worn
strip of carpet on the rough cobbles of the street,
she presented a pathetic figure in the gold of the
afternoon sun. She was old and wrinkled; the
rouge would no longer stick to the sunken cheeks;
the wrinkles were become clefts; the shrunken
but still muscular legs were clad in a pair of tights,
a very caricature of the silken webs that must once
have encased the poor old creature's limbs, for
these were knitted of the coarse thread the commonest peasant uses for the rough field stocking.
Over these obviously home-made coverings was a
single skirt of azure tarlatan, plentifully be-
sprinkled with golden stars. The gossamer skirt
and its spangles turned, for their *début*, a somer-

sault in the air, and the knitted tights took strange
leaps from the bars of a rude trapeze. The groups
of peasants were soon thicker about this spectacle
than they had gathered about the improvised altars. All the men who had passed the day in the
taverns came out at the sound of the hoarse cracked
voice of the aged acrobat. As she hurled her poor
old twisted shape from swinging bar to pole, she
cried aloud, "*Ah, messieurs, essayez ça seulement !*"
The men's hands, when she had landed on her feet
after an uncommonly venturous whirl of the blue
skirts in mid-air, came out of their deep pockets; but they seasoned their applause with coarse
jokes which they flung, with a cruel relish, into
the pitifully-aged face. A cracked accordion and a
jingling tambourine were played by two hardened-
looking ruffians, seated on their heels beneath a
window—a discordant music that could not drown
the noise of the peasants' derisive laughter. But
the latter's pennies rattled a louder jingle into the
ancient acrobat's tin cup than it had into the
priest's green-netted contribution-box.

"No, madame, as for us, we do not care for pilgrimages," was Madame Poulard's verdict on such
survivals of past religious enthusiasms. And she
seasoned her comments with an enlightening
shrug. "We see too well how they end. The
men go home dead drunk, the women are dropping with fatigue, *et les enfants même se grisent de
cidre !* No; pilgrimages are bad for everyone.
The priests should not allow them."

This was at the end of the day, after the black
and blue swarm had passed, a weary, uncertain-

footed throng, down the long street, to take its
departure along the dike. At the very end of the
straggling procession came the three acrobats;
they had begged, or bought, a drive across the
dike from some of the pilgrims. The lady of the
knitted tights, in her conventional skirts and womanly fichu, was scarcely distinguishable from the
peasant women who eyed her askance; though decently garbed now, they looked at her as if she
were some plague or vice walking in their midst.

The verdict of Madame Poulard seemed to be
the verdict of all Mont St. Michel. The whole
town was abroad that evening, on its doorsteps
and in its garden-beds, repairing the ravages committed by the band of the pilgrims. Never had
the town, as a town, been so dirty; never had the
street presented so shocking a collection of abom-
inations; never had flowers and shrubs been so
mercilessly robbed and plundered—these were the
comments that flowed as freely as the water that
was rained over the dusty cobbles, thick with refuse of luncheon and the shreds of torn skirts and
of children's socks.

At any hour of the day, of even an ordinary, un-
eventful day, to take a walk in the town is to
encounter a surprise at every turning. Would
you call it a town—this one straggling street that
begins in a King's gateway and ends—ah, that is
the point, just where does it end? I, for one, was
never once quite certain at just what precise point
this one single Mont St. Michel street stopped—
lost itself, in a word, and became something else.
That was also true of so many other things on the

hill; all objects had such an astonishing way of
suddenly becoming something else. A house, for
example, that you had passed on your upward
walk, had a beguiling air of sincerity. It had its
cellar beneath the street front like any other
properly built house; it continued its growth upward, showing the commonplace features of a door,
of so many windows—queerly spaced, and of an
amazing variety of shapes, but still unmistakably
windows. Then, assured of so much integrity of
character, you looked to see the roof covering the
house, and instead—like the eggs in a Chinese
juggler's fingers, that are turned in a jiffy into a
growing plant—behold the roof miraculously
transformed into a garden, or lost in a rampart,
or, with quite shameless effrontery, playing deserter, and serving as the basement of another and
still fairer dwelling. That was a sample of the
way all things played you the trick of surprise on
this hill. Stairways began on the cobbles of the
streets, only to lose themselves in a side wall; a
turn on the ramparts would land you straight into
the privacy of a St. Michelese interior, with an entire household, perchance, at the mercy of your
eye, taken at the mean disadvantage of morning
dishabille. As for doors that flew open where you
looked to find a bastion; or a school-house that
flung all the Michelese *voyous* over the tops of the
ramparts at play-time; or of fishwives that sprung,
as full-armed in their kit as Minerva from her sire's
brows, from the very forehead of fortified places;
or of beds and settees and wardrobes (surely no
Michelese has ever been able, successfully, to

maintain in secret the ghost of a family skeleton!) into which you were innocently precipitated on your way to discover the minutest of all cemeteries—these were all commonplace occurrences once your foot was set on this Hill of Surprises.

There are two roads that lead one to the noble mass of buildings crowning the hill. One may choose the narrow street with its moss-grown steps, its curves, and turns; or one may have the broader path along the ramparts, with its glorious outlook over land and sea. Whichever approach one chooses, one passes at last beneath the great doors of the Barbican.

Three times did the vision of St. Michel appear to Saint Aubert, in his dream, commanding the latter to erect a church on the heights of Mont St. Michel to his honor. How many a time must the modern pilgrim traverse the stupendous mass that has grown out of that command before he is quite certain that the splendor of Mont St. Michel is real, and not a part of a dream! Whether one enters through the dark magnificence of the great portals of the Châtelet; whether one mounts the fortified stairway, passing into the Salle des Gardes, passing onward from dungeon to fortified bridge to gain the abbatial residence; whether one leaves the vaulted splendor of oratories for aërial passage-ways, only to emerge beneath the majestic roof of the Cathedral—that marvel of the early Norman, ending in the Gothic choir of the fifteenth century; or, as one penetrates into the gloom of the mighty dungeons where heroes and the brothers of kings, and saints and scientists have died

their long death—as one gropes through the black
night of the Crypt, where a faint, mysterious glint
of light falls aslant the mystical face of the Black
Virgin; as one climbs to the light beneath the
ogive arches of the Aumônerie, through the wide-
lit aisles of the Salle des Chevaliers, past the
slender Gothic columns of the Refectory, up at
last to the crowning glory of all the glories of La
Merveille, to the exquisitely beautiful colonnades
of the open Cloister—the impressions and emotions excited by these ecclesiastical and mili-
tary masterpieces are ever the same, however
many times one may pass them in review. A
charm indefinable, but replete with subtle attractions, lurks in every one of these dungeons. The
great halls have a power to make one retraverse
their space I have yet to find under other
vaulted chambers. The grass that is set, like a
green jewel, in the arabesques of the Cloister, is a
bit of greensward the feet press with a different
tread to that which skips lightly over other strips
of turf. And the world, that one looks out upon
through prison bars, that is so gloriously arched
in the arm of a flying buttress, or that lies prone
at your feet from the dizzy heights of the rock
clefts, is not the world in which you, daily, do
your petty stretch of toil, in which you laugh and
ache, sorrow, sigh, and go down to your grave
in. The secret of this deep attraction may·lie
in the fact of one's being in a world that is built
on a height. Much, doubtless, of the charm lies,
also, in the reminders of all the human life that,
since the early dawn of history, has peopled this

hill. One has the sense of living at tremendously high mental pressure; of impressions, emotions, sensations crowding upon the mind; of one's whole meagre outfit of memory, of poetic equipment, and of imaginative furnishing being unequal to the demand made by even the most hurried tour of the great buildings, or the most flitting review of the noble massing of the clouds and the hilly seas.

The very emptiness and desolation of all the buildings on the hill help to accentuate their splendor. The stage is magnificently set; the curtain, even, is lifted. One waits for the coming on of kingly shapes, for the pomp of trumpets, for the pattering of a mighty host. But, behold, all is still. And one sits and sees only a shadowy company pass and repass across that glorious *mise-en-scène.*

For, in a certain sense, I know no other mediæval mass of buildings as peopled as are these. The dead shapes seem to fill the vast halls. The Salle des Chevaliers is crowded, daily, with a brilliant gathering of knights, who sweep the trains of their white damask mantles, edged with ermine, over the dulled marble of the floor; two by two they enter the hall; the golden shells on their mantles make the eyes blink, as the groups gather about the great chimneys, or wander through the column-broken space. Behind this dazzling *cortège,* up the steep steps of the narrow street, swarm other groups—the mediæval pilgrim host that rushes into the cathedral aisles, and that climbs the ramparts to watch the stately procession as it

makes its way toward the church portals. There
are still other figures that fill every empty niche
and deserted watch-tower. Through the lancet
windows of the abbatial gateways the yeomanry
of the vassal villages are peering; it is the weary
time of the Hundred Years' War, and all France
is watching, through sentry windows, for the approach of her dread enemy. On the shifting
sands below, as on brass, how indelibly fixed are
the names of the hundred and twenty-nine knights
whose courage drove, step by step, over that treacherous surface, the English invaders back to their
island strongholds. Will you have a less stormy
and belligerent company to people the hill? In
the quieter days of the fourteenth century, on
any bright afternoon, you could have sat beside
some friendly artist-monk, and watched him
color and embellish those wondrous missals that
made the manuscripts of the Brothers famous
throughout France. Earlier yet, in those naïve
centuries, Robert de Torigny, that "bouche des
Papes," would doubtless have discoursed to you
on any subject dear to this "counsellor of kings"—
on books, or architecture, or the science of fortifications, or on the theology of Lanfranc; from the
helmeted locks of Rollon to the veiled tresses of
the lovely Tiphaine Raguenel, Duguesclin's wife;
from the ghastly rat-eaten body of the Dutch
journalist, who offended that tyrant King, Louis
XIV., to the Revolutionary heroes, as pitilessly
doomed to an odious death under the gentle Louis
Philippe—there is no shape or figure in French
history which cannot be summoned at will to refill

either a dungeon or a palace chamber at Mont St. Michel.

Even in these, our modern days, one finds strange relics of past fashions in thought and opinion. The various political, religious, and ethical forms of belief to be met with in a fortnight's sojourn on the hill, give one a sense of having passed in review a very complete gallery of ancient and modern portraits of men's minds. In time one learns to traverse even a dozen or more centuries with ease. To be in the dawn of the eleventh century in the morning; at high noon to be in the flood-tide of the fifteenth; and, as the sun dipped, to hear the last word of our own dying century—such were the flights across the abysmal depths of time Charm and I took again and again.

One of our chosen haunts was in a certain watch-tower. From its top wall, the loveliest prospect of Mont St. Michel was to be enjoyed. Day after day and sunset after sunset, we sat out the hours there. Again and again the world, as it passed, came and took its seat beside us. Pilgrims of the devout and ardent type would stop, perchance, would proffer a preliminary greeting, would next take their seat along the parapet, and, quite unconsciously, would end by sitting for their portrait. One such sitter, I remember, was clad in carmine crêpe shawl; she was bonneted in the shape of a long-ago decade. She had climbed the hill in the morning before dawn, she said; she had knelt in prayer as the sun rose. For hers was a pilgrimage made in fulfilment of a vow. St. Michel had granted her wish, and she in return had brought her prayers to his shrine.

"Ah, mesdames! how good is God! How greatly He rewards a little self-sacrifice. Figure to yourselves the Mont in the early mists, with the sun rising out of the sea and the hills. I was on my knees, up there. I had eaten nothing since yesterday at noon. I was full of the Holy Ghost. When the sun broke at last, it was God Himself in all His glory come down to earth! The whole earth seemed to be listening—*prétait l'oreille*—and with the great stillness, and the sea, and the light breaking everywhere, it was as if I were being taken straight up into Paradise. Saint Michel himself must have been supporting me."

The carmine crêpe shawl covered a poet, you see, as well as a devotee.

Up yonder, in the little shops and stalls tucked away within the walls of the Barbican, a lively traffic, for many a century now, has been going on in relics and *plombs de pélerinage*. Some of these mediæval impressions have been unearthed in strange localities, in the bed of the Seine, as far away as Paris. Rude and archaic are many of these early essays in the sculptor's art. But they preserve for us, in quaint intensity, the fervor of adoration which possessed that earlier, more devout time and period. On the mind of this nineteenth century pilgrim, the same lovely old forms of belief and superstition were imprinted as are still to be seen in some of those winged figures of St. Michel, with feet securely set on the back of the terrible dragon, staring, with triumphant gaze, through stony or leaden eyes.

On the evening of the pilgrimage our friend,

the Parisian, joined us on our high perch. The
Mont seemed strangely quiet after the noise and
confusion the peasants had brought in their train.
The Parisian, like ourselves, had been glad to escape into the upper heights of the wide air, after
the bustle and hurry of the day at our inn.

"You permit me, mesdames?" He had lighted
his after-dinner cigar; he went on puffing, having
gained our consent. He curled a leg comfortably
about the railings of a low bridge connecting a
house that sprang out of a rock, with the rampart.
Below, there was a clean drop of a few hundred
feet, more or less. In spite of the glories of a
spectacular sunset, yielding ceaseless changes and
transformations of cloud and sea tones, the words
of Madame Poulard alone had power to possess
our companion. She had uttered her protest
against the pilgrimage, as she had swept the
Parisian's *pousse-café* from his elbow. He took up
the conversation where it had been dropped.

"It is amusing to hear Madame Poulard talk
of the priests stopping the pilgrimages! The
priests? Why, that's all they have left them to
live upon now. These peasants' are the only
pockets in which they can fumble nowadays."

"All the same, one can't help being grateful to
those peasants," retorted Charm. "They are the
only creatures who have made these things seem
to have any meaning. How dead it all seems!
The abbey, the cloisters, the old prisons, the
fortifications—it is like wandering through a
splendid tomb!"

"Yes, as the curé said yesterday, '*l'âme n'y est*

plus,'—since the priests have been dislodged, it is the house of the dead."

"The priests"—the Parisian snorted at the very sound of the word—"they have only themselves to blame. They would have been here still, if they had not so abused their power."

"How did they abuse it?" Charm asked.

"In every possible way. I am, myself, not of the country. But my brother was stationed here for some years, when the Mont was garrisoned. The priests were in full possession then, and they conducted a lively commerce, mademoiselle. The Mont was turned into a show—to see it or any part of it, everyone had to pay toll. On the great fête-days, when St. Michel wore his crown, the gold ran like water into the monks' treasury. It was still then a fashionable religious fad to have a mass said for one's dead, out here among the clouds and the sea. Well, try to imagine fifty masses all dumped on the altar together; that is, one mass would be scrambled through, no names would be mentioned, no one save *le bon Dieu* himself knew for whom it was being said; but fifty or more believed they had bought it, since they had paid for it. And the priests laughed in their sleeves, and then sat down, comfortably, to count the gold. Ah, mesdames, those were, literally, the golden days of the priesthood! What with the pilgrimages, and the sale of relics, and *les bénéfices* —together with the charges for seeing the wonders of the Mont—what a trade they did! It is only the Jews, who, in their turn, now own us, up in Paris, who can equal the priests as commercial

geniuses!" And our pessimistic Parisian, during
the next half-hour, gave us a prophetic picture
of the approaching ruin of France, brought about
by the genius for plunder and organization that is
given to the sons of Moses.

Following the ⸜Parisian, a figure, bent and
twisted, opened a door in a side-wall, and took
his seat beside us. One became used, in time,
to these sudden appearances; to vanish down a
chimney, or to emerge from the womb of a rock,
or to come up from the bowels of what earth there
was to be found—all such exits and entrances became as commonplace as all the other extraordinary phases of one's life on the hill. This particular shape had emerged from a hut, carved, literally,
out of the side of the rock; but, for a hut, it was
amazingly snug—as we could see for ourselves;
for the venerable shape hospitably opened the
low wooden door, that we might see how much of
a home could be made out of the side of a rock.
Only, when one had been used to a guard-room,
and to great and little dungeons, and to a rattling
of keys along dark corridors, a hut, and the blaze
of the noon sun, were trying things to endure, as
the shape, with a shrug, gave us to understand.

"You see, mesdames, I was jailor here, years
ago, when all La Merveille was a prison. Ah!
those were great days for the Mont! There were
soldiers and officers who came up to look at the
soldiers, and the soldiers—it was their business
to look after the prisoners. The Emperor himself
came here once—I saw him. What a sight!—Dieu!
all the monks and priests and nuns, and the arch-

bishop himself was out. What banners and
crosses and flags! The cannon was like a great
thunder—and the grève was red with soldiers.
Ah, those were days! Dieu—why couldn't the
republic have continued those glories—*ces gloires?*
Aujourd'hui nous ne sommes que des morts—instead
of prisoners to handle—to watch and work, like so
many good machines—there is only the dike yonder to keep in repair! What changes—mon Dieu!
what changes!" And the shape wrung his hands.
It was, in truth, a touching spectacle of grief for a
good old past.

An old priest, with equally saddened vision,
once came to take his seat, quite easily and
naturally, beside us, on our favorite perch. He
was one of the little band of priests who had
remained faithful to the Mont after the government had dispersed his brothers—after the monastery had been broken up. He and his four
or five companions had taken refuge in a small
house, close by the cemetery; it was they who
conducted the services in the little parish church;
who had gathered the treasures still grouped together in that little interior—the throne of St.
Michel, with its blue draperies and the golden
fleur-de-lis, the floating banners and the shields of
the Knights of St. Michel, the relics, and wondrous bits of carving rescued from the splendors
of the cathedral.

"*Ah, mesdames—que voulez-vous?*" was the old
priest's broken chant; he was bewailing the woes
that had come to his order, to religion, to France.
"What will you have? The history of nations

repeats itself, as we all know. We, of our day, are
fallen on evil times: it is the reign of image-
breakers — nothing is sacred, except money.
France has worn herself out. She is like an old
man, the hero of many battles, who cares only for
his easy chair and his slippers. She does not
care about the children who are throwing stones
at the windows. She likes to snooze, in the sun,
and count her money-bags. France is too old to
care about religion, or the future—she is thinking
how best to be comfortable—here in this world,
when she has rheumatism and a cramp in the
stomach!" And the old priest wrapped his own
soutane about his lean knees, suiting his gesture
to his inward convictions.

Was the priest's summary the last word of
truth about modern France? On the sands that
lay below at our feet, we read a different answer.

The skies were still brilliantly lighted. The
actual twilight had not come yet, with its long,
deep glow, a passion of color that had a longer life
up here on the heights than when seen from a
lower level. This twilight hour was always a prolonged moment of transfiguration for the Mont.

The very last evening of our stay, we chose this
as the loveliest light in which to see the last of
the hill. On that evening, I remember, the reds
and saffrons in the sky were of an astonishing
richness. The sea wall, the bastions, the faces of
the great rocks, the yellow broom that sprang
from the clefts therein, were dyed as in a carmine
bath. In that mighty glow of color, all things
took on something of their old, their stupendous

splendor. The giant walls were paved with
brightness. The town, climbing the hill, assumed
the proportions of a mighty citadel; the forest
tree-tops were prismatic, emerald balls flung beneath the illumined Merveille; and the Cathedral
was set in a daffodil frame; its aërial *escalier de
dentelle*, like Jacob's ladder, led one easily heavenward. The circling birds, in the lace-work of the
spiral finials, sang their night songs, as the glow
in the sky changed, softened, deepened.

This was the world that was in the west.

Toward the east, on the flat surface of the
sands, this world cast a strange and wondrous
shadow. Jagged rocks, a pyramidal city, a
Gothic cathedral in mid-air, behold the rugged
outlines of Mont St. Michel carving their giant
features on the shifting, sensitive surface of the
mirroring sands.

In the little pools and the trickling rivers, the
fishermen—from this height, Liliputians grap-
pling with Liliputian meshes—were setting their
nets for the night. Across the river-beds, peasant
women and fishwives, with bared legs and baskets
clasped to their bending backs, appeared and disappeared—shapes that emerged into the light
only to vanish into the gulf of the night.

In was in these pictures that we read our
answer.

Like Mont St. Michel, so has France carried
into the heights of history her glory and her
power. On every century, she, like this world
in miniature, has also cast her shadow, dwarfing
some, illuminating others. And, as on those

distant sands the toiling shapes of the fishermen are to be seen, early and late, in summer and winter, so can France point to her people, whose industry and amazing talent for toil has made her, and maintains her, great.

Some of these things we have learned, since, in Normandy Inns, we have sat at meat with her peasants, and have grown to be friends with her fishwives.

www.ingramcontent.com/pod-product-compliance
Lightning Source LLC
Chambersburg PA
CBHW030955110726
47900CB00004B/1287